R J Dillon was born in the North West of England. He taught history and visual culture for over ten years. He now writes full-time, and is the author of five novels, a poetry collection and a book examining the portrayal of history on British television. He is married with two children and lives on the Lancashire coast, where he devotes his time to writing and walking.

For more information, visit rjdillon.com

Point of No Return is the fifth in a series of novels based around the British Secret Intelligence Service's (SIS), Covert Operations Directorate, CO8.

By the same author
The Oktober Projekt
The Fanatic
Hunted and the Damned
Network of Lies

Poetry
Midnight's Revolution

Non-fiction
History on British television: Constructing nation, nationality and collective memory

R J DILLON

Point of No Return

REVIDION BOOKS

First published by Revidion 2016
Second edition published by Revidion 2020

British Library Cataloguing in Publication Data. A catalogue record for this book is available from the British Library.

ISBN: 978-0-9572651-6-5

For Jeffrey

Thank you for inspiring my guardianship of the past. As a historian, I hope I have never let you down

Courage, however, is the best slayer, courage which attacks: it slays even death itself...

Friedrich Nietzsche — *Thus Spoke Zarathustra*

One

The deep crush of evening stole around the Audi intent on taking it prisoner. Raked partway up a meagre incline on a rutted concrete pad the Audi Q5 rested in a thicket of shadow. Its nose pointing towards a stretch of road cut in a sharp line through the flat countryside, the Q5 was prepared to get out of the Czech Republic in a hurry. Twenty-two miles outside the capital, close to Liběchov, this laying-up spot chosen as an ideal means of escape through Central Bohemia, then on across the German border to safety. A hoarding on rusty metal legs listed at an angle beside the car. In two foot blistered letters it urged passing drivers to call at '*Restaurace U Jelinka*' for a most satisfying experience. No one had accepted the invitation in the hour since Nick Torr had manoeuvred cautiously into position.

Slung hopefully on a snow heaped verge beside the opposite lane, another raucous billboard: this one for the breakfast show on *Frekvence 1*. But by morning Nick would be waking up in London and have no need of a Czech radio station as an alarm call. Ahead of him hanging in dense tatters over winter scrubbed fields, curtains of cloud graciously backlit by a waxy moon.

Slouched down into his seat, Nick listened through his concealed earpiece to the latest update on the defector's progress before the next vehicle change at Mělník. Peering ahead into the viscous gloom he tensed at the rare approach of headlight clusters, fastidiously monitoring every passing vehicle, concentrating on identifying any hint of suspect activity.

Nothing during a high-octane operation could be ignored. And Nick's nerves racked up another notch when a flame red Zetor tractor made a howling return in the opposite direction less than fifteen minutes after its first pass. A father and son bounced happily together inside the cab: towed behind them, a trailer packed with bales of fodder. Coming through his encrypted Motorola, a stream of priority talk group commentaries from his CO8 teams as Operation Julius moved up through the gears. One of the feeds provided coded confirmation that the defector – codenamed TAURUS – had successfully feigned acute stomach pain at the closing event of a science convention on this, his last evening in Prague.

'Sanction,' said Nick, giving the green light.

In the overall scheme of things, Nick should never have set foot in the Czech Republic. As Director of the Secret Intelligence Service's Covert Operations Directorate, he should, by all rights, have been a mere observer inside CO8's tactical basement control centre during the high risk extraction of Taurus.

That was before the incident.

During a final, dry surveillance run along the route out of Prague, a pivotal member of the CO8 team took a punishing side blow from a car driven by a reckless drunk, spilling him off his motorcycle at a junction, breaking a collarbone and his pelvis. Unable to call-off the operation Nick stepped in, accepting the role of an emergency replacement to operate as the in-country anchor and final leg driver. Despite voluble requests for Nick to take a well-earned rest from front line activities, principally from Rowena, his deputy controller of operations, he insisted on filling the vacant role.

Regardless of Nick's faults – of which his enemies agreed there were many – he was that rare type of director, a hands-on operator well versed in the turbulent world of hostile intelligence gathering, demanding of no one what he could not deliver himself.

Scanning the road he peered into the darkness, searching for the local community bus on its run between Česká Lípa and Mělník. Glancing at his watch he noted the service was running behind schedule. In the frost tinted darkness slinking across the fields, Nick worried if the Czech security service *Bezpečnostní informační služba* – the BIS – might be ready to pounce, smother their operation and catch them red-handed despite their loose assurance of no interference. At almost a minute and a half late, a pair of bulging headlights meandered towards the Audi.

Tucked low, Nick picked out the familiar profile of the advancing bus. Blissfully unaware of its importance this January evening, it trundled merrily along on its mundane journey, its windows fogged into ragged patches concealing the passengers. And any footpads along for the ride, thought Nick watching as its tail lights were snuffed out by the gloom.

Through his earpiece, a pair of CO8 wire mechanics hunkered inside their stationary support vehicle on a drab side street close to Prague's Congress Centre verified they had intercepted the call requesting medical assistance. During a tense phase of secure airwave activity, Nick acknowledged a flurry of callsigns and short burst radio traffic as a CO8 team pulled up in an ambulance to scoop up Taurus from the Congress Centre.

A garbled flash update brought Nick sitting bolt upright. He demanded a 'repeat', receiving a series of 'confirm' clicks from his team supporting the initial transmission. Unable to intervene, he listened intently to a developing crisis from a number of live operational feeds.

'The package's minder is demanding to ride along,' a CO8 watcher reported, adding that an unseemly tussle at the rear of the ambulance threatened to get out of hand.

'No additional baggage after first base,' Nick snapped into his command channel. 'Bin it. Lose it,' he insisted, not wanting to risk collateral intrusion.

'Will do,' a disjointed voice acknowledged through a shimmering whisper of static.

Rapidly attempting to contain this minor interruption, Nick concentrated on the familiar extraction formula of time and distance. How much head start would they manage before Taurus was reported absent? How would Taurus's babysitters react? On maximum alert and visibly tense, he glanced frequently at his watch.

As the freezing night tightened its hold Nick adjusted the volume on his scanner, hearing only routine police chatter.

'Pick up completed at first base,' one of Nick's team reported.

'The additional baggage?'

'Jettisoned. Package loaded in the hold,' came the reply, affirming the transfer of Taurus into the concealed compartment of a van for the first phase had gone to plan.

And who, exactly, is our package? Nick wondered, allowing himself a rare moment of retrospection. Until the actual transfer took place, he had no idea of Taurus's identity and maybe never would: their operational status was designated 'black' which gave Whitehall and the Service more than enough room to blissfully deny any knowledge of Nick, his team, and more importantly, any involvement in the transportation of illicit 'cargo'. During his final briefing in a dank Prague safe house, Stape the Deputy Head of the Middle East Desk, would only disclose to Nick on a need-to-know basis that it was a 'ultra priority lift and run'.

'In that case we'll prepare for a hot reception,' Nick had reasonably countered.

'That would be advisable. The JIC has leant its voice to the FCO's shrill chorus pleading for us to get the package out regardless of risk,' he'd retorted obliquely.

'What's behind the urgency?' Tight windows of operational opportunity concerned Nick. He knew how the Joint Intelligence Committee inevitably sided with the Foreign and Commonwealth Office's reckless tendency to cut operational corners for the rewards and glory high value defectors brought with them.

'We have very good reason to believe that the heat is going to be turned up on our package. His loyalty to his masters is being questioned. This light touch chaperoned trip to Prague happens to be our only opportunity; hence the timing is critical. Miss this available window, and we may not have another chance for the stars to come into alignment. It became a mad scramble to hoist all sails and run for a friendly port. Hence CO8 being called out at short notice, and that dear Nick, is your lot. Take it or take your reluctance to C,' Stape had curtly challenged him.

Now his second phase delivery team were somewhere out in the darkness: Calcot driving, Wilsden riding shotgun and Leiston – Taurus's nominated Head Office escort – lending support. Offering a muted grunt at the memory of the frayed encounter with Stape, Nick returned to stoically monitoring his scanner and radio. Around him a brutal wind dashed through the trees. Snagging against stripped branches it shrieked of an advancing storm playing hide and seek in the darkness.

The last update Nick received from the van had come some ten minutes ago. Since then, he'd had nothing. Each acknowledge-transmit call he sent went unanswered. In return he heard only an undulating, ethereal hiss. Finally, in what fieldmen burrowed deep inside a covert operation term their 'Hallelujah moment', Nick's earpiece filled with the brevity code confirming the van and its cargo were a less than a quarter of a mile away. Shifting into reverse Nick eased the Audi farther back up the incline, sheltering in the deeper, dull block of shadow beneath the hoarding.

Releasing the magazine from his bobbed hammer HK P200, Nick rechecked the alignment of the first round. Satisfied, he returned the magazine and tucked the semi-automatic pistol under his left thigh. The van, a snub nosed much travelled TAZ 1500, slowed and flashed its headlights before bouncing heavily as it rode the ramp's lip. According to the timed schedule inherited by Nick, the changeover should have lasted no longer than a minute. As with so many tactical plans, the reality happened to be optimistically wide of the mark.

Emerging from inside his concealed compartment in the TAZ's rear section, Taurus decided then and there – between van and car – to air a string of grievances. Rejecting attempts by Wilsden and Leiston to calm him, Taurus brushed off their concerns with venomous, outright disdain, bullishly issuing a set of demands. With his patience verging on completely fraying, Nick gave Taurus the ultimatum of climbing aboard or taking his chances by being abandoned on the spot.

'I must speak to my family in Damascus,' Taurus demanded. Clutching his small leather satchel, he directed his clipped order to Leiston beside him at Nick's lowered window.

'We can arrange that later,' Leiston offered.

'Why not now? You people are behaving as if I were your prisoner,' Taurus volubly complained.

Puffing out an irritable sigh, Leiston's exercised her only option given the constricted protocol of being Taurus's escort. Pursing her thin lips, Leiston opened the rear door, forcibly nudging her charge into the Audi, Taurus muttering all the while as he shuffled along on the back seat.

'You'll have no contact with anyone,' Nick snapped over his shoulder when everyone was aboard. Easing the Audi out onto Highway 261 he glimpsed the brief glint of the van's rear lights through his wing mirror when Calcot swept away on his return dash to Prague.

'It is essential,' Taurus brusquely maintained to anyone who would listen as they headed off towards Ústí nad Labem.

'You're in isolation,' Nick told him, assuming the sole right to reply. Through his rear-view mirror he watched Taurus glare at him. In his late forties Taurus was jowly with small, mocking eyes. A fat nose sat imperiously above large lips accentuating a diplomatic sheen of self-importance that Nick guessed came from something besides postings as a senior embassy bureaucrat. As so many vain men do when they hit a certain milestone in life, Taurus had dyed his hair a respectable jet-black along with his full military moustache.

'And who are you to give orders?' Taurus leant forward, his wide body charged with resentment.

'Your ticket to freedom,' Nick retorted.

Still bristling and very much volatile, Taurus slumped back. Transferring his satchel to his lap, he accepted a set of new documents from Leiston.

'So I am to be Jordanian,' he announced in a theatrical impression of amusement, skimming through his passport. 'Maybe you should consult me before giving me a new nationality.'

'Should we also have cleared it with your Ministry of Foreign Affairs?' Wilsden challenged him from the passenger seat.

'Is this the respect I can expect from my hosts?' Taurus protested, his rich tobacco voice bearing a surly, indignant tone.

Ignoring Taurus's professional bid to assert control, Nick concentrated on the route he'd committed to memory – the various detours for emergencies, each connection; beginning with the 253, before picking up the main route 8 to the border then swinging north-west to Altenburg. But in the distance he spotted a more immediate and pressing problem. Dead ahead, and certainly not easy to avoid without causing a major incident, a traffic officer astride a Yamaha FZ6, a blue strobe light spilling into the night from its rear pillar. Directing Nick with a reflective baton, the rider swept the Audi into a coned off slip road marked with a portable fold up sign declaring: '*Policie*: Traffic Control'.

'Do we make a bolt for it?' Wilsden asked, her throat tight, her breathing sharp.

There are decisions that take a split second to make and a lifetime to relive: each moment replayed over and again in minute detail; a painful analysis of what went wrong, a lonely and miserable consideration of every single action. Nick faced one now.

'We'd never clear the border,' he said, reluctantly slowing.

In the back Taurus feverishly drummed his fingers on his satchel, Leiston attempting to calm him, bring him down from the edge of catastrophic panic. Framed square in Nick's rear mirror like a miniature landscape with all the proportions flattened, he watched the motorcycle behind them draw across the road, its uniformed rider bringing it to rest at an angle. In the skein of darkness its blue pulses bounced off the rider's white helmet then faded when Nick followed a tight curve.

'Anything?' he demanded of Wilsden.

'Track... it's a rail line... two lines.... that far down it's a leg breaker,' she answered, squinting hard through her window. 'You?'

Glancing down an uneven gully a foot from his door Nick glimpsed the Elbe rushing headlong towards Cuxhaven and the North Sea. Under the spectral glare of a high, full moon free of cloud, the coiled, dark skinned river opened into a foaming band of mercury as it tumbled over a formidable weir. 'No go,' he admitted.

Picked out by the Audi's headlights, a course, rough tongue of land opened up into a temporary storage dump used by highway maintenance crews for hard core, rock salt and piles of torn out kerbstones. Ahead of him Nick saw a VW T5 traffic control unit van pulled over by a clipped, narrow exit road. Mounted on its stand, the second Yamaha FZ6, its rider waving the Audi into a coned inspection bay behind the van. Fanning in around the maintenance area a tight ring of spruce and elder.

'It's fine. We'll take care of it,' Leiston assured a jittery Taurus.

With Leiston continuing to soothe Taurus's raw nerves, Nick's attention remained on his left as the police motorcyclist pushed back his visor during his measured walk over to the car. Out of nothing more perceptive than a crude, fieldman's survival instinct, Nick rested his hand on the centre console and eased the weight off his left leg, allowing a much easier rapid draw for his HK.

Agreeing to the rider's demand to lower his window fully, Nick enquired if anything was wrong: '*Neco není v pořádku dustojniku?*'

'*Jen rutinni kontrola.*' The oval of face compressed inside the helmet never shifted from unfriendly, insisting on examining Nick's driving licence: '*ridicsky průkaz.*'

In one deliberate move Nick dipped into his inside jacket pocket, his right hand withdrawing his Czech licence. Slipping his left hand between the seat and his thigh, he cupped his hand around the HK's grip. At that very moment, what the military minded members of CO8 deem the 'opening contact' rapidly flowed in a stream of stop-start, jerky motion scenes.

Whether it was Nick who opened fire first, he wasn't sure. He didn't see the canister or where it came from – he just felt the sticky blast of pepper spray coat his face, hearing Wilsden curse as it hit her. Inside the Audi was complete mayhem. Leiston's screams were drowned out by a bellowing rage of a battle cry from Taurus scrabbling inside his satchel. Nick attempting to throw the Audi into gear, managed to get off one round into the rider's shoulder. With the pepper spray in his eyes he had the distinct impression of trying to aim and fire underwater.

Swarming around the rear of the car, three figures in boiler suits and hockey goalie masks grabbed for the doors. 'Down,' screamed Nick, struggling to throw the Audi into reverse. Driving blind he slewed it no more than a couple of feet before hitting a bank of rock salt. He felt the cold air swim in through both rear doors when they were torn open, then the instant pain in both of Nick's ears after Taurus fired a Smith and Wesson .44 Magnum revolver he'd concealed inside his satchel. In a return of automatic fire that Nick only heard as an extremely fuzzy, mundane pop... pop...pop... Wilsden slumped heavily against his shoulder.

Throwing open his door Nick stumbled away, blinded, crouched low. With snot and tears streaming down his cheeks, he groped around the Audi. Hugging down close to the bonnet he raised his HK to aim. Unable to focus, all he could distinguish were blurred movements and indistinct flashes of white goalie masks. Outgunned, attracting automatic bursts from Vz.58s, Nick offered wild, inaccurate fire in return. He made an all or nothing break for a gap in the tree line. That's when the VW van rammed him in his back, spilling him over the lip of the gully in a flailing bundle towards the river.

Two

Without her second floor window, *Pani* Raisova's life would be unbearable. It gave her an unobstructed line of sight down V mezihoří where it branched off from Sokolovská Boulevard in Prague 8. She sat by it daily in good weather and foul – the activity on the other side of the glass always tingling her bowsprit spine with a little voyeuristic shudder of delight. Nothing went unobserved. Her memory at seventy-eight – thank the merciful Lord – still served her with impressive and unfailing clarity. Visitors and locals were stored in a mental scrapbook with the organisational precision she'd applied to her Rolodex as a production manager's secretary in the old Ringhoffer factory.

Today she had a new face to add. She had glimpsed him arriving quite by chance during her vigil for her weekly frozen food delivery from Family Frost. Not that she ever missed collecting her provisions after she'd complained to the stupid boy that he didn't need to play his idiotic jingle when it wasn't summer. Didn't he realise he was delivering groceries not selling ice cream? Who couldn't fail to notice his van painted brighter than a canary? Since she'd confronted the ignorant oaf of a boy, he'd played his van's crazy tune louder than ever just to annoy her. Instantly she knew she'd made a mistake, cursing her own foolish action. The next day she discovered Family Frost were extending their deliveries late into the evening. Then she'd suffer, she'd not receive an ounce of peace when the boy raced his van around the corner towards her apartment block, his jingles blaring louder than a dance band orchestra.

But it was this new visitor keeping her occupied, a corner of her net curtain surreptitiously raised. Gawping about him like a rabbit in a hunter's lamp, *Pani* Raisova *knew* at once he didn't belong in Libeň. Even with his unshaven appearance – expertly noted through her pair of opera glasses she kept on the sill – *Pani* Raisova noted his unease and discomfort. 'Move,' she silently urged him as he loitered between the only two good working pavement lights getting his bearings, reading something in his hand.

In her efficient filing system, *Pani* Raisova slotted this visitor under her lost soul category; a man of some worth, she estimated, clearly blighted by sorrow. 'Move', she implored him, her sickly mint breath wafting a corner of the curtain. 'Go before the local *vytrznici* who patrol after dusk sniff you out. Go before they rob you of everything. Maybe even your life.' Why she should have such an impending vision of doom for this man, she didn't know. But she did.

He was different from the other men who slinked by making their calls to the foreign whore who rented a cheap attic apartment at the rear. The regular visitor she had christened the 'gypsy' because of his dark looks, the way he crept from his car like a wolf in the night, young enough to be the whore's son. The whore had put out the word to some of her stupid neighbours that the gypsy was her adopted child. But she'd seen them together, down by the trees, and mothers and children don't kiss like that, she tut-tutted to herself.

Here was a man who visited for another purpose, she decided. This one had dignity, he had breeding and bearing and she watched him disappear down the side of the building, knowing even when he moved out of range he meant to go straight at the road crossing.

If this one had sense he'd use the rough path that hugged the building and save himself the long walk around the back. Then he'd see what neighbourhood he'd landed himself in. He'd pass the scrawled insults under the dolt Mialhkov's window who did nothing but watch sex all day on his satellite television. Then he'd be at the electricity's company's distribution box the street children beat with sticks. Then if the *vytrznici* who sniffed glue in their den in the trees hadn't spotted him, he would have access to the block where the kept whore lived.

During this introverted bout of speculative concern – an unusual occurrence for *Pani* Raisova – she picked out the distant Family Frost notes jingling towards her building. Sliding her opera glasses back into their little nook on the sill, she shook her head as the stupid boy made a meal of parking his van across from the stranger's car. Plucking her walking stick off the wing of an armchair she ground off towards the front door.

In the hallway she caught a glimpse of her crooked frame in the mirror and in a rare mood of conciliation, had to agree that the brats who taunted her for being a witch had a point. All she needed was a wart on the end of her nose and pointed hat. One day she'd wake from her disturbed nights of sleep and her warped old backbone would finish its work, leaving her head touching her swollen, arthritic knees. For a long five minutes she waited leaning against the corridor wall, her gaze fixed on the framed Madonna, praying the idiot boy would be sharp, that he hadn't forgotten anything off her order. But his insolent whistle never carried up the stairwell.

Swearing to God and all the saints that she would carry out her threat to ring and report the Family Frost boy, *Pani* Raisova made the return to her window hoping to catch the boy idly chatting or doing some other misdemeanour the company would punish him for. The van remained where he'd parked it, but she could see not a breath or hair of him. What did catch her attention was the stranger's car.

Placed on the bonnet she recognised one of those brown bags the *vytrznici* always dumped in the alley, the sort from American food chains where they bought their meals because their drunken pigs of mothers and fathers drank away the larder money. Reaching for the phone *Pani* Raisova stooped to one side of her window. The visitor had returned. This time walking fast, his fists clenched and his face a work of fury. Praising Jesus and his family of angels that the visitor hadn't fallen prey to the *vytrznici*, she willed him back to his car like she did when her father took her to a sports event as a child, and she sided always with the underdogs.

Let that be a lesson to him that this neighbourhood is not for his type, *Pani* Raisova decided when the visitor spotted the bag on the bonnet of his car. Looking around like an innocent fool, the visitor did nothing but stare at it. Brush it off. Swipe it to the floor, *Pani* Raisova silently urged the visitor. Do something. Thanks be to Joseph, he has a brain, she decided when the visitor lifted the bag off the bonnet. A man of upbringing who will deposit the rubbish at home she thought, wishing him happiness as he climbed into his car. The last thing *Pani* Raisova saw before the explosion was the headlights come on. Then she heard thousands of tiny bells tinkling together as slivers of glass diced her face and the stupid boy's Family Frost chimes rang eternally on. On her back with a mouthful of dust, she stared up at the ceiling as if she was ready to give birth to her selfish, ungrateful children all over again.

•••

Every particle of Nick roared in pain. He remembered nothing of his fall into the gully – only of coming round, of agonisingly clawing his way back to the top. His ears persistently rang. He reasoned he would be partially deaf for several hours after Taurus had fired his handheld canon inside the Audi. His leather jacket had taken a good deal of punishment. He could feel the dried blood on his face, his hands, in the cool patches on his legs where his jeans snagged, ripping on his plunge towards the Elbe.

He'd woken wrapped around a tree and that, he assumed, accounted for his shoulder on his left side feeling inflamed, hot and tender. Breathing in through his mouth, out slowly through his nose, he aimed to limit the after-effects of the spray that had inflamed his lips, throat, tongue, his nasal passages. His eyes had stopped streaming but they were gummed shut in the corners and his field of vision came through a stinging letter box slot. On his hands and knees he retched twice. The second time felt as if he was bringing up fire.

Cautiously he picked himself up, staggering like a drunk until he mastered his balance. In front of him the Audi where he'd left it, reversed against the mound of rock salt. There was little for him to do but carefully pick his way through the carnage. Shivering one moment, burning hot the next, he checked for a pulse on Taurus and Wilsden. Neither of them had one, their skin cold against his fingertips. Leiston, though he searched everywhere, was gone. The only evidence that she'd been there was a shoe, sized seven – from a right foot – he found close to where the VW van waited to launch the ambush. It was here too that he located two trails of blood in the light film of snow.

Maybe I hit one and Taurus inflicted some serious damage on another he speculated, not remotely satisfied. Maybe the blood isn't from the imposters in police uniform? After that uncomfortable possibility Nick concluded Taurus wasn't meant to come out of the ambush alive. He'd been green lit for termination. Did they take Leiston as consolation or as a prize? Not knowing the answer he returned to the car.

Slowly and with methodical precision, Nick went to work on the Audi's interior finding no trace of Taurus's satchel. The scanner had gone and so too had his radio. What glass remained in the doors, windscreen and rear screen, held blooms of blood and dribbles of tissue, most probably brain. So did the upholstery. In the foot wells amongst the diamonds of glass, he found more 7.62×39mm casings. Not the weapon of choice for common highway robbery he decided, going through Taurus's pockets, removing any identification, including the set of Jordanian papers. Moving onto Wilsden he went through the same ritual, claiming her purse, passport and phone from her handbag and jacket: the unspoken CO8 ritual of sanitising the dead.

An overwhelming wave of tiredness broke over him during the emergency call he made on Wilsden's phone to the Service's Prague Station Duty Officer. He gave the brevity code for an immediate abort of the operation then requested support.

'A major breakdown... The engine... Seems like fatal damage... I definitely saw a lot of oil and parts... Best if we could have a covered transporter...'

When the Duty Officer was debriefed afterwards by a thumbscrew sent out from her base at the Service's training establishment at Aspley, the Duty Officer swore Nick's emergency call was the most disconcerting he'd ever taken; adamantly insisting when asked how Nick had sounded: 'Obviously in shock and not a happy bunny.' Reliving the moment with a raised eyebrow the DO vowed how Nick had bawled each coded request as if he was trying to make contact from Mars.

Pushed and prodded into assessing if Nick's reaction sounded genuine, the perceptive DO agreed that in his experience it most definitely was. Astutely he added that there was something in Nick's tone to support his claim. When corralled into expanding on his point, the DO admitted that he couldn't really describe it: only that Nick's voice contained a sinister remoteness to it; a chilling quality that despite the yelling, Nick had made up his mind that someone would pay. Relentlessly pursuing the thread, the thumbscrew squeezed the DO into summing up Nick's mood. 'A Horseman of the Apocalypse someone has seriously pissed off,' the DO told her. 'And if I was responsible, I wouldn't be turning the lights off at night anytime soon.'

•••

In normal circumstances after any demanding extraction of a defector, Nick would have returned directly to his home in Putney or taken a few days off at his cottage in Devon to adjust, to 'come down off the mountain' as the wise hands have it. But with a disaster of such magnitude, he did what other countless professionals caught cold in the murky, twilight world of covert operations deem safe procedure, and that was cool his heels far from the scene of what was being claimed by Head Office as an out and out act of sabotage and brazen betrayal.

Cursed by death's long shadow once again, he crossed the border ready to strike back, his mood positively malicious. Not from any long held preference or singular attachment, Nick started on a carefully charted withdrawal to Berlin; his reasoning derived out of a purely practical consideration that the city provided a relatively secure haven from the tainted core of the compromised action. A quarter way into his drive, his work phone delivered him a succinct coded text from Head Office – 'Proceed Nürnberg. Wait for instructions.'

Against who or what, Nick didn't know, but changed course to Nürnberg anyway. He took up residence in a humble hotel with baronial pretensions close to the round tower on Königstraße, presenting a set of escape papers issued in the name of Herr Rees-Mehr. According to standing orders, Nick, having aborted the operation, was meant to remain incommunicado with his own HQ affectionately known as the Mad House, with Head Office, its satellite stations, friends, allies and assets – contact in any form and description, strictly prohibited. Ignoring the directive, he turned his third floor room into a temporary tactical outpost from where he tirelessly coaxed, chivvied and harassed a loose collective of CO8 illegals into buying up information on Leiston.

Reclusive and legendary for being unable to pin down, Harry Bransk eventually broke surface on Nick's eighth call.

'Nick, I got to tell you this isn't a good moment.'

'Who've you ripped off this time, Harry?'

In the years Nick had worked with Bransk – a nomadic hustler who operated out of Helsinki – Harry as a broker of intelligence and all-round merchant of valuable information, possessed contacts CO8 could never reach. Harry's active network of assets and freelance traders of secrets covered most of Europe. If not of criminal inclination themselves, they certainly knew their way around the underworld maze. Harry, as their proud ringmaster, not only bought up sources Head Office classed as off-limits, he'd amassed a fabulous number of enemies.

'It's personal. A medical condition, okay? I'm recovering, Nick. I've had to rest.'

'They've actually found you have a heart?'

'If it's just a chat about the good times, call me next year.'

'I've got a missing person.'

'Where?'

'Czech Republic.'

After a lengthy, unbroken silence, Nick had to demand twice if Harry was still there?

'Sure, I was thinking who I got in the neighbourhood who might help. This person important?'

'One of my team and I want her back.'

'It's going to cost. I have to make the deal attractive to my contacts.'

'I don't want bounty hunters, just reliable leads, Harry.'

'Sure, I'll make the arrangements personally. For an old friend like you, I'll start right now.'

'So what *are* you suffering from Harry?'

Taking a moment to compose his reply, Bransk eventually admitted 'Ulcer,' somewhat shamefacedly.

Achingly fatigued, sorely close to exhaustion, Nick dragged his bruised body off for a shower. Barely refreshed, he went through the old, tiresome routine of assessing the latest damage: a wonderful collage of rich purple and sunflower yellow had blossomed on different parts of his body. Using the hand basin as a dressing station, he attended to his cuts and grazes using a pack of antiseptic wipes on his hands and face. For the deeper grazes and gashes down his side and legs, he liberally doused them with Betadine that stung like crazy.

Using the palm of a hand to fan a porthole in the misted bathroom mirror, he stared at his features as if they belonged to a proxy he barely knew: the telltale scars of a veteran campaigner were still there, the old mementoes of previous battles – broken nose, the dark hair peppered with an odd strand of grey, the piercing, unforgiving eyes, weathered creases and sincere laugh lines. But he had that vivid sensation of looking at a 3D portrait without the benefit of the ridiculous glasses, and his slightly out of sync overlay was ageing too fast. Pretty soon he'd become a total stranger on the outside, quite convinced that his skin had a life of its own.

More than anything he wanted to sleep. But that hinterland of peace and rest refused his entreaties, despite painkillers and two neat glasses of Laphroaig. Slouched in a chair by the window he watched the square beside the round tower, the late afternoon sun gradually thawing the post-operational tension screwed tight into his muscles. At some point he must have dozed, then rudely awakened by the window slamming closed by a fist of cold wind.

Wondering if after so many vicious operations he was finally teetering on the edge of a meltdown, what Head Office euphemistically labelled a 'personal event', he spent the rest of the evening locked in his room. He had clean sheets, modern, feature wallpaper and nothing more to do but sink headlong into his whisky, reminding himself he was alive, others were dead. He aimlessly watched television; strangely fascinated by a quiz show seemingly broadcast straight out of the Eighties, including a blonde presenter hosting a bizarre game of chance no one seemed to win.

Sunk in its hollow on his pillow, his phone chimed with a clear, incoming text that insisted: 'CT24 News channel. Now.' Flicking through the predictable and inane, he caught a final segment of a breaking story on a series of IED attacks. Eight all told. Car bombs every one: the targets British or Israeli. He stared at a montage of static shots, some clear, some blurry from eyewitnesses' footage after the events in London, Paris, Amsterdam and Berlin. Over this grim spectacle of burnt out twisted vehicles, the news anchor quoted an unnamed source confirming the latest attacks were linked to a car bomb in Prague that claimed the life of a British diplomat's husband. Glancing at his phone, Nick's next text was just as stark: it read – 'Developments. Contact shortly'.

Three

The call from Head Office gave Nick an hour's advanced warning. It also contained a chain of coded directions. Leaving his hotel before nine, he hit the bars around Frauentormauer, never hanging around for more than one drink. Nick's eyes, even with his glass level to his lips, always found the door, keenly appraising who left, the intentions of those arriving. Feeling anything but in rude health, Nick headed north across the Karlsbrücke, the river a wide, dark scar. Along its banks, glass and stone faced apartments dripped bold squares of lights into the slow moving current.

Mollified that he'd done enough dry cleaning to ensure it was safe to continue, he sheltered in a corner of the Trödelmarkt. He picked out the landmark he'd been instructed to look for: the four-star Pension Gustav run by one of the Service's emergency irregulars. A sparse biographical summary offered nothing more than: 'British Council, rtd. Snr Pos. Clearance Grading – Accommodation of senior personnel and priority assets.'

They say that about every irregular housekeeper on the books thought Nick, making two discreet passes. The stores ringing each side of the square were exclusive, reserved for Nürnberg's affluent consumers of style. Luxury he'd never need – chronograph watches, furs, designer denim, artful vials of perfume costing more than an apartment. He strolled on down an *allee* and a narrow flight of steps emptying into a courtyard. Young trees had strings of lights threaded through their branches; a thousand tiny starlight bulbs synchronised into a galactic display.

Dawdling outside a gallery dealing in mural sized chromogenic prints commencing at a thousand euros, he made one final assessment of his destination. Cosseted between a café and a men's emporium, the period hotel was a sliver of a building tucked under a sleek Dutch gable; one corner completed by a Rapunzel tower. In place of a princess, each curved window contained vases of cut flowers.

Scanning in an anticlockwise sweep he checked each viable position where footpads may be lurking, his eyes alert for the giveaway tokens of a team playing him in sequence from the shadowy sides of the square. He found nothing that in tradecraft jargon 'raised the temperature'. As an additional precaution he formed basic escape routes along two *allees*, one with stone stairs fanning down to the river.

Having nothing more to worry about, Nick took his chances and entered Pension Gustav. Slewed at an angle in one corner of the reception a baby grand piano. Lining the black and cream walls life-sized prints of Brahms, Wagner, Vivaldi, Beethoven in garish Lichtenstein imitations, complete with speech bubbles mouthing the greeting *'Willkommen! Lassen Sie Ihren Aufenthalt beginnen.'*

Not planning on a stay or knowing how welcome he would be, Nick struck a triangle bell mounted on a wooden stand with a miniature silver rod. Responding to the bell's muted peel, a tall, reed of a man locked resignedly into his sixties stepped through a black wall panel disguised as a door. Adapted as a sort of contemporary canvas, the panel held a pair of surreal purple lips proffering a generous kiss.

His craggy, starved face, a good deal of it forehead, made Nick think of a defrocked priest for some reason. The owner clasped his bony hands then balled them into fists, shifting from foot to foot reading Nick. He nodded, he smiled, but it only made him seem totally ill-suited to working front of house.

'Willkommen... Willkommen,' he announced bereft of enthusiasm. *'Willkommen im Heimat-und Gästehaus von Tarvin.'*

'Ich habe einen Freund, der hier wohnt und wir haben verabredet, uns hier zu treffen,' Nick explained. *'Vielleicht hat mein Freund, Herr Münden eine Nachricht für mich hinterlassen?'*

Sympathetically clicking his tongue at Nick's friend having let him down, the irregular automatically switched to a pre-arranged safe house protocol, agreeing that Herr Münden had indeed left a message for Nick to join him in his room. *'Er bittet darum, dass Sie zu ihm kommen. Zimmer 12.'*

'Danke.'

'Bitte sehr!' And he passed Nick a key card, directing him towards a curved staircase, sending him on his way with a desultory last glance from tired, mournful eyes.

At a sharp landing turn on the stairs a woman waited for him to pass, her narrow eyes flicking over Nick with the hostile contempt reserved for inferiors. He continued upwards, through her cocktail of perfume lingering above the oak treads like a mist. He followed the scrolled directions to Room 12 down a main corridor covering the length of the hotel, then three steps to its own isolated landing; a staging post in an expedition into the unknown. Inserting the key card, Nick waited for a couple of seconds. Pushing the door fully open he treated this entry as the first gateway towards an act of resolution.

Not taking his eyes off Nick from his position sloughed in a squat club chair, Paul Rossan's furtive, lean face diligently scanned his visitor.

'Dear God… you said you had only minor scratches,' Rossan said, on his feet, looking Nick over, his expression one of pure alarm.

'I'll live.'

If Nick wanted conclusive proof that he hadn't been hung out to dry, he got it at that very moment: a couple of loping steps and Paul Rossan, the Services' Director for Requirement and Production was cranking Nick's hand tightly, the grip bestowed on an old, dear friend who also happened to be a valued colleague.

Despite his fatigue Nick's trained eye did an unprompted, instinctive appraisal of his surroundings. The room, certainly not large enough to be regarded as a suite, had handsome proportions to accommodate discerning middle-class travellers. The furniture came from the heavy, reliable Biedermeier school. It had left deep footprints in the grey carpet following what Nick guessed had been an impromptu reshuffle.

'Not much of a welcoming committee,' said Nick idly picking his way around the room. 'Hope you got a refund when you cancelled the band.'

'Nick… Nick… I understand what you're feeling.' Worn and creased by his own battles within the secret world, Rossan stood framed against the decadent wallpaper; silver and gold flowers growing wild on a charcoal background. His bristling demeanour was that of a manager called to deal with a guest's complaint.

'Do you. That's good, because I don't.'

This would have been the first taste of freedom for Taurus after the final vehicle change in Altenberg, Nick realised. The room had been thoughtfully prepared for the opening round of Taurus' debriefing: the claw-foot writing desk and extra chairs forming the centrepiece for the Services' prime exhibit.

'Roly is doing his damnedest to contain the situation,' Rossan said in that sort of eager way some men have of trying to talk their way around a confrontation.

'It's beyond containing,' Nick answered, peering into the bathroom. He pulled the cord for the light and fan, turning it on then off, listening for an extra mechanical whine or electronic sniffle from recorders.

'This might be too major even for Roly to sweep under the carpet,' he added, imagining Roly's disappointment at missing his opportunity to be master of ceremonies. Good old Roland Blackmore, the Service's Director Global Affairs and Security never gave up the chance of playing to a full house.

'You're drained, you just need to rest,' insisted Rossan.

'Do I?' Nick tried the sockets and lights around the room. 'Are we mute or live?' he wondered. He casually glanced where he thought the wire mechanics would have placed their wares for rolling twenty-four hour coverage, the concealed devices to steal every decibel of sound. There were dozens of available positions he realised: the broad cherry wood wardrobe where Rossan's overcoat dangled on a wooden hanger off a lip on one door, the flat screen television, lamps, the PIR sensor; it was amazing where GSM infinity devices could be installed.

'It's all disconnected,' Rossan stated. 'They packed away their toys.... Didn't seem any point them staying on.'

'No,' agreed Nick.

He had witnessed other defectors go through the quaint merry-go-round of debriefing in similar requisitioned interrogation chambers. The first open house taster session began with the emotional process of stripping away a defector's reluctance to bare their souls. The atmosphere and surroundings had to be just right, Nick remembered. It was like a first date. Anywhere shambolic or too stark gave the impression of a miserly attitude that rubbed off on the defector. Too comfortable or luxurious suggested to the defector they had bargaining power. For Taurus they had got it more or less balanced. The opening round would be led by Aspley thumbscrews, with invited guests from sister services who had brokered their way in or paid the ultimate fee, a pledge of full cooperation later on another operational route.

'Can we proceed?' Rossan suggested, sorely tried.

'Don't let me hold you back.'

Nick slipped off his overcoat, sitting wearily on a plump corner of an antique cast-iron bed its corner posts topped by brass finials. A white duvet complete with a treble clef had one corner turned down below a bank of red pillows. He thought give me ten minutes alone and I could sleep for a month. But he'd things to discuss. Just minor details, he thought. Clearing my team of blame for a compromised operation, trying to forget the cold print of death left on his fingers from Wilsden's skin, pushing against the barrier of exhaustion to locate Leiston.

'The Chief is coming out to see you,' Rossan announced. His narrow brow ruffled in perplexity, he glanced distractedly about the room, as if hunting for something he'd misplaced. 'He's asked me to reassure you he isn't intending on carrying out a witch hunt or interrogation,' he continued.

'I'm sure that will stop Leiston worrying.' He stared hard at Rossan.

He's putting too many hours in, thought Nick. Small puffy hammocks of skin were strung under Rossan's eyes, the usual vitality that nipped his cheeks with a ruddy, country tint was missing, replaced by the lacklustre and dull pallor of a man confined inside the sterile atmosphere of one too many emergency meetings.

'The rest of your teams made it back, by the way,' Rossan disclosed, trying to sound upbeat.

'Except for Wilsden.'

'It's an occupational hazard.'

'Is it?' Nick snapped, watching Rossan, his back to the bed.

It's the little rituals that keep us normal he thought, as Rossan uncapped a bottle of Laphroaig, dispensing the familiar safe house rites of hospitality for the 'ghosts' who arrived and departed at strange hours.

'Has anyone claimed responsibility for the attacks?'

'The usual cranks, no one we'd class as serious,' Rossan admitted, irritated. He poured two glasses of Laphroaig: his own measure modest, and for Nick, a bracing reviver deemed suitable for survivors. 'Damascus did release a statement claiming the terrorist atrocities were carried out by the agents of imperialist British and Zionist intelligence,' he continued, handing Nick his glass.

'For any particular reason?'

Leaning back against a chest of drawers Rossan cupped his glass, both hands held slightly out in front of him. He stared remotely down into his drink.

It's not a debriefing, but a secret Benediction, decided Nick as the first warm pulses of Laphroaig seeped through his veins in a heady reunion. We just need candles, a thurible, the body and blood of all those who meant so much to me and I'm free of death's shackles, Nick thought. Rossan should be offering up a chalice not a glass of malt, and I then I would have a simple recitation to save my soul in preparation for my absolution.

But Rossan, locked in his own cloud of pessimism, resumed with a précis of the statement issued by Damascus. 'Our murder of innocent British citizens and Jews is alleged to be a diversionary tactic,' he explained. 'A smokescreen to hide the fact that we kidnapped the Syrian Second Secretary to Moscow who was to be smuggled to Tel Aviv,' Rossan added, with a sneer of outright disdain. 'According to Damascus, the operation was foiled by the brilliance of the Syrian External Security Division. But before they could intervene and save their loyal patriot, the imperialist assassins butchered him in cold blood to save their own necks. They are offering a reward for the repatriation of their noble, martyr's body.' Rossan stared hard at Nick. 'There's no chance they're likely to get Taurus back is there?'

'He's been disposed of,' Nick said flatly. 'Permanently.' He took a deeper hit of whisky, the alcohol acting as an accelerant, touching off his unspent fury and frustration. 'Don't worry, Paul, I've had the mess cleared up. Part of CO8's remit isn't it? Specialists in all aspects of dirty work, remember? The car's been crushed and Ganton is having Wilsden flown home as diplomatic freight.'

'Dear God, Nick, you're impossible,' snapped Rossan in a flash of temper.

'It's Head Office's definition of what's possible that's the problem,' countered Nick draining his glass. 'Taurus must have been blown the moment he decided to defect. We walked into a set-up. Who was he, Paul? Why didn't we have a guide to his value? An indication that there might *just* be a chance of more than hostile countermeasures?'

'Taurus...' Rossan began grudgingly, 'enjoyed a colourful reputation as an *Akab 1* commander before his appointment as Second Secretary to Moscow. Unfortunately,' he continued, returning to the club chair, 'portions of the mud flung from Damascus are sticking. We did have friends in Tel Aviv extremely keen to talk to him.'

In a single rush of angry energy Nick was off the bed, doling out another glass of Laphroaig, in no mood to offer Rossan a refill.

'Who wouldn't be,' he fumed, striding past the club chair. Lounging a little to the side of a window facing down into the square Nick recalled the arrogance of Taurus, his rush to defend himself with a concealed weapon. Viewed from this side of the extraction, Nick realised Taurus would be a crucial key to unlock the workings of *Akab 1*.

In the last eight or nine months, *Akab 1* featured consistently on the Joint Intelligence Committee's target list; an urgent appeal for a priority increase of product to be included in its Red Book assessments. An autonomous branch of *Shu'bat al-Mukhabarat al-'Askariyya*, the Military Intelligence Directorate of Syria, it consisted of covert operational units formed to detect, protect and neutralise any dissident threats to the Damascus regime. And that included sponsoring and supporting terrorist groups to operate overseas.

'We didn't go out on a limb because he was just handling diplomacy and enjoying the cocktail circuit in Moscow did we?'

Staring once more at his untouched drink, Rossan shook his head. 'Taurus cut his diplomatic teeth in Lebanon. He was the pivotal mover in forming alliances with a bagful of militant groups. In return for their undying devotion to Damascus' geopolitical ambitions and ideological call to arms, he ensured they were top of the list for funding and Russian weapons.'

'Taurus was the catch of the year, a defector we couldn't afford to turn away. That a fair assessment, Paul?'

'It has its merits,' Rossan sniped defensively.

'Who made the approach?' Dug in, Nick refused to yield any ground.

'Before he took up his post in Moscow, he made contact with one of our representatives in Beirut,' Rossan explained warily. 'Taurus was utterly disillusioned, painting a picture of how his masters were pushing his beloved country into a no-win situation. His increasing paranoia was that he might be left on the wrong side of the fence if the Damascus regime started to tumble.'

'No one thought to push a little deeper why this brilliant, celebrated walk-in volunteered his services?' Nick fumed, 'Come on Paul, it has all the hallmarks of a dangle, and we just might have royally bought it.' It wasn't the first time Head Office had raved over a new asset who happened to be a planted defector remembered Nick.

'Dear God, Nick,' Rossan snapped, 'of course the possibility of Taurus being a dangle was assessed. He was rated genuine.'

'Who by?'

'We landed him, Nick, at least give us credit for that.' Rossan waspishly stung back. 'The courting of Taurus was compartmentalised, his potential product rating A1. Bardney seduced him for over six months in Moscow, playing him hot and cold. Approach and back off... Approach and back off... until he had the measure of Taurus. It wasn't a question of having to talk him over the line, Bardney had to hold him off. Taurus' motivation was venal, pure greed; he held the winning hand but we were going to decide when he played it. We were in control.'

'He was given a very generous rating,' observed Nick, his demeanour exuding that of a clerk querying minor details.

'It was fully deserved as far as the Middle East Desk was concerned,' Rossan countered. 'They assigned specialist handlers.'

'Leiston?' Nick didn't turn from the window. He heard Rossan sigh followed by a weary 'Yes.' If she wasn't already dead she'd be sold on to the highest bidder, reasoned Nick. Along with Taurus there would be other premium assets she'd ran, and for all he knew, she could have another 'live feed' on the go: someone unaware that their life was also about to slip out of their control. How much she disclosed depended on maintaining the pretence she had value. Nick estimated – not out of cool disregard, but operational experience and expediency – Leiston had seventy-two hours to hide behind her legend.

'Roly... God help them... has personally visited both sets of relatives,' Rossan disclosed.

Nodding distractedly, Nick's thoughts were running counter-current along another trajectory. He asked: 'Which of the cranks who have claimed responsibility for the ambush stand out? Have Head Office amber lit any of them as capable of disrupting the extraction?'

'*Komunistická obranná síla Československa, the KOSC,*' Rossan admitted.

'I thought the Communist Defence Force of Czechoslovakia were only active online?'

'It's too ridiculous to contemplate.'

'It just might make sense,' Nick disagreed.

'Theoretically? Ideologically? Speculatively?' Rossan demanded, quite out of sorts.

'Empirically... The little welcoming party that we ran into were Czech,' confirmed Nick.

'None of it adds up.'

'Neither does targeting the husband of a British diplomat,' said Nick. '*Who* is she?'

'Celia Rewall, Deputy Head of Mission. She was the Prague end of the FCO's liaison input on Operation Julius…'

'Have we talked to her?'

'We can't locate her. If she *was* the intended target, she could have gone to ground. She may even have been abducted like Leiston for all we know.'

'Maybe she and Leiston have already been shipped out?'

'Dear God, Nick,' Rossan thundered, 'don't go there… Rewall had been nominated as one of Taurus' tertiary debriefers when he reached here.'

'How many active projects did Leiston have on the go?'

'She has her usual caseload which you know we're not permitted to discuss,' Rossan acidly revealed.

'Have they been warned?'

'Not all of them, Roly's people are working on it. They're getting word out to anyone with past or present dealings with Leiston – assets and irregulars,' Rossan explained.

'They need to work faster.' Nick's ire was well and truly up. 'What material had Taurus promised us?'

'One of his Moscow remits was as principal liaison between Damascus and militant factions operating in Europe. He *was* the controller, Nick. He tasked them, he approved finance, he nominated targets, he green lit assassinations requested by the regime.'

'He handled these terrorist groups alone?'

'For routine servicing and face to face meetings he used a Palestinian,' admitted Rossan, not caring to look at Nick.

'Who?'

'Zaid Khallet.'

'Khallet…' Nick slammed his hand against the window casing. 'Remind me, Paul, just so that I can get this straight. The Zaid Khallet I'm thinking about was a workname, owner unidentified. We couldn't put a face to the name and neither could any of our friends. Mention him to our Palestinian assets and they'd run a mile. In our estimation he was either a phantom bogeyman created so we'd chase our tails or a seriously deadly high-ranking operator.'

'Taurus named Zaid Khallet as his influential asset. That's what we have to work with, Nick.'

'It isn't just the Syrians we need to be looking at, Paul.'

'If we go after a Palestinian target without any absolute evidence, our detractors in Whitehall will have a field day,' Rossan sighed.

'That's outstanding Paul,' Nick raged, 'Is that an official veto or have you skipped a couple of chapters ahead?'

'We still have a chance to penetrate militant cells and networks operating in Europe,' countered Rossan.

'Really? What with... Taurus is dead.' Nick stared at his good friend.

'Then you'll have to find a way.'

After that admission, Rossan kept his own counsel during an indecently charged silence. Nick remained fixed by the window like a small boy returned as a man, familiarising himself with the lay of the land, remembering long days of festering arguments from his youth that torched friendships. He stared ahead through the snow beating hopelessly against the glass. Below him Nürnberg ticked remorselessly on.

Coming in steady waves, the swirling flakes broke over the sharp pastel gables of the pretty Baroque houses circling the Trödelmarkt like covered wagons anticipating an attack. Down under the pitched eaves of a triangular courtyard, a young woman's steps clicked smoothly away, beating the retreat as the city settled into its evening routine. Normality everywhere he glanced, and it grieved him to think of Leiston and Rewall cut off from these incidental moments; life's trivial details reminding you being alive actually counted for something.

'Before we go off at half-cock chasing shadows, perhaps you might find if... how... and why the KOSC *are* involved,' Rossan adamantly stated, resurrecting his original thread, sternly assessing Nick. 'Our Prague Station insist the KOSC remain a fringe group. Lunatics and charlatans who couldn't progress beyond issuing threatening statements they didn't have the means to follow up.'

'Well someone's decided that it's time they grew up,' Nick proposed, finally turning from the window, his vigil complete. His spine stiff, the Laphroaig drained, he rested his back against the wall. 'They've had training,' he added, grimacing as his shoulder protested. 'Someone's using them as freelancers.'

'If you mean the Syrians... yes, that might be more logical,' said Rossan tartly.

'None of this is logical, Paul. This style of European operation just isn't the way Damascus does business,' countered Nick.

'So who is it?' flared Rossan. 'Please don't suggest the KOSC are included in a Palestinian orbat.'

But Nick refused to dismiss the possibility of the KOSC having a role in a Palestinian faction's order of battle. 'The ambush, the IEDs,' Nick continued earnestly, 'It matches the strategy of Palestinian militants.'

'Come on, Nick. Those groups are unlikely to risk any political fallout likely to strengthen the Israeli position.'

'The new radical factions don't care. Political considerations aren't high on their agenda.' Restless, his anger growing, Nick mooched off on another slow circuit of the room.

'Surely if it was a Palestinian militant group, they would have claimed credit by now,' Rossan objected.

Nick paused at an espresso machine on a long, extravagant dressing table. In neat clusters cups, saucers, and a small basket of individually wrapped biscuits. All the vitally important essentials for the smooth running of a clandestine gathering thought Nick, his exhaustion deepening.

'Exactly how much evidence do you need, Paul?'

'Enough to convince the Prime Minister and Foreign Secretary that we have legitimate reason to mount a valid operation,' said Rossan. Reproving someone or something with a curt shake of his head, he was on his feet, pacing the room's length: a prisoner getting the measure of his cell.

'They'll have to use their prudence.'

'That's asking for the impossible,' Rossan speculated, refilling both glasses. 'If we have Palestinian militias loyal to Damascus hell-bent on drawing Israel into a new conflict on British or European soil, the Foreign Secretary will want immediate, rolling updates.'

'He'll have to join the queue.' Nick gave a little sway as he accepted his whisky and downed it in one. 'I've things to finish.'

Shrugging on his overcoat, his head feeling far too flimsy for his body, he dipped his fingers into an inside pocket. 'Give him those,' he suggested, dropping two passports into Rossan's lap – one belonging to Wilsden, the other Taurus, both covers smeared in dried blood.

Walking out he heard Rossan call out something, but Nick continued without turning. On a floor below a woman laughed uproariously. From another part of the hotel, the stirring Prelude to Bizet's *L'Arlésienne* swept him down to reception.

Buying a coffee at a café with prominent views of the river, his eyes were bleary, half closed. His appearance drew wary stares from the waiters. You should see me after a six month operation he thought, leaving a meagre tip, clattering the table as he left.

Reaching his hotel he steered clear of the front desk, trudging up to his room, a dishevelled combatant returning from the front line. Dumping his overcoat he went into the bathroom and hitched up his shirt, examining his deep grazes down his side in the glare of the mirror strip light. The one giving him the most pain, a three inch scar curving towards his stomach. Under the light it shone pale and fine: his very own strip of mercury in a diagonal line.

Maybe they're infected, he thought, clutching his bottle of Laphroaig and a tumbler. What did it matter he reasoned, I'll either keep going or fall flat on my face. Dragging his legs up on the bed, he jammed a pillow behind his head, adjusting his neck into a comfortable position before the important matter of absolving his mind, body and soul with whisky. Ten minutes of sleep, that was all he needed.

• • •

Twice they'd moved her across the city trussed in the boot of a car, then a van. The car she noted was old, the chassis squeaked in a hundred different places and a rear spring needed replacing. The van stank of lubricants and grease as if she was actually riding in the engine. Each transfer came as a rapid, brutal handover. Not a word spoken, just the blunt nudging, pushing and lifting as they hauled her from vehicle to vehicle. Keeping track of night and day was a problem.

Dragged into her latest holding area, the initial rush of freezing air swallowed every inch of heat from her body. She felt it more on her shoeless right foot even though they'd bound it with some sort of material and taped it tight. The same binding wound around her legs up to her knees, the same tape they'd wrapped around the plastic ties pinning her wrists together behind her back.

Discarded in a corner, a coarse blanket draped haphazardly over her shoulders, she'd picked out certain sounds – the rush of an express train, the banging, scraping of a distant object falling, the dull voices from a radio, laptop, television, tablet or phone murmuring in a distant room.

What worried her was the thick stench of petrol, diesel and oil vapour that clung to the inside of a thick hangman's bag they'd hooded her with. Peculiarly, she wasn't afraid, confident when the interrogation came, she had the training to cope. All she'd volunteered so far was that she worked for the Foreign Office as a diplomatic resettlement officer: enough, she hoped, to convince them she was a commodity more valuable alive than dead.

She flinched badly when a heavy door slammed somewhere off to her left and behind her. Tensed, anticipating another change of location, waiting for the hands snatching for a hold under her arms, a rush of whispered commands, she prepared herself, but nothing happened. So slowly, her confidence returning, she angled her head forwards. Using her shoulder like a novice escapologist, she started to work the hood upwards just a fraction. If she could get a glimpse of the floor she could start to map her surroundings. Not to attempt anything stupid, just as evidence, a future reference.

The footsteps took her by surprise and to her annoyance she actually gasped. Aimed straight at her in a furious burst, they pulled up smartly and she felt the blow to the side of her head; an open hand swung downwards in rage. Another solid cuff rocked her head back. She realised her stupid mistake. Not considering that someone had been watching her, allowing her to transgress, break some unwritten rules, relishing a chance to punish her, inflict pain.

Stood over her, the guard – a woman, young – yelled for reinforcements between shrieking abuse. Afraid more than she'd ever been, she counted more footsteps slap... slap... slap against what she guessed was a concrete floor. Grabbed by her hair through the hood, a strong and determined pair of hands dragged her into another corner. As another blow partly set her ear buzzing and burning, a furious argument broke out in Arabic above her head. For the first time she felt alone and doomed. That's when the music began: the whump of base from albums or tracks played non-stop somewhere high, on a distant floor.

Four

Cars and delivery vans lined the square outside Nick's hotel where, the next morning, he did a meandering tour of all four sides at a sedate pace, casually checking out each vehicle with the ruthless patience of a parking warden. In tradecraft jargon he did a 'turn around the block', coming back in reverse direction, his pace fluid, each step brisk. Assured his back was well and truly unmarked, Nick went about making his transport arrangements.

All the way from the Hauptbahnhof rich folds of heavy cloud gathered in packs threatening sleet as Nick's tram glided serenely through the city, gently swaying out into the neatly ordered suburbs where spies never ventured unless summoned. The route belonged to a different era, marking the final stage in a journey undertaken by the faithful when they trooped to the *Reichsparteitagsgelände* to parade before their *Führer*. And I'm about to do the same but on a much smaller scale Nick thought, close to a drowsy peace as his tram sneaked nearer to the old Nazi Party Rally Grounds.

The sleet eventually came in long, drifting bands, cascading across Bayernstraße when Nick, with his shoulder tingling, alighted at the *Dokuzentrum*. Cursing Rossan's oblique instructions, he paid his entrance fee then dutifully spent a couple of minutes amongst depressing exhibits. He started on a clockwise circuit of the outer colonnaded horseshoe walkway, moving through dark, vaulted stone spans dripping with severe blocks of shadow. Both hands were drawn, poised at his side. For there is nothing a fieldman hates more than the unknown and the corpus of wisdom runs along the line of: if you're entering a location that hasn't been swept clean, you operate on a strictly offensive basis.

Which Nick did, moving with diligent care through each of Speer's dismal chambers lining his grandiose, unfinished *Kongresshalle* main arena. Two arch spans along, he glimpsed movement. Fast on her feet, Sir Martin

Bailrigg's personal protection officer vetted Nick, nodded solemnly behind her before stepping graciously aside. A former diplomat with his own take on how and where the Service should be guided, Bailrigg rode over fools in a merciless display of power. Trim and fit, he paid a premium for his suits and wore them with the panache of a prisoner carrying out hard labour. Nick had only witnessed him truly happy in his Barbour, a Tattersall shirt of faded gold blue and brown checks, heavy corduroys careworn at the knees, a holed cable stitched sweater and Cumbrian boots. Topping off this weekend ensemble he habitually carried a shotgun broken under one arm when he fervently hunted vermin on his Suffolk estate.

'It's become a dog's bollocks and I'm not having it, Nicholas,' announced Bailrigg, Chief of the Service.

Fully stretched, Bailrigg might have topped the scale at an inch over six foot, but his shoulders were increasingly bowed noticed Nick: it's the burden of fighting on all fronts – politicians, the poaching parties from Security, allies demanding to be cut-in, and they were just the Service's friends he thought.

'I'm not overjoyed,' said Nick.

Concealed deeper inside the colonnade's shadow, Nick caught the outline of another figure taking cover: a mystery guest wrapped snugly in an overcoat as he shifted restlessly awaiting his cue in the wings.

'Callerton, Director of the FCO's Diplomatic Security Directorate,' Bailrigg seethed, spitting out the introduction, his words a barbed flail. 'He's fretting, Nicholas. He wants to get his pennyworth in. Oh, *he'll* have his moment,' vowed Bailrigg, casting a firm glance over his wide shoulder, rounded like a tail fin.

Pacing between the colonnades Bailrigg's babysitter flitted in tight, controlled circles. Nick recollected how she had been at the Chief's side from the opening hour of his appointment. Where C found her, he never disclosed. She just arrived, calling herself Flin. First name, workname, surname? No one knew. She was Flin and Flin she stayed. She can't hold still for a moment realised Nick, glimpsing her springy pace when she ventured out on patrol, her coordinates taking her no farther than the railings and back.

'No one had a chance... that the gist of it?' Bailrigg resumed. 'No one could be saved? No lifebelts to hand around?'

Nick shook his head in a sorry affirmation. 'But Leiston might have a chance.'

'Quite.' He crooked his finger and beckoned forward his very own guardian angel. From inside her thickly padded jacket, Flin produced a single sheet of photo paper before promptly retreating. 'Received by the Prague Embassy,' he continued with distaste, handing it over.

A print taken from all action, moving footage decided Nick, mulling over the image. At the edges of an unusual group portrait there were slight blur lines from when motion is transferred into a still. The figures, four in total, were crowded into a shell of a room faced in brick with crumbling threads of mortar. The room was lit sparingly. Three walls were visible and Nick supposed it to be some sort of cellar or industrial storeroom. Two female figures sat with their hands bound in their laps, staring impassively ahead at the camera's lens. The abductors, in oddly matched surplus combat shirts, red berets, sunglasses and keffiyehs, had squeezed in on either side of the hostages making sure they were in the frame. They posed in a stiff revolutionary style, treating the camera as if it were an enemy, their Czech Vz.58s aimed at a hostage. A banner tacked up in the background added nothing but stage dressing, giving the scene its chilling verisimilitude. Beneath the proclamation – '*Komunistická obranná síla Československa*' – spaced pedantically in black capitals, a clenched fist was entwined through the workers' symbol of a hammer and sickle.

'What are they demanding?'

'The KOSC have generously issued an ultimatum,' Bailrigg said, as though still coming to terms with the sheer audacity. 'The release of all political prisoners held throughout Europe in exchange for Leiston and Rewall. It's all a piece of flummery and I'm not buying it.'

'It's a false flag operation, the KOSC are providing the front,' Nick suggested.

'Full marks, Nicholas, go to the top of the class,' Bailrigg answered. Tapping Nick's forearm, he pointed out a route along the walkway. 'Too damn cold,' he added on the move, Nick in step at his side. 'At my age, you freeze up if you stand still for more than five minutes.'

The tidy little group led by Bailrigg set out like a deputation. Behind them Nick glanced at the unhappy Callerton slipstreaming a good head and a length forlornly in Bailrigg's steps. As to Flin, he could see no trace. She's part woman and part shadow, Nick decided, Bailrigg's very own succubus.

'We can't just write the KOSC off,' warned Nick.

'No, Nicholas,' Bailrigg snapped, his ire rising, 'we cannot. They're marionettes, a single act in a gala performance. We take them seriously we pay them respect. We flatter them with attention until *you* find the true impresario behind our woes. As of this moment everyone with an iota of anti-British feeling and their dog will be ready to bid on Leiston and Rewall if they're offered up for auction. The controller of this dirty little venture will want a handsome reward for their efforts.'

'What's the official line?'

'We would not have one if it were not for a cretin at the Embassy,' Bailrigg declared, directing his obloquy at Callerton with a noxious stare.

'I'm sure it was a misunderstanding,' Callerton claimed from a safe distance.

'Bollocks,' snarled Bailrigg. 'Misunderstanding my arse.'

'The Acting DHM assured me the leak could not be deliberate,' Callerton protested.

'Hear that, Nicholas. We have a faceless whistle-blower inside the Embassy and *he* only got as far as the *Acting* Deputy Head of Mission for an explanation, when *he* should have been twisting the Ambassador's arm for answers,' Bailrigg seethed, gesturing to the FCO man.

'How much is out in the open?' Nick wondered.

'What isn't?' ranted Bailrigg. 'Our whistle-blower, assuming the rights of God Almighty, started their own campaign to petition for clemency on Rewall's behalf. They leaked her predicament to a Czech journalist of a certain anti-establishment persuasion. The result, Nicholas, is that he could merrily flout the DA-notice we have in place, running with an exclusive, front page splash claiming the Embassy was up to its ears in an illegal operation. He *claims* the British Government has washed its hands of a valued diplomat kidnapped along with a MI6 agent. That has placed the Embassy and its masters at King Charles' Street firmly in the media headlights,' Bailrigg explained, inchoate with rage. 'Downing Street has seen fit to deny any knowledge of an operation on Czech soil. The Foreign Secretary has issued a statement confirming that the UK Government will not respond to terrorist demands. Our missing diplomat is not a saint, nor is she going to be a martyr,' Bailrigg railed. 'Not if I have my way.'

'What's the concern with Rewall?'

Lunging over to the balustrade railings, Bailrigg clamped the top rail tight in his gloved hands. He glared away into the open bowl, his eyes fixed in the distance where the Nazi Party delegates gathered: his expression set; a senator waiting for the opening fight in what could very well have been the Coliseum.

'Tell him,' Bailrigg decreed, not even bothering to turn and find the hapless Callerton. 'Tell Nicholas what you have.'

Compact and hollow cheeked, Callerton's sallow skin had the cool sheen of a church candle. 'The Acting DHM confirmed that Mrs. Rewall has...'

'Been a model diplomat,' Bailrigg jumped in, unable to contain his wrath. 'But according to our brothers in Whitehall she's not earmarked for an Ambassadorship,' he added, his anger raising florid, streaky patches on his cheeks. 'Apparently there are doubts about her suitability for a top table posting. You haven't heard the best bit,' he said to Nick.

'Compartmentalised briefing notes on Operation Julius were circulated by yourselves per our standing agreement, and distributed on a strictly limited need-to-know basis...' Callerton rushed out his prepared statement. He paused, waiting for an interruption. When it didn't materialise he filled his chest with a long gulp of air, seizing his chance he bolted for the finishing line. 'Rewall possess satisfactory clearance to be fully indoctrinated at the appropriate level. She was added to the operational list, code word protected.'

'She's more less got the operational crown jewels,' Bailrigg cut in, his breath popping in condensed ack-ack bursts against the icy air. 'Our Mr. Tysoe is reporting directly to me in the morning,' vowed C, the most vexed Nick had seen him for at least a month. 'He may be young. He may be headstrong. He may be versed in wheedling his way around his Section Head, but Tysoe is going to explain to me – fully, in person – why he allowed so much of our classified wares to be shared. Continue...'

Obeying Bailrigg's directive Callerton swallowed, plunging in once more, a daring swimmer not knowing if he'd make landfall. 'For the latter stages of her career Rewall has held a number of sensitive postings, based on and around the Middle East Policy Unit. Her record is actually quite outstanding. She has distinguished herself in all her recent posts. Following a period as Deputy Head of FCO Liaison Department and Deputy Head of the Counter-Terrorism Policy Department, she was on loan to the Cabinet Office providing Middle East Assessments. Before taking up her posting to Prague, she did four months in London as Head of the Lebanese Desk in our Middle East and North Africa Political Directorate. Her value cannot be overstated...'

'To the KOSC or us?' Bailrigg grumbled.

'With the best intentions...' Callerton objected.

'That's what the Devil started out with,' Bailrigg snapped, furiously closing Callerton down.

Off on his travels once more, Bailrigg covered the curving walkway in the measured sway of a man who has mastered the art of inner control: a feature Nick recognised in numerous interrogators who knew the answers in advance of their questions.

'So who's been slyly dipping into our back pocket? Who's our Phaeton?' Bailrigg demanded of Callerton, stopping without warning. 'Loose lips pass on secrets. Someone's been talking out of turn, and they will pay for their treachery. We need to know when Rewall fell into the clutches of the KOSC. Was it before or after the husband met his explosive finale? Something's rotten, I can feel it in my water,' concluded Bailrigg, his damning summary complete. 'Rewall being nabbed because of her links to the operation makes sense – just. But it's the spectacular demise of her husband that troubles me. That's for what? A mistake? Wrong car, wrong place? To cover for someone? To deceive us? Make us look in the other direction as our Attaginus shows us a clean pair of heels?'

Callerton stiffened his slender shoulders, sighed and returned to the point he was about to make. 'At this juncture, perhaps we shouldn't be drawn to assumptions that may very well turn out to be false.'

'I am not making assumptions, I am working from fact,' Bailrigg forcefully stated. 'Rewall knew of the operation in Prague – fact. That operation was compromised in Prague – fact. The ambush took place on the outskirts of Prague – fact. The reason for the termination of her husband is unclear – fact. Rewall is being held by the KOSC – fact. We've done some preliminary footwork, took soundings, checked the pulse. And for all our considerable efforts, we found nothing to suggest any problems or any inkling that *we* leaked like a sieve anywhere other than Prague – fact. Is that all the facts, Nicholas?'

'It's the facts,' agreed Nick, making a rare contribution.

'I've more facts for *you* to mull over,' Bailrigg announced to Callerton, his mood darkening. 'Our Middle East assets have been placed on emergency protocols – fact. The Embassy in Prague is locked down and virtually out of play – fact.'

Not waiting for clearance following Bailrigg's stricture, Callerton plunged automatically on. 'As far as I can ascertain, our officials carried out everything according to the pre-operational protocols supplied by yourselves.'

'We haven't reached the cherry on top, believe me,' pledged Bailrigg, seething. 'Tell him,' he ordered Callerton.

'Rewall's personal life...'

'Is an unholy mess,' Bailrigg impatiently added. 'Before her London posting, Rewall was recalled from Beirut with six months of her three year posting still to complete. Whilst in this delightful ancient city, her husband threatened to expose her for having a torrid affair.'

'A friend or someone we should know about?' Nick turned to Callerton who seemed entirely lost when asked for an opinion.

'We don't know,' railed Bailrigg. 'And that resulted in her stay becoming untenable. But the husband attempted to save his marriage for what it was worth. He went to the Ambassador who had a word on the quiet with the errant wife. And *we* have only now discovered this as hearsay because the Ambassador never filed a report. For this ne'er-do-well behaviour, Rewall was actually promoted on her arrival in London. I kid you not, Nicholas,' Bailrigg disclosed incredulous.

'Is that it?'

'No, Nicholas, that is not *it*,' fumed Bailrigg. 'She's also garnered a name for herself as a liberal free thinker,' he added. 'Her enthusiastic *premiere jeunesse* seemingly has no bounds. And they,' he nodded severely at Callerton, 'flatly deny that she went native in Beirut,' he simmered, turning wrathfully on the FCO man. 'We have been granted winged clearance to personal records of course. We can glut ourselves on the life, times and indiscretions of the whole Prague Embassy. But not it seems, on Rewall's *ménage à trois* in Beirut.'

Not waiting for another censure, Callerton defiantly went onto the offensive. 'With respect, just because one of our people has a personality or lifestyle that doesn't always sit comfortably within the orthodoxy of Government policy, does not necessarily preclude them from carrying out their duties effectively. Rewall's affair was fully investigated by her Ambassador in Beirut and at no time were her actions considered to have compromised official policy or Embassy security.'

'That's a blessed relief,' said Bailrigg with disarming charm. 'That's why she's never been considered Head of Mission material is it? I think you've earned yourself some refreshment.'

Cheered by such a painless dismissal Callerton strode off back down the walkway, a prisoner returning to solitary confinement.

'It stinks, Nicholas, the whole affair,' admitted Bailrigg, his head turned, watching Callerton slink back into the visitor's centre. 'With their customary nimble footwork, the FCO have shunted all the blame squarely onto our shoulders.' As they turned into the wind he flattened wild strands of greying hair flapping above both ears. 'I will not tolerate the Service, nor our partners, being used as whipping boys for the failures of others,' he declared. 'Our American and Israeli friends are running through possible leads for the KOSC's newly found thirst for making a name for themselves.'

The anger had flowed out of Bailrigg and he suddenly seemed remote and flat as the walkway came to a dead end.

'I have put in a request to Tel Aviv that our joint venture continues,' he disclosed, a man who inexpediently finds himself a winner, but the prize is only a consolation. 'You have a quite different goal.'

'The KOSC?'

Out in the arena a heavy gloom crept out over the open ground. Coming in spirals to meet it, the first tentative, probing, fingers of snow.

'We know fringe groups are always volatile, unpredictable,' said Bailrigg. 'Security and ourselves are always playing catch up until we have the leadership and operation structure within our sights. We cannot be seen to overtly engage in a bloody vendetta with a terrorist group, whatever their persuasion. You are on your own. No direct support, you remain in the black. If your name appears anywhere other than on a final post-operation report, we will deny that you were even conceived let alone born.'

'It's hardly likely that the KOSC guessed about Operation Julius.'

'You find me the culprit that tipped them the wink and I will personally walk them to the Gemonian Stairs,' Bailrigg insisted. 'They had inside help to fabricate this revolutionary illusion.'

'Obviously it was someone linked to the operation.'

'Don't be facetious. If I wanted comedy, I'd have put Teddy in control,' Bailrigg snapped, raising the alarming prospect of Edward 'Teddy' Hawick, his Deputy Chief of the Service playing an active role. 'That what you wanted?'

'No.'

'Thought so.'

In the cold air and miserly light, Bailrigg's features held a tired and pasty rinse; a country squire who'd lost his rude colour after being too long mired in the city.

'Do I include Rewall as a suspect?'

'You do not rule anyone or anything out. Rowena has prepared a package on our missing diplomat for you. Her life, her hobbies, her husband, her pets, her motivations – what little we officially have on record. I want Leiston and Rewall found, Nicholas. I want an inquisition. I want whoever did the dirty on us to squeal so hard I can hear them from my office.'

'Expedient disposal?'

'The damned lot. The works, every twisted turn you and your unofficial partners have to take, you follow it. Whoever is responsible is for the Tarpeian Rock. And you will ensure that we do not suffer any stigma through association. We cannot wait for the hue and cry in Prague to abate, so you make sure you operate so far below the radar you're underground.'

'What's the connection with the IED victims?'

'The only common denominator we can establish is that they were employees of Israeli companies based in Europe or in the case of the Britons, they did direct business with Israel. We're putting out white noise to throw off the pack.'

Coming silently forward, Flin touched Bailrigg on the arm, so softly it was almost a caress. 'I have another appointment, Nicholas...'

'If the KOSC have Middle East backers, you know what that means for Leiston and Rewall,' said Nick.

'Of course I do. The KOSC are stooges. They could not have advanced beyond idle Internet chatter without a guiding hand or two. They are cut from the same cloth as the Red Army Faction in the Seventies. Whether they appreciate that is a moot point. I'm not buying the KOSC as solo operators. You get to the bottom of this, Nicholas. You find Leiston and Rewall and find them fast.' Leaving this codicil hanging behind him, Bailrigg dug his hands deep into his overcoat pockets sweeping imperiously away.

Lost inside the temperamental light that ran in impish waves through the colonnades, Nick watched Bailrigg go at full tilt for the exit. Bouncing not far off her Chief's heels, his devoted protection officer Flin stopped every few yards for a full panoramic sweep.

Five

The fighter they called Hāru had slipped across the border ahead of a milky dawn. All his life had been spent in preparation for martyrdom in a patriotic war – a loyal soldier of God and his people who respected no frontiers. Before setting out on his present campaign pitting himself against the European tyrants, he had immersed himself in his father's words of faith; grew to loath and despise the ignorant fools doing the Jews' bidding. And through God's mercy and inspiration, he was ready to continue leading the worthy into action against the enemy. So many miles travelled to reach his latest temporary home where he could witness fellow believers shape their own struggle for a glorious victory. For a full hour after sunrise he contentedly observed batches of fresh recruits obeying their instructors' orders. Standing alone on a high, crumbly ridge, he once more felt that sense of place embrace him after climbing up to his rocky platform.

At twenty-nine he already owned the distant gaze of a veteran; a man quite comfortable in his standard issue Syrian Army fatigues. He carried the weapons of his trade with the blasé air of a professional – a 9mm MP-446 Viking pistol holstered on his belt and an AK-47 slung around his broad back. After each of his recent trips to the training camp nestled in a protective fold of the Khanaser Plain, Hāru returned to Europe knowing the sacrifices his brothers offered could not be squandered.

As a small boy he listened intently at the feet of his father as the wise, battle hardened veteran explained Hāru's duty when he grew into a man. If he failed the call to arms, his soul would join those of deserters condemned to roam and seek out a resting place on the plains and in the mountains because they were cowards, not true martyrs.

Spread out around Hāru an open, wind rippled desert encampment sheltered by long, barbed ridges. In one roped off sector, small groups of fighters went through their final exercise before leaving for the front line. Hāru offered a prayer to God, silently despatched up into the searing morning air. Behind Hāru, an order curled high into the stark, blue sky. Rapid bursts from AK-47s on automatic kicked up snickers of dust and rock fragments as squads practised street combat. Punctuating this rapid tattoo of sustained firepower, he heard the stark, clinical retort of an OSV-96 sniper rifle.

As he absorbed these sounds from the hell of battles to be fought, Hāru felt a swell of pride from assisting his *fedayeen* brothers, the men of sacrifice who would be the brutal upholders of resistance against the rebels and their foreign mercenaries. A rabble of turncoats and invaders who had pledged their allegiance to the wrong side, they were proving no match for the loyal warriors he had helped to inspire – resolute combatants bloodied in their own struggle against the Jews who denied them a homeland. By his own examples of valour and acts of war, Hāru gave his brave brothers a demonstration of how their strength as defenders of their people would give them hearts of lions; spur them on in each attack.

Here in this slab of Syrian wilderness, criss-crossed by dirt tracks winding through clusters of tents and huts like seams of crystal, Hāru appreciated the training camp's role in sustaining government held territory. One of many camps built to further the Palestinian struggle and assist its Damascus allies; Hāru knew the layout intimately. Away to his left the assault course twisted in and out of ditches, zigzagged through mounds of tyres, over stacks of logs, under razor wire obstacles, finishing at oil drum blockades.

Off on his right the nursery quarters that housed volunteers during their schooling in the arts of urban combat, their introduction to the basic skills of guerrilla warfare. In each of the recruits' communal huts a plywood partition faced the bunks – the 'wall of hate'. It held images of Western imperialists stapled in target groups: vivid reminders of each recruit's duty to eliminate their enemies. Hāru remembered his own devotion as a novice fighter over ten years ago when he had been selected for God's work at nineteen. A different camp, a different country, but the principle had barely changed. After washing and prayers he studied the bank of faces pinned up by his instructors. An hourly ritual he performed with such intensity that bitter tears from his passion to die in the struggle for freedom, to sacrifice everything for independence, would tumble down his cheeks.

That pain of devotion he never forgot, a cleansing of mind and soul preparing him for life as a warrior. Now others were sharing these stages of initiation. Behind him, the restricted compound run by diligent bomb makers who had perfected their craft in the Bekáa Valley – patient tutors holding master classes with assistance on new improvised devices given by Iranian technicians. Even in these classrooms the trainees would be surrounded by posters of their leader, their allies' leaders and slogans of defiance and victory. Messages broadcast through the camps' tannoy at every opportunity praised and reinforced the duty of sacrifice expected from chosen martyrs.

It was this strange world apart Hāru had chosen to devote his life to, accepting that nothing else counted but being a warrior on behalf of his people. Deep in thought, he followed the trainees' dust veiled silhouettes below his rocky ledge; their devotion and dedication would soon be turned into action. They had been taught well.

Chosen volunteers arrived each month. Screened for their loyalty in Beirut and Qusayr, suspected spies were ruthlessly weeded out to face summary execution. Once accepted, each new intake gathered in the late afternoon on their first day in camp. Young Palestinians recruited from besieged districts drawn into a horseshoe to hear their call to arms, clutching their Kalashnikovs, rocket launchers or grenades for the first time.

Reverently they would listen as the training director pointed them down their road to freedom, their first steps as brave martyrs their battle hardened instructors would praise. Clear, sharp as a bell, the training director's voice always rose sharply when he told them the Zionists wanted to eradicate Islam from the earth. From these volunteers, those that survived front line action, the training director would select his very best warriors to join the elite cadres working overseas carrying the war to the enemy as Hāru's own father had done.

He heard footsteps on the flint topped path behind him, then a solid hand kneaded his shoulder. 'God be praised, we will soon secure another victory,' the training cadre's Chief Instructor vowed, gripping Hāru's arm. The fingers were hard, short and stubby, each one a band of steel pressed firmly around the young Commando Director's solid muscle. He wore the same combat fatigues, the woodland pattern faded, its colour washed into blurred stains by the sun. On his right arm like Hāru, a red arm band identifying his fealty to the regime, a means of identifying his militia battalion. His face, his skin, his hair appeared grey as if the desert had begun to claim him, seep into his core, his very being.

'Their courage will grow after they spill the first blood of their enemies,' Hāru said, nodding down towards the recruits dividing off into smaller training groups.

Overhead the sky screamed when a MIG-21 banked low and fast on its final low run towards rebel positions outside Aleppo.

'*Allahu Akbar*,' the chief instructor said, releasing his grip.

'*Allahu Akbar*,' repeated Hāru.

Turning together they watched a rolling pall of smoke tumble high into the lazy, calm, blue morning.

'The new recruits will bring you credit,' suggested Hāru.

Accepting Hāru's appraisal of his men, the chief instructor slowly nodded. 'Your operation – it has not gone as planned?'

'The opposition was greater than the intelligence my comrades on the Armed Struggle Command received,' Hāru answered. 'We still achieved our objectives, we even surpassed them,' he insisted.

'With your leadership and example, we have achieved a swift victory my brother. There must...'

Hāru put a finger to his lips silencing the chief instructor. 'The time is still a dangerous one for us. Our enemies are cunning. They run together like a pack of wild dogs in the night. They will not be permitted to disrupt our campaign. You must sacrifice everything to safeguard our goal – this is a battle that we cannot concede,' Hāru declared, squeezing the chief instructor's shoulder. 'Our enemies have sought to seek salvation, but we will send them to hell. Your mandate has not changed, my new recruits need to be ready in three weeks.'

'So soon? But why? What has changed?'

'The links that may be used to trace us in Europe are to be severed,' Hāru pledged. 'Our enemy will still be unsure who they are fighting after we strike again. A decision has been taken by your respected brothers of the Armed Struggle Command. You are to advance the training for my recruits, you will ensure they are strong fighters available for the next phase of my operation.'

'But the commandos I have provided should be capable enough,' the chief instructor countered. 'I have personally supervised their selection and training. They are prepared for this task.'

The whipping cuff delivered to the chief instructor's head by Hāru stunned his comrade.

'We must respect the wisdom of our senior officers, my brother,' Hāru declared. Calmly, he stroked the chief instructor's cheek, a gentle atonement after his abrupt punishment. 'We have been chosen to carry out God's work in the name of our people,' he explained. 'No one must prevent our future from being formed out of Zionist ashes. You will personally ensure that we do not fail,' he insisted. Months of operational advances would not be lost because the chief instructor despised the bonds Hāru had created with his chosen commandos, because the chief instructor loathed the recruits from Europe forever clinging to him – *lambs bleating for their mother* as the chief instructor mocked them. But Hāru would teach him that daring was sometimes more important than restraint, all Hāru's recruits who operated as death stalkers eventually did.

'My *advisor* has provided all the details. Nothing has been held back.' Kicking out at a loose pebble, Hāru sent it tumbling down the steep rock face towards the range where snipers conscientiously tuned their Russian KSVK 12.7s.

'We have passed on the names of the traitors to Damascus,' the chief instructor admitted, tensing as each retort shook the air around the range. 'Is there more work I can do to exploit your unexpected bonus?'

'In good time, my brother, in good time.'

'Your other successes have been celebrated – the enemy do not know where you will hit them next.'

'You will show patience,' Hāru suggested, his warning blunt. 'You have done well, my brother. The Armed Struggle Command has expressed its congratulations for the way you have carried out its directives. But the Command reminds you that my advisor is not to be underestimated, you must use my advisor's knowledge as a powerful weapon. The route we travel is difficult and dangerous, so we cannot afford to lose any assistance. Remember that, my brother. Even those who we distrust must serve their purpose.'

'Of course,' vowed the chief instructor. 'Go back among the enemy, reveal to them our strength, reveal to them the fires of hell.'

'It will be done.'

'All your commando brothers will be inspired by your wisdom and courage.' Clutching the brave commander to him, the chief instructor left his sweet breath in Hāru's nostrils as he strode off back down the trail.

Swinging the AK-47 off his shoulder Hāru waited until the puffs of dust from the chief instructor's footsteps gradually settled. Racking back the AK's cocking handle he fired a burst into the dazzling, immaculate sky – a rapid song of thanksgiving for this opportunity to inflict further pain on Western imperialists. Threading his way down into the camp, he spoke with an instructor before summoning a bunch of trainees together. Herding them into a semicircle before him, Hāru lectured them only as a wise veteran could: how they must double their efforts, how average was not good enough, how they were not fast enough. And after each criticism, he offered a demonstration, regaled them with examples and accounts from his own operations.

Late in the afternoon as the first cool winds crept in off the desert plains Hāru returned to the rocky outcrop. There he sat until the evening covered him, a martyr perhaps witnessing his final sunset. He sat and smoked, listening to mortars and rocket launchers snake away on a makeshift range, targeted on wrecks of abandoned vehicles, throwing silver and flame into the charcoal sky. Licks of tracer snaked in bright beautiful hoses down along the ridge.

At his side tucked into a cradle in the rock, a two-way radio relayed the urgent orders from instructors. He cocked his head to one side, waiting for a heavy machine gun to bark, snapping round after round into a gully. When prolonged bursts of AK-47s opened up, Hāru slung his own Kalashnikov casually over his shoulder and began his final descent into the camp. Tomorrow he would venture overseas to inspire his fighters again, raise their spirits as he emphasised how they would heap more destruction on the true enemies of Palestine.

Six

If omens count for anything, Nick's return to Prague coincided with a severe drop in temperature accompanied by arctic blasts of snow, buffeting him all the way into another of the city's discreet, economy hotels. Hotel Kaspar was a Nineteen-Sixties confection of concrete, stone and glass dumped at the end of a cul-de-sac in the Old Town. His room reserved under the workname of Hrádek lay at the end of long airless seventh floor corridor, its patterned carpet soiled, its pile flattened into a bare trail. The lighting had an autumnal woodland tinge too, giving the same shady twilight sensation as if Nick was strolling through a copse.

A flock of watercolour birds were randomly scattered down the corridor. The prints jaded, their frames poorly fitted, the glass patterned by greasy smears. A fire door was wedged open with a grotesque ornamental cat, its bloated, purple head chipped, missing its right ear. He'd stayed in worse establishments Nick decided, surveying his room. A scuffed rudimentary sideboard, its veneer skin lifting from its chipboard frame blocked access to one half of the double bed. From a two foot wide balcony in his room he had the glorious vista down onto a frantic junction. Set opposite, over a reef of red tiled roofs, a baroque clock tower stole most of the natural light leaving his room in perpetual gloom.

It took Nick less than ten minutes to unpack the sparse possessions he'd brought from Nürnberg. A couple of changes of clothes, shaving kit, toothbrush and laptop stuffed carelessly into his leather messenger bag – that was it. Setting a series of telltales to detect any uninvited visitors, the last in the outer frame of his door, Nick made a start on his quest to find Leiston and Rewall.

He avoided a direct route on the Metro, choosing instead to stagger his journey. When he entered Staroměstská Station the sky was already deepening; thick wads of cloud pressing in over the city gave the late afternoon a pale pink glow. When he stepped out at Jiřího z Poděbrad a curtain of light snow had rolled in. He headed back north on foot, boarding a tram behind a couple of drunks at a stop on Lipanská. The drunks punched each other playfully on the shoulder until one of them fell asleep, his head bumping against the glass as the tram picked up speed.

At Palackého náměstí a fractious ticket inspector stepped out of a blizzard sweeping through the square, working through each carriage ejecting the homeless riding out the snow. On the seat opposite Nick, a middle-aged man layered against the weather, his fur ushanka tugged low at a rebellious angle. Every time the tram jolted, a rabbit stuffed down the man's padded jacket raised its angry red eyes at Nick. Big dabs of snow brushed against the tram's windows and the air was dispiritingly cold. He got off at Krymská; headlights and streetlights turning the frost tipped mounds of snow blue when he crunched over ruts set hard in the frozen ground.

He obeyed the directions guiding him to the *K Rotundě* and the church of St. Peter and St. Paul, slipping into the castle grounds through the Tabor Gate. When he reached the Baths of Libuše on the cliffs above the river his shoulders and head were liberally dusted with snow. To his left he had a view of the islands on the Vlatava: long, tapered fingers pointing accusingly towards the Charles Bridge. Below him, to his right, Prague shimmered like a scene in a winter diorama. He mingled with the few hardy visitors circling the church, quietly slipping in behind a couple packaged in matching thermal layers. At the Slavín Pantheon, Nick went his separate way, picking a route through graves topped by a squadron of angels permanently grounded.

No more than five yards in front of him sheltering in one of the arcade's Gothic arches, the stocky, thickset shape of Harry Bransk covertly tracked Nick's arrival. Lean faced with the born survivor's quick, furtive movements, Harry had barely started on his fifties but appeared a decade older. It's the burden of constantly looking over his shoulder in a ruthless underworld thought Nick; always fighting to remain ahead of the pack had finally ambushed Harry.

'Risen from your sick bed just for me, Harry? That's very touching.'

'I still got pain, okay,' retorted Harry. 'I do this out of friendship, Nick. Maybe you should appreciate my sacrifice more, huh? "With the right helper, a thousand things are possible"... A Russian proverb, okay,' explained Harry, extending his hand.

'Very true,' agreed Nick, though with Harry a lot was sometimes left behind in the translation. 'What have you got for me?' Nick, accepting the firm greeting, stepped inside out of the snow.

'Serious problems, Nick, that's what I got,' Harry admitted. 'Your missing friends... they already got a premium value tag,' his tone suggested this might pose an additional dilemma. 'This is no damn stroll along the beach. I got to be careful who I do business with. You get what I'm saying?'

'Yes,' agreed Nick, slipping deeper into the arcade.

The arches housed memorial tablets, slabs of worked marble as waymarkers for the dead; each one guarded by mute carved figures inside the open mausoleums. On the inner plaster skin of pillared cross vaults, a compilation of religious frescoes composed in soft hues.

'Could be that I have a contact who can be persuaded to work on your problem,' admitted Harry. 'This isn't going to be done for peanuts, okay. London has to accept that this isn't the normal bazaar. Usual rates don't apply, Nick. It all depends on how much you're willing to spend.'

'Do I get a hundred per cent guarantee that your contact can light the way?'

'Nick... He's solid, okay,' Harry assured him. 'Reliable. Believe me, my contact is a dynamo,' he insisted, an astute businessman who had cleared a major hurdle.

'I want intel Harry, not a power source,' Nick icily retorted.

'You want your friends back or not, huh? Nick... Nick, this guy can get you connected. He paddles in all the right pools, okay. It's this guy or nothing. You want nothing, huh?'

And what Harry could be conveniently omitting in his glowing testimony of his source, is just how much Harry's contact may be involved in the abductions, thought Nick.

'Head Office would prefer that details of our deal remain private,' Nick explained, patiently. 'If, for any reason, your contact became careless it would put me in a difficult position. I'd have to intervene, Harry. That clear?'

'Sure,' accepted Harry uncomfortably, recalling that Nick's previous interventions were often messy, painful and often fatal.

In a slow, reverential procession they began a tour along the arcade. Sidestepping bowls of flowers left as offerings, they paused at each memorial stone like two old friends seeking out a familiar inscription.

'Now *you* got to level with me, Nick,' demanded Harry. 'No one's willing to talk face-to-face except my contact, okay. That makes me nervous Nick, sets off my alarm. Then I hear scared whispers that these KOSC losers suddenly grew operational balls. Talk of how they might have tapped into some serious outside support. It's two and two making five all day, Nick, know what I'm saying, huh?' Harry shrugged, a heavy overcoat lifting off his sturdy, narrow bladed shoulders, a hustler baulking at a confidential agreement.

'We think they're just the front for a false flag campaign,' Nick admitted. 'I'm no wiser than you, Harry.'

'You wouldn't be holding anything back from your old friend would you Nick?' Harry wondered, making it into a light-hearted aside.

'Not this time.' Nick stared hard at Harry.

And for a couple of scary seconds, the cold, dark look in Nick's eyes, the menace in his denial convinced Harry someone would surely have their neck broken the mood Nick was in.

'These whispers, Harry... what else is doing the rounds on the KOSC? There must be more.'

Harry agreed with a single nod.

'What's their profile?'

Ahead of them along the colonnade, ornate lanterns and candles on Gothic curled holders honoured departed spirits.

'KOSC... Complete cranks... That's for number one,' conceded Harry. 'Anarchists... Pseudo Commies stuck in Sixty-Eight...,' he added. 'They don't know what they ought to be. They've always been complete nuts, making crazy threats from laptops. One day it's demanding a workers' revolution. The next, they call for an attack on capitalists. Then they decree the army mobilise, return democracy and government to the people and then disband. Nick, this group, it's always been a bunch of total cuckoos.'

'Well they're well and truly out of the nest now.'

'Nick, listen okay. My contact insists they don't even have the brains to organise a big score like this.'

'Someone's written their instructions,' Nick insisted.

Meandering through the cemetery's set pieces, the last straggling tourists fought against the weather, cherry picking their way around the prominent shrines of artists, philosophers and politicians; an all-inclusive tour of the great and not so great, supposed Nick, leading Harry down the arcade.

'Leave it to me, okay,' Harry pleaded, his stealthy eyes warily tracking

Nick's every movement.

'I can't afford any blowback on this Harry. You make sure your contact understands the consequences.'

'For you Nick, I'll run him personally, okay,' offered Harry, his compact face rising into a smile.

They stood beside a primitively carved obelisk encasing the ashes of one of Prague's notable citizens. Perched on the pinnacle of an ornate rock face, a full-sized figure of Christ, his arms outstretched in forgiveness.

'I can expect top results then, can't I,' decided Nick, extending his right hand to confirm Harry's generous offer.

Concluding his deal with a wry shake of his head, Harry turned to leave. 'As soon as I get a lead you'll have it, okay Nick. You rely on me, huh,' he pledged sincerely, relieved at escaping Nick's dark, simmering fury.

• • •

The latest journey they'd inflicted on Leiston she wrote off as sheer, bloody torture. Hooded, gagged and heavily trussed, she'd suffered, in her own vague estimate, at least a numbing four hour drive. In the back of a van? The boot of a car? Some other vehicle? She didn't rightly know – only that she'd been lifted into something and wedged tightly on her side. Before her departure, she'd been dragged out into arctic air, each breath chilling her lungs.

Someone had tied a strip of cloth over her eyes, overlapping it with bands of tape. She guessed it would hurt like hell when they ripped them off. Then they gagged and hooded her, their voices low, fuzzy, indistinct.

She'd kept her movements to a minimum, straining to pick out any sounds of the other hostage being loaded before the engine started, but heard only the driver's and passenger's door slam. The last she'd seen of the other woman was when they were herded together for the video. In the few seconds they were left alone, the woman had smiled, gripped Leiston's hand and whispered – 'Celia' as they exchanged names. In Leiston's dark world of isolation, logic barely played a part. She had no idea about anything – not even if Celia would share the same bone cracking journey.

Hauled out at the other end, she felt rain or snow on her exposed hands before they hustled her inside. Snow, she guessed from the stillness that always arrives with a heavy fall – and the cold... too cold for rain. Carted up a staircase, she'd been jabbed in a prisoner's manacled shuffle into a corner. One big hand locked onto her head, others – lighter – on her shoulders forced her down onto a blanket reeking of dog. In the background an eerie fizzing. Fainter still, she heard the low, drifting groans of someone coping with pain. Celia?

The first interrogator spoke in a blurry, hard voice that brushed around the edges of her role. Mature and Middle Eastern, she reasoned from his indifferent grasp of English. When he lifted her head up by the chin she caught the bitter tang of his breath – a heavy cigar smoker.

Gradually like someone getting to know her, the interrogator applied more pressure as he chatted happily away. He questioned her about the operation as if he didn't require any answers but simply needed her to confirm the facts. She clung to her cover as a Foreign Office diplomatic resettlement officer. Not pushing or disagreeing, he thanked her and left her in peace. In the patches of sleep she'd taken sitting up, the faces of her parents tumbled over and over in her mind.

She knew that another of her captors came to monitor her, observe, watch; a periodic drill spread in a measured routine. The watcher's steps were distinct from those that delivered her tray of food and bottle of sparkling water. Comfortable and controlled, they were sure of their surroundings and her. Each time they'd stop outside the door, its dry hinges cracking and screeching until her watcher had walked a few paces into her room. The first time it happened she had begun by firing off her own fusillade of repressed anger. 'The British Government will not negotiate. I am of little value. Contact the Embassy in Prague. They will confirm everything,' she'd told the silent observer, turning in a small radius, speaking to a point in front of her where she assumed someone stood.

'You talk... you speak... we punish you,' the interrogator's grainy voice warned her. 'You got that?'

Nodding that she had, Leiston worked on his thick accentuated order: definitely not European, she decided, recalling elements of voice analysis training. From the Mediterranean rim... the Middle East again?

After that mini confrontation they hadn't bothered with her until today's little adventure.

The hood came off with a single, violent tug racking her head to one side. She edged back into *her* corner where the cold from both solid walls leached right into her core. In one rapid movement she intuitively followed across the wooden floor, someone came towards her. A click, and her hands were grabbed roughly, a blade split the tape. Then the same fingers, slender and thin, rummaged in her hair in a callous attempt to remove the gag. When the tape was yanked off Leiston gasped. Prepared for a rush of light, her muscles, her nerves stiffened and she scrunched her eyes tight like a child scared of the night.

When the strip of cloth fell away she opened each eye tentatively. But there was no glare, no shock to her bleary vision. Three or four gas lanterns fizzed happily away, bathing a narrow, lozenge room in a yellow, gauzy light forming dusky, shaded outlines. Through this shimmering mirage a woman strolled over carrying a folded grey jumpsuit clamped under her left arm like a student toting her file to a lecture. An instant visual crude appraisal stuck hard in Leiston's mind; she now had her first label to store the details about one of her captors. This woman would be the *student*. Nipped between the fingers of one hand, a pair of canvas ankle boots with Velcro fasteners swung from the student's right hand.

'Get undressed. Put these on,' the student commanded.

She pitched the items at Leiston. An arm – or a leg – uncoiled when the jumpsuit hit Leiston's chin. One of the boots glanced off her shoulder. The other caught her a swiping blow below her ear.

If orange jumpsuits are for terrorist hostages, what does grey signify? Leiston asked herself, gathering together her uniform. One round, that's all I'd need, she promised herself undressing, her fingers cold – awkward slabs making a mess of her buttons and zip. Just you and me on our own, no holds barred. It would give her great pleasure to wipe the smirk off the student's face. Leiston consoled herself by planning the opening strike as she wormed and wriggled the jumpsuit over her underwear. She had an overpowering sense of resentment that this humiliating removal of her clothes marked only the beginning of peeling away her individuality, the first attempt to claim her mind, body and soul.

Iraqi? Iranian? Syrian? Leiston played through the possible options, attempting to pin down the student's background, her motives, her psychological composition. Her summary gained in focused glances gave Leiston only a starting profile of the student: Twenty-eight, younger by a couple of years? The du haut en bas of a Parisian model – sculpted cheeks, smooth clear skin and light body to go with it. The long, revolutionary's black hair that matched her temperament, how it played off the hatred wound deep in her brown eyes. The choice of a casual sweatshirt screaming NEW YORK, the hugging taper fit of the jeans worn out of familiarity: the choice of someone enjoying Western design and influence.

The student yanked Leiston's head up by her hair. Forced to look at her captor, Leiston stared into the calm eyes of a fanatic: a warrior who didn't understand mercy; a young woman devoted to revenging past generations.

'We know all about you. Remember that,' the student whispered into Leiston's ear. Bent forward, brutally retying the strip of cloth over her captive's eyes, the student's long hair brushed Leiston's forehead.

Soft and rich it smelt of almonds.

Returned to her own dark prison there was nothing Leiston could do but listen. She heard the student call for assistance. She heard the tape peel off the roll as the student and her helper rebound her ankles. Plastic handcuffs were sealed tight around her writs, biting into her skin. With the student pulling, the helper pushing, she was shuffled out. The student called ahead when they'd manoeuvred her clumsily down eight steps.

'Sit,' the student instructed her.

Tentatively Leiston bent her legs not knowing how far she had to go. The palm of a hand pushed her backwards into a chair held from behind. Whoever prevented the chair from bowling over now hung a sign over Leiston. She felt the board against her chest, the cold metal links on her neck. Even behind her blindfold her eyes blinked when a powerful light shone full in her face. More footsteps entered what she supposed must be a low, box of a room, because they echoed like crazy. One set heavy and regular belonging to a male. The others lighter, those of a woman. Her hair – always her bloody hair – was grabbed in a tight clench. The retort of the 9mm close to her head brought up the watery soup she'd been fed the previous evening.

The student taunted her when they dragged her out to the upstairs room. Mocking, prodding and laughing at each clumsy step made by Leiston. Two of them planted her back in her corner. She would not damn well cry, she sternly instructed herself. When the second pistol retort tumbled away in the distance she broke, silently weeping inside. Holding back her fear she braced when a gang of footsteps entered – one pair definitely not walking, but slurring, dragged along. Not daring to move, barely breathing, Leiston waited until the footsteps retreated.

'Hannah?'

Her name came in a sob from her right. 'Celia?'

'Shh...'

In a gentle steady pattern Leiston heard movement, the unmistakable scuffing of arms and legs inching towards her.

Seven

Awoken on the quarter and at every hour by neighbouring clock bells solemnly tolling at the night's passing, Nick had surrendered any notion of sleep by five the following morning. In sporadic lulls between each set of chimes he'd managed to fitfully doze: a grazing sort of rest trapped between the extreme polarities of being neither fully awake nor dead to the world. He ran a bath as a much-needed elixir to coax out the weariness in his muscles and joints, convinced that every inch of him creaked. The water fastidiously refused to run faster than a splutter; his temper climbing, his patience close to breaking before he even began his remedial soak. He tended to his wounds and was in the middle of brushing his teeth when his phone shrieked for attention. Pitching his toothbrush into the chipped basin he made a barefoot dash for his bed.

'Nick... Nick... you hear me?' Harry Bransk demanded.

'Yes, Harry, I'm here.'

In Harry's shady empire of backstreet deals, results counted for everything, particularly if you were in one piece and able to enjoy the fruits of your labour. Which, that morning, Harry indeed was.

'I got you a lead, okay. I got you a break in the clouds, I got you a foot in the door,' Harry said with a measure of pride. 'I came through for you again, don't forget that, Nick. Did I ever let you down, huh? I'm arranging the other extras as you requested, the whole package.'

'I hope so, Harry, I really hope so,' Nick replied, storing Harry's instructions and directions on his throwaway phone, a text that would never leave the device.

Forsaking his overcoat Nick set out in a dark, grey padded jacket he'd picked from a winter sports outlet a block from his hotel, gracefully declining the assistant's offer of a discount on matching salopettes. From surrounding stores he'd completed his change of wardrobe – selecting black jeans, sturdy boots and a woollen hat complete with a bobble. As a distraction and a virtual wing mirror covering his back, Nick carried out a routine dry clean through the Old Town: stopping, starting, abruptly kicking off on devious short cuts through streets and squares until he was assured that he hadn't acquired a single footpad.

On the Metro platform at Staroměstská Nick let three trains go on their way before he seemed to reach an impulsive decision to board the next, an inbound service to Strašnická. Here the fieldman's instinctive need to lay a false trail led him through a bitter wind that gnawed at his skin as he dallied and lounged at a number of different stops like a tardy postman doing his rounds. He halted at a tabák kiosk making a specious enquiry about tram tickets until the owner flapped a hand dismissively, studiously returning to reading his morning newspaper.

He pushed on through side streets with his head down, but possessing the fieldman's all seeing, alert vision. In this hinterland, the old, worn traces of Prague stubbornly remained, resisting attempts at being included in the modern city's rush for revival. The scrubbed, grey render walls of depressingly familiar socialist apartment blocks, the central cobble strips nursing tram tracks, the plain dour local bars most of them an unloved brown: all of it an austere landscape that had surrounded Nick on his many trawls through desolate back alleys in the relics of former East European Iron Curtain states.

One block stood out: a lighthouse in the stormy sea of a plain, drab district. Coated in a soft shade of white, its woodwork offset in grey, Nick matched the number with Harry's directions. Lace nets screening the ground floor windows were strung in front of heavy, brocaded curtains partially closed.

On each side of the communal entrance, two identical bay trees in coordinated planters wore red ribbon bows around their necks. Between them, an unremarkable plain, high glossed black double door watched over by a sleek pair of security cameras. Beside the left stone pillar a frosted acrylic panel lit from behind promised *Decadence* in blue powder coated letters.

On the opposite pillar, Nick read the house specials presented in a polished steel menu case, an appetising selection that omitted *entrées*, listing only the mains:

Cocktail Bar

Main Dance Bar

Restaurant

20 Rooms

Sauna

Steam Bath

Sports Massage

Girls! Girls! Girls!

And if Harry were to be believed, one of the girls would be Jana, thought Nick. One half of the street door was permanently sealed. The other operated on a security release activated by a gleaming buzzer set tastefully below an intercom. Nick pressed it three times in a rapid sequence, surrendered his workname, and as Harry promised, he was admitted. He entered a pre-war vestibule unable to shake off its imperial, stark grandeur – the air roaming in stiff cold peaks, a resident left over from a different period. He followed a low, wide flight of stone risers to another casement of double doors, their upper sections of opaque glass etched with the block number in Gothic numerals – *87*.

All the doors at this level were signed '*Soukrome*' each of them locked enforcing the privacy. So Nick, once again, resorted to the stairs – a filigree ensemble topped by an ebony banister corkscrewing around a latticework lift humming and whining as if consuming power for the whole district.

He emerged a floor higher into a panelled, moody lobby: all dark original oak, complete with tastefully positioned immaculate crimson leather sofas. Subtle mood lighting picked out framed ink caricatures of personalities Nick didn't recognise. A flourishing parade of indoor plants had their polished spear leaves lit by soft, blue strips of LEDs. To its clients the club distilled the exclusive cachet as one of the city's 'gentlemen's clubs'. Or as Harry crudely put it – *Nick, the place is a cathouse for VVIPs, okay. It's got protection from on high, okay; its clients don't want anyone spoiling their fun. The owner has gold standard connections. So take it easy, huh?*

He'd promised Harry he'd do just that.

Boxed into a red velvet walled recess, a receptionist with a model's precision shoulder length blonde hair acknowledged Nick with a dashed glance of her cool eyes. Ignoring him entirely, she focused on a screen as she scrolled through bookings. The air was clean, sanitised like the cabin of an aeroplane, and he doubted if all brothels went to so much trouble to filter out the animal smells.

Muting her headset the receptionist tartly beckoned Nick over. She had the advantage of a raised platform putting her out of reach from dissatisfied clients. Behind her on the velvet wall, a clear, engraved panel welcomed the use of all major credit cards.

'I've got a meeting with Ondřej,' Nick explained.

'Ondřej isn't seeing anyone today,' she claimed, bubbling away on automatic, shooing Nick back to the exit with her cervine eyes.

Mouthing a silent 'Thanks,' Nick headed in the opposite direction, striding fast for the double doors etched 'Members Only', the receptionist's protests bouncing after him.

Partway down the passage the whole ambiance changed. Nick felt it as if the very air around him had instantly become charged. The gentle, decadent lighting of the lobby intensified. Tongues of brash violet, orange and blue writhed vertically in LED panels caged in aluminium screens above the dimpled, rubber flooring popular in baggage reclaim halls. Pulsing from concealed, overhead speakers a compelling electronic number pummelled out.

The same mix of vocals, drum and base met him in the club's lounge. One full translucent light wall behind a chrome barrier squirted out abstract shapes, a montage of surreal psychedelic patterns.

Two figures coordinating the light show were in a conference huddle around a laptop opened on a crescent bar. Suspended in steel pulpits at staggered heights over the main floor, dancers in tracksuits testily attempted to coordinate their routine. Below them, a stern choreographer clapped his hands with the manic rhythm of a frenzied backing singer.

Despite the club's modern, sleek and sophisticated skin, Nick picked up that tawdry undercurrent of women for hire.

A dancer petulantly stepped out her routine, pointing out Nick to one of the men at the bar.

'*Co chceš?*' he demanded. His head was shaved close, leaving a dark tonsure of stubble.

'I'd like a word with Ondřej,' called Nick, not moving. Slowly he removed his hat, clutching it in his hands held very deliberately in front of his body. If you didn't want to set off a firestorm, first impressions were important Nick reminded himself. 'In private,' he added.

The other male concentrating on the laptop turned as an afterthought, disinterestedly staring at the visitor.

'You here to discuss Jana?' He swivelled fully round, mildly curious. He had a closely trimmed cultivated beard much favoured by affluent entrepreneurs. 'You are Peter?'

Yes, Nick admitted he *was* Peter and that he was *very* keen to discuss Jana, deciding which one of the pair would be most likely to play the hard man, step up as the hero.

Loafing against the bar, his elbows tucked behind him on the counter, one foot – his left – on the brass rail, Ondřej Libáň received Nick's workname with a grave smile.

'I'm busy right now,' Libáň announced, his English adequate in a prep school sort of way. 'Call tomorrow. If I'm not available, ask for my manager – Karel,' he decreed, nodding towards his shaven headed companion.

He swung back to the laptop, starting an earnest discussion with his manager.

As Libáň and Karel cued up another track meshed to a fresh lighting sequence, Nick stood his ground. On the plasma screens, jerky segments of mouths, lips and eyes in hypnotic colours melted, reformed into the background under a set of pulsing opening bars and vocals.

'*Co mas za problém?*' Karel yelled glancing over his shoulder. 'You got problem, Peter?' he repeated as much for himself as Nick. 'Ondřej tell you to leave. You try some other time,' he bawled, distinctly unfriendly. 'Fly away, Peter. This no time to play or I snap your wings.'

Hopelessly distracted from their routines the dancers watched motionless from their pulpits: the visceral beat waiting for no one: a runaway train thundering on. The choreographer stood with his arms folded, a detached but fascinated observer. And not for the first time, Nick was the star of the show. He walked towards the bar as if he had all the time in the world. His eyes hard, focused, had what old soldiers describe as 'the kill' in their fierce, unflinching stare. It carried with it the same unwavering symptoms – the tingling in every nerve, the prickliness that grew inside before the timed release, the controlled explosion.

When it came, Karel seemed to lift and fall in the same second. Dragging the manager to his feet, Nick struck at least twice more and although the choreographer swore every punch was a blur, he was unwavering in his praise of Nick's dexterity in one particular move – definitely one – involving a furious headbutt timed to coincide with the fluid, coordinated use of a rising knee.

'I don't have time to waste,' Nick told Libáň, a tad breathless, his shoulder spitting fire through every tiny nerve. 'Perhaps I didn't mention that?' He slammed the laptop closed. 'We need to talk.'

Eight

It had never been Libáň's intention to treat Nick with any disrespect, the *Decadence's* owner resolutely affirmed, transformed into the cordial guide as they journeyed up the same soulless stairwell to his office on the floor above his adult playground.

'I have many friends,' he explained as if this in itself was a rarity. Ensuring he remained two strides ahead of Nick, he put down a marker: 'Some of them will be interested to hear of the trouble you caused, my friend,' he confided over his shoulder.

'I'm not your friend.'

The stairwell counted out their steps; sharp, clapping echoes against its stone treads, the air frigid. The ancient caged elevator shook itself awake below, shuddering no farther than the first floor. Nick smelt the baked dry layers of grease, the heat from its cables, the stale oil off its winding gear seeping down the stairs.

'You are what to Jana?' Libáň wondered.

'My company are working for a friend of hers.'

'What... like some private investigators... detectives... snoops?'

'We're just doing someone a favour.'

'You been in a war, maybe?' Libáň stopped, twisted his head for a full review of Nick's grazes.

'A disagreement.'

'It happens.'

Every inch of Libáň's sharp, inclined face had a driven intensity, noted Nick. Dressed in a white shirt, waistcoat, black jeans and pointed Chelsea boots he was one of Prague's determined, rising band of millionaires if Harry could be believed. And taking Harry's word for anything brought the same risks as gambling: you paid your money and took your chances,

Nick remembered ruefully.

'My company operate a full, non-disclosure policy on information we receive,' explained Nick.

A strict frown rolled out into tight waves on Libáň's brow.

'And there is payment?'

'As usual it is based on results... bonuses apply for extras. No payment until we are satisfied that the information is legitimate.'

Libáň nodded as if he required some conditions of his own. He turned off the final landing through a considerable pair of wooden swing doors. 'My contract with Jana is perfectly legitimate,' he admitted.

And he was still covering his back with all the possible angles as he deftly entered his PIN into a keypad outside his office.

Marring the clinical modernist tone, a stuffed brown bear backed into one clean, stark corner had a three quarters winter overcoat hung from one outstretched paw, a gentleman's brolly from the other.

'We had Krumlov in our forest room,' Libáň explained, waving a hand towards the bear. 'Our guests found it disturbed their concentration,' he added, permitting a momentary brief smile.

He pointed Nick to a cream leather chair braced in polished steel. Tactically slewed at an angle, it faced his desk consisting entirely of glossy white cubes.

'Her friend believes that Jana is in danger,' explained Nick, making a point of bypassing the chair. 'Do you have *anything* for me?' He'd decided on a more convenient position beside a long sash window from where he had a discreet overview of the street, and more crucially, a full line of sight to Libáň's office door.

'My involvement is purely third party,' he emphasised squared off ten paces from Nick. 'That is accepted?'

'Yes.'

'Then we have a deal.'

He dropped into his high backed chair – also white leather – like a pilot resuming control after a break during a long haul flight. He keyed an extension on his desk telephone; receiving no answer, he tried another number. He used the dial pad as if wielding a pen or using a keyboard; occupying his fingers with precise little curls, his wrists delicately poised and balanced. '*Zadne telefonaty*,' he commanded to someone who eventually responded. '*Ani od Karla*,' he insisted, snapping the handset into its cradle.

Gliding around to Nick, the sole owner and director of one of Prague's most exclusive gentlemen's clubs dedicated to ungentlemanly entertainment, opened with a frank admission: 'I'm not motivated by politics, but profit. This can sometimes cause issues. I don't always look at the backstory. I prefer to concentrate on creating margins that work in my favour.'

'Is this an issue that concerns Jana?'

'I am not directly involved, this I'm making clear.'

A nerve in Libáň's top lip pulsed between his admissions.

'What's the connection?'

Composing his reply, Libáň spun a slender remote control around on his sparse desk, and like a navigator he watched it intently before making a decision on which bearing to follow. 'Jana,' he disclosed slowly. 'She *was* a member of our client team. Very popular, but outside work she mixed with people who don't appreciate the nature of my business.'

'They hold different views?' proposed Nick.

'Capitalism... it's their enemy. They believe it's a disease that has to be eradicated,' he said with disdain, giving the remote another compass spin. 'Jana got the bug, started to lecture her guests. And that's not what they want to hear. They pay for a good time and they started to complain being with Jana was like going to a political rally. I had no alternative... I had to talk with her. "What's with the attitude?" I asked her. "Who's giving you all this bullshit manifesto crap?" She sat there...' he stared at the empty chair, '...and warned *me* it was none of my business. "That's classy," I told her. "It's *my* business that's paying your rent... filling your shopping cart..." But she didn't want to know. I had few options, so I let her go.'

When Libáň spoke, his voice was all lows and highs, a melody in its own right – deep serious, sincere, light, and sometimes drifting free. He had that cultured, philosophical edge that verged on the passionate: an inquisitive, playful voice that he acoustically explored.

'Who was influencing her?' Nick, already a page ahead, waited for Libáň's confirmation, his gaze drawn to an impressive canvas of red dribbles installed on an entire wall.

'Her boyfriend, a bum, a dreamer who thinks he's a big, bad, revolutionary,' admitted Libáň.

'Is he part of a group?'

'Group...' Libáň allowed himself an economy smile. 'Call themselves the KOSC... *Komunistická obranná síla Československa*... Most of them are layabouts who object to other people earning serious money.'

'Are Jana and her boyfriend still a couple?'

'Who knows… maybe… Her guy's called Strizov and he always bums around the university posing as a radical,' Libáň finally admitted. 'I heard he's a mechanic… car repairs. Has a workshop in Nusle that's run as a collective. Jana did leafleting with him, calls for strikes, advertising meetings where some old Commie would be the red star speaker. She even tried to hand out flyers to the other girls denouncing capitalist exploitation.'

Across the street a dark Skoda caught Nick's attention.

He watched it crawl along through pockets of wind shipped snow and he knew mobile surveillance required a command vehicle. The type depended on what footpads and watchers determined as 'atmospherics' – the location, traffic patterns and other variables. If the Skoda came around again or did a quick switch with any of the other cars and vans keeping the parking spots warm, he knew he had trouble.

'So Jana was fully behind the KOSC cause, whatever it led to?'

Infected by Nick's sudden alertness, Libáň pushed himself out from behind his desk as though he recalled a much-needed chore requiring his immediate attention.

'Sure, but that's her concern. Jana knew what she was getting into.'

'What was she getting into?'

'Trouble, totally, one hundred per cent. Jana turned up on Tuesday,' he admitted, on his way to a cubed storage display stacked in an obsessive, precise staircase formation. 'She was completely wasted,' he revealed, resting one shoulder against a cube storing glossy books. 'She'd loaded up on vodka… maybe hit a few lines too many… her head was a shambles and she started screaming the place down that she needed to see me. It took us an hour to talk her round. Her big scene was all down to Strizov not showing up,' he disclosed with a dismissive shrug of his shoulders. 'She was ranting that he'd been lifted. Not the local crime busters, okay, but the secret cops.'

'Did she give a reason?'

Pursing his lips, Libáň recounted how Jana, 'Pounded out this wild story that Strizov's revolutionary plans were really taking off.' Not looking at Nick, he glanced at a row of black and white photographs decorously hung in a recess, reacquainting himself with each stark, moody scene. 'Strizov and some of his buddies were going to make a major, five-star statement. He wouldn't let Jana in on the big deal, but she'd know when it went down.

Everyone would. Then everyone would start taking the KOSC seriously, pay them the respect they deserved. I told her go home, to come and talk to me in the morning, but she never showed up. No one's seen her since.'

'You have the address of this workshop?'

Glancing back down into the street Nick saw the Skoda enter the block again. He watched it drop to walking pace, then draw to a stop in the main through lane outside a corner grocery store, just long enough for a middle-aged woman to load her shopping and children. Decoys? Distractions? Surrogates drafted in for cover? Nick couldn't be sure. In the art of hard surveillance it is the skill of creating smoke and mirrors that matters.

'I can get it for you.'

'I'll be outside on the street,' Nick decided, preferring to take his chances in the open.

'This counts as a bonus, right? Libáň, the entrepreneur right to the end, belted out his demand as Nick closed the door behind him.

• • •

In Praha 4 the morning snow had lessened, spilling across the city in intense flurries. When Nick reached Nusle after a tedious journey split between bus and tram, he sought out the landmarks provided by Libáň. The combat clothing market with enough stalls to equip a revolutionary army, the Pleasure Garden sex shop, each of its full plate windows obscured by a modesty film of decorative vinyl – its smooth surface crinkled, its corners lifting in its own modest uprising. And after a couple of wrong turnings, the high-speed rail line to Brno.

He passed a down-at-heel hotel slipping fast towards total ruin. Littering its front steps a drunk in his sixties instead of a doorman. Nick followed a trail of weak footprints in a layer of new snow cut between the patched gable wall of a tenement and main railway line. Deep tyre tracks had churned up the iced edges, exposing patches of cobbles cut into deep grooves by iron rimmed wheels on handcarts.

The embankment rose in a high, rough overgrown ridge above his left shoulder closing out the daylight inside a hazy hollow. Low branches from feeble saplings and wild thickets bent almost double by snow shone fiercely in the bitter air, his very own clandestine lighting. He came out onto a stone sided ramp. Below him there were dozens of vehicles abandoned in a big, ugly patch of scrubland in the lee of two tenements married corner to corner in an L resembling a wing of a Victorian prison.

Cordoning off the other two sides, the parapet walls of a factory met a sheer faced embankment buttressed into steep terraces. Here, straggly limbed trees and bushes had grown fat and thick by pilfering all the light. It's a fortress for all Prague's anarchists Nick reasoned, descending the ramp. Glancing around the rows of windows on each block's seven floors, he glimpsed shadows of life monitoring his route, but no firm shapes lingered for longer than a couple of seconds.

Gathered around this tiny inlet of devout revolution, a handful of collective ground floor workshops for those seeking an alternative life: a printer of radical pamphlets, manuals and other subversive reading, a furniture exchange, a food cooperative, a squatters advice bureau, a clothes bank – none of them open.

Perhaps they operate on an appointment only system? Perhaps they are taking cover because they know someone is going to come calling? With those possibilities to consider, Nick hurried on.

He passed the shell of a dismantled fire truck, its axles propped on plastic beer crates. Picking his way over a clump of tow chain bleeding rust into the snow, he avoided a minefield of empty gas canisters.

Slashing through each block's column of shared balconies, metal chutes descended in vertical umbilicals to allocated bays for wheeled collection bins. Nick noted most of these had either been stolen or damaged beyond repair, leaving pyramids of rubbish leaching a rank, sour odour into the air. Midway in one of the blocks a rough workshop for vehicle repairs was shoehorned behind double, mismatched doors.

And Nick made straight for them.

Fashioned out of scrap timber boards the doors were decorated with floral garlands using left over cans of paint. Stacks of spare wheels lined the sides of the entrance like replacements in a pit lane; cannibalised from the decaying fleet, their tread barely roadworthy. Bubbling from an open window in one of the apartments, Soundgarden's *Hands All Over* played high to drown out any disturbance. Fear: it's the constant they live by – the fear of conformity, the fear of authority, the fear of friends who visit in the night, decided Nick, tugging against a padlock on an industrial hasp protecting both doors. Solid and tight he rattled it vigorously one more time in frustration.

Looking around he went to the nearest row of vehicles. He rummaged through the gutted hulk of a Renault van, finding a tyre lever half buried under a crust of rusty snow. Clutching the lever like a baseball bat Nick strode back to the workshop, starting on the lock and hasp. He split away a tongue of wood, jammed the lever in again to work away behind the padlock. Pivoting his good shoulder against one of the doors Nick heard the wood splinter then give with a jolt that pitched him sideways.

He took a count of five before prying the door open. His breath snapped out in relief when it parted from the lock. He entered slowly, two vigilant steps at a time, allowing his eyes to adjust to the drowsy midwinter light trapped inside. He made out a flat panel of switches, flicking each one in succession, the tyre lever laid to rest against a tool trolley.

The starters for each fluorescent tube hummed awake, roused into a crisp buzzing. Then in flickering surges they sporadically lit each quarter of the workshop. Crammed into the stale air top heavy with oil, fuel and the open guts of engines he recognised the pungent smell of death. No matter how much you'd encountered it, the putrid, ripe stench of decay and cloying aroma of body fluids mixed with blood always caught you unawares like an unorthodox punch. It was something you could never prepare for, and Nick was no exception. It lodged in his throat, in his nose: he had the impression of it clinging to his skin and that no number of showers would loosen its grip.

He moved quickly knowing that time was against him. Thrashing out from a floor above, the brutal chords of heavy metal, punk or grunge. He didn't know which; only the obscure, growled lyrics seemed to be a portent of doom. Slewed upright against a brick wall, the Yamaha FZ6 motorcycles used in the snatch of Leiston. In a nest of cardboard boxes he found the scanner and his Motorola radio. Towards the rear of the workshop he parted the curtain of a makeshift polythene spray booth. That's when he found Jana.

What a waste, Nick thought, staring at her body. Partially on her back and side, her legs buckled from the knees under her, he estimated they'd whipped upwards when one fatal round entered her forehead. Dribbled across the concrete floor from a crimson halo around her head, her blood led in abstract trails across patches of dried paint where the VW T5 van was given its police colours. The remaining cans of paint were dumped beside a compressor.

She was expecting a journey to the promised land of anarchy and revolution Nick reasoned; his logic derived entirely from the pathetic scene. By her body, its strap in her long fingers, a leather travel bag. Searched in a hurry its contents were dumped in careless spoil heaps.

So where's Strizov? he wondered, returning to the main workshop, kicking open the door of a meagre chipboard partition office. A lean-to hunkered up against the rear wall, its flat roof a disorganised store of exhaust pipes. In a roll-top desk he tugged out boiler suits and ice hockey goalie masks stuffed amongst flyers for anarchist meetings and rallies. He went through each pocket of the boiler suits, finding nothing. Methodically, with a nagging awareness that he was overstaying, Nick picked through a notebook covered by smears from oily fingers. In a last page to bear an entry he found several folded till receipts from a camping store in Třinec.

Keeping the receipts he retreated from the office as another pounding track thrashed into action. Having nowhere else to look for Strizov, Nick concentrated on a vehicle tucked under a dust sheet. Grabbing one corner he whipped the sheet clear like a magician, exposing a M-class Mercedes SUV, its condition and lack of plates suggesting it was stolen. Clenching his mouth tight, breathing shallowly through his nose Nick tugged the passenger door open, his grim discovery propped in the front seat. He started to rifle through the uniform pockets of one of the fake motorcycle policemen that yielded nothing.

On the man's wrist a chunky gold identity bracelet engraved with 'Love from Jana'. Fatally wounded by Taurus, he'd been dumped to bleed out. The blood from where the .44 Magnum round tore into Strizov's abdomen had percolated around his feet and congealed into a dark, sticky pool. He'd been finished off with clear bag taped around his neck. Did your own comrades sacrifice you to safeguard their identities? Was this repayment by a different group using you and your KOSC friends as disposable contractors? Nick softly wondered aloud, never anticipating an answer.

Scrabbling through a tool caddy he took a screwdriver, and taking a deep breath made a rip in the bag. Exhaling hard, twisting his head from the stench, Nick peeled the bag down around Strizov's bloated neck. Standing back he took a full set of photos of the head and body from different angles with his phone. Making one last trip around the workshop Nick scoured each corner, each inch of the place for an indication that Leiston or Rewall had been here during their first hours of abduction.

With nothing to back up his theory other than his intuition, he collected the tyre lever. The remaining happy band of KOSC urban guerrillas will have closed ranks, preferring to remain ignorant of anything that has happened to two of their own comrades he decided, pulling the door closed behind him. *KOSC are stooges. They have not advanced beyond idle Internet chatter. They are cut from the same cloth as the Red Army Faction in the seventies. Whether they appreciate that is a moot point*, Bailrigg had decreed. Tossing the lever down into the snow Nick walked calmly towards the ramp, the crash of guitars filling the scrubland with an electric dirge.

•••

On his return journey from Syria the fighter they called Hāru, stopped over in London before flying on to the Czech Republic. He had spent his life in transit, travelling from country to country acquiring a mixed bag of Western customs. This, amounting to his acquisition of a cultural veneer, lay lightly on a deeper and more pronounced political bed of radical ideology. Educated in Europe, Hāru never lost sight of his roots or his father's wisdom. 'In every Palestinian's heart there is a permanent stain, a sorrow that cannot be bleached or purified by happiness,' his father once told him. 'The joy of a woman, the accomplishment of a great battle; they will always fail to remove this reminder of the Jews' control. Go. Go live amongst the Western imperialists; hear... see how the capitalists assist the Jews' to suppress our people. Remember my son we have the bargaining counters; the dice is in our hands. To throw badly is no dishonour, not to throw at all is cowardice and should be met with death.'

At fourteen years and two months he had settled into the growing adulthood of a boy deliberately cut adrift. Welcomed and educated firstly in Athens, the philosophy of how freedom had become corrupted by the satanic breath of Western capitalism deepened his hatred of his enemies, heightened his devotion to his father engaged in commanding the war against the Zionists and their imperialist friends. During his father's absences, arrangements were made for Hāru to attend an exclusive school as part of his formal education. In the evenings, he visited a private tutor for his moral education; a grizzled Palestinian fighter stronger than a stallion with a face puffed and inflamed from wounds taken in battle. The fighter's skin he would always remember; a mottled brown forming a rough terrain baked by desert sand with scars sealed deep into the solid flesh.

On the first of his many visits to his evening tutor, the fighter had cuffed Hāru with a closed fist, on his second, he chipped the boy's front tooth, on the third he offered his hand in friendship as a sign of courage. On a fine summer evening when Hāru had reached eighteen, the fighter took him to a lake, made him empty his pockets: money, phone, his forged identity. 'Your wits will always be your provider and protector,' he instructed him. 'You must survive for four nights in the city, boy. No money, no friends' homes. Live as you mean to go along. I will be watching you. If you weaken I will crush you.' He made his point by doubling Hāru in two with a stunning blow to his abdomen. 'Go.'

So Hāru, his belly and ribs racked by pain after vomiting, his eyes swimming with tears, walked off through a tapering woodland trail. For three hours he sat on a bench opposite the bus station shrouded in fumes, surrounded by the rich smiles of people returning home, the lucky pilgrims sure of a bed and a decent meal.

At a quarter to ten he knocked on the rear door of a restaurant, explaining he wanted to wash the dishes in return for something to eat. They threw him out. He tried again, a different restaurant and got his chance. He also got his bed from a waitress who thought his nose sexy, his eyes romantic. He never forgot those nights of food and her warm body curled beside him, the fragrance of jasmine oil dominating her small, hot bedroom. He'd been born with quick wits, good looks and youth as a means of showing his potential, his tools for survival. And he intended to use them without mercy as he intensified his war in Europe.

Nine

It was a good four hour drive to Třinec and it snowed persistently for three quarters of the way. Nick left Prague after ten in the evening, the dusk imitating dawn with streaks of fiery red, the radio offering a handful of ballads recalling a different way of living. He'd collected the Skoda Superb from a steep mountain of a street behind the FK Viktoria Stadion, the keys taped in a polythene bag under its rear nearside wheel arch. The logistics taken care of by Harry also included a Fobus paddle holster complete with a Glock 32, a tactical light fitted, plus two seventeen round magazines.

Leaving Prague Nick remained on the E50 through Velká Bíteš, his route pre-planned for skirting Brno, aiming up the D1 to Vyškov. At the gates to a truck stop a young woman in a thick padded pink coat and pink boots twirled a pink umbrella, drumming up custom for lay-by sex. Which gave the concept of love in cold climate a whole new twist, thought Nick.

He halted once for fuel and coffee before continuing on the R46 to Olomouc, concentrating on staying in tracks cut by a plough. Finally he obeyed signs for the E462 leading him to Třinec, a sports talk channel on the radio providing a non-stop debate on ice hockey. He remembered the goalie masks stuffed in the roll-top and thought how somebody was using the KOSC for a different play, how it really had turned into a game of life and death.

Hitting Třinec he verified his directions against the thick lines inked on a map Harry had folded into the glove compartment. Cross-referencing his destination on his phone's GPS, Nick undertook the final act of dusting his trail, his route vague and fluid along a winding series of roads emerging in a pocket of woodland as the flimsy first stirrings of dawn shrugged off the night. Staring through the Skoda's wiper blades as they beat away granules of fine snow he made out a rough, potholed lane running parallel to the iron and steel works. Calling Bransk to confirm his final coordinates, Harry made his usual outrageous assertion that he'd never supplied anything to Nick that turned out to be a dud.

'You got to have more faith, Nick, huh?' Harry urged. 'The favours I'm calling in, they're hurting me... if I'm absolutely honest.'

'The only thing that's hurting is your pocket.'

And for several minutes after he'd reassured Nick the coordinates were correct, Harry lectured him on what he regarded as his friend's need to consider the bigger picture.

'Nick... Nick... listen, okay. You got to slow down, you need to let me check out these reports my contacts brought in,' he urged. 'Give me a couple of hours to chase the details down, verify the product, take some back-bearings.'

'We haven't time, Harry.'

'Then better make sure you're not walking into a trap, huh.' Harry had advised, ending the call with a grunt of disapproval.

Pledging silently that he would observe Harry's directive Nick eased down the lane, swerving to avoid its ruts and craters. He chose a partially hidden spot under the overhanging limbs of an elder, the bark on one side of its trunk caked a rusty brown by dust from the smelting plant. He reversed up a slight bank beside a chain-link fence, the low tips of branches scraping the roof panel.

Beyond the fence a forgotten railway siding partially capped by snow overlooked by an obsolete concrete signal control tower. Tightening the zip pull on his jacket he tugged it down over his holster as he abandoned the Skoda. His steps brisk, he pounded out his anger, counting sixty paces before he came to a gate and single overgrown roadway stopping abruptly at a branch line in an island of old sidings.

Taking the dull tracks and points at a crouched trot, Nick's left shoulder ached and gnawed with each jolting step. He picked out sets of tyre tracks cutting through the snow on a crossing leading to and from the signal control tower. A river sluiced through a spur of land on the other side of the tracks, its dark brown frothy water sealing off the yard from the works. Clots of steam and ribbons of smoke curled from cooling towers and thin, pencil flue vents. Nick could taste sulphur blown across the yard by a mean wind. He ducked in behind a rusted lighting stanchion when a diesel shunter hauling wagons of scrap to the furnaces crossed a set of points on a distant line. Clear to move, he sprinted towards the tower.

One of the early concrete pre-war models, the double storey tower shared a wire fenced compound with a generous prefabricated store that had holes smashed into its panels. Hitting the fence Nick set it shivering, whirring and rattling. He tugged on a heavy chain and formidable lock looped around a pair of reinforced gates.

I should have a team, he thought. Not one but two, he reasoned fastidiously. A pack of watchers who would have warned in advance of what to expect before the breachers went in.

Keeping tight against the fence he worked slowly around its perimeter. He worried about his fingers nipped by the cold if it came to a sudden contact. He fretted about what he might or might not find.

At the rear he squeezed through a diagonal tear in the fence's wired bands. Using his good shoulder Nick heaved one of the store's split back wall panels sideways, shattering it with a bang. For a good twenty seconds he listened for any response but all he heard was the slamming and beating of raw metal in the works.

Once through the gap he drew his Glock. Half the store's roof was missing; inside snow had steadily fallen. It had built up in small drifts against one wall and the side of a VW T5 masquerading as a police traffic control unit. Swirls of footprints led from the van's rear hatch. Left in a wavy line like an erratic furrow through the snow, the heels of bound legs dragged in the direction of the tower. Scattered alongside them, unmistakable drops of blood. Leiston's? Rewall's? Giving himself a count of three, Nick tried the rear hatch. The mechanism released, he levelled his Glock as the door swept up.

Empty from its tail to the front compartment, Nick went about seeking evidence under the beam of his tactical light. Smeared partway down a side panel a patch of dried blood. In Nick's brisk estimation, it corresponded to a casualty slumped in a slouched position who'd taken a bullet to the shoulder. And he recalled the single round he'd fired during the sham traffic stop. Out of the rear compartment he went around to check the front cabin. On the inside of the driver's door he made out the original colour, a vibrant yellow, before a hurried respray added a police livery. Going through the interior he smelt the tint of chemicals from cleaning agents after a thorough valeting wiped the van clean. Apart from that, he came across nothing of note. Perhaps the KOSC have done their homework Nick reasoned, leaving the way he came in: the Internet is full of useful tips for anarchists, for would-be revolutionaries, including manuals on indiscriminate killing.

There were perhaps a couple of yards between Nick and the tower. He negotiated them at a sprint. He held his position at the foot of a metal stairway cantilevering up the tower, giving himself a hundred reasons for not proceeding. As much as he took each tread carefully, the solid metal steps clanged out each foot of progress like an accusation.

The main door was faced with steel plate, the exterior handle removed, a single, wide slot cut as a keyhole. From the rebate Nick could tell the door opened outwards. Rivets rather than screws held the plate. He noted one missing at the top right corner. He ran his finger over the hole feeling the tiny rib of clear nylon line passing out, then back over the door's top edge. If you don't know what's on the other side of a door, you don't use it unless it's the last resort, the Aspley directing staff never tired of preaching. For once Nick heeded their wisdom. He continued around onto a metal gantry running the length of the tower's top level. At the rear, one of the corrugated sheets slapped lazily over the windows flapped loosely on its mounting brackets.

Levering back a corner of the sheet he gradually pried a large enough gap to expose a rectangle of smutty Perspex below. The original glass had been smashed years ago he reckoned, replaced by a sturdier barrier. But from scorch marks and names scratched into its surface, this hadn't worked either, so they'd added metal as a final deterrent. He cleared away a film of dust ground in with years of furnace smoke with his forearm, though it gave him nothing to look at; just an impenetrable dimness as if he were staring down a mineshaft. Standing back he kicked hard with the base of his boot. He heard splintering from the edges when the Perspex cracked. After five more strenuous kicks, the panel burst free along one side.

Holding it ajar with his elbow Nick stepped over the low base concrete lintel, starting to wriggle his way in. The familiar perfume of decomposition met him like an old friend. In amongst the clamour of the iron and steel works, he picked up the buzzing shrieks of mopeds over revved as they belted closer to the sidings along a different route. Would this be some of the KOSC's friends coming to clear away any evidence? he wondered.

Twisting his torso to ease the tight fit he used his tactical light in fast swoops, holding off entering until he'd illuminated a clear path into the main control room. Half in, half out, he surveyed the litter left behind – camping lights, food wrappers, a pail, and beside a panel bursting with switches and dials, a space in the dust where something or someone had sat. One hostage here and one elsewhere? he wondered.

At first he mistook a dark pile in one corner by the door as rags, old clothes – a blanket, a boot tossed idly aside until he joined the dots. The boot was one of a pair attached to feet. The rest he made out in short order; a jacket sleeve, a trouser leg – the uniform of a motorcycle policeman. Spreading out from the body, a dark tributary of blood formed into a lake after Strizov's comrade had been abandoned to a painful death. In one of those moments that raise an instant, hot flush, Nick ran the beam of his tactical light to the door. He picked up the returning tail of nylon snaking across the floor, running up into the blanket. Down below, the mopeds came to a rapid halt.

On the other side of the tower he heard the clank as three sets of boots hammered at full stretch up to the door. Pushing back through the gap his jacket snagged tight on a corner of the corrugated sheet. Writhing, fighting to break free Nick used his arms and knees as levers. The sound of a key grating through the steel plate echoed through the whole tower. Using all his weight, his upper body strength and leg muscles, Nick gave one last almighty pull. He came tumbling out, throwing himself flat onto the gantry, his hands and arms covering his head.

Contained by the concrete walls acting like a pressure cooker, the Perspex and corrugated sheets blew out over the gantry in a blast wave that seemed to pick up the tower, shake it from side to side and drop it. Nick, his face nestled into his shoulder remained prone as debris peppered the gantry. In his nostrils he had an acrid tang of explosives, the back of a hand felt scorched, in his throat he felt dust lodging into a ball.

On his feet, a pain traversing through his skull, he wove along the gantry, the numbing fatigue in his arms and legs requiring double the effort to make it down into the yard. Slamming into a side wall on the store he sucked hard for air, choking on the dust. His ears rang and everything he heard came from within his own body: his breathing, heartbeat and pulse, as if he had inadvertently switched on internal speakers.

He gave himself a minute, realising that in all the chaos he still gripped his Glock. Holstering it, regulating his breathing, he watched for the first sign of anyone responding. Across the river caught in the smoky haze, a dozen steel and iron workers were gathering in little knots, a couple of them running along the fence to get a better view. Recovered and fully charged, he ripped over the sidings, not stopping until he reached his car.

• • •

At some point during Leiston's latest transfer from her noisy concrete prison, she sensed the mood change. When they had dragged her once more bound and blindfolded during a rapid departure to bundle her into another van, she caught a rise of anticipation in those around her. Something important was happening: she'd heard the student walking behind snap out the name 'Hāru' in response to a question and the very air seemed to tighten. Lost in this random stream of thought, she flinched when she bumped against the arm, then the leg of someone already loaded up against the van's bulkhead. She waited until the doors slammed, the engine started, regulating her breathing, timing it so that she could be sure she had a companion.

She had the urge to whisper 'Celia?' but rejected it, not sure if this other passenger might be the student, slyly observing, waiting for a misdemeanour that would give her chance to deliver more pain.

'Hannah?' Her name was barely audible, murmured close to her ear, a snatch of warmth dashed against her cheek.

Soft fingers landed on her sleeve; then in fluttering, constrained moves of another bound prisoner, sought out Leiston's hands. 'Hannah, it's me, Celia,' came the familiar low soft melodic voice in a reassuring lifeline. 'I've decided that I'm going to tell them everything...'

Lurching to an unexpected halt the van idled as the student bawled for silence from behind the partition. The command drove the hostages apart, no more contact, nothing but an invisible bond to counteract the fear consuming Hannah Leiston. Returned to her own dark space against the van's cold metal, Leiston rode each bump on a drive that never seemed to end. When they hauled her out into a blast of bitter air she had a sensation of being in the countryside miles from anywhere.

Manoeuvred, pushed and pulled, they led her through corridors leading to rooms with high ceilings that gave their steps a resonating, drumbeat echo. Dumped in a corner they cut her wrists free, a gentle grip that she hadn't encountered before took her hands and guided them around a bottle of water. Startling her, a gentle hand stroked her cheek, tugged trapped strands of hair from her mouth.

'Thank you.'
'We'll talk later.'

The promise rocked Leiston. It came from someone she immediately assessed as cultured – not too old, not young – a confident male on the right side of thirty. His accent, his tone, had that hybrid English-American pitch derived from an education taken outside his homeland.

'I'm not going anywhere.'

She was answered by the soft patter of retreating steps followed by a deliberately slammed door, a keynote reminder of her status. Left by her new visitor – to Leiston he would be the *professor* – a lingering tail of soap and fragrant lotion.

During her resistance to interrogation training Leiston had willingly suffered a taste of inhumanity first hand, accepting it as a means to an end, the completion of her new entrant phase allowing her to progress as a Service probationer. She'd been humiliated, taunted and mocked after being stripped naked, deprived of light, warmth, food, water; they'd distorted time, employing it as psychological weapon. The directing staff had introduced each and every method of interrogation, some in theory, many in practice. But nothing they touched on came close to the acute pain from seriously wanting a pee.

Real hard-hitting discomfort surged across her abdomen from her bladder. She'd ignored it for long enough. Sitting up, she bit her lip as she gingerly felt with both hands for a metal pail they'd left at her side against the wall. A surge of nausea clogged her throat as she uncovered its lid and lifted herself to squat. If they'd intended this as punishment, to see how long she could suffer they'd wait a good few days yet.

Taking the freeing of her wrists as neither a truce nor softening of attitudes, Leiston sat draped in her blanket crying quietly in despair and relief. She'd been exactly six years, seven months old when she'd sobbed like this during her first term away at school. *We'll talk later.* Then what? What came after the 'final chat'? Fighting to hold her composure, she channelled her anger into a refusal to give in: she concentrated on her family, determined not to let them down. At that moment she started preparing; determined not to be stranded in a dark void of not knowing. Repeatedly she cautioned herself that if she didn't begin to assert control over her wild thoughts, the fear would destroy her.

Ten

Nick counted twenty steps down to Oskar's Bar; all of them sensible, all faced in robust tiles fired in a hearty blue lustre. Inside dark oak doors the main bar had pine cladding stained a shocking black. Towards the lavatories, behind a plastic chain barrier, a twisting small flight of steps led Nick deeper underground; to a vaulted cellar made up entirely of red brick. An unofficial command post during the Russian invasion of Sixty-Eight, Oskar had converted it into a private guest area, reserving it for business meetings between his friends. On rare occasions he could be coaxed into an impromptu performance on his saxophone; one number Nick remembered was a seductive version of Handy's *Hard Work*.

The atmosphere was positively mellow. Lit by candles twisted into the necks of wine bottles, layers of wax smothered the glass in coloured roots and tubers. The tables were meagre, intimate, all of them oddly shaped and sized. But only one concerned Nick. Berthed with his back to a wall, László Ercsi lounged with the supreme ease of a man who could afford to enjoy his leisure. A teardrop of a man, his head was long, courting a sharp face that no one naturally trusted, but he possessed a strange captivating aura that could somehow fill a room.

'How is Mr. Arrowsmith? You are well? I did okay on fulfilling Harry's order for the pistol? I hope Mr. Arrowsmith appreciated the effort I made. When Harry ordered Glock and paddle, I thought this for someone special, this for guy who knows the tools of his trade.' Ercsi rattled out his opening burst in rapid snatches as his guest sat opposite.

'Everything was fine, László,' said Nick. 'Who else has been shopping? Anyone approach you for automatic rifles?'

Diverting Nick's question into a show of hospitality, Ercsi poured two respectable glasses of Talisker 18.

'Rifles?' he eventually responded. 'You discussing longs?' His face twisted in a quizzical, perplexed frown, he offered a salut. '*Na zdraví.*'

'*Na zdraví.*' Nick raised his glass, barely wetting his lips. 'Yes, longs László. Assault rifles…Vz.58s for instance,' he added.

A Hungarian who divided his time between Prague and Brussels, Ercsi blatantly encouraged the myth that he was a successful international arms trader. To Nick's knowledge, the only major deal he'd negotiated involved twenty-four Javelin anti-tank missiles that happened to be dummies, supplied by CO8 and intended to derail a coup in Africa. His real genius, the mainstay of Ercsi's regular trade, came as a purveyor of small arms. As a lucrative sideline he marketed duty free cigarettes and alcohol as diplomatic goods through a website based in Lichtenstein.

'Swear on my sweet, dear grandmother's shrine, Mr. Arrowsmith,' vowed Ercsi, his face taught in a sanguine appeal. 'Not a Vz.58 gone out my warehouse to a user I not been able to verify.'

'So what's the word on the backstreets? Any rumours circulating on black orders and crash cash purchases?'

Ercsi had slipped fast into has late fifties, perversely returning to the heady, blasé days of his youth wearing the top three buttons of his shirts open, a gold crucifix nestling at the base of his bull neck. His upper body was muscle; the remainder down to his waist and thighs had long since surrendered to flab. His tight, curly hair was waxed into a sparse parting, once more proving that he was no devotee or respecter of fashion.

Draining his remaining drops of Talisker, the ersatz arms trader went for a pre-emptive refill before offering Nick a recharge that he studiously declined.

'Harry told me that Mr. Arrowsmith had two leads, two individuals,' Ercsi complained. '*Na zdraví.*'

Nick ignored the salutation, pushing aside his glass still fully charged. 'I haven't spoken to them, László – they're dead.'

Ercsi dwelt on Nick's information, his eyebrows – bushy, wild affairs – nuzzled up against the deep, gouged lines on his forehead when he frowned. He pinched his marble cheek between his left thumb and fingers as if attempting to massage away the trench system of thin, broken veins.

'Collateral damage?'

'Casualties.'

'Your face tell me that you no here to award medal.'

'Just checking the facts,' proposed Nick.

'Facts? You want facts?' Ercsi snapped. 'I give you facts, for sure.' Reaching out across the table he slid the bottle of Talisker closer. The tips of two fingers on Ercsi's right hand were fractionally shorter than the rest; to anyone who had time or the inclination to listen, he spun the legend of how he'd lost them during combat. Nick learnt from Harry that the injuries were from a foolhardy prank with fireworks when Ercsi was a boy.

'I got everyone working for Mr. Arrowsmith. I make calls of personal nature, reel in fish I have dangling on line. Call in IOUs that I been storing for rainy day,' he offered, his voice dull, deep, seeped in one of the brands of tobacco that his website purported to ship within twenty-four hours.

'Course you have.'

'It's true, every word, no lie. Swear on grandfather's shrine and every shrine of every damn ancestor.' Ercsi poured more than a healthy shot.

'Met him at all?' Nick brought up the image of Strizov on his phone. He held it close for Ercsi to study. 'Seen him with friends... associates... looking for supplies?'

Pushing the phone out of his face, Ercsi downed his whisky in a single rush. 'A guy called me up,' he confessed slowly, 'an acquaintance, based in Prague. Asked if I could get him a handshake on reconditioned Vz.58s in a hurry. I say to him – "What? You tell me you can't pin any down? Your whole damn life you been supplying them! They're Czech, you got crates of the damn things on your doorstep". Do you believe this guy!'

Nick didn't believe Ercsi either, so he remained silent until the arms trader felt compelled into resuming, braced by another good measure of Talisker.

'This acquaintance insists this deal is Vz.58 only. His client will have no other way. No serial numbers, no paper clip trail, just Grade-A condition with enough 7.62 rounds to begin war. I laugh, Mr. Arrowsmith. I say to this to guy: "I get your shipment, no hassle. Just let me contact associates in Sudan and Mali. They have Vz.58s coming out their ears." He didn't see my joke,' Ercsi ruefully admitted, his moist lips pursed. 'The guy told me to try, so I did. During second day of calling up people I should never do business with, the guy texts me. He got better offer and so I need no worry.'

'Anything else on the original shopping list?'

'Not much, but enough,' Ercsi disclosed confidentially. 'It what you don't see that tell story.' He cast a conspiratorial glance around the cellar, hopelessly looking for an accomplice to bolster his point.

The bare plaster walls housed a personal Cold War museum. Maps, photographs, lines of newspaper headlines amassed from when the Russian's came calling. Rumour had it that Oskar had somehow been caught up in it, remembered Nick. In what capacity no one felt like saying.

'What *is* the story?'

'It's like a dumb kid put order together to start insurgency. Vz.s... RPG-7s... Grenades...'

'Type?'

'Polish...RGZ-89s.'

Nick recalled the IED at the signal control tower, visualising how the grenade could have served as a primary charge for other explosives packed around the body.

'Wouldn't this guy who called you... this dealer... surely he would have his own inventory of available stock without turning to anyone else?' proposed Nick. 'Between you and me, László – it sounds like you were being set-up.'

Pouncing on Nick's suggestion, Ercsi became animated. 'Exactly – that what I tell myself, Mr. Arrowsmith. "László, you being used as pretty dumb mark." On the grapevine, I hear whispers,' he continued. 'The guy in the market for Vz.s and other dumb crap, he think he top man. I just listen, Mr. Arrowsmith. He runs his mouth off when he go socialising, always bragging to impress other associates. He claiming that he hit pay dirt with this deal,' he explained, huddled forward. 'His new client is so happy at service he provide as broker, he going to recommend him to some special friends who are big users and spenders.'

'Don't suppose he provided details of his new client or the special friends?'

Shaking his head to imply that Nick should know better, Ercsi rounded off his disclosure with a final decent top-up of Talisker. 'He'd be pretty damn crazy. Who'd want your competitors muscling in on every deal?' he admitted in a rare burst of refreshing honesty 'This guy's slick, does business using only mail boxes and throwaway phones.'

'Can you arrange a meeting?'

Taking his time to consider Nick's request, Ercsi finished off his whisky as if it might be his last for a considerable time. 'For you, Mr. Arrowsmith, I make exception,' he volunteered. 'But don't say I no warn you. This guy is pond scum. Jiří Cista has expenses fever; even claims for licking postage stamp. He charge you fortune for telling you his name.'

And with Ercsi's perpetual vow that on their next meeting he would come bearing gifts – *Cartons of Dunhill... Diplomat... Marlboro... you just let Harry know and László do rest* – Nick shook hands and to the arms-trader's amazement, left without bothering to drain his Talisker.

• • •

Most cities were remarkable at how they contained multiple personalities – distinctive quarters, districts, neighbourhoods that changed so dramatically within a few miles. During Nick's ride that took him west across the river, he read the signs like an old experienced adventurer, aware of how the sense of security gave way to something darker. He read the increase of graffiti, the swarms of fly-posters blighting every corner, how the tarmac stuttered out to end in tattered patches, the old worn, smooth cobbles exposed where a biting, ice edged wind drove lying snow into ridges. Flanking Nick on his trudge up a road snaking towards a wooded escarpment, rows of harsh, dark grey apartment blocks loomed upwards into an even greyer sky. The whole neighbourhood had the twilight gloom of permanent winter.

Another redoubt stormed by Soviet forces, Nick decided pushing open a low mesh gate barring his path to a sturdy villa isolated on a twisted crook of land where the blocks abruptly halted their climb. Hardy stone ribs held vivid bullet wounds concentrated around a ground floor window and second floor balcony, where he supposed, an attempt at upholding democracy had been violently suppressed.

After the signal control tower he didn't even bother with the dark lacquered main door. Pulling his leather gloves tighter, Nick went off around the rear, down a fenced side passage to a garden left to its own devices. Heaving himself over a section of fence, Nick stayed in the shadows working his way up to the villa. Steps and railings led to a higher terrace level, a three foot by three foot paved area where Nick listened for any sounds from inside. Below him the din of the city came in muffled, blends of noise; the strange sounds from another world. A kitchen window at shoulder height stood open, a piece of curtain limply swaying.

With the rear door locked, he chose the window as his point of entry. Resolved to eliminate any possible snags, he removed the Glock from its holster, tucking it into his waistband where it sat nudged up against his spine. Scrabbling over the ledge Nick pulled himself through, his gloves slipping on greasy tiles above a sink.

Grabbed by his hair and his jacket Nick shot crudely forward. Crashing into a pyramid of cups, pans and plates he landed hard on a tiled floor. Out of an immediate need for preservation, he automatically rolled on his side. An instinctive move saving his life, it also dislodged his Glock, sending it skittering under a large pantry cupboard.

He saw only a blur of movement, a brutal downward thrust, hearing the blade tip strike against floor tiles. Up on his feet Nick's vision rapidly adjusted, making out vague objects in a darkened kitchen. One of them a balaclava masked attacker closing in on him, a hunting knife in his gloved right hand. Scything the air he made probing lunges at Nick's arms, his face, his torso.

Sidestepping, twisting his body, Nick dodged each swing of the blade like a matador. His nerves alight, fizzing on adrenalin he worked around the kitchen in a deliberate pattern, his back resolutely to the cabinets. With his breathing heavy taken in nasal snorts, the attacker spat snatched Arabic curses each time Nick swiftly changed position.

His latest preselected move brought him to a section of worktop where he spotted the foggy outlines of a set of old scales, a toaster, a kettle, a jar of wooden utensils. It was all or nothing he reasoned, yelling at an imaginary friend in the hallway. He needed less than a second and got it. When the attacker cast a fast glance over his shoulder Nick grabbed a hefty spatula, using the utensil's thick edge like a machete. He hacked once against the attacker's bony wrist bringing a howl of pain, a lessening grip on the weapon. Nick rapidly struck at the same spot again and again, harder, fiercer, hearing a heavy metallic clack as the knife clattered away onto the tiled floor.

Launching his counter-attack Nick sent the blade scuffing off under a cabinet with a rapid kick. Abandoning the spatula he snatched a large weight from the side of the scales, smashing it into the man's jaw. Screaming in rage the attacker made a grab for Nick. In a fierce assault, Nick's feet, elbows, fists and knees became his primary weapons.

Using a lethal combination of blows, punches, kicks and strikes he inflicted serious, bloody damage. In a series of punishing body blows, Nick aimed coordinated strikes at the attacker's liver, a rapid series to the chest below his heart. One ferocious, piston-fast punch using his mid-finger knuckles in a power line, delivered a fatal blow to the attacker's throat.

Standing back from the prone body, Nick's pulse raced, his breathing greedily taken in deep surges. Toppled into a twisted face down position, the attacker's body began its pre-death overture, the nerves in the arms and legs gave spasmodic twitches; escaping air bubbled in the damaged, restricted throat.

Planting his feet either side of the body Nick ripped off the balaclava, rolling the figure over onto his back. He estimated his attacker to be between twenty-five and thirty; from his deep, carnelian eyes, his distinct features, Nick guessed his roots were closer to Beirut, Gaza or the West Bank than Europe. Considering he now had a strong possibility of Palestinian involvement, Nick rummaged through the killer's pockets at some haste, starting with the zipped closures on a leather motorcycle jacket.

From the top right pocket he extracted a wallet and tossed it onto the worktop. Slipped into the man's black jean's pocket Nick discovered a quarter of an A4 sheet ripped from a pad folded in a tight square. Opening it out he read Cista's address written in a hurry. It's the KOSC's handler closing all the doors, Nick decided. The fledging revolutionary group were encouraged and financed to make their own arrangements for weapons, now a different kind of terrorist cadre were clinically erasing the traces.

Turning his attention to the wallet Nick worked through each compartment: nine thousand koruna, a clutch of store receipts, a couple of condoms, a driving licence, a set of debit cards in different names. He'd even gone to the trouble of having a business card printed describing himself as a civil engineer. But there was nothing civil in the way he'd behaved thought Nick, straightening the head, adjusting it for portrait and profile photographs using his phone. He shook out the wallet to see if anything else remained, but nothing did. Nick's energy levels began to dip rapidly, the sweat wrapping his body grew cool, clammy. Even though his senses and every nerve buzzed, he knew he'd crossed the outer boundary of exhaustion. Retrieving his Glock he crouched over the body. Aware that his attacker was beyond recovery, Nick fired once into the dying man's head.

In the doorway he held every muscle still, determining the threat level. Deciding the level was close to nil he padded softly out of the kitchen into a ground floor high on perfume and body spray. On down the hall, its runner coming apart at the edges, Nick stopped every couple of steps to listen, hearing nothing except the eager mumble of long distance traffic. He took the set of doors in turn, working from the sitting room back towards the kitchen. Each room he found trashed after a crude hunt for incriminating evidence, particles of fine dust shimmering in the beam of his tactical light, silently protesting at being disturbed.

Cursing as each tread on the stairs creaked, he resumed his search on the upper floor. In the bathroom he met a trapped sweet odour, noting a stack of dirty laundry tossed across the floor presumably by the attacker. Partway along the landing Nick gripped a brass handle to a plain door, what he supposed must be the master bedroom.

He stood inside the doorway for a couple of seconds, the room turned upside down, dim, pungent. It bore the same abandoned second-hand feel of someone who could never settle, making do with furniture chosen for convenience. What Nick also recognised as a feature that by no rights ought to be there, the strong rusty metallic odour of fresh blood. At the centre Cista lay across a double bed, and from the way his slashed neck hung to one side, Nick was absolutely certain he wasn't sleeping. Along with the ragged, slit throat, Nick counted four stab wounds to the arms dealer's chest and one to the left eye. He tugged off a glove using his teeth, felt Cista's flabby wrist, the skin faintly warm. Hardly any daylight penetrated through heavy, velvet curtains. But the shadows failed to hide a young woman slumped with her back against a wardrobe, bloodied from multiple stab wounds. A wide splatter pattern had sprayed outwards in a flamboyant shower covering one of the mirrored doors.

Going around the bed Nick gazed down at the woman's helpless eyes, her skin pale, turning an unnatural white, her lips coated in a shiny gloss matching her eyeliner. Her make-up, not too heavy, had been applied with a natural finesse. Her blonde hair barely covered her shoulders. Cista's wife? Partner? Girlfriend? Maybe a hired companion for the night? considered Nick, her flesh lukewarm. From the way her hands were splayed down by her sides, her feet planted square, knees drawn up into her bloodied chest, she had backed into the corner, nowhere else to go.

Assessing the room, the condition of each body, Nick's senses became hyper alert. He prodded through Cista and his female friend's possessions dumped on the bed by their killer. There were the contents of a cosmetic bag, bedside and dressing table drawers whisked together. Nick diligently sifted through them all, sorting, analysing each scrap of paper, every receipt. *This guy is pond scum. Jiří Cista has expenses fever; even claims for licking postage stamp*, Ercsi had disclosed. Yes he did, agreed Nick, holding a receipt – the last Cista added – dated a week ago for fuel from a service station outside Chyňava.

Absolutely weary, convinced he hadn't overlooked anything Nick retreated to the terrace. Where, over a cigarette, he made a call to Harry.

'We need stain removal specialists,' Nick explained.

'That bad, huh?'

'Full clean and removal.'

'That's going to cost you, Nick. This is going to be an additional extra, okay. I'm not running a charity, know what I mean, I got to get the right personnel that I trust.'

'That's fine, Harry, just do what you need to do,' agreed Nick.

'London are going to have a fit when I tot up my final bill, know that, huh? Anything else?'

'I need to find a property around Chyňava. It's going to be isolated, perhaps empty... even derelict. Big or small, it's somewhere where our friends wouldn't be disturbed.'

'How much time I got to look for this place?'

'An hour at the most.'

'Any other miracles you like Harry to perform?'

For the moment it appeared Nick didn't have any, he simply provided Cista's address. Regretting how other victims had become trapped in the rotten fallout of a failed defection he headed back down off the terrace, slipping off his gloves. Weary of more senseless deaths and destruction he unbarred the garden gate, walking smartly out, prepared for another house call, and after that, if he was lucky, he could look forward to more nights of restless sleep in other economy hotels.

• • •

Calming herself, Leiston blotted her damp cheeks with a corner of the blanket, took deep breaths and ridiculed herself for being so weak. After her latest painful interrogation she kept the blanket round her shoulders, an itchy, stinking second skin. Twice she'd asked politely for a cigarette when her food arrived. Twice she ran her fingers around the tray's lip praying to find her request answered. Each disappointment only deepening her anger at being so helpless, trapped in a void she couldn't control.

To keep her spirits up she composed letters in her head to her parents, her brother, anyone. Angry letters to politicians she'd never officially be permitted to send, dissecting their ridiculous policies line by line: a cathartic release in imaginary ink and paper. Torn apart by the hunger clamping her stomach open, she paced her way through each piece of rye bread, forcing herself through a layer of margarine topped by coarse salami.

This latest question and answer session had been the worse. That was when reality struck, the sheer hopelessness of knowing that outside these cool walls the beat of normality never missed its rhythm; day followed night, high tide after low, lunch before dinner, people loved, people hated, they sulked, ran their lives blissfully ignorant of how she longed to rejoin time's endless, mundane routine. A prisoner's blues that's what she had come down with, a maudlin virus infecting her system after the grinding hours of visualising how the world could get along just fine without the presence of Hannah, Abby Leiston. When she bumped along these low points she'd choke up; recounting lost days she'd never recover.

What intrigued her was *actually* knowing this final phase of yelled insults, demands, beatings and having a 9mm pistol loaded and discharged next to her ear would inevitably lead to some sort of conclusion. If it was to be an execution, then she had prepared for it. She had accepted the approaching point of no return with a sense of calm that amazed her. No longer did she tense for hours listening for footsteps, no screech of nerves when the door opened.

Somewhere close to her she'd picked out the slapping of branches against an exterior wall, visualising the place as her own secret, winter palace. The longer they tried to extract every piece of information she carried in her head, the more she crammed it down, willing it, urging it deeper, forcing it right down to her numb toes. Each threat she reasoned would come from their lack of patience; the end, from one of them – probably the student – trying something aggressive or foolish.

Assuming that none of them had compassion, she'd no reason to put herself at their mercy, plead for clemency. Not even the voice or presence of Celia disturbed the shrieking silence. Not since Hannah had jumped, startled at the rounds from a semi-automatic pistol fired somewhere in the distance. These were followed-up by the intense booming, the crisp retort of snap, snap, snap from an automatic rifle. If they'd disposed of Celia, then it would soon be her turn Hannah reasoned, confident there were no other options remaining.

Eleven

Leaving Prague behind on a bitter Saturday afternoon Nick crossed the river by way of the Jiráskův Bridge. In his mirror the cathedral of St. Vitus seemed to squat on top of the castle as he headed west on Plzeňská, the city gradually shrinking behind him, until only the tip of the lookout tower on Petřín Hill remained. Partway through the journey it began to snow, fine grains rolling towards him in waves. He turned on the wipers, one blade lazy, juddering across the windscreen, leaving a fine glaze behind after each erratic sweep.

Gradually the landscape changed after he passed through Rudná, the factories clotted along the highway fell away, replaced by islands of farmland sealed between bands of spruce woods and denser, higher arms of forest steeped in hostile shadow. At Loděnice he turned north on small meandering roads, scarecrow limbed trees in tight pockets lining his route.

• • •

Her, face, neck, back and legs were inflamed, racked with searing pain. She'd be deformed after a couple more of their heavy-handed chats, unrecognisable even to her family. 'What are you like?' Leiston muttered to herself. Some victims of torture suffered in silence for years and their determination and courage far outstripped her own. She had entered a state of dull, grudging acknowledgement during the last severe beating they inflicted after kicking her awake; how she actually represented more than a physical manifestation of an enemy; how she was a symbol of a loathed ideology that had to be exterminated. And they enjoyed it.

This gradual acclimatisation towards the moment she would cease to exist had taken her captors by surprise. They had broken her, they had humiliated her – she had expected it and so had they. What they failed to understand was how they could never unravel her psyche, come to terms with it, reach into the territory of her soul. Occasionally she wondered if any of their demands had brought a response from London? Had her parents been informed? Her father no longer someone she could call a friend; their difference long rooted and beyond repair, defences dug, strengthened. Neither of them prepared to accept a middle ground, their stubborn positions entrenched and hardened over the years into conflict. At least there would be peace now for one of them.

During her first hours of being a prisoner she realised how much her mother must have hurt if she knew of her predicament, of not being there for her, how she'd disintegrate inside each day. Her own endurance had hit its limits, her self-deception at convincing herself she was a valuable hostage rapidly fading. Before long she'd give up biting her tongue and give vent to her fury.

She heard them coming from what seemed miles away. Two or three, she couldn't tell exactly how many, only that their rapid footfalls were stark, loud, filled with an assertive pledge, smacking purposely against bare floorboards. Dragged for what seemed miles she was thrown against a wall; cold, bare bricks pressing against her back. The blindfold came off in rough tugs and the student slapped her – for old times sakes? wondered Leiston, squinting through her swollen eyes.

The screech of a chair came from somewhere in front of her. Blinking away what she thought must be a hallucination; she vaguely made out figures sitting behind assorted tables pushed together – four of them wearing keffiyehs and sunglasses. One of them overweight, reverently conferred with a slender young Arab at his side who didn't turn or speak, he just sat observing. In the centre, a female wearing a headscarf adapted into a hijab looked along the table and cleared her throat.

'The court of the Military Front of Palestine has found you guilty of crimes against its people,' Celia Rewall declared.

•••

In another couple of days the road from Chyňava to the abandoned asylum would be snowed over. No way in, no way out, Harry had warned him. Nick drove with a fierce determination, a desperate resolve spurring him on. The road cut across a remote landscape in a zigzag through forests desperately clawing their way up steep hillsides. In places the road was barely wide enough to allow two cars to pass. He had his lights on full, the snow making it seem as if he were driving through a fitful dream, the lazy wiper juddering with every dash of the blades. On this raw evening the isolation closed in around him, and he felt the nerves in his hands stiffen on the wheel as he rounded each torturous bend. He drove with a fear of failing urging him on, his resolve focused on not coming off the road, not here, not now.

Pulling his Skoda onto a gravel apron serving as a passing place, Nick traced the final leg of the journey on Harry's hand drawn map through a natural wilderness of forests. Snatches of burly clouds raced above dense cages of pine, cedar and birch ushering in the night over what used to be part of the Hapsburg Empire. As he prepared to rejoin the deserted road, a big deer bolted out from the trees disappearing in a whirling tunnel of snow. His grid reference fixed and confirmed he pushed the car as hard as he could, the temperature rapidly sinking. In front of him a freezing mist added to the sense of permanent dusk, settling lazily in the trees. On steep exposed clearings, summer cottages and chalets stood out like dark ugly warts against the snow. Farther on, the odd hunched crow flapped laconically between treetops.

Running into a partial clearing, the road carried him over a crude rail crossing rattling and bouncing the car. Pushing on through the snow he broke out of a final shield of trees, his headlights playing across a set of high stone gateposts marking the start of a winding carriage drive. The gates were severe, tall and padlocked. Tyre tracks ran all the way up to the asylum, patches of its red roof and top three floors glided above a series of hummocks and a screen of mature woodland.

After reversing the car over a rough verge so that it nestled amongst a crescent of roadside saplings, Nick cleared and readied the Glock, added an extra magazine to his left pocket. Pulling down his hat, tightening his gloves, he slipped into the woods at a crouch, his bearings not fixed nor fast, just a wild scramble beside the stonewall marking off the institutions' grounds. Every few yards he passed warning signs attached without finesse into the moss smeared slabs:

Soukromé vlastnictví

Zadny pristup

Vstup zakázán

Each of them displayed a silhouette of a figure within a red circle, the broad diagonal slash enforcing the message of prohibited entry.

He dragged out two mossy log stumps from under a canopy of branches

– one short, the other a good foot higher – jamming them tight against the wall. Testing one with his left foot, he scrabbled up onto the second with his right. And like a climber feeling out a route, he used his fingers and toes to drag himself up and onto a broad ledge. Laying flat he swung his legs over, then gradually lowered himself using his hands and arms so that his body dangled four foot off the ground. Dropping, he automatically bent his knees cushioning the landing.

Seventy, eighty, yards ahead the asylum's careworn barrack wings jutted away from a baroque château with its soothing view of a curving lake. The front windows had wriggly tin sheets slapped up in place of glass. Heaps of snow lay in dunes and drifts on an expanse of lawns tapering away to an ornamental pond: its central feature, a Cupid fountain missing its bow.

Nick made his first run to a stone gazebo: a folly complete with a pepper pot dome. When he made a break for the main door a couple of herons lifted off towards the lake, the mist running in cold spikes straight into his face. Under a portico, its stone columns pocked and shedding flaking paint, a rust eaten sign gave instructions for visitors. Beneath it a notice complete with an arrow pointed to the rear. Finding the main door bolted, he gratefully accepted the instructions. He followed car tracks towards two small granite annexes forming a loose enclosure; the roof on one had collapsed, on the other there were missing tiles exposing scorched, charred rafters.

There were no vehicles just a trail of footprints, dozens of them leading to and from a rear terrace door prised open. He pulled it wider, its hinges screamed, racing away inside into the gloom. Skittering chunks of plaster and broken lathes out of the way with his foot he moved on into the old main building, entering a ward that faced the formal garden. Moving slowly between metal bed carcasses, some still complete with leather restraining straps, Nick swept the tactical light from his Glock in a wide arc, disturbing nothing but murky shadows lurking in dark corners.

Racing in through gaps in each window's tin sheets, the wind screamed along long corridors disturbing a counterpane of dust. He roved cautiously on a grid pattern search of the ground floor, tracing a route along dark, tiled passages through wards, offices, equipment stores and pharmacy. Each long corridor piled with rubble had a pervasive fusty stench clinging to the damp air.

Out in the main hallway Nick sidestepped metal lockers, smashed furniture and chairs pitched down the central stairwell like jetsam. His muscles taut, he shone his tactical light up the winding stairs, moving slowly up each stone tread, concentrating on every yard ahead.

Pushing himself on, he picked out the faint tail of coffee coated with stale cigars, following it all the way to the third floor. Turning onto the landing he stepped around sheaths of papers strewn in sodden clumps between wreaths of fallen plaster. Rounding the corner to a long, formidable corridor, Nick abruptly halted. At his feet, a body half in, half out of an arched vestibule ward entrance. He counted seven entry wounds between shoulders and waist, all of them matching the sort of damage he'd witnessed when high velocity combat rounds rip into a body. Only the shot to the back of the head differed, and Nick reckoned it to be 9mm and overkill, though it had still made a significant mess to the right side of the skull.

He moved on, his pulse and breathing rapidly increasing. Two thirds down the corridor in a small red brick opening, a block of stone steps rose higher. Locked in the corroded, powdery air the aroma of tobacco was stronger. He took the stone treads fast, coming out onto a vaulted isolation wing. Not caring for subtleties or entry protocol, Nick traversed down a narrow passage, his back hard against the walls, paring away slivers of plaster with his shoulders as he edged along. He pushed open one door at a time, their reinforced glass panels set behind protective bars. He probed each derelict workroom, each office using his tactical light, a measured assessment revealing only wreckage from years of vandalism – the torn out fittings, scattered stationary, shattered window glass, cabinets and desks passionately destroyed.

In a passageway that came to a full stop, a block of four seclusion cells. In the very last cell he found Hannah Leiston. Held in the sharp pin shaft of his tactical light she was propped lopsided in a corner. He barely recognised her. Letting out a voluble: 'What have they done to you ...' Nick needlessly felt for a pulse. Sliding down the wall, he sat beside Leiston his knees drawn up. His hands loosely gripping the Glock rested across them, the tactical light randomly striking a spot on the flaking, calloused ceiling. Fishing in his pocket for a pack of cigarettes, he lit one, resting his head against a patch of brittle plaster. Leaning across, he snatched at a sheet of A4 attached to Leiston's bloodied top with a safety pin.

Found guilty of imperialist crimes
Executed by the
Komunistická obranná síla Československa

Nick screwed up the proclamation, pitching it one side. From different angles he recorded Leiston's injuries on his phone: the mutilated fingers on her right hand, the bloated, mashed face, the single 9mm round to her left temple brutally ripping away an upper section of her skull. And where, he demanded of himself, is Rewall?

Consumed by a sense of absolute rage he hadn't experienced since the murder of his wife, he returned to the body in the vestibule. Kneeling on one knee, he rapidly turned out the corpse's pockets, finding a wallet sticky with blood naming the victim as Jáchym Herálec. So where are the other gallant members of the KOSC? he wondered. Has there been a disagreement between the heroes of the revolutionary committee? Spurred on by Leiston's ordeal he entered a side ward, his tactical light pinpointing a body partly snuggled inside a sleeping bag under a blanket patterned with bursts from an assault rifle.

He'd woken when someone entered, estimated Nick, noting how the body was flopped down the side of his bed, its white paint chipped, covered in rusty scabs. The fingers on the right hand remained splayed open, a belated move for the Vz.58 resting under the bed frame. Splinters from cupboard doors and oddments of board placed on the bed's wire base for insulation created a bloody fretwork on the tiled floor beneath the body.

Reacting to a noise from his right, he swung his Glock in a controlled offensive aim, his tactical light catching a rat scampering along metal shelves built into a wall nook, its lithe body slinking between a camping stove, kettle, dried milk, packs of sugar and coffee. Another secure door opened into a plain, small tiled antechamber. At its centre, a reclining wooden treatment chair centred under a twist-strand light cord. There wasn't a bulb or a shade. Slouched uncomfortably in the chair another home-grown KOSC revolutionary. In no need of the waist restraints or head clamp, the dozen or so rounds shared between the head and torso counted as his final treatment.

Retracing his route back along the corridor to the main stairs, his path lit by his Glock, Nick ascended slowly and surely. The next floor had suites of day rooms; some he passed through still contained ripped apart armchairs in semicircles aimed at empty, smashed TV cabinets. Television is the opiate of the people he thought, borrowing heavily from Marx. In what he supposed must have been a therapy room, a potter's wheel hunched opposite long bench tables bolted down. Back on the corridor he stepped over IV drip stands tipped out of a storeroom.

Could this be an improvised alarm to warn of an intruder approaching, or a simple act of vandalism? In conflicts of any kind, there were no rules, he warned himself, pressing on.

Around a turn in the corridor Nick hit more of the bitter, acrid punch of cigars bolshily clinging to the greedy shadows. Every couple of feet he stopped, listening, his own controlled breathing deafening in the silence. Edging slowly into a recreational hall he moved cautiously, running his tactical light in diagonal sweeps to reveal any tripwires. Down one side of the hall he roamed freely through what remained of another temporary base; this one coordinated, arranged with a semblance of military precision, including the folding canvas camp beds.

On one of them, a half dozen Café Crème cigar tins all empty. He started on a savage hunt in two adjoining side rooms. The first, the smallest had clothes scattered in a panic evacuation: a silk blouse, jeans, T-shirts, a pair of red keffiyehs, each of them speckled with blood. There were old stacks of packing cases, plastic tubs and wicker laundry baskets that he ripped through in a search fed by brutal anger. He paid for his temper, petulance and frustration, his minutes of havoc with red-hot lava streaming inside his shoulder.

He picked up a blood trail by the door. Rewall? From the quantity and spacing of the drops, Nick guessed they came from someone moving under their own steam. The pain in his shoulder became so bad that returning up the main stairs he winced with each step, gripping tight to the banister, dragging himself on.

When he reached the attic the blood led off in a continual, meandering smear across filthy, rough sawn planks. Nick traced its path, a drawn out route through piles of cluttered equipment once required to imprison the insane.

Moving softly along the thin beam of his light, Nick stopped where the blood did – at a hatch giving access to a crawlspace in the eaves. Kicking the wooden cover inwards, it flew less than six inches before stopping abruptly. Stooping, Nick peered inside. Grunting, he reached in, his fingers brushing against a trembling body. Dragging out a badly shaking figure, he rolled the severely wounded male onto his back. A round had entered his body in a diagonal line – in the thigh above the left knee, up into the hip – exiting through his right arm. Resting a boot on the skinny arm where a jagged splinter of bone peeped out of the elbow, Nick began his direct, no-nonsense field interrogation.

'Who set your group up? Who's been using you?'

Smiling plaintively back, the KOSC man put a good deal of effort into shaking his head. 'Palestinians...'

'Name? Who was your contact?'

He had trouble answering. Each word, each breath a choked effort. 'Shadia... Hatab...' he eventually confessed his voice perished.

'Did she run the operation?'

Attempting to answer he gave up, moving his head in a perceptible nod.

Nick increased the pressure on the wounded arm. 'Don't you die on me,' he insisted. 'Celia Rewall? Was she here?'

Gulping, attempting to clear his dry throat, the KOSC man once more grimaced. 'With... with... her friend Hatab...'

'Who killed the young English woman? Who did it?' Nick ferociously demanded.

'Hatab... Rewall...'

'How did you contact Hatab and her friends?'

He flapped his good arm across his body in an attempt to latch hold of Nick's leg. '... Place in Vinohrady...' he whispered, beckoning Nick lower. 'I... I got... address... I give you details... Tell them... tell them that... that Petr Rybná helped you...'

Barely able to hold down his rage Nick plodded back down after receiving Rybná's heartfelt, unabridged confession. And why not betray your handler, Nick conceded, replaying Rybná's information on a safe house used to contact Hatab via a courier. When you realise how you've been used, how all your friends were executed and you've been left for dead it's the least you owe yourself. Returning to the seclusion cell he shrugged off his jacket, laying it gently over Leiston as he started on a number of urgent calls.

Twelve

After slipping discreetly out of his modest lodgings Nick spent forty minutes purging his trail along a dummy route. Sometimes pounding the pavement in short and long bursts, mostly choosing bustling tram and Metro lines, he practised his own tradecraft variation on 'collapsing the box'. Assured he was thoroughly clean he adopted a slow, vigilant push towards his destination in Prague's staid, old bourgeois Vinohrady quarter.

The overnight snow soiled by passing traffic formed miniature ranges along the footpaths' edges. Nick kept to the clear valleys from the Jiřího z Poděbrad Metro Station his vigilance maintained at the same heightened level. Outside a Thai restaurant and bar on U Vodárny he trod cautiously across a bed of ice set rock hard where melt water escaped from a burst down pipe.

Across the road from a third floor apartment Rybná gave up as the Palestinians' safe house, Nick remained in the tree line marking the boundary of a lozenge shaped urban park wrapped around a bright Noah's Ark of a playground.

You don't... contact Hatab... direct, Rybná painfully confessed, you make... arrangements with... courier... guy named... Jafar... Nick vividly recalled.

From a bench he swept clean of snow, he kept watch on the apartment's front windows. Most of Nick's attention focused on the main one; an elaborate baroque affair supported by a full-sized sculpted nymph joining hands with her handsome lover. Keeping track of any movement, however slight, he counted one shadow grow in strength as it repeatedly patrolled close to the scrolled net curtain before drifting away like vapour.

What's the vigil all about? wondered Nick. Part of the safe house routine, maybe? Maintained for a visitor expected to call? Perhaps it's the Palestinians' early-warning system? Not sure if had pinned down anything close to a satisfactory reason Nick launched his venture into the unknown. Dark, metallic grey clouds came to close out the sun, a rapid filling in of the morning as instant as blinds being pulled. Small specks of rain grew into hard storm drops of hail ricocheting off roofs, pelting vehicles, pelting Nick during his dash through the traffic.

Set squarely in his sights a merchant's grand town house reduced to low-income apartments, the austere exterior rising pessimistically a full five floors. Its lower stone façade clad in washed-out green tiles owned a pair of glass doors banded by a distressed, mottled black wooden frame. The bottom rail scuffed clean of paint from tenants' feet holding it open. Some residents had taken the trouble to go over their faded names in black biro on cards slotted into their mailbox panels, but Jafar wasn't one of them.

The hallway had a drab, unloved aura of no one caring. Its easy clean roughly painted walls were doused in stark yellow from economy ceiling tubes humming their very own in-house rhapsody. Added in a rash on one wall he glimpsed names of lovers, affirmations of hatred, a smattering of random philosophical musings. *Life is a universal enigma* one of the coherent ones declared. On his right, a padlocked cage for bicycles held a fleet of infant strollers, a solitary shopping trolley parked in a hurry at their centre. Skulking in intense shadow the grand staircase carried a lifetime of bruises and gashes; its treads covered in practical grey tiles, its black spindles capped by a handrail adorned by carved initials; a census of past and present residents he read on his way up.

The air as he ascended had that composite aroma of dank washing, cigarettes and ribbons of disinfectant. Hanging around the open stairwell like a permanent tenant he met the tail of basic cooking; wafts of warm oil, garlic, potatoes, pork and sauerkraut. On each sparse landing he passed through stilted conversations, bleary snatches of music, clipped sounds from laptops, tablets, televisions and God knew what else; each floor ready packaged with the discordant echoes of lives lived at full volume.

Listening outside a top floor apartment Nick picked out nothing but the awkward strain of silence. He banged hard three times with his palm against the pale brown veneered door panel, a finger plunging the bell push just as the police do when they call unannounced, demanding immediate entry. Receiving no answer he tried again, louder. A minute or so passed and he glanced at the other doors facing him on a miserable landing where, he guessed, the merchant's junior maids had been stored when not on duty.

Perhaps not answering is a regular everyday feature he decided, holding his finger on the bell. An intuitive response to visitors who came and went inside the protective arms of the night he thought, visitors who it made sense not to notice.

From inside came the trill beat of short steps clacking towards the door. Giving one last determined slap with his palm, he flattened himself against the landing's wall, out of range of the door viewer. A safety chain slid into place, a lock turned disengaging its bolt. And before the courier could ask the caller's business or demand an explanation, Nick went for broke. He put all his weight into the kick, followed by a full-on charge.

With the momentum in his favour, the chain tore free of its mounting. There was a dull thud, a yell of surprise when the door followed by Nick slammed violently inwards.

Banging the door closed with his heel Nick realised he had a major problem.

Sprawled out, tangled in a coat stand wasn't the courier, but a woman in her early twenties out to the world, her forehead gashed. Checking her pulse, he decided that she was no worse than mildly concussed. Gripped firm under one shoulder, Nick dragged her unceremoniously along, her heels squealing across the parquet flooring.

He dumped her on the sofa in the main lounge. Lifting her legs, propping her up like a patient recovering from a minor operation, Nick set about securing the apartment. Clearing each room in one fast loop, he returned with a damp tea towel from the kitchen and two pair of tights left out to dry in the bathroom. He applied the tea towel as a rough dressing for the gash above a sleekly pencilled curved eyebrow. He used one pair of tights on her wrists, binding them behind her narrow back, the other pair he lashed around her ankles. A silk scarf from the back of a chair he tied loosely as a gag.

Sitting across from her on a cream armchair, its grubby leather fissured, Nick tipped her shoulder bag out onto the heavy lacquered coffee table; a replica banded carriage chest complete with dubious padlocks. As she slowly recovered he went through her purse, discovering she was nineteen, her name: Michala Hostokova.

On the walls, a spread of iconic posters, and the one given pride of place celebrated Che Guevara. He set his Glock down next to her empty shoulder bag aware of Hostokova's flickering eyes tracking him. The smell of cannabis stuck fast to the room, a stubborn late-night guest overstaying their welcome. In a glass ashtray he saw the remains of several scorched stubs. Resting in one of the ashtray's half-round cups a perfectly rolled spliff ready for lift-off.

'Where is Jafar? Who is he to you? Where is he? When is he due back? Where is Jafar?' Nick landed each question without a pause, verbal punches heaping on pressure from the opening round. Leaning forward, his elbows on his knees he conscientiously monitored Hostokova when she began to recognise her predicament.

She tossed back her head and screeched out an answer, a muffled curse she repeated, hissing and spitting behind the gag. She roared, yelled, fought against the restraints on her wrists, on her ankles, wriggling and thrashing to break free.

'Do you speak English? Yes or no?' Nick had an implicit need to establish his facts, confirm his priorities.

Hostokova swallowed in gulps under the scarf; her dark, ringed eyes snapped wide open in hostile assessment. She lashed out with her bound legs somehow getting enough momentum to pitch herself off the sofa.

Standing over her in no mood to play, Nick fitted the suppressor to his Glock. When she managed to grunt out: 'English... okay... I understand,' Nick raised an appreciative thumb.

'Jafar your boyfriend?'

On her side glowering up, Hostokova's eyes brimmed with hatred.

Nodding 'yes' to Nick's question, Hostokova snarled out another mumbled curse.

'You cooperate and you're going to be fine,' Nick assured her, hauling Hostokova back onto the sofa. He loosened her gag, allowing the wet scarf to slither down around her neck. He undid the tights around her wrists, retying them with her arms at the front. As a show of goodwill he removed the tights from her ankles.

'*Jdi do hajzlu*,' she yelled – the same muffled curse thrown at him before, now all too audible. She made a drama of wiping her lips against her upper arm, flinging a loathing, deadly stare as he holstered his Glock.

'Where's Jafar? When is he due back?' Nick tried once more, his manner brutal, his expression downright mean, scary.

Dipping her head, Hostokova looked at her T-shirt splashed with blood. Its stencilled message urged: STOP ALL WAR.

'He's wanted for murder,' he continued. 'Jafar is a terrorist. He's a killer. You, Michala Hostokova, are in a lot of trouble. It could be that you go to prison. For how long is up to you.'

She began to tremble. She snatched for air, her teenager's face running out of natural colour. She tried twisting the bottom edge of her T-shirt into a ball around a fist, her bound wrists preventing her normal childish comfort mechanism. A pleated skirt rode up over her purple leggings, the right leg torn into a ragged hole over her knee, a testament to Nick's forceful entrance.

'I'm not really interested in you,' Nick explained slowly, watching Hostokova's wary reception. 'But I will help you if you help me,' he assured her.

'Okay.' Hostokova had a regular figure, her attentive, chubby face swathed by long, curling blonde hair. Her pale, laconic eyes were too young for her, seeming to anticipate a rebuke or a command at any second.

'Where is Jafar?' Nick asked. This time he framed the question slowly, his body quite still as he lowered the threat level, minimising any risk of intimidation. 'You know, don't you?'

Hostokova nodded, her long false eyelashes curling at the corners fluttered in confused uncertainty.

'Where is Jafar?' He'd supplied the opening, he'd walked her to the boundary and he could do nothing but sit back to see if she crossed the border for a full disclosure.

'He doesn't tell me where he is going,' she admitted. Looking up at Nick tears streamed down over her rounded cheeks, dashing into patches beside the blood on her T-shirt.

'But you know?'

'No,' she answered as if Nick really was dumb. 'Sometimes I wait for him get off tram that come from Praha Six when he's been on errand. We walk down to buy lottery ticket from Fortuna booth at Metro.'

'What sort of errand?' wondered Nick. '*We* do not intend to harm him,' he told her. 'Do you understand?' Guarantees for the innocent and false hope for the damned; this was the tarnished currency Nick traded in.

She only just stopped herself from crying as she spat: 'Sure... what I care. It's errand, that all he tells me. He says I must never ask about his business, it private, so I don't.'

Across her nose she had a fine translucent scar. Nick wondered if it came from asking one too many questions of Jafar. When she compressed her lips, her mouth curled into a default position of disillusionment.

'Has he gone on an errand today?'

'I Guess... I not ask, I told you.'

'Does Jafar always return at the same time?'

'I guess.'

'Does he always use the tram?'

'I guess.'

'And he gets off the tram at the same place?'

'I guess.'

'I don't want guesses, I want what you know,' Nick snapped. 'Is it the same tram stop every time?'

Hostokova nodded.

'When Jafar goes on his errand, is he away for long?'

'Sure... always about four hours.'

'When you meet him off the tram from Praha Six what time does he arrive?'

'He get to Korunni around five-thirty-seven.'

It had already turned eleven-thirty Nick noted, glancing at his watch. Which might just leave a viable window to make and finalise operational arrangements. He set about it straight away making a call from the hallway; Hostokova kept permanently in view.

'Omri... I'm going to be arriving around five-thirty, usual stop on Korunni. I'll have that large package I told you about, so I'll require a hand...' Nick explained, his voice low, discreet. 'My girlfriend is going to be lonely while I'm out, so I thought you could send that nice girl you know to keep her company...Great...'

His call for immediate assistance complete, Nick collected Hostokova off the sofa. Grabbing a dangling length of the tights binding her wrists, he began a more detailed search, tugging her along behind him.

'How long have you been with Jafar?'

'Seven months I guess,' she sullenly disclosed, trailing down the hallway until they came to the kitchen.

Dragging a chrome stool away from a breakfast bar built to seat one, he motioned Hostokova up onto its flat leather cushion. Positioning himself with a clear view down the hallway to the front door, Nick ransacked cupboards, tipping out the contents of each drawer.

'Where did you meet?'

After a moment of making up her mind, Hostokova petulantly flung out her answer. 'A store... I worked there.'

In a base unit beside the sink Nick rummaged through plastic tubs storing bottles of cleaning products promising an instant, brilliant shine, scourers and bin liners. At the rear of the unit dropped hastily into a box of light bulbs, fuse wire and fuses, he located a roll of duct tape and a magazine for a 9mm semi-automatic.

'He's never told you what he does to earn money?'

'No... he never say... He a refugee...'

'Refugee? So why does he need these?' Nick demanded straightening up, holding out his finds. 'You know what he's mixed up in, don't you?'

He slammed the tape and magazine down onto the counter.

'Well, do you?' he yelled, an inch from her face, a provocative and crude form of interrogation the American's sometimes call 'Fear-up'.

Minutes passed – maybe two, perhaps three – but they brought no response from Hostokova. A tense silence spread through the kitchen, only broken by a steady whine of traffic dreamily skimming through the square. Nick standing perfectly still in deep concentration reacted a fraction of a second too late when Hostokova lashed out with both legs in a single move, her feet slamming into Nick's abdomen. He made a snatch for her arm and missed, left in Hostokova's slipstream as she galloped down the hallway for her front door. Nick grabbed the upturned stool, pitching it under arm with full force after her. It bounced once, catching Hostokova behind the knees tipping her off balance. Recovering, she had the door part open when Nick crashed into her, their combined weight thumping the door closed with a bang.

'*Dej ty pracky pryč, hajzle,*' her breath and protest came in gasped snatches. Then a scream and '*Co to sakra je?*' uttered aloud as Nick hauled her all the way back to the kitchen.

Panting from her failed escape, Hostokova contemptuously watched Nick reapply the tights to her ankles.

'Move,' Nick insisted, bundling her out into the hallway once more, nudging her along in a chain gang of one.

'Okay, I help you,' she promised shuffling ahead.

'No.'

He stopped abruptly at a plain, narrow door without a handle.

'What's in here?'

Hostokova shrugged. At the same time she twisted her lips in a 'who cares' declaration of insubordination.

'Do you have the key?' Nick ran his finger over the escutcheon, felt around the frame for any sign of a command wire.

'It got lost.'

Severely out of patience Nick dragged her back into the kitchen. Taking the power cord from the kettle he looped one end through a pull bar handle on a cabinet, the other – the one with the plug, he pulled through the tights around Hostokova's wrists. Bumping her close to the cabinet he tied the power cord in an ugly knot. Smiling as he passed her, Nick rummaged through a total of six drawers and five cabinets before he found a plastic container of tools buried deep in a cupboard.

Back in the hallway he hammered in a screwdriver between the narrow door and its frame. Prying open the door slightly, Nick forced the hammer's claw into the door's side edge. Straining hard he began levering back and forwards in a rocking action, his shoulder acutely burning. The wood around the lock started to split, then gave completely when Nick piled on the pressure, swinging back on its hinges. So where do they keep the vacuum cleaner? he wondered staring at an arms cache consisting of Vz.58 rifles, a couple of 9mm pistols, a stack of empty and loaded magazines.

He stretched in dragging out a Vz.58, and from the assault rifle's condition, it was one of several recently fired. *This acquaintance insists that this deal is Vz.58 only. His client will have no other way. No serial numbers, no paper clip trail, just Grade-A condition with enough 7.62 rounds to begin war*, Harry's good friend Ercsi had claimed.

It wasn't the grenades that spiked Nick's interest. What stopped him in his tracks was a canvas camera bag resting in a corner, its flap thrown back, its zip open. In the main compartment besides a couple of spare magazines for a 9mm pistol he recognised the guts of a quite sophisticated improvised explosive device in the penultimate stage of assembly.

Stooping forward to reach the bag he noticed tremors in his right hand. He paused. Relaxing the tension in his arms, breathing in through his nose, exhaling from his mouth Nick gripped the shoulder strap, ever so gently lifting the bag clear.

He carried it tentatively in front of him at arm's-length, knowing that some bomb makers include secondary activation mechanisms to kill disposal technicians. If it became dynamic it would be a futile gesture, making little difference how he transported it.

Taking a pace at a time he moved in a slow journey to the bathroom. He set it down with maximum caution on the lavatory seat. Wiping his hands down his sleeves he prised open a pop stud fastener on one of the bag's outer pouches, tugging out a phone charger lead. Cut into a shortened length, the wall socket plug had been removed and a narrow, electronic pin type of connector fitted.

Peeling back the sides of the main compartment Nick studied the contents. Taped around a plastic milk container packed with ball bearings, he recognised a slab of pure, unmarked military grade plastic explosive resembling marzipan. The other components secured by strands of duct tape he ticked off one by one: a modified throwaway phone in close proximity to a nine-volt battery powered circuit board adapted to receive the connector on the phone's charging lead.

One final connection, that was all it needed to bring the device to life, he realised, a sticky film of sweat on his neck and chest. Once in place at a target location the device would be triggered by a call to the throwaway phone. Placing the bag in the bath he grabbed a handful of towels – large and small – draping them over the bag until the device was fully jacketed – creating, he sincerely hoped, a barrier between the throwaway phone and any incoming signal.

Thirteen

Late in the evening Nick made a return journey back across the river to Praha 6. Outside Rewall's FCO owned villa in Dejvice a sturdy van straddled the kerb. Sapped, every muscle knotted tight with fatigue, he lingered in the heavy shallows of nightfall finishing a cigarette. He wanted a mental overview of Celia Rewall, create points of reference to help him understand her: locate her in some context; anchor her in space and time, a palpable entity to pursue rather than a ghost.

Cascading down the road in a shimmering line, the white-hot dazzle of street lamps. He paced slowly along the footpath visualising Rewall pulling out of the drive on her daily commutes. Did her husband suspect her treachery in anything other than love? he wondered.

In a break between packed ranks of larch he glimpsed the city unrolled below him in brilliant clusters: occupied territory marked on the night's dusky chart. Across the road in Rewall's villa the blinds in each window were fully drawn. In every room the blazing lights announced Head Office's team of scavengers hard at work.

Nipping through the freezing air Nick joined them.

'Anything?'

'Bits and bobs,' Miriam the team leader said, bearing Nick off down the hallway.

Attractive and tall with long straight hair to her shoulders complemented by a neat square fringe, she glided rather than walked, the protective forensic suit swishing against her arms, her legs.

What Miriam had achieved inside the pre-war property in less than forty-eight hours with her team of six specialists was impressive. He decided it was also utter carnage. They had dismantled furniture, lifted carpets, prised up sections of parquet. And that just counted as a warm-up in the

"

preliminary routine Nick remembered, passing a large reception room in a complete state of deconstruction.

'The Embassy finally confirmed her official laptop is missing. Not surfaced here has it?' Nick wondered when they'd reached the dining room.

Here too the table and chairs were nothing more than a mess of disjointed pieces stacked in an alcove. Along one wall a regular line of holes were drilled into the plaster for the insertion of flexible cameras to sniff out anything buried in the cavity.

'No, but we've located two others. His and hers – for personal use,' Miriam stated mundanely. 'Just like hand towels.'

He saw them set out side by side on one of those foldaway decorator's tables – this model made of sturdy laminate on metal legs. Both computers had been 'remotely interrogated' their hard drives breached. Some of the forensic hardware he recognised from the portable field kits used by CO8: the duplicators, the bridging links, the write-blockers synchronised to harvest the laptops' hidden treasure. Other devices were custom in-house tools the scavengers had developed for replicating the systems as authorised users, allowing them a clean interface to recover deleted files, the scavenger's holy grail.

'Anything useful?'

'Could be a footprint on our target's device.' She nodded towards one of her team curled in a scholastic slouch over a rugged laptop triaging the 'take' for further analysis. 'Can we have the scrubbed emails, Ryan?'

Clearing his throat in deep grunts Ryan gave a hoarse, 'No problem.' He retrieved a folder. 'First six months are intense. Grooming long distance by a smooth operator, a pro,' he disclosed, ill at ease at having an audience.

Terribly thin for his considerable height, his stubble beard accentuating his sharp jaw, Ryan's actions were rapid and jumpy, his taciturn manner those of a twenty-something lacking social confidence, someone who found face to face interaction a total discomfort.

'Grab a coffee,' Miriam told him.

'Cool.' He rose from his spot at the end of the table, glanced down at his laptop, then Miriam and finally Nick. 'Love conquers all, I guess. Everything else comes a poor second,' he suggested, stretching, cracking the joints in his fingers. 'She didn't care how much damage she inflicted,' he mumbled, loping off, his head sunk into his hunched shoulders.

Some of us never do, thought Nick, slipping off his overcoat. He draped it along the back of a floral covered sofa, a garden of roses and climbing garlands. Waiting in line for being ruthlessly dismembered, the cushions were stacked in a neat column ready for their turn in front of the portable X-ray scanner.

'Holler if you need me,' offered Miriam swishing off.

The tranche of emails resurrected out of the hard drive's soul coincided with Rewall's arrival in Prague nine months ago, Nick noted. They were composed in the same romantic prose he'd read in a letter recovered from Rewall's strongbox in the Embassy's chancery. All the missives, electronic and paper, began 'My Dearest Jasmine Flower...' and signed 'Firas'.

Nick traced the mechanism of entrapment for himself amongst the ripe sentimental yearning. As a prelude to betrayal, it seemed to have been drafted several times and then systematically edited: '...my heart races when I know we're going to meet...' reoccurred in a variety of forms as a standard epistle in the one-way traffic. The more emails he read, the same syrupy theme intensified '... your body makes me see the seasons with a new intensity...' This is the weakness of love, Nick decided; it's all the meaningless scraps that we leave behind, the letters written in passion, forgotten notes. The personal asides and soliloquies we discard, forget about; a paper trail of evidence for someone to pore over, to discover our sordid secrets, how we are burdened by the imperfections we prefer to hide.

So why didn't Rewall reply? he asked himself. Having lifted the shutters on the diplomat's relationship with her mysterious lover Firas, Nick wanted everything, the entire stock – every item underpinning their romance. *My Dearest Jasmine Flower... just being near you makes me alive...*

A composer of sentimental drivel and very possibly a killer, known so far as Firas, but who is he? Nick demanded of himself. Someone who knows Damascus as the fragrant city, the City of Jasmine, using it as the covername for his beloved Celia? So who's using love as a weapon? Where is *Jasmine Flower*? In the arms of Firas or does she share her affections with other terrorists?

Away from the laptop on a second foldaway table he picked through a line of exhibits bagged up by Miriam and her scavengers. One of them a photograph of Celia Rewall: her short, dark hair layered in a style that would barely change over the years, just slowly succumb to fine, spun grey and eventually blanch to white.

'It's the husband's,' Miriam called from the doorway.

He was holding up a clear evidence bag as if presenting it to a jury, containing a ball of chunky wool replete with needles and a few part knitted rows.

'We've got the patterns on his hard drive if you don't believe me,' she confirmed, rustling her way over to the table.

'That the sum total of his sins?'

'Do you mean did have a passion for filth? Obscene downloads? Weird and wonderful habits and cravings?'

'That sort of thing.'

'You've been mixing with dark side for too long.'

'Part of the job.'

'Poor fella was cool wash clean,' Miriam said, wriggling her shoulders out of the protective suit.

'Not a blemish?'

'Who hasn't?' she shot back, resting against a bookcase carcase to tug the suit off her legs. 'Couple of minor sins,' she grunted, one foot caught in the lightweight material. 'He's enjoyed some low level online flirting. The other?' She taunted Nick with a quizzical, raised eyebrow. 'Giving his wife the benefit of the doubt, I'd say.'

'Doesn't that count as love, not a sin?'

'Depends on what you mean by love, and how you classify sin,' she said, bundling up the suit. She wore tight black Levi Strauss jeans, combat boots and a furious red fitted top that set off her raven hair and angular face.

'How much did he know?'

'A fair amount. We recovered two deleted letters from his hard drive, composed when he was in Beirut with his wife. All the dates match, we've checked. The first was addressed to the Ambassador. It basically laid out his concerns that the delightful Mrs. Rewall was carrying on with an undesirable. He gave no firm details; it was really a way of airing his angst, a warning shot, I presume. Two months later he let his feelings fly in a letter to the FCO's Conduct and Discipline Section. This was full-on, no mercy shown. He dished the dirt on his wife, naming her love interest as Firas Sahil...'

'A workname ...'

Giving Nick a circumspect glance she wound her shoulder length hair tight into a tail, and fastened it high with a plain scrunchy kept conveniently on her wrist.

'A workname... and fake cover ID for a field team leader for the UN's Refugee Agency working the Palestinian Shatila camp,' she continued. 'The husband didn't spare any details as he went into what he described as a "torrid, sordid liaison" he claimed could leave his wife open to compromise. We think he used the letter to reign her in, a nuclear option that was never sent. We'll never know. King Charles' Street *claim* they never received it. They acted on the report submitted by the Ambassador which brought about an immediate recall and a couple of weeks on the naughty step.'

Loud bumps and bangs increased on the upper floor. Over this song of destruction, Nick heard the eager voices of scavengers calling out tips to each other as they systematically ferreted for more damming proof of Celia Rewall's secret life as a traitor. But what Miriam's team had amassed was already enough to confirm Rewall's defection decided Nick, browsing along the recovered items laid out along the table like assorted bric-a-brac at a car boot sale.

'And these?' Nick pointed to a dozen photographs of the sort tourists routinely capture on their rush to tick off Prague's top sights.

'The original stego images are on her hard drive. We picked them up as suspicious files because of a distortion in the embedded algorithms.'

'That some kind of code?' Nick flicked through the top three photographs – the Castle, the Dancing House, and a neatly framed shot of the Astronomical Clock no set of Prague would be complete without.

'Bog standard concealment... a secret key software using pixel values as the carrier. They were uploaded onto a photo-sharing site. Once Rewall and her handler had the shared keys to lock and unlock the traffic they were chatting like old friends. That was their mistake, the message length was too long.'

'Transcripts?'

'Help yourself,' Miriam suggested, gesturing to another cluster of documents in clear wallets.

Sliding out a top sheet Nick scanned down the mundane 'table talk' keeping the channels of communication open between agent and handler. There were greetings, dates and locations of brush contacts, action signals for dead drops and on a sheet towards the bottom, a string of frequencies.

'Emergency hotline?'

Directing Nick's gaze along the table with the accomplished air of a proud curator, Miriam singled out a transceiver. In what Miriam termed 'goody corner' he picked through a shortwave radio, dawdled at a set of USB flash drives displayed beside a compact digitizer compatible for hooking up to a laptop. Set aside as a star exhibit, a burst transmitter capable of firing data packets over a short distance.

'She used the laptop and transmitter on an ad hoc network,' stated Miriam. 'Probably somewhere public for a quick handshake with a waiting receiver. We've identified a phone, tablet and unknown device on her router. Cheltenham are working on the electronic tailings for ownership and call locations.'

After a thunderous crash from overhead a pair of boots slapped against the bare stairs bringing a scavenger racing down, and screwdriver in hand, back up again. The FCO Estates Department are going to demand an outlandish sum in compensation, thought Nick when methodical hammering started up. They have a traitor but will expect someone else to foot the bill; all part of Whitehall's slick pedigree he supposed.

'Light reading?' He'd worked his way down the table, a guest at a finger buffet. He shook out a photocopied pamphlet from a sealed bag – *Ben Gurion... the Liar* by Muhammad Husayn Sha'bān.

'A statement of intent,' said Miriam, her arms folded. An impulsive gleam surfaced through the satisfaction in her green eyes. 'Her loyalty is pretty clear.'

'Yes,' agreed Nick picking up on a section framed in mellow pink highlighter: "The land of Palestine will utterly spew out all that is on it... and none will remain except the Arabs..." He lifted the first book from a mound of titles to be shipped back to Head Office for fingertip inspection. Read and read over again, its mottled, faded boards had parted from the spine where *Zionism: the Greatest Crime of the Age* stood in faded gold. Beneath it, Fanon's critique of imperialism and colonial power – *The Wretched of the Earth* – had FCO complimentary slips as bookmarks.

A loose photocopied sheet had several paragraphs bracketed by the same highlighter, one paragraph denouncing the Palestinians' isolation from the global economy as an imperialist, Zionist conspiracy. If Palestine possessed high value raw commodities, it too would have protection and support from its trading partners, the author vehemently argued. It's the old democratic centralism philosophy decided Nick, returning the sheet.

'They were kept in a locked trunk in her wardrobe,' Miriam disclosed. 'A genuine closet traitor.'

'Now she's out in the open.' He recalled the shattered bodies of Wilsden, Taurus and Leiston; wondering just how far Rewall had participated in planning the ambush, how she justified her own ruthless part in Leiston's torture and execution. 'Let me know if Cheltenham get a hit on the tailings,' he suggested, dumping the book back on the pile. 'I'll let you get on with it.'

'We should have it all wrapped up in another day,' Miriam admitted with a smile, showing him out.

Walking back down the hill he took a last look at the villa as Miriam's team toiled on with their forensic dismantling, oblivious of the hours they burnt. The last task, and the most unpleasant, which is why it was left to the very end, involved a hunt through the drains for the residue of evidence hastily disposed of, Nick remembered. Now the pursuit of Rewall could begin by stripping away her outer skin as a decent, loyal trusted diplomat to reveal the dark core of a hardened traitor. He pulled up his collar against the sub-zero night, taking another calculated route to his car and a ponderous drive back to his meagre lodgings.

•••

He deposited the Skoda in a corner parking bay down a lane in the Old Town, opting for a ticket covering a month's duration. His temperament barely hovering above morose, his thoughts constantly returned to Rewall's act of betrayal as he indifferently browsed the food sections of Supermarket Albert. What *had* drawn her into embracing Firas Sahil's cold-blooded brand of ideology? The mask of love or reasons of a darker persuasion, he really wasn't sure. With barely any appetite to talk of, he left with a chicken pasta salad, bottle of wine – white, no sense of the label, no idea of how it would taste – packs of plastic tumblers, forks, knives, serviettes, bread rolls and butter.

With his haul in a carrier bag he ventured out into náměstí Republiky braving the light snow pursuing him back to his hotel. A teenage night porter who regularly scowled at Nick from over the top of her criminology textbook, tracked him in measured, fulsome scowls all the way to the stairs, pushing back strands of greasy hair off her sour face.

She thinks I live a secret life, that I'm a creature of the night up to no good – and she'd be right he decided, carting his supper up to his room.

Setting out his victuals he delved into the known facts on Rewall, seeking out any missing pieces on Firas Sahil, the mysterious lover of Jasmine.

The hourly chimes from the Astronomical Clock in the Old Town Square worked their way into his room, punctuating his review of what little evidence he had amassed. For three quarters of an hour Nick thought of nothing but Rewall somewhere out there on the loose – and free to share her haul of secrets. So using what materials he could find in his bedside cabinet's drawer: a chewed biro and a headed hotel pad badly faded, he set about constructing a timeline of betrayal.

And still the same question appeared as an unsolved equation – who did Celia Rewall actually meet in Beirut? Firas Sahil was a workname; Nick had no doubt of that. But he needed the bones under the legend, the real identity of Rewall's lover. So he set about collating a trail stretching from Lebanon to London with Prague anchored at its centre; a sprawling endeavour written in his very own code. Outside the wind picked up, hurling big dabs of wet snow in dashing charges against his window.

Each time Nick thought he had a semblance of clarity, a direct route, a possible connection, he found himself denying his very own logic, dismissing his half-formed results. He screwed up page after page and spun them low into a metal bin with the indefatigable knowledge that he desperately wanted to believe he was wrong. Six, seven, or more attempts he had at joining his theory together in ink, a simple matter of expressing ideas and facts, a compelling case that misguided love lay behind Rewall's craven behaviour Nick refused to accept.

Balancing the bin on the freezing balcony, he lit the balls of paper and felt the heat race round the metal until all he'd left were layers of flimsy, grey ash. Back on the bed he called Rossan who promised him anything if he could just have some sleep. He made at least another four calls as he picked at his chicken and drank his tepid wine. Sure at last of what he must do, he used his coded phone like a one time pad, passing on details for endorsement.

A remote drowsiness eventually claimed him and he dipped into a series of dreams succeeding each other, all of them with Nick engaged in frantic hunts for Rewall and her perfidious boyfriend Firas; a Sisyphean task complete with untold guilt. And that was when he'd realised this meant a thorough reworking of every event, taking his newly found insight into consideration.

At some drowsy point after three in the morning he was awoken by a call from a CO8 Duty Officer who confirmed that Nick's flagged searches were bearing fruit. And then a moment's hesitation before she informed Nick that Taurus's wife had been executed, the children remained unaccounted for. So why did you set it all in motion at this precise moment in time? he wondered of Rewall, going over the facts from Head Office slowly. What *is* your motivation? Acting on your beliefs or having to prove yourself in the eyes of your lover? Maybe one fed the other? Nick reasoned. Ordering his thoughts into a logical sequence, he attempted to fight off the heavy hand of sleep, his head lolling gently forward as the five o'clock chimes struck out across the Old Town.

•••

It had proved a crazy day for Lewis Martens. His meeting had overrun by twenty-eight minutes. But if every trip meant closing deals as lucrative as this one he didn't care how long they overran. Ten... Eleven... Midnight... who cared when they ended, he cheerily decided waiting at the corner of Rustom Pacha and Phoenicia for his taxi to Beirut's Rafic Hariri Airport.

In the rear of the white Mercedes his jubilant mood evaporated. The reality hit him, a sickening ball knotting tighter in his gut. Suffering from tunnel vision in the run-up to the meeting, Martens had put blood, sweat and capital into securing this contract. Too much, he thought, realising that everything else had taken second place. That, to his horror, included the sharp realisation that his wife Judy had booked a couple of days at a beach resort on Dubai's Palm. If he missed his eight-twenty flight, the last to leave that night, any chance for rare family downtime would be ruined. He'd be made to suffer by Judy and the kids. He'd no intention of taking that gamble. No crisis, no drama, he reasoned in a rapid case of self-reassurance.

Hadn't the driver sworn he'd have him, his bags included, all present and correct at check-in with time to spare for his flight to Amman? Well he'd better start shifting thought Martens; the traffic around them on Baalbek was noticeably slowing. After the bonus he'd paid up front, he wasn't going to settle for tailbacks or excuses.

Normally he relished each trip into Beirut's living, breathing spectacle. He prided himself on his negotiating skills, the knack of steering contracts through the bureaucratic maze, the family connections, the clans, the militias. It was a miracle developers ever got anything off the ground with so many bickering after a cut, 'a fee for introductions' they jokingly termed it. Always count your fingers after shaking hands with a Lebanese he thought, recalling advice issued on his first visit eight years ago.

Eager to celebrate with his Jordanian staff, Martens now seriously considered if he'd make it home that night. He gave a deep, loaded sigh, sitting heavily back, his frustration peaking. Up ahead he recognised the familiar chaotic Beirut pageant following a collision. Nothing moved in front or behind. Cars, vans, scooters and light trucks blocked the one-way street. The urgency of wanting to catch his flight heightened Martens' senses. He wished to God he'd paid more attention to the monthly 'advisory sheet', he cursed his arrogance for treating the twice yearly refreshers as holiday excursions.

The double, triple parked cars of residents lining the kerbs, the shouted accusations and vehement rebuttals carrying back from the warring drivers triggered a nervous tension in Martens. He had an overriding impression this wasn't a typical Beirut snarl-up capable of bringing a whole block to a grinding halt. A crowd gathered at the collision started to drift towards Martens' taxi.

Glancing to his right he saw him. The big, flabby individual he'd noted on a corner across from the developer's office earlier that afternoon. Martens had no doubt it was the same footpad, carrying out the same surveillance routine, his suit jacket looped in a thumb draped over his shoulder, a phone to his ear as he stared directly into the taxi. He'd glimpsed the footpad again from the restaurant's pavement table where Martens lavishly wooed his prospective client. An acute wave of fear washed over him, the taxi had become his prison.

Crushing around the Mercedes one of the crowd leaned in, spoke quickly into the driver's ear. Nodding once, without any sign of resistance, the driver abandoned his taxi leaving his door wide open. Alert to his fate Martens shakily got out his phone, his fingers trembling, he tried calling Judy, receiving no answer. Praying for his wife to pick up, Martens jerked and flinched when the first 9mm round struck him.

Fourteen

Nick picked at a light breakfast after rising wearily at seven before setting off into a morning barely formed; a mean blustery day still not sure if it would bring snow, sleet, hail or rain. In the parking bays close to the Kotva Department Store a couple bitterly locked in the midst of a heated row concerning an overstay charge; the husband hotly disputing that he'd forgotten to purchase the appropriate ticket. Just admit defeat thought Nick, heading for his Skoda, it will save a lot of pain down the line. Tucked under the wiper, an out-of-date flyer advertising a day of ecumenical prayer in Libeň – his the only vehicle singled out – and Nick knew his meeting was a confirm.

There was to be no let up to the filthy weather with a freezing wind slapping Nick hard in the face when he parked in Libeň. Sprinting across the road he entered V mezihoří, a short narrow street, its apartments imperiously dressed in stone. Facing them, a belt of trees hugging the road where it made a sharp left turn.

The ground level apartment walls were painted in a neutral cream, the floors above in a lighter shade, something not far from pink. Graffiti covered the wall closest to the pavement, a veritable diatribe under one window. Some of it crude, and for an original twist, a few unruly insults were in English. Further on he saw tails of police tape whipping from a tree trunk and lamp post, the tatty souvenirs of a major crime scene.

There were scorch marks on one section of wall. The apartment windows here had taken a good deal of the blast and were boarded still, awaiting new glass. Chunks of stone were pocked with shrapnel along with tiny smears of paint from Graham Rewall's car. Some debris from other vehicles parked too close reached higher than Nick. In one place a considerable trace of paint was worked into the stone, a fine sparkling trail in gaudy canary yellow. At a set of steps an ancient, shrivelled woman bundled up in padded layers watched Nick pass; her street coat, a mangy long fur, had moulted many seasons ago. Her chubby face was bitten from the wind, clawed red by the cold. She jammed back her knitted hat, kicking open the communal door with a deft swipe from one of her booties.

Nearing the corner the door slammed behind him.

This is where you came to find the truth about your wife, isn't it Graham, but Celia had set you up, reasoned Nick.

Standing by a neat grey Mondeo parked where the building took a sharp left curve, Omri Ni'ram laconically monitored Nick's arrival, his breath impelled above his close-cropped head in curt white bursts.

'Always Nick, it's good to see you. But the circumstances I could do without for once,' Omri conceded, one powerful hand extended, his tanned, lined soldier's face bitter at the nature of their meeting.

'And you, Omri.'

'Someone chose a good base for liaisons, my friend,' Omri said, taking a couple of paces back to scan up towards the top floor, a mountain guide assessing the route.

He had that watchful alert nature of someone born into a troubled land, which he had been. Possessing all the right credentials as a native born Israeli to qualify as a true *sabra*, Omri had willingly pledged to sacrifice himself for his homeland. Like Nick, he possessed the watchful eyes of combatants that spoke of a heavy toll amongst friends and colleagues.

'Rewall paid the deposit and the rent, cash up front every month,' Nick admitted, his hand tingling from Omri's fierce welcoming grip. 'We don't even have a credit trail.'

The Israeli swivelled his stocky body in the manner of a commando dodging a punch. Wrinkling his stubby nose, he nodded, taking in the scene across the street where a part demolished brick shell of a factory and office rested in a fenced off compound.

'Not overlooked. Easy counter-surveillance. She was good, my friend, she followed the tradecraft she had been taught,' Omri proposed, nodding in grudging approval.

Sunk into his overcoat, his check scarf folded tight around his muscular neck, Omri had the natural élan of adapting to his location. Today he furnished the demeanour of an insurance assessor, complete with a modest, soft briefcase.

'But this time her tutor was Palestinian,' said Nick, the needle sharp air pricking his cheeks.

'I believe so too,' admitted Omri.

'Anyone in mind?'

Comfortably settled into his early forties Omri's compact body was hunched, braced against the cutting, freezing wind rushing headlong down the street.

'The Military Front of Palestine are a very strong possibility,' Omri disclosed. 'Monitoring recorded a statement playing on Lebanese radio. An MFP spokesman issued a decree stating they have opened a new front in their continuing war against Zionist imperialism, against Israel and all those criminal allies foolish enough to stand behind her. Anyone deemed to be supporting the expansionist regime will be treated as a legitimate target.'

'Well that's cleared that up,' decided Nick.

'So I have appointed myself as your liaison,' Omri announced. 'This is a very politically sensitive time, my friend. It is agreed in Tel Aviv and London that formal assistance is not being offered or received.'

'It wouldn't be the first time we've worked in the shadows, Omri.'

'Officially, operationally, our response will be minimal,' he confirmed, his tone that of a fellow combatant relaying an unpopular order. 'Our actions will, for reasons of diplomatic expediency, be measured.'

'Washington?' ventured Nick.

'We have to be seen to honour standing agreements with close friends,' Omri stated, 'particularly those who believe in their own ability to broker peace out of thin air.'

Parked either end of the street Nick identified two vehicles: a filthy red Mercedes van and white Skoda with a buckled wing as the likely positions for Omri's mobile 'stand-off' security teams. There would be more deployed, he reasoned. For Omri in his latest role as Mossad's Head of *Metsada*, its Special Operations Division, an inner and outer perimeter came as standard.

'Informally, my friend, you continue to have our full hands-on support,' he pledged.

'And I continue to take all the responsibility. That it Omri?'

Disregarding Nick's point, Omri smiled benignly. 'You have seen the seat of the explosion?'

'Imported techniques,' he plunged a hand into his pocket emerging with a set of keys. 'Very effective.'

'But also adaptable,' accepted Omri.

Banging open a redoubtable panelled main door freely decorated in layers of banal, multi-coloured scrawls Nick set the pace with Omri at his side. Who would believe this to be a love nest, he glumly thought as they stepped into a dreary lobby bound from floor to ceiling in sallow chains of light. In the stale air a smell of dust and blocked drains lingered wilfully after the explosion.

In a matter of fact manner, Omri rolled-out the ground rules for what he termed 'prudent interaction' as they scaled the stairs. On the top floor he vowed that he would do everything possible to ensure their backchannel arrangement remained off Washington's radar.

'I'm already beyond deniable,' reasoned Nick as they hit the final landing. Peering through the condensed arms of shadows he located Celia Rewall's rented safe house, a garish number 16 stencilled on its door. As far as London is concerned, I definitely don't exist, he thought.

'Better to be deniable than liable, my friend,' Omri wisely observed.

'It's a complete shift in strategy for the MFP...' He stopped, a key supplied by the letting agency turning stiffly in the lock.

'Really? Did you not receive the assessment provided by our Political Action and Liaison Department? I assumed it was issued to your Head Office and colleagues in Security?'

'I've been away from base for a while, Omri. I haven't checked my inbox recently,' said Nick, leading the way inside.

'That is a pity, my friend,' Omri admitted. 'We have worked together now on how many occasions?'

'A good few,' admitted Nick. And without any hesitation or invitation, walked straight into the main room. Three, four paces, and he had arrived at the centre of a meagre, plain bedsit.

'Personal... Professional... on any damn level, did I ever let you down?'

When Omri became charged, animated, he lost the melodic calm that had steeled him against devious rivals during his rise through many of Mossad's uncompromising departments. His voice, his rugged mannerisms emerged as always from the brusque, rude survival mode of his hardy childhood and youth on *kibbutz Alonim*.

'No, Omri, you haven't,' Nick admitted, assessing the modest bedsit.

Equipped for nothing more than solitary living except perhaps the occasional bout of lovemaking, the bedsit was stark, a vapid box. Along one wall a single bed with a brown Dralon headboard, above it a fluted wall light giving off a soulless, wistful glow. Opposite, a wardrobe also for one, Nick noted. Beside it, a high bow-fronted chest of drawers in a dark oak veneer intended to mirror the original twisted beams: two of them running across the crushing slope of the eaves ceiling.

'So you lost good officers,' Omri observed on his way to a rectangular window in slow rhythmic paces. 'It happens,' he added. There were close calls on shared missions with Nick too when Omri seriously doubted he'd ever make it home; crazy operations in Paris and Beirut that still brought him out in cold sweats.

'It's the circumstances, Omri. You should know that,' Nick retorted, striding off towards a primitive kitchen.

'A device came into our possession,' Omri offered, admiring the view. 'It was brought in by friends.'

'Israeli?' Nick wondered, slamming his way through cupboards and drawers.

'Of course.'

Turned back into the attic bedsit Omri tracked Nick's hunt through cutlery, dishes and a set of brand new pans.

'Our friends from Czech Security will have removed anything of value,' he offered sanguinely.

'They assured London it was left untouched,' muttered Nick unconvinced, clattering through a wall cupboard stocked with tins of soup, cans of herring, packets of pulses, jars of instant coffee, some opened and some part full. 'The friends who brought you the present,' he added, sniffing a base layer of murky seeds in a container. 'Did they purchase it or borrow it?'

'A permanent loan.'

'Is it going to be missed?' Definitely fennel, he decided recapping the spice container.

'The owners are not in a position to complain.'

Not if it involved an Israeli Defence Force's *Sayeret Matkal* unit who lifted the device Nick decided, moving on to the wardrobe. No one would be in a condition to object.

Behind the doors a perfume of mothballs and ancient dust sat trapped. He didn't expect any clothes; safe houses rarely contained personal items.

He rattled a lonely pair of coat hangers; one reserved for Rewall and one for her lover he supposed, the little foibles to calm the nerves during their rendezvous as agent and handler.

'The device in our possession contains a recognisable method of assembly,' volunteered Omri. Claiming a green spindle-back chair, one of a pair at a tiny matching faux café table, he tracked Nick from behind the briefcase set prim and square in front of him.

'Unique?' Nick on his hands and knees dragged out a set of drawers under the wardrobe base, one of them missing a swan neck handle.

'So, so,' said Omri with a shrug. 'It has similar features to devices we know originated in the Bekáa Valley. It is derived from advanced techniques, training and original designs provided to the Continuity-IRA in 2000.'

'Hezbollah selling on their skills to recoup their original investment,' grunted Nick, jamming his arm into the wardrobe's foot well after he'd jerked out the last drawer. He groped in the space, retrieving a couple of buttons, along with a crumpled 1989 samizdat edition of *Lidové Noviny*.

'Terrorism is a self-serving business. *We* know the Bekáa training operation is a franchise, my friend. You pay a lump sum or instalments and you get the know-how and ingredients. Now you're in the bomb making business. The more you pay for franchise rights, the louder your protest becomes.'

'The MFP have bought themselves a loud voice, that it, Omri?' Nick tossed the newspaper and button onto the bare mattress. Back on his feet, he slapped patches of fine dust off his knees.

'They've had it for years, Nick. It is only now that they are screaming in your direction that London suddenly hears them.'

'You know the franchise holders?'

'We have neutralised several of their bomb makers,' confessed Omri. 'Over the past five years a new cadre has come through the MFP ranks. Some we have eyes on, others remain more elusive.'

'Like the current bomb maker.'

'The technical forensics from the MFP attacks in Europe and the UK corroborate a new signature. The initial analysis of recovered fragments from several sites confirms a distinct symmetry between IED components.'

'It could be a bespoke kit,' said Nick recalling the device in the courier's apartment. 'There were some sophisticated adaptations to standard circuit boards on the device I looked at,' he added, setting course for the chest of drawers. 'Once bombers have achieved an effective design, they don't change it. It's the mode of delivery they can experiment with.'

In some of the statements he'd read from eyewitnesses, most of them from that very building, a recurring fact emerged. Every one of them recalled seeing a brown takeaway bag sitting on the bonnet of Graham Rewall's vehicle.

'In this case, what do you have, my friend?'

'Fast food bags,' Nick suggested.

'Which our technicians believe are a magnetic arming device. The bag is removed from the vehicle placing the device in the engine compartment on standby. The device is activated by the vehicle's own battery completing a circuit.'

'So who is our new bomb maker?'

'Amatulla Salhab,' disclosed Omri, and for once, became resolutely taciturn.

He was one of those enigmatic men like Nick with a remote, forceful aloofness that dissuaded enquires as to how they made their living. They just did; they were tough, they were trouble and you *just* didn't ask.

'That it?' Nick demanded, every drawer in the chest empty, the carcasses musty.

'More or less.'

'More or less what?'

'She's British,' admitted Omri. 'Birth name is Lydia Hallam. She's twenty-two. Parents middle-class professionals, separated. Never bothered with the divorce.'

His steadfast gaze barely wavered as Omri recited file details Nick suspected he'd probably memorised on his drive from the Mossad safe house.

'A true technician?'

Staring at his briefcase as though he had the ability to read the contents inside, Omri bobbed his head in agreement.

'She has a degree in electrical engineering. A good two-one, but she chooses to waste it.'

'When did she join the MFP fold?'

'Full-time... as a *fedayeen*, maybe only nine or ten months,' Omri volunteered, balancing the probability by rocking his hand. 'Before that she worked evenings and weekends at the London office of the European

Foundation for Palestinian Refugees. A couple of summer vacations she spent at the Shatila camp in Beirut south.'

Above Nick's head the wind soughed through gaps in the roof tiles, retreating and advancing like vague whispers from a different era. He remembered Celia Rewall's mysterious lover. Did Hallam fall under Firas Sahil's recruiting spell in Shatila? he wondered, venturing to a window set in the gable. Maybe it was an MFP team effort; talent spotters touring the camps with a recruitment quota for impressionable foreign nationals besotted by the Palestinian cause, he reasoned.

'Firas Sahil is a name that keeps flashing up on the trail, Omri. You got anything on him?'

He focused on the footpath going back towards the corner, satisfied that anyone occupying that very same spot at the window would have advance warning of Graham Rewall's arrival. So who exactly *did* he meet? wondered Nick.

'Our *katsas* have pushed their assets but always, always hit the same wall of silence. They complain: "Why not ask us to keep records on feathers blown by the wind too?" No one is giving us anything except riddles,' Omri explained.

'There must be something.'

'Firas... He may even be a ghost, Nick. Nothing but a workname providing a false trail... A myth created by the MFP maybe? None of our Stations, Nick, not one, have come close to pinning a firm identity on him. We checked with our asset in the UN's Refugee Agency. Nothing... they never heard of a Firas Sahil in Beirut.'

Breaking from his position at the window Nick joined Omri at the table; two passengers forced uncomfortably together, unlikely companions waiting to depart a terminus. After a sticky pause, Nick broached the subject Omri had smartly dodged like a patrol leader fearing an ambush.

'Jafar cooperating?'

Nick's prescient observation stirred Omri from his reverie.

Unclasping his briefcase Omri extracted a buff folder, laying it out with meticulous attention. Turning back the outer cover he wet his forefinger, industriously rustling through the loose pages until he reached an A4 black and white portrait.

'The courier has used two worknames we know about – Qasim Jafar and Farzad Takāb. We have identified him as Jalbun Sanur,' he said, sliding the portrait around to Nick. 'He is a committed *fedayeen*, a tough individual and resistant.'

'But in one piece?'

'So far,' Omri said, his face contorted with the problems of handling a difficult business.

Staring back at Nick from the enlarged photograph a tousled haired twenty-something Palestinian. His cheeks appeared swollen, his eyes inwardly lit by an unwavering belief in his cause, were sunk deep beneath puffy quarter moon bags Nick guessed came from sleep deprivation.

'We knew of him on the West Bank,' admitted Omri. 'He operated as a MFP command runner. Mostly he made regular trips between *Akab 1* contacts and his Armed Struggle Command's base in Damascus. He reported directly to Khaled al Fawar the chief. From our sources we established Jafar left Nablus nineteen months ago,' continued Omri. 'Flew to Cairo on a Moroccan passport, made his way from Greece on Syrian papers, then he washed-up in Frankfurt requesting asylum. Now he is here some six months. You have an interesting find, my friend.'

'He's not only here to feed, water and manage a safe house for MFP cells,' speculated Nick.

'No... He hasn't yet disclosed his purpose here,' Omri admitted, sitting back into the chair. 'We found no documents, no electronic signals or contact details on his phone. It is not even clear if the MFP are using the typical three volunteer cell structure.'

Licking his finger Omri slid a number of contact sheets across. Each sheet contained nine frames, three of them featured Jalbun in Jerusalem putting down a false trail mingling with crowds, then alone in parks. On the final sheet Nick went over several frames; most of them long-distance surveillance recording Jalbun being admitted to an apartment by a fifty year old male with heavy jowls and a robust, portly figure.

'The friend?'

'A distinguished professor of engineering... Wasif Al-Ruwaili. We gave a high probability to him being a MFP coordinator and began surveillance. He too moved to Prague, he was our target, not Jalbun. He became the spokesperson for the European Foundation for Palestinian Refugees, an MFP front. Respected member of staff at the technical university. Has very a nice house in Praha Six. We were too late, my friend, Al-Ruwaili has departed.'

'They've ordered a strategic evacuation,' suggested Nick. 'Or they've started severing their weak links. Sanctioning the elimination of MFP cell members.'

He recalled Hostokova's declaration on her boyfriend Jafar's secret trips: *I wait for him get off tram that come from Praha Six when he's been on errand*. Al-Ruwaili was probably Rewall's local handler and Jafar the cut-out, thought Nick.

'Loyalty is sometimes rewarded by death,' admitted Omri with a woeful shrug.

'No mercy shown.'

'Sure. None expected. It's heritage... tradition... a way of life. People forget that. Israelis kill Arabs, big story. Palestinians kills Palestinians, somehow it's always our fault too. *Esek Bish*, my friend, *Esek Bish*.'

'It's always been a dirty business, Omri. This time it's more than faction against faction,' decided Nick.

'The team are waiting for you,' Omri disclosed. 'They ask that you should be there for the next session.'

'I don't want him unable to cooperate. I want the network, I want Rewall and I want Firas Sahil.'

'Of course,' agreed Omri, reaching for the photographs. 'I will make the arrangements,' he pledged, returning the glossy sheets into the folder. 'Nick, listen. You... me... we're the tip of the spear. We respond, we react, we take no unnecessary prisoners. That still our deal?'

'Yes, Omri,' agreed Nick. 'Those are our rules of engagement,' he added, leaving the table as Omri packed away his folder.

Fifteen

A soft snow continued to feather Prague, slewing in from the north in random, wispy squalls. The warehouse unit in the district of Kačerov stood back off a single track roadway Nick negotiated with caution, slowing at each fissured rut, steering diligently around rough craters gouged into the tarmac by heavy trucks. Away to his right a sprawl of rail tracks looped into a freight terminus. Above them the candy stripe towers of a heating plant. Behind a humpback ridge of stunted trees, lazy coils of steam wafted up from an industrial bakery capable of feeding half the city.

A member of Omri's *Kidon* team admitted Nick to the workshop after they'd danced through a coded greeting when he'd stored the Skoda close to the unit's rear wall. She gave her name as Shiran and in the accepted spirit of black operations Nick took it at face value. Pale, her slim body toned and fit, her hair was sensibly twisted into double fishtail plaits tailing over each bare muscular shoulder. She wore the uniform of a protester – black vest, combat trousers and paratroopers' boots, chosen purely for practical reasons. Out of sight beside a plain, blue van, she'd made her one and only introductory briefing.

'Has he given you anything else?' Nick wondered, trailing behind Shiran down a lane of empty metal racking dividing the unit into storage zones.

'More basic denials.' Her answer cannoned off the unit's galvanised skin, and she'd given it with an impatient sigh. 'We've still a little way to go with him.'

To hell and back, Nick thought dismally. The place was undergoing a refurbishment with painter's scaffolding erected in one corner. He followed Shiran down an aisle between reinforced crates stuffed with oily gears; in others there were untidy piles of what seemed to be second-hand machine parts – bearings, axles, sprocket drives. They've used one of their irregulars, a *sayanim*, to loan them secure premises suitable for this phase of the operation Nick reasoned, a location where they can go about their business undisturbed. Projecting out from a back wall, Omri's team had constructed what in the jargon of brutal field interrogation is christened a 'spray booth' – a studwork timber frame formed a cubicle shrouded in heavy gauge, blue polythene.

Streaming towards him Nick felt the high-octane beat from a CD, some sort of electronic thrashing played to soften up the 'candidate' before each session. And frequently employed as twenty-four hour brain numbing punishment, a technique Nick had intimately experienced for himself in Moscow. Controlling the sound and a perimeter ring of LED panel lights on stands, another of the four-strong team waved as Nick passed, then turned the music low.

Nick pulled up at a section of racking set close to the booth where the team stored an assortment of items used as inducements and rewards – plastic bottles of Coke, Fanta and water along with chocolate bars, snack bags of dried fruit and nuts. Arranged neatly on the shelf below Nick noted the supplies of clothing. Some of them military, some typically Palestinian: an accessory bar of props for costume changes required in a successful cycle of disorientation.

'Does he know Sahil's identity?' Nick asked, accepting a pair of sunglasses and keffiyeh.

'No. Definitely no,' Shiran regrettably announced. 'He does admit to knowing Shadia Hatab,' she added.

'What's does he fear most?' Nick wondered, selecting a Fanta.

'Camp 1391,' Shiran disclosed, parting an opening in the booth.

The double layer of polythene carpeting the concrete floor let out a soft whisper when Nick stepped inside the booth. Behind him the lights were upped along one gantry so that he appeared as a vague, fuzzy outline. In opposite corners wearing all black, the final two *Kidon* members in sunglasses nodded from their plastic foldaway chairs. With the lights around the booth balanced, the effect produced a surreal experience. For Jalbun positioned centre stage, the sensation must have come close to being held inside a glacier, Nick reasoned. Except for the stench of sweat, urine and soiled clothing. The MFP safe house courier squatted painfully on a low, three-legged wooden stool. His hands bound behind him by solid handcuffs were padlocked to heavy restraints around his ankles by a length of taut chain passing under the stool. A second short chain secured to his ankle restraints ended at a shackle attached to an eyebolt welded to the base of a steel stanchion. Forced into a permanently arched stress position, all the pressure centred on his neck, his shoulder sockets. Racked backwards in this way, the courier struggled to force air into his chest and had closed his swollen eyes to escape the continuous light.

'Jalbun... Jalbun...' Shiran called, standing in front of the courier. 'Jalbun... time to talk,' she continued, clapping her hands as though he were a stubborn child late for school.

Rising from their corner, Shiran's colleagues stood either side of the courier as she knelt on one knee releasing the padlock and chain.

'I accept that you do not know Sahil's real name,' Nick gently opened, the session officially underway.

The courier's eyes, which were nothing more than slits, peeled reluctantly open. He squinted up at Nick, inhaling a long deep breath as he drooped into a crooked slouch. Breathing hard through his nose he drew again for air. Then he spat meaningfully at Nick. Lacking any real force it landed short. Before Nick could intervene one of the team had whipped the chain around Jalbun's neck in a chokehold using his knee in the courier's back as a fulcrum.

'I think he understands,' Nick suggested, moving out of range.

'Listen to me, Jalbun,' insisted Shiran as her colleague slackened the chain. 'You can have it easy, or you can have it hard. You make the decision,' she warned him, leaning in close.

'Can we lose the cuffs too, please,' Nick suggested.

Receiving a nod from Shiran, her colleague took out a key from his combat trouser pocket, unlocking the handcuffs in a fast manoeuvre.

For a moment or two Jalbun never stirred. Then in stages he brought one arm up, then the other until his hands slowly met like strangers in his lap.

Twisting off the Fanta bottle's cap Nick held it out. 'Drink?'

Nodding sullenly the courier attempted to raise his hands. Wincing, he managed to ease them out of his lap before they dropped again.

'Let me help you,' offered Nick. 'Is that okay?'

Receiving an affirmative, apprehensive nod, Nick placed the bottle into Jalbun's hands. Cupping the courier's stiff, bloated fingers inside his own, he gently eased them, and the bottle up to Jalbun's lips. He drank far too fast, choking, spluttering out excess Fanta he couldn't swallow. Nick prised away the bottle, handing it to Shiran.

'This is no way for a proud *fedayeen* to end his fighting days,' he observed with gravitas.

Massaging his wrists Jalbun stared non-committally back, his eyes apprehensive, hostile, working on figuring out Nick's motivation.

'I can make you an offer that would make life easier,' Nick continued, pacing around the stool. 'Should we discuss it?' He used his handkerchief to dry off the sticky soft drink residue clinging to his fingers.

'You want for me to betray my brothers?' Jalbun delivered his rebuke with a sneer, his dry voice carrying his total commitment to loyalty.

'I want you to enjoy peace and a long life,' said Nick, accepting a hand wipe from Shiran. 'Tell me about Wasif Al-Ruwaili,' he suggested amiably.

'A friend,' Jalbun cried becoming animated, bringing restraining hands onto his shoulders. 'I tell them... I tell them, he a friend.'

'Tell me,' suggested Nick. 'What sort of friend? A close friend? A good friend? What type of friend is Wasif Al-Ruwaili?'

To everyone in the booth, including Jalbun, there was no pressure, no impatience to force an answer.

'Family...' yelled Jalbun. 'Al-Ruwaili... he friend of family.'

Absorbing this point as though it raised complex irregularities Nick broke off eye contact, retreating to one of the chairs behind Jalbun. For fifteen or perhaps twenty minutes – no one was precisely counting – Nick remained in a state of what interrogators term, 'out of play', sitting ruminatively in a world of his own making. From time to time Jalbun would peer over his shoulder at Nick as some sort of guarantee against a return to his painful stress position. Obstinately refusing to engage with Jalbun, Nick noted the gradual increase in these reassurance checks until they reached a level of acute dependence.

'What concerns me,' Nick announced from his corner as if he'd spent time considering nothing else, 'is how someone as bright as Jalbun has been used. You have a wife... a son... a daughter. Do they even know anything about your important work as a *fedayeen*, fighting for what you believe in? If they did,' Nick continued, pacing slowly out of his corner. 'Would they be proud that you are now used to run messages? What would they think of Jalbun the courier? Jalbun who is given orders by men and *women* who have never tasted battle? Jalbun who looks after an apartment like a housekeeper? Jalbun who takes many risks and is left exposed... abandoned.'

'Wasif Al-Ruwaili has left Prague,' said Shiran, crouched, her hands on her knees as she gazed at Jalbun. 'Gone. Runaway.'

'That's a lie,' cried Jalbun, his passion turned at vilifying the accusation.

'All we have is you,' said Nick, standing beside Shiran. 'Terrorism... murder... someone has to pay. It isn't going to be your *Akab 1* friends. It isn't going to be your fake KOSC revolutionaries... they've all been eliminated to prevent them talking. It isn't going to be your MFP comrades.'

'Jalbun pays,' said Shiran straightening up. 'A martyr pays for the cowardice of his military leaders,' she added, slowing backing out of range.

'I think I'd prefer to be martyr in a British prison,' suggested Nick, 'much better than being a martyr in Camp 1391. How can your wife visit you at somewhere that doesn't exist? A place that isn't on any maps? In Britain we have to take care of prisoners... but Camp 1391...'

Turning his back, Nick heard the whipping, rapid clink of chain. There was the sound of scuffing feet rippling the polythene floor, the impact of fists – all denoting a brief, violent commotion.

When order was once more restored, Nick faced the courier. 'You see my dilemma, Jalbun – in Britain that wouldn't happen. But I can't help you if you don't help me. Why did you think you were betrayed?'

Bleeding from the nose, his left eye totally closed, Jalbun vehemently shook his head. 'You are wrong,' he announced, breathing heavily as he rejected Nick's allegation.

'Wrong? What am I wrong about?'

'I am not playing your games,' he spat, not prepared to recant on any of his ideology.

'It isn't a game,' Nick insisted. 'I am trying to save your life. Give you a chance to see your wife and children again.'

Lifting his head from where it had slumped onto his chest, Jalbun critically appraised Nick; his one good eye warily following Nick's movement backwards and forwards, his face twisted into an apprehensive scowl.

'There is an alternative,' proposed Nick. This time he paused close to the *fedayeen*, gaining his full attention. 'Cooperate and we will protect you. Of course your comrades already know you have broken off communication. They will believe Al-Ruwaili, who is probably denouncing you as a traitor right now. How can your Armed Struggle Command trust you? They will execute you to be certain of your loyalty. Is that what you want for your wife and children? For them having to live with the taunts, the pain, the embarrassment of Jalbun as an Israeli spy?'

Nick glanced at Shiran who nodded.

'We can arrange for your family to move to Europe,' Nick continued. 'You will have new identities for you and your family. It will be a time to live in peace after the sacrifices you have made. No warrior can fight for ever,' Nick assured him.

For some minutes Jalbun played over the sincerity of Nick's offer. 'My family... I really see them again?'

'You will have a new home, a new beginning,' stressed Nick. 'Your Military Command thinks nothing of sacrificing *fedayeen* for political advantage. It was their carelessness that sold you out.' He looked directly at Jalbun. 'They use *fedayeen* like pawns, and you were expendable. Arrangement will be made for you to meet one of our friends on a regular basis to discuss your MFP work...'

'My work is important...' Jalbun trenchantly stated, a spark of pride lifting his muzzy voice over his cracked lips. Momentarily undecided, the *fedayeen* stared into Nick's eyes probing his sincerity. 'There is an attack planned for London,' he disclosed tentatively. 'Shadia told me,' he added. 'She should not have spoken about the operation, but she excited, she boasts how it will be spectacular.'

'Shadia Hatab is a gifted warrior,' Nick stated, his voice, soft, mellow. 'She must have been impressed by a strong *fedayeen* like Jalbun? Perhaps she was secretly a girlfriend?'

Shaking his head, his split lips twisted in a wry smile, Jalbun explained: Shadia ... she cell leader in Prague. She is gone, she travels to London, she uses many different names. Sometimes she uses European Foundation for Palestinian Refugees as cover.'

'Then we have much to discuss.'

There were no shared glances, no recognition between Nick and the *Kidon* team that they had crossed the finish line. But in the booth the whole atmosphere had subtly altered. The tension had diminished; in its place an air of purpose brought a burst of rapid, controlled action. Having tempted Jalbun out into the open with the 'convincer', Nick literally opted for a back seat as Shiran patiently led Jalbun through a prepared list of subjects, her colleague on the other side of the polythene assiduously recording every word, each heavy sigh.

• • •

Bleary, half asleep, Paul Rossan's secure work phone stirred him from a troubled dream a couple of minutes after midnight in a Pimlico flat set aside for senior officers rostered as principal watchkeeper. His eyes sluggish, slow to focus, he yawned, raked a hand through his hair as he concentrated on a coded text. A flash alert notifying him of two incidents – ULTPRI/INDIA-BRAVO TWO – trade shorthand for an ultra-priority report of suspected terrorist attacks on operational Intelligence Branch staff – permanent and irregular. On the edge of his bed in boxers and a crumpled Blues and Royals' T-shirt, Rossan logged onto an encrypted mobile network, receiving the first scant details from his deputy, Jenny Rowton.

'What have we got?'

'Chaos and mayhem,' Jenny breezily replied. 'First strike in Beirut is a confirm... Lewis Martens... one of Leiston's early recruits... influential asset based in Amman. Owner and MD of a refrigeration and air conditioning concern, he'd built up some promising government contacts during his travels. On route to catch his flight home his taxi was boxed in... they hit him on the back seat... twelve rounds estimated,' she explained, swallowing a mouthful of coffee.

'And the other?'

'Mmm... Port Said... also a confirm...'

Rossan heard the rustle of pages as Jenny flicked through several preliminary reports.

'Andrew Croxton... Civil engineer... employers are... a Dutch company... supplying and installing port equipment. He was an access agent, a roving talent spotter. Originally from Leeds he'd just returned from Haifa... Primary indicators suggest this wasn't amateurs or a crude technician. The device was complex, constructed by a pro, powerful. Delivered by courier... most probably inside some sort of package, parcel or box. Addressed to Croxton who was due back from Haifa. His wife signed for it... they've recovered the slip. Looks like they opened it together after he got back. The wife's in a bad way... seriously maimed... lost a hand... blind in both eyes... they've put her in an induced coma. She hasn't been informed her husband is a fatality.'

'How did he fit with Leiston?' Rossan demanded, genuinely fearing a catastrophic hammering of assets, illegals and networks.

Lost in a background murmur as if she were stranded in a packed airport,

Jenny repeated '... An irregular she initially handled...' before cutting down the racket by plugging in a headset. 'Better?'

'It's sufficient.' Though Rossan could barely distinguish any improvement. 'Why didn't they act on the alerts?'

'We're not sure... Roly's team is watertight. The circulars were all flash priority and anyone connected to Leiston received one... I've seen the transmit log.'

'Well we cannot nursemaid everyone Leiston had direct contact with,' Rossan decreed, his irritability rising. 'Dear God, they have to take some responsibility for their own security.'

'What action do you want on our long-term ops Leiston indirectly contributed to?'

'Reinforce the security alert,' decided Rossan, furious years of work may have to be abandoned.

'That it?'

'For now.'

Dressing for his dash back to Head Office on what already threatened to be a grey, cold, disreputable morning, Rossan's phone rapidly delivered a further coded flash alert. He scanned through it standing at his modest Hugh Street flat's window, its glass dotted and mottled by flecks of traffic dust. After an inordinate wait Rossan's call found a tense Liz Shepeau, Head Office's Director of Signals Intelligence. Trying to make sense of a fluid situation, Shepeau in disaster mode, delivered the most recent monitoring updates.

'Rewall has given an interview outlining the reasons for what she termed as her moral duty to defect. Went live about twenty minutes ago as a MFP webcast. We're working with Cheltenham on identifying the source location.'

'Dear God.' Rossan stared at the dour, glowering rear exterior of the National Audit Office, listening grimly to Shepeau scything off details in a mechanical staccato as if announcing train departures.

'She more or less basically set the scene; this public outing is her ideological prologue. Provided a brief profile of her career that she will divulge in more depth in her next interview.'

'Her next?' Rossan could barely contain his fury.

'She's pledged eight more when she'll reveal how the UK and Israel are complicit in covert operations targeting Palestinians.'

'Do we have toxic shockwaves?'

'A limited amount, but this was a teaser of what's to come,' she disclosed. 'As a sign-off she named two individuals as oppressors of the Palestinian people. One, a director of a political lobbying group, the other a partner in a risk management company.'

'Why them?'

Taken aback by the force of Rossan's blunt question, Shepeau patiently explained: 'The common denominator appears to be they feathered their nests at the FCO where they dealt extensively with the Israelis...'

'How?'

Responding to Rossan's demand, Shepeau's response came back in a rising state of agitation, relaying how the lobbyist had served as Deputy Head of the Israeli Desk, the risk manager as Deputy Director of Counter-Terrorism, Middle East. 'I'll initiate traffic analysis and ask the DO to open primary and secondary jackets for yellow striped trawls, shall I?' suggested Shepeau.

'Before Rewall names the entire FCO's Israeli Desk,' proposed Rossan ending the call, absorbed by a number of terrifying scenarios.

No matter how he turned over the potential outcomes, Rossan was quite horrified at the damage Celia Rewall had managed to inflict and this he feared would only be the beginning. He recalled his own warning to Nick during the Nürnberg debrief: *If we have Palestinian militias loyal to Damascus hell-bent on drawing Israel into a new conflict on British or European soil, the Foreign Secretary will want immediate, rolling updates.* If only it could be that simple he thought, preparing to leave for what he realised would be an absolute nightmare of a day.

Sixteen

Mrs. Santon heard Nick out with the fortitude of a saintly head teacher who hadn't risen through the higher echelons of her profession by accepting half-baked explanations. She would not accept them from her staff nor her students. She would most definitely not accept them from an official of the Foreign and Commonwealth Office, especially one who turned up without an appointment at *her* door. The door in question was attached to a Methodist leaning boarding school for girls in the wilds of Sussex. Priding herself on her attention to detail she proved it by accepting Nick's card, framing it between thumb and forefinger, calling the number listed beneath Nick's workname.

'Been in an accident... Mr. Aylestone?'

'Tumble from a quad bike,' Nick said affably, quietly concerned at the delay it took for Rossan's unofficial admin team to answer the dedicated line. He sincerely hoped it had been linked to the appropriate script he'd agreed after his arrival from Prague via Dublin.

'No serious injuries, I hope?'

'Only to my pride and wallet,' laughed Nick.

'Ah... Good morning...' Mrs. Santon swivelled her back to Nick, lowering her voice as she gazed out over the inner quadrangle of an academic beacon fashioned by the ideals of faded eras.

Beyond the ivy walls opposite, Nick picked out the familiar landmarks of another vaunted educational establishment: an array of towers, brick turrets; a redoubtable chapel spire and a flagpole that stood naked except on founder's day. Entering the drive he experienced the same terrible sinking feeling as he did on his own return to school from holidays when each cold, stone façade seemed to be ingrained with the marks of further misery; a taunting reminder of another bleak term to be endured. For the first six months of each new quarter he read the *Count of Monte Cristo* as a practical survival guide.

'I understand... Thank you... Goodbye.' Mrs. Santon said, much louder, spinning around to replace the handset. 'Your department makes the vetting of applicants for sensitive roles within the Diplomatic Service sound *so* mysterious,' she chided Nick. 'It must be very rewarding work. The school has always provided, how shall I put it, suitable Establishment material. None of them has let us down. Not that I know of,' she thoughtfully added.

'It's quite mundane actually,' smiled Nick, seriously concerned that someone had ad-libbed with the script.

'Really?'

'I just harvest the background so it can be checked,' he conceded. 'The candidate is...' He delved into his overcoat pocket and removed a small notebook and pen. Flicking through pages filled with random, undecipherable jottings, he stopped and read out: 'Lydia Hallam,' with conscientious precision.

A grimace rolled down over the pleasant smile and Mrs. Santon stared slightly open-mouthed at Nick. 'Lydia Hallam? Are you certain it is *our* Lydia Hallam?' she demanded, puzzled.

'That's the information I have,' confessed Nick, wondering if Omri in his haste to proceed had provided the correct name for the suspected MFP bomb maker known also as Amatulla Salhab. 'I do hope I haven't run into a serious problem already? Lydia Alicia Hallam, the only daughter of Selina and Felix?'

'Goodness... Yes. She *was* here as a boarder right through to completing the sixth form. You must think me very rude, but really it is quite a shock that *our* Lydia would consider a government career. It's just... well, I never considered her to be a team player. Please do forgive me if I suggest you seem to have a wasted journey, Mr. Aylestone,' she commiserated and looked off into the distance.

'It really would be useful if I could speak to someone who had contact with her on a day-to-day basis during her time here,' Nick suggested, not accepting his cue to leave. 'Everything will be treated in the strictest confidence.'

'Quite.' She briskly swung her attention back into her study. A room with high ceilings and intricate plaster mouldings that over the years had served the purposes of education without the slightest prejudice, a nerve centre for taming and rewarding young febrile minds in equal measure. 'Someone obviously must believe Lydia has potential to fit in,' she grudgingly conceded. 'Her time with us was, shall we say, not without incident. Rules and regulations were not amongst her forte, Mr. Aylestone. *Independent* and *headstrong* constantly appeared on her reports. Bright, academically gifted in some subjects, in others she would withdraw completely and obstinately refuse any type of engagement. Some parents, many from overseas, do maintain regular contact to check their children's progress. In Lydia's case, she was more or less abandoned into our care. It was very distressing. Are you sure you still want to continue with the assessment?'

'If I failed to do each candidate justice, I would be doing them a disservice.'

'Of course... naturally.'

Her face ran to a point, every inch of its sharp angles reminding Nick of a yacht's prow, her nose its racing pulpit. At some stage of her successful career, she had discarded the need to smile and stared impassively at Nick with pursed lips tastefully smeared with a pale lipstick. Modern and smart, her style seemed out of place with the generations of past boarders held captive in serried ranks of school and house photographs cloistered about the room; a roll call of triumph and failure.

'One has to be careful that is all,' she continued, handing back his card. 'We never allow school access without carrying out thorough background checks. Only authorised visitors are permitted admission to the grounds and buildings. The school has a password system to ensure that undesirables do not masquerade as parents. I'm pleased to say that it is most effective in keeping the ne'er-do-wells out.'

'Absolutely,' agreed Nick.

'I don't know if this is valid, but Mrs. Hallam caused a considerable scene,' she admitted, tapping a pencil on her desk, a secret Morse message of her disapproval. 'Quite disgraceful. If it had been *my* decision alone, I would have most definitely called the police. But the member of staff involved – whom I trust implicitly – requested that no action should be taken, despite his black eye.'

'If we were all judged by the actions of our parents, perhaps not many of us would remain unblemished,' Nick suggested, for once quite the forgiving type.

'If it impacted on the suitability of a candidate for a particular post, I thought it would matter a great deal.'

'If the mother's continued behavioural pattern is a cause for concern in her relationship with Lydia, that would be something that the selection panel would have take into consideration. *Is* there a member of staff I could talk to about Lydia Hallam?'

'Miss Bonby, I suppose. She was Hallam's housemistress. But she has a heavy teaching and pastoral schedule. I'll have to check if she's free,' Mrs. Santon confided with a petty sigh.

'If it's not too much trouble.'

Using the pencil she tapped on her keyboard to wake her computer. Clicking her way through timetables she delved into the logistics of academic delivery: 'I thought we had arranged temporary cover... That is a clash... This won't do...' she muttered in the best tradition of a pursuit driver giving a blow-by-blow commentary. 'Bonby... digital media club... no, no... that's extra curricular. This morning she should be... Yes... Cross-country... Netball... How strange, she's down for Fourth Form coaching.' With the pencil used once more as an aide, she entered the number of an extension into the upright desk phone, her high backed chair used once more as a shield. Nick wondered if it was school policy not to openly communicate in front of visitors?

'Michael... A favour,' she pleaded in that saccharine tone some women have refined into a persuasive art for dealing with recalcitrant men. 'I realise you're on a free period, but *could* you do escort duty? I have someone who wishes to see Miss Bonby. She is out on the hockey pitches. I'm sure the staffroom *curia* will survive until you return.'

Waiting for Nick outside the study, one foot crossed over the other, a young lively member of staff who introduced himself as 'Mike. I'm Classics.'

'Alan. Foreign Office,' said Nick in return.

Down each side of long high, corniced corridors the classroom doors were stripped back to bare wood heavily varnished, each coat high gloss. Filling the air in churned echoes, the buzz of excitable, immature voices; and here and there, the strident soliloquies of good, old fashioned teaching. As they travelled a meandering route through the main building, sets of doors acted as frontiers between departments. Nick caught his own reflection before reaching for the ebonized beehive turned handles, imagining the stares of other generations trapped in the layers of mellow varnish.

'Julia's not been forging passports again has she?'

'If she has I'd better contact my Border Force colleagues.'

'It was a joke,' the Classics master hastily offered.

'I know,' Nick assured him pleasantly.

Nick presumed 'Mike' had only recently entered the profession, for he had that naïve fervour in his eyes not yet dulled by the brutal front line struggle of engaging with the enemy. His eager all or nothing vitality hadn't yet been fully tested, burning as two vibrant red patches on his cheeks.

'Don't suppose *you* know anything about Lydia Hallam by any chance?' Nick casually enquired when they'd cleared the art annexe, stepping out into the grounds.

'Before my time, I'm afraid. But there are rife stories to be heard in dark corners about the school's all-time political activist.'

'That sounds intriguing?'

'Not that I heard anything that wasn't already public,' he stressed, halting at a flight of stone steps, a crude modification cut into the upper bank of a ha-ha. 'But she apparently possessed the true genius and knack of stirring up a hornet's nest, then leaving others to be stung.'

'Rumours are legion when the truth is a scarce commodity,' Nick observed primly, selling himself as a truly pompous bureaucrat.

'Oh... absolutely... please don't think that I was being malicious.'

'Do you have a reason to be?'

'No... no... not one bit. I suppose it is her reputation as a committed rebel that continues to define her,' Mike admitted, a touch apologetic. 'As far as I know, her worst offence brought her within a whisker of being asked to leave for using the chemistry and physics labs for dark experiments. Of what type, I couldn't tell you,' he admitted slightly crestfallen. 'Follow the path,' he advised. 'You'll hear them before you see them. *Fas est et ab hoste docēri*,' he added flatly.

'Thank you,' said Nick, descending alone. And he doubted if Mike would ever change; his 'school personality' already formed, an eccentric classics master sprinkling quotes from Ovid to illuminate the darkness in ignorant minds.

The hockey pitches were reached through an avenue of ornamental trees pruned like flat topped skittles, then a zigzag path down onto another plateau set aside as mini sports arenas for tennis, hockey and netball. In the distance, the Newmarket Ridge half obscured by a flimsy cradle of mist. As the classicist predicted, the cutting wind drove the sounds of girls engaged in ferocious play back towards the school. Coaxing orthodox and cunning moves out of her charges under the glare of floodlights though it stubbornly remained mid-morning, Miss Bonby raised a languid arm, acknowledging Nick strolling towards the touchline.

'Defence... defence...' Miss Bonby shrieked, and shook her head in dismay. 'There's not much I can tell you,' she said, glancing sideways at Nick. 'Stella... STELLA... WAKE UP!'

Santon's issued a warning Nick decided; she's sent a runner from the Lower Fifth by a secret route, issued a coded text, or call, released coloured smoke from her study chimney: anything to safeguard the school's reputation.

'You must have come to know Lydia Hallam fairly well as her housemistress?'

'Enough to know the last career she'd follow would be diplomacy,' Miss Bonby scoffed. 'Keep up Grace, stay with the play,' she bellowed, skipping off down the touchline.

Pursuing her beside the synthetic pitch, Nick paused, watching an attack fizzle out with a hopeful shot bobbling wide of the goal. 'People change,' he proposed when he'd caught up.

'Not Lydia Hallam,' Miss Bonby flared, her frown and tone adamant. She raised an arm to attract a player's attention, her wristwatch slipping down her bony wrist into the sleeve of her tracksuit.

'What makes her so different?'

Reacting to screams of 'foul' with a stern 'play on' Miss Bonby rounded on Nick. Slim, barely over five feet in height she had that aggressive determination of an extreme adventurer, someone who revelled in her agility, her mastery of hostile environments.

'A self-centred rebellious core,' she called, tearing off down towards a corner flag shouting encouragement to defenders and attackers.

She would be at home at a high camp on a difficult peak decided Nick, revelling in the challenge of testing herself in the death zone.

Stopping play at Miss Bonby's double blast on her whistle, the girls gathered in a pack around the games mistress, some of them panting hard after a last minute charge down the pitch. Flung back towards Nick on the scouring wind partial remnants of Miss Bonby's tactical analysis praising the efforts of every player. She finished with a 'Don't dawdle', clapping her hands to disperse the circle of admiring faces.

Filing past Nick the girls seemingly paid Miss Bonby's distinguished visitor no attention, but they all made sure they saw him; memorising details to be stored as house currency – the seeds of school rumours. After lights out they would flower into myths and unsubstantiated legends of how one raw morning during Lent term, the games mistress was proposed to on the touchline by a grizzled, handsome army officer who had been her fiancé before casting her aside to serve his country.

Ignorant of how her popularity and kudos was set to rocket, Miss Bonby jogged back to Nick, her long straw blonde hair streaming out in curled strands from under a green beanie hat.

'She only accepted authority on her own terms. If it suited *her* ideals,' she declared, resuming where she had left off.

'Which were?'

Plucking at a loose hair trapped in her lips, she gave Nick the full power of her captivating eyes, an intense Nordic blue. 'The downtrodden victims of imperialist, colonial capitalism.'

'Anyone in particular?'

'When she joined us, it was the Kurds in Turkey,' Miss Bonby explained, step-by-step with Nick in a slow march as they set out for the path. 'By the end of middle school, Lydia and Sophie's room resembled a shrine to separatist causes – the Tamils, Tibet, Bolivia. We assumed it was part of Lydia *finding herself*, or as the educational psychologist's report that arrived as Lydia's additional baggage on her first day made clear, it is the "transfer of a repressed neurosis into an empathy with fellow sufferers of real or imagined oppression." Apparently it's a common syndrome developed by children from dysfunctional homes as part of their coping mechanism. No one is unteachable, it just takes a lot time and effort.'

And money to pay the fees, thought Nick. 'None of this was a passing phase?'

'It could have been until she and Sophie fell head first for the big one,' Miss Bonby confessed a little sadly.

'Palestine,' proposed Nick, curling up his collar against the brutal wind. 'Sophie was her best friend?'

'Acolyte,' Miss Bonby, smartly corrected him. 'They were poles apart in personality and outlook. Sophie was the thinker, introspective, the conscience of the two. Lydia had more of a radical streak, a doer, always going to the boundaries and didn't care if she went beyond them. And yes, it was Palestine. In the Lower Sixth Lydia organised fund raising events for refugees, organised protest campaigns. She started an online blog, contacted the PLO, Hamas, Fatah. Even landed herself vacation work with a charity supporting the *dispossessed*. Sophie, poor girl, just slipstreamed along behind Lydia's flaming chariot.'

'What happened in Hallam's home life to make it so unconventional?'

'Curse of the aspiring middle classes,' Miss Bonby suggested.

They halted at a small wayside sheltered terrace of crazy paving. Its main feature a wooden bench sited towards the sports pitches with glorious views of open country. For a couple of minutes they stood in silence, two intrepid surveyors memorising the trail already taken.

'The mother was actually a respected interior designer with a very bohemian spirit,' Miss Bonby continued. 'She accepted a brief in Morocco, loved her work and the client so much she never returned. The father ran a legal company in Brussels before becoming an MEP. He was caught cheating on his expenses and received a two year sentence. For Lydia, the school became her main home, a sort of protective custody.'

A feature Miss Bonby could relate to, Nick suspected. In an adjacent field a cloud of seagulls pitched and rolled behind a tractor opening the earth into neat furrows.

'The charity she worked for,' said Nick returning to an earlier point. 'Would you happen to remember which one it was?'

'Something along the lines of friends or supporters of Palestine,' she disclosed turning for the school. 'I know there was a mention of Europe in it somewhere. That, I guess, was her father's influence. Or her boyfriend's. It was a few years ago.'

'Boyfriend?'

'Came to collect her once at the start of the holidays. Another idealist she'd recruited during her campaign probably. She did have a habit of attracting the dreamers. Gathered them to her like a magnet in a pin factory. A couple of years older,' she added, a fleck of information in her memory resurfacing. 'I only met him because he'd blocked the Head's parking bay with his van and I was nominated to sort it out. I think he said he was at university doing some sort of electronic engineering degree.' She snapped her fingers recalling another detail. 'The van – his van, it had all his band's instruments in it. James, that *was* his name. I made some joke how that it was very apt when he told me the name of his band – the *Burning Apostles*.'

'How serious was Hallam about this boyfriend?'

'Serious enough to run-off to London whenever she could,' Miss Bonby disclosed. 'Lydia had to be escorted back quite a few times. I suppose he was like her other loyal acolytes, he would do anything for her.'

'Where did they stay?' Nick wondered, playing the perplexed Civil Servant perfectly.

Smiling at Nick's naivety in understanding the mysteries of teenage girl boarders, Miss Bonby explained. 'They had their own dedicated anti-imperialist headquarters. Lydia told Sophie how James' father owned the place, a flat above some sort of shop dealing in second-hand guitars, drums; all that band sort of thing. The father apparently owned the whole row, and knowing how Lydia only cast her golden rays of revolution on those who could be useful to her, it could be true. I don't have the actual address, but it was somewhere in the Battersea, Wandsworth area I think.' Miss Bonby added, still annoyed at the memory of her errant charge.

Up and out of the ha-ha first Miss Bonby waited for Nick.

'The vetting process is quite confidential,' he said, reaching the upper bank. 'If the candidate should...'

Miss Bonby cut him off with a wry smile and shake of her head. 'Whatever Lydia's got herself involved with, I hope it's not serious,' she decided. Turning abruptly she struck out back along the path, covering the distance in the long, smooth bursts of a dedicated sportswoman.

•••

'It is the true believer against the Jew. It is the Arab against the Jew. It is the Palestinian against the Jew. There will soon be a day gleaming with the brightness of a Palestinian sun to celebrate our return, to honour the reclaiming of our homeland. The moment when your eyes witness how our enemies cower, can no longer withstand our fire, is close. We will have victory for Palestine; we will have victory through the sacrifice of our MFP *fedayeen* brothers. Never lose sight of those words Hassan Maghazi,' the intimate voice of Hāru had urged in a gently whispered farewell.

He sat back allowing a moments rest from his preparations, not wishing to blunt his concentration. In front of him a line of documents and sections of maps spread out on an old drop wing table in his rented Plumstead property, his dossier on Donald Heligan almost complete. Every cell in Maghazi's body buzzed, inflamed with pride at his selection for this important task.

His life now had real purpose; there would be no more lonely hours dreaming of seizing back their homeland, of showing no mercy to Zionist occupiers or their Western imperialist friends. This was not another wishful dream; this was real. From the moment Hāru chose him for this mission, Maghazi focused on each stage of the conquest with renewed energy, a passion he had never experienced during his other projects.

Returning to his preparation, he smoothed out the folded creases on a section of his London map with the palm of a hand; bold red crosses and blue circles spread out in a spidery patterned web. Identifying the corresponding location from the latest intelligence supplied by his cell commander, Maghazi pulled on nitrile gloves, verifying his specifications against the sample components delivered by his comrades.

Seventeen

Holly's Café stood shyly back from Goldsmith's Row in London's East End; being something of a local institution, it served homemade cuisine until eleven in the evening. Two prickly weekend waitresses in their teens zipped between Formica tables and a chest high counter, ferrying mugs of teas, coffees, plates of cheese on toast or the odd full English, though it had already gone one in the afternoon. Nick took a table squared up to plastic wood panelling, giving him a free view of the door and the street through the window. His order came as a dark, bitter coffee and an insipid bacon roll.

Dim silhouettes flitted outside along the grey pavements, a steady ebb and flow from the Columbia Road flower market, some of them clutching huge potted plants they could barely carry. Stirring the dregs of his coffee, Nick seemingly lost in thought, glanced up when Paul Rossan made his entrance wearing a flat cap in sporting check to go with the lining on his mackintosh. Looking briefly around the tables Rossan delivered his dismissive shrug, following it with a smooth departure. With the 'all-clear' given and received Nick set off, keeping a healthy distance behind Rossan turning sharply into Haggerston Park.

'The Foreign Secretary is requesting action. Right now, not tomorrow, not next week, Nick. C is coming under intense pressure from the political jackals for results, for a suitable conclusion and fast. He has been warned that if we continue to lose any more assets and irregulars as a result of Rewall broadcasting Leiston's disclosures, our standing in the marketplace is going to be irreparably damaged. Not just amongst friends and allies,' Rossan began as he and Nick commenced on a slow circuit of an all-weather football pitch.

'Leiston didn't make her *disclosures* over a coffee, Paul. They tortured her, slowly, thoroughly, they didn't leave a bit of her out,' Nick furiously responded. 'C will have to hold off the jackals, buy some time.' He read the disquiet gathering on Rossan's face, collecting in his eyes. 'What's the problem?'

'We don't have time, Nick,' Rossan declared, shaking his head in weary acceptance of the burden he was expected to carry. 'Rewall has issued a press release through a Beirut news bureau. She asserts the elimination of Martens in Beirut and Croxton in Port Said are not terrorist attacks, but legitimate military targets in the MFP's war to liberate their homeland. The press release also promised further revelations of our complicity in the Zionist suppression of Palestinian freedom.'

'Is she capable of inflicting more damage?'

'A considerable amount, actually.' Halting behind the goalposts they played the parts of two avid spectators engrossed in a friendly Sunday League game of football. Rossan stared down the pitch as though following an entirely different match only he could see.

'Haven't all Leiston's remaining contacts adopted countermeasures?'

'You know what assets and irregulars are like, Nick. They adopt the security protocols but after a while become lax, start to believe the threat has passed, that they are somehow immune,' said Rossan, and it sounded too much of a hostile indictment.

Suspecting Rossan of avoiding a difficult decision of some kind, Nick bluntly confronted him with: 'And?'

'King Charles' Street has completed its security audit on Rewall,' he began head down. 'It's not good, Nick,' he admitted looking straight at his good friend.

'For who?'

'Operation Nomad.'

'How?'

'Rewall *had* access to the Nomad Directory. Apparently... and Roly has demanded serious sanctions on those cretins he holds responsible within the FCO's Syrian Steering Group. Without any adequate checks, Nick, without adhering to the box system, it was mistakenly bound in the tertiary appendices as part of a debriefing package for Taurus issued to Rewall.'

'That's wonderful, Paul, absolutely impressive,' Nick shot back. His demeanour definitely stormy, he glared hard at Rossan.

Nick had been the driving force of Operation Nomad, the recruitment of prime assets within Syrian, Palestinian and Lebanese militant factions allied to the Damascus regime. Nick had personally wooed Nomad's prime Palestinian asset operating under the workname of Omar. Controlled entirely by CO8, the operation had expanded to include a combat school for the secular opposition commanders in Jordan.

'*They* can't just up and clear out,' Nick snapped, openly furious. 'Other than warn them, what solution am I meant to offer them? Arrange a mass extraction for them? Pull the plug on all communications, all channels of support to prevent major blowback? We can't write every Operation Nomad asset off,' said Nick. 'You know the difficulties of establishing deep cover assets,' he added.

Accepting Nick's point, Rossan nodded and in a moment of contemplation examined a veneer of dust that had accumulated on his immaculate tan leather loafers. 'Of course deep cover assets are the ones you never want to write off, but we have to accept some are going to be a lost cause,' he decided, returning his attention to his good friend. 'Some will already be compromised, it's the law of the jungle, Nick.'

'So what option should I go for, Paul?'

'Rewall seems to be spinning out her disclosures,' offered Rossan, 'There is every chance you can reach her before she opens up on Nomad.'

'Ask her to call me, arrange a mutual time for a chat,' Nick angrily countered. 'I have to find her first and she hasn't left a forwarding address.'

'I want this fiasco brought to a conclusion as much as you do,' Rossan admitted waspishly. 'We have to prevent the spectacular the MFP have planned for us,' he added, his ire up. 'We need to find Rewall and her controller. We need to find Lydia Hallam and Shadia Hatab. We need them stopped before they inflict any more death and suffering. Tell me what assistance you need?'

'You need Security to get a move on with the trawls I've requested,' suggested Nick, pulling up smartly as the referee's shrill whistle blew for a foul. He held off completing his request until the yelled protests from players and spectators faded away. 'Anything on Firas Sahil and Hatab would be useful,' he proposed, 'do they own any other worknames? Do we, or Security, have any traces of them crossing our paths?'

On the pitch, solid, repeated whistle blasts grew louder after the player committing a sinister tackle refused to approach the referee.

Glancing curiously at the incident Rossan nodded in tentative agreement:

'They're probably a month behind on liaison requests,' he disclosed. 'They have admitted to dropping the ball on Palestinian factions. Security placed them as a low flag concern in the Syrian scheme of things.'

'Well they're not,' stressed Nick. 'Did we get any hits on this alleged specialist from Bekáa the courier Jafar introduced to Hatab?'

Waiting until they cleared a group of spectators packed on the touchline, Rossan began reciting a profile package of a notorious Palestinian IED instructor.

'Hassan Maghazi, a freelance consultant available for hire to any revolutionary council with deep enough pockets.'

'Or any group who use a charity front to build up their war chest,' Nick said above a round of jeers aimed at one of the teams. He thought of Lydia Hallam's involvement in charity work, wondering if all the donations were really earmarked for *fedayeen* operations?

'Maghazi is a highly competent technician originally tutored by Iranian Revolutionary Guard instructors,' disclosed Rossan.

'Any allegiances in his past?'

After a peevish shoulder charge, two players crashed heavily into the fencing. Nick and Rossan never flinched, continuing their sedate walk.

'Initially from pieces we have assembled, Maghazi *was* a devout, paid up member of the MFP. Either in-house fighting over operations, or one too many putsches to gain control saw Maghazi disillusioned. He abandoned the MFP ranks offering his services to the highest bidder.'

'So what's brought him back into the fold? An irresistible offer or has he regained his revolutionary zeal?'

'Six of one and half a dozen of the other,' disclosed Rossan, pulling up at Nick's side behind the opposite goal.

'And he has the experience they need?'

'We believe he's been working with *Akab 1* on fuel-air devices.'

'That *would* be the type of device guaranteed to create a spectacular,' admitted Nick.

'The ingredients could come courtesy of *Akab 1*,' Rossan suggested, furling his shoulders against the blustery, cool wind. With heavy steps he followed Nick off along a side walkway beside the fence. 'The Revolutionary Guard probably tutored him on hexogen, nitro, oxidisers, plasticizers and freezing point depressants. They've no doubt paid special attention on the formula of a wax coating capable of buying time for a suicide run. Maghazi is good, he learned fast.'

'Now he's here to supervise a front page job,' speculated Nick.

At the other end of the pitch a cheer erupted from a knot of spectators after a goal. Nick watched the scorer's celebration perfectly aping the antics of professionals.

Rossan waited for the match to resume, falling in step with Nick heading away from what was turning into a one-sided game.

'Our contacts confirm eighty-four kills can be attributed to Maghazi. His talents are so highly regarded he was offered a seat on the MFP Armed Struggle Command. A year ago he returned to school in Damascus for a six month refresher, mastering new techniques with his old Revolutionary Guard tutors. We found his executive signature on the device you came across in Prague.'

'He could be anywhere Paul. We need Security to start shaking their assets out of the trees,' proposed Nick.

In front of them batches of leaves scurried across the dull grass, pushed, pulled and tumbled by icy cones of wind streaming through the park.

After taking an age to consider the details, Rossan stated flatly: 'I'll make the requests officially and via the back door.'

'I can't wait for them to dither about clearance,' said Nick, stuffing his hands into his pockets.

'Since when did that stop you?' called Rossan, walking off, taking a path for the city farm, tugging at the peak of his cap.

• • •

Pushing her into the SUV's passenger seat, Abu Talib, the MFP's Head of Security punched her, a low blow severely winding her, strategically placed to leave no visible evidence. During the drive she sat silently, visualising a dozen ways she'd prove her loyalty. She massaged the burning spot where his fist caught her under the ribs on her left.

'You are our *guest*, remember that,' Talib barked. 'You are only of value because of your treachery. We... we... decide, not you, who will have access to the Nomad material,' he added.

Closing her eyes after this latest physical attack, Rewall tried to block out Talib's simmering dark stare. Her mouth had a dry, sticky taste, a nasty stale film coated her teeth, her neck pulled and ached from the way she'd forced her body away from Talib, her head lolling on the door during the first stage of their journey. She wanted to show she was still valuable, the anger rapidly fermenting when a half dead sign for Homs signalled they had a good part of the route remaining. Her nerves were flayed, felt as though they ran on the surface of her skin. Lifting her shoulder bag from the footwell she reached in for a pack of Lucky Strike, her hands letting her down; rocking as she put a flame to the cigarette.

Against the hammering tyres on the patched tarmac, Rewall contemplated the moment when she'd die, quite ready to accept sacrificing herself as a martyr. Sitting back she put her bag beside her, momentarily closed her eyes for a taste of the eternal darkness she'd *definitely* experience. Stubbing out the cigarette she sighed, wanting this journey never to end. Anything to prolong her existence as Talib drove deeper onto the dark plain.

* * *

A puff of red dust floated into a prism of light on the top floor landing of a disused, vacant shop; the fourth along in a parade of small industrial units proving difficult to let. Seasoned and rotten, the gritty dust tickled the back of Hassan Maghazi's throat. He fought the impulse to cough: holding his breath, swallowing hard.

The danger passed.

To make it this far undetected surprised him. He moved silently forward, his gloved fingers tensing around a lever handle, its mechanism sloppy, loose, having lost its tension. Listening, his ear pressed close to the door, he picked out the buzz of her voice wrapped in idle chatter. His fury aroused, his body primed, Maghazi stormed in.

Reacting fast Shadia Hatab reached across the workbench, snatching up her machine pistol.

'Hey, you're meant to call,' she raged, lowering her Z84, flicking off the safety.

'Why you not keeping watch?' Maghazi yelled, his mood dark, his anger rising. 'Where is he?'

'Out... buying provisions... okay,' she shouted back, resolved she would not back down.

Striding across to the workbench he delivered a fierce backhand blow to Hatab's face, followed it with two full fisted punches.

'Who you been talking to?' He stood over Hatab, his features wound tight in open fury. Snatching her phone off the workbench he reviewed the last call made.

'Brother…'

'You were told no external communication,' he roared, crashing her phone into the far wall with a powerful overarm throw.

'My brother is sick,' she protested angrily. On her feet she squared up to him, not for one moment cowed.

'Buying provisions… Sick brother…' Maghazi sneered, pushing her aside with a firm hand. 'These are a serious breach of our security protocols.'

Swinging around he launched a couple of vicious, whipping slaps bursting her nose busting her lower lip, immediate punishment for daring to answer back, for her impudence in questioning his reprimand.

Stepping out of range, Hatab visualised a dozen different ways she'd pay this lowlife back. She raised a hand to her swollen eye, ran the tip of her tongue along her lower lip. When she got the right opportunity, Hāru would be told; quietly informed Maghazi was seriously, seriously crazy.

Moving slowly along the workbench Maghazi inspected the assembly line, stopping in a couple of places to examine separate groups of components. Rotating individual parts in his gloved fingers he spent a considerable amount of time scrutinising the manufacturing process of his design, on this, his final quality control visit.

Eighteen

Nick glimpsed the big top circus tent from half a mile down the road. Pitched on the outskirts of Brentwood it dwarfed everything around it in the grounds of a former Catholic convent, chapel and school. A huge weather beaten board leaned awkwardly at the bottom of the drive offering building plots for sale, as well as promising the development of a luxury hotel with nine-hole golf course. The opening date was over two years old and from where Nick parked by piles of bricks marking where the school once stood, it seemed the scheme had never progressed beyond a vague planning stage. The Victorian convent with its small chapel was boarded up; mounds of plaster churned with rubble lay dumped outside in spoil heaps, a miniature continent dotted with assorted mountain ranges.

Rising in the centre of this developer's dream, the blue and white striped big top. Strung over its entrance a jittery rainbow sign flashed 'mission of light' on and off into a frost tipped evening. A handworked wooden cross smothered in glittery gold paint stood proud on the big top's central mast; an attempt to connect earth with the stars assumed Nick. Draped around it, pulsing light tubes moved in anything but a heavenly rhythm. Music, clapping and praise boomed across the site.

A couple of caravans, converted coaches and a retired Routemaster bus were herded in a circle round a crackling fire. Plastered across their windows, some straight, others at different angles, stickers pledged the faith of total believers for all to see: 'Lighten Up, Lighten Up for Salvation' and 'Belt-Up For A Celestial Journey'. Sitting on plastic tubs guarding the heavenly convoy, three hardened members of the travelling road show, one of them cradling a pickaxe handle. When Nick walked past, the armed apostle craned his neck, following Nick with his eyes.

Packed inside the big top's canvas walls Nick estimated there were close to a hundred in the congregation, none of older than thirty, stamping and swaying to a synthesiser led by a drum machine. On a chrome podium a thin preacher in his mid-forties, slick and buffed as only cult elders can be, mixed cosmology with Old Testament, promising salvation with the arrival of a comet. Not in a mood to be converted, Nick recrossed the empty slice of land filled with humps of tough weeds. Snagged plastic bags swayed like flowers in the coarse, pallid brown grass. In a festering pyramid, tyres from buses and trucks were jumbled between saturated cardboard boxes and sacks of rubbish dumped by previous visitors on their pilgrimage.

'I'm looking for Felix,' said Nick back at the campfire.

Getting slowly off his tub, the apostle with the pickaxe handle barred Nick's way. 'Why?' he demanded. His smile fell well short of being remotely friendly. 'You press? TV?'

Nick guessed the media hadn't given the cult good reviews and his colleagues got to their feet waiting for Nick's answer.

'I'm a starship trooper. Where is he?'

Whether it was something in Nick's eyes or the way he scanned each of them, slowly forming his defensive strategy, the pickaxe handle was raised only as an indication of which direction Nick should take. 'He's in the stellar base,' said the apostle, pointing to a building standing alone.

Outside a detached presbytery finished in ornate Victorian pretension, a customised Mercedes GLE that no stipend and weekly collection could ever afford. A solid gate led to a closed porch with a choice of day and night bells. Nick rang them both together. His experience of religious housekeepers was of women chosen for their homeliness, devotion and resilience to temptation: the one who opened the door to him had blonde hair in a ponytail and a deep Scandinavian tan. Bare footed, she wore tight jeans, a T-shirt and no bra.

'Is Felix in?'

For some reason Nick's question caused her to recoil in horror. Frowning, her jet white smile fading, she turned back into the house for assistance, calling for 'Ricco.' Ricco was Italian, no older than twenty-two. He came bounding up in bare feet, long dark hair to his shoulders. If it hadn't been for his jeans and vest he could have stepped straight out of a Renaissance fresco thought Nick, tensing his hands, redistributing the weight in his legs. Standing to one side they spent a minute in a whispered conference before returning to Nick, their pious delegate smiles in place.

'I am Astrid, a Maiden of the Light,' she announced, 'and this is Ricco, a Knight of the Light. Please, this way.'

Astrid skipping ahead – Ricco following on behind – showed Nick to a bare boot room, a simple pine settle the only furniture. From outside in the big top Nick heard the sound of synthesisers above the bump and crash of a rehearsed dance routine. Coming and going along the corridor past the open door, a procession of young men and women, none of them close to twenty-five. All good looking, all wearing jeans, T-shirts, vests, all barefooted, all having the same sharp smile they turned on for Nick.

'Do you want to make a donation?' Astrid asked.

'Our maybe you'd like to be a volunteer,' suggested Ricco.

They worried Nick with their smiles, their routine, their pantomime pitch; so rehearsed it became a thoughtless refrain.

'Where do I find Felix?'

Screwing up their faces as though Nick had set off a high-pitched alarm, they looked at each other for solace, a cosmic way forward.

'You mean our Spiritual Assessor,' Ricco corrected Nick.

'If you require an audience with our Spiritual Assessor, this can only be booked four months in advance after we have verified your background,' Astrid explained, her smile not completely formed.

'My soul's in a pretty bad way,' said Nick, making for the door, 'so I really can't wait.'

Proving his credentials as a Knight, Ricco jumped on Nick's back, his arms locked around his neck. Swinging his head back Nick smacked Ricco viciously on his nose, then repeatedly slammed him backwards into the wall until he felt Ricco's grip loosen. Grabbing Astrid by the arm, he pushed her through the door. 'Felix, I want to see him. Now.'

Her smile had simply frozen. She guided Nick through the house, barging through Maidens and Knights, leading him up two floors to a landing swathed in incense. Digging her heels in, Astrid would go no further.

'I am not permitted to approach,' she said in a whisper, 'my time for anointment has not been set.'

'Where is he?'

With a hesitant hand Astrid pointed to the farthest door. Marching off, Nick could hear her let out a soft cry of alarm, her bare feet clapping down the thick oak stairs. Nick pushed open the door, stepping smartly into an old study painted completely black with Day-Glo stars, scriptures and planets covering walls and a ceiling pared back to the plaster. Lying on a Bedouin king-sized daybed with fitted black satin sheets, Felix Leverton smoked a large spliff surrounded by three of his Maidens in various stages of undress.

'Stand by thyself, come not near to me for you are troubled,' Felix decreed, a portly figure propped up on a bank of cushions, his well-formed fist punching the air. His voice resonated with a fake transatlantic intonation designed to make sinners and converts blush and burn.

'I need a quiet word.'

'Who is this that cometh from Edom in the stars with false words?' Felix boomed.

'Out,' Nick ordered Felix's Maidens, helping them up off the daybed.

'Leave ye not and assist me to cast him out. For he is amongst ye and thou must face thine enemy.'

Pushing the last Maiden of Light out, Nick kicked the door closed. 'Quite finished?'

'Nicholas, what a delightful pleasure...' drawled Felix, recovering his syrupy Home Counties accent.

'How's the saving of souls going, Felix? Still profitable?' wondered Nick.

'It keeps the wolves from the door.'

'I bet it does,' said Nick.

In the years since Nick had last run into Felix, the former FCO Arabist had barely altered. He was like a river boulder that the fast moving current of life flowed around – subtly modified but largely untouched by the rigours of a celebrated career as one of Whitehall's 'go-to' mandarins.

Crashing open the door two Knights made for Nick but were stopped by Felix's raised hand. 'Thou rest assured, the stranger has sought the truth and I will talk with him yet longer. He is no longer thy enemy, but a friend of the cosmic powers. I will see to the door,' he told them.

It must be something he puts into the water decided Nick watching them retreating, heads bowed, grateful vacant smiles flashed in recognition of their cosmic leader's power.

Swinging his legs around off the daybed Felix stretched as he ambled over towards the corridor. Keeping his eyes on his departing Knights, Felix prepared for a private audience. 'I was fortunate to have the momentum to change my life through an inheritance,' he divulged having locked the door. 'It allowed me to buy this prime plot. The plan,' and he gave an ironic laugh, 'was to eventually redevelop most of it, keep this place and some land as our winter quarters. Solitude allows us to recharge our life energy before we set off on our mission of light tour during the summer.'

And it gives you the opportunity to snare some more wealthy, gullible cosmic believers, thought Nick.

'What brings you calling, Nicholas? You appear tetchy. Let me guess. You're in a spot of bother, possibly with some of our Arabian friends?'

Elegantly tall, his thick grey curly hair was left long, adding to the Byronic charisma his ready smile made quite dashing. At some point as he'd tripped into his sixties he'd gone for a younger look, the attempt not quite flattering, more of a pastiche. He nodded Nick to a plain course fabric sofa, his charm guarded, a miracle he dispensed sparingly.

'I was thinking about converting,' said Nick. 'Called in to check out the power of your gris-gris.'

'Sorry to disappoint, my dear, but voodoo is terribly passé,' countered Felix, his smile taut, flexing the charm of an old bureaucratic campaigner. 'State your business or piss off,' he added in a sham earthy accent he hid behind for hard-nosed credibility. 'I gave up on the fun and games after Gabby... when Gabby didn't return home – remember?'

Nick certainly did. He'd watched the unfinished documentary shot by Felix's eldest daughter of a night-time clash with settlers close to the Palestinian village of Bil'in on the West Bank. After an ugly stand-off, Gabrielle started a speedy retreat when multiple tear gas canisters were fired like *Katyushas* from a launcher on the roof of a Border Police Sufa. The final scenes were of her running, the picture shaky, blurred, before a mighty blow swung from the side or behind killed the camera and Felix's daughter stone dead.

'This isn't about Gabrielle,' said Nick, knowing personally how grief took many forms, how violent death could tilt some people from reality to a dark world of their own making.

Their last chance encounter came in Jerusalem where a disgruntled Felix had decided to hold open court in the American Colony Hotel's cellar bar. In one of his dour, morbid moods, Felix was already part way through a bottle of Jim Beam Black when Nick and a junior diplomat walked in. 'Here's to Her Majesty's finest,' Felix gauchely toasted them. 'God Bless them and all who sail in them,' he boomed, throwing a drunken salute.

Rocking the table as he was tugged back down, he returned to his acerbic lecture on how radical settlers spectacularly refused to understand the basics of Arab cultural sensibilities. Goaded by a Dutch news crew, he roundly condemned Britain's disastrous intervention in Iraq; very publicly denouncing the evidence of weapons of mass destruction as base, oil-baron propaganda – and a momentous folly to boot compounded by the slick PR of Downing Street. He resigned the following morning.

'What *does* bring you darkening my door?' He strode over to an antique desk, bare but for a phone, gold fountain pen, a foolscap pad and a realistic model of a Saturn V rocket.

'I thought you might be able to dispense some of your wisdom,' proposed Nick.

'Retire. Go find yourself a spiritual plain,' Felix offered magnanimously. 'You've earned it, honestly, no bull,' he suggested, sitting on a strip of the desk's ample top.

'Secular wisdom of a Middle Eastern kind,' said Nick.

'Whitehall got its collective head in the sand once more, has it?' scoffed Felix shifting into a comfortable position. 'If it's Syria, then we can rule out FCO revanchism, thanks very much,' he huffed. 'Regime change? Been there, done that, cocked it up – twice. Change one pack of cards for another and there's still a queen, king, joker and jack in the fresh deck ready to flow seamlessly into the vacuum. Surely you can't have forgotten our inglorious campaign in Basra? As I recall, you and your CO8 brethren were left rudely exposed when the *people's darling* in Downing Street heroically led the charge for the exit.'

'Everyone on the ground was exposed,' countered Nick, avoiding being press-ganged into sharing Felix's credo.

'Try as I might to educate those boors who dominate King Charles Street, I came up against intransigence on every step of the Grand Staircase when it came to matters of Middle East policy,' Felix surged on, not only warming to his theme, but positively glowing. 'Would they heed my warning that it wasn't Muqtada al-Sadr's *Jaish al Mahdi* running the show, but thugs from the Iranian Revolutionary Guard. No, the chumps would not. If...'

'It's a Palestinian issue,' Nick impatiently cut in.

Fixing Nick with a bitter stare, Felix nodded to himself as if in preparation for a painful journey. 'Grudge match or they just upset you in some way?'

'Military Front of Palestine have crossed the line,' said Nick.

'And you would like me to do what exactly?'

'A second opinion on their family tree.'

'After eighteen years of being trapped in Whitehall's machine, Nicholas, I can spot a blatant fib from a thousand yards,' declared Felix. 'I thought I'd seen the last of you and your hallowed fellowship. Breath of fresh air when I shook off the shackles,' he admitted. 'Surely all your own Arabists have something to offer? Head Office is packed with young experts, so my moles confess. So what has brought you fishing in my lake?'

'You came to me for advice once,' Nick reminded him. 'After Gabrielle's second or third West Bank trip, you thought she'd been propositioned by a talent spotter.'

'Gabby was her own person, she knew the risks,' Felix snapped, curtly closing that door in Nick's face.

'After you'd done some of your own sifting, you ranked it as a clumsy attempt by a new extreme MFP faction to bag useful idiots sympathetic to the Palestinian struggle. Do you happen to remember the leadership structure and main players?'

'Possibly. It's not the sort of treasure that I covet now. The Middle East belonged to a phase that I sincerely hope is consigned to the past,' Felix decided. 'But I will admit that I saw things in a completely different perspective,' he added. 'After I found the cosmic light in Jerusalem you understand.'

'Of course.'

'Don't patronise me,' warned Felix. 'My conversion was an ideological awakening and made me wonder why I'd had my head in Plato's dark cave for so long,' he added.

Of course you did, thought Nick, wondering how much the cannabis and the Maidens played their part in his cosmic shift in beliefs.

'Was Gabrielle a convert?' he pushed. 'Who's that delivering the big top performance?' He needed to know who Felix might be sharing his bitterness with over a post-performance spliff or two.

'No, Gabby was a non-believer,' Felix said. 'Our celestial guide today is my brother in the stars, Morgan. He joined us from Connecticut two seasons ago. Any other questions?'

'Is that cosmic time?' Nick felt a terrible urge to grab Felix, to shake him out of his fantasy.

'You can mock, but our cosmicgration have been robbed of belief and I just help them rediscover it.'

Robbed is right, thought Nick. 'The radical MFP faction,' Nick pressed once more. 'Who is the driving force?'

'Oh do give it a rest,' Felix snapped. 'You're beginning to sound extremely dull.'

'I'm two officers down,' insisted Nick.

'That's very careless of you, old boy.'

'You still do your banking in Switzerland, Felix?' Nick asked, making an elaborate effort of recalling further details. 'A branch of the UGP in Zurich, wasn't it? Is Lucca still the manager?'

'Touché, Nicholas, touché,' Felix admitted. With a defeated sigh, Felix reverted once more to being an Arabist. 'From the very beginning the MFP were divided,' Felix volunteered after a silence, a weak, painful smile subsiding. 'The MFP per se, evolved as a breakaway Shia faction unable to stomach Arafat's pedantic democratic centralism. The split with Fatah and the Palestinian Liberation Organisation came in Sixty-Nine, and even at the time of its conception, a flaming row over the MFP's covenant threatened to consume it, actually.'

'About policy?'

'About everything,' he said with an angry wave of his arm as though erasing a dubious memory. 'The leadership was turning into a cabal until Wasfi al-Dibwan asserted order by securing Syrian and Iranian funding. Any romantic infatuation with peaceful negotiations ended when al-Dibwan issued the group's founding ethos – *Al-qada' 'al-isra'il bi-al-tha'r.*'

'The liquidation of Israel with a vengeance.'

'Al-Dibwan had never been a shrinking violet. He cut his teeth in Arafat's sordid world of undemocratic power. He enjoyed its resonance, its aura. As the self-appointed MFP founder, he began mixing in dangerous circles.'

'Which circles?'

'Syrian Ba'ath Party,' Felix disclosed, 'Internal tensions within the MFP boiled over in Eighty-Two when the Israelis invaded Lebanon. Al-Dibwan and his supporters legged it to Tunisia to maintain their comfortable lifestyle and avoid the inconvenience of dying for the cause. Out of a hard core group of fighters that remained behind, a new cadre emerged.'

'And they broke all ties with the old leadership?'

'Their first act was to accuse al-Dibwan of losing his revolutionary zeal. Denouncing the MFP for being mired in bureaucracy just as the PLO had been was another stone the young hawks cast at the old guard of the

Armed Struggle Command. The other charge levelled at al-Dibwan and his followers really did rip the MFP apart. They were accused of betraying the people; they'd usurped the struggle as a personal vocation to provide a livelihood as professional Palestinians. It became a popular refrain in Gaza and the West Bank,' he explained, his smile on simmer, his eyes becoming still and wary. 'The old guard were denounced for being infected with the PLO virus. They were showing all the symptoms and didn't care – greed, laziness and a real embracing of bourgeoisie values. The young hawks demanded change and made sure they got it.'

'What's the reasoning?'

Fully immersed in his subject, Felix had gained a passionate inflexion: 'In Ninety-Five, the die is cast. A new hard-line Armed Struggle Command refused to agree to the Oslo accords, objecting to accepting Israel's right to exist. The Accords, they claimed, turned the old MFP into true Israeli puppets who cared only for their own elevated positions, *their Swiss* bank accounts and a healthy grip on retaining power. The young hawks predicted that conditions for the majority of Palestinians would grow worse, and they did. They proclaimed in Article 9 of their newly minted covenant that armed struggle is the only means to liberate Palestine. I assume you're attempting to prove that this extreme Armed Struggle Command is connected to the recent bombings?'

'This latest faction, are they still controlled by the Syrians?' Nick countered with his own question.

'Who else? Damascus has always played the numbers game. It's used the Palestinian conflict for years to deflect attention from its own internal strife. No single militia is allowed to be top dog. One season it might be the Popular Front for the Liberation of Palestine – General Command, the next the Islamic *Jihad* Movement in Palestine or the extreme, young avengers behind the MFP. It's all part of Damascus's strategy to maintain the balance of weakness amongst its anointed *fedayeen* so as to assert total control. If it's to their advantage, they unite Shia and Sunni, persuading them put aside their differences to fight together – the concept of *umma* – a joint community ready to eradicate Israel.'

'All differences are forgotten?'

'Haven't you been listening, Nicholas? Of course differences are put aside. It's the culture of Arab terrorism, always has been, it's dominated by individual and collective shame, complicated by tribal affiliations and feuds.

Shaming rivals and the fear of being shamed makes the groups paranoid. Comrades they suspect of betrayal are hunted down. It's vengeance, Nicholas, a question of honour. Pride is essential to Arabs of all faiths. They are waiting for a new champion, another Nebuchadnezzar to tear down the walls of Jerusalem. Until then, no terrorist organisation operating from Syrian soil carries out an attack without tacit approval from Damascus.'

In the big top the cosmic gathering neared its climax and Nick heard the synthesisers rise into a messianic wail backed by a screaming wall of chants.

'The Battle Command is run out of Damascus and is led by Munahid Surif,' Felix continued. 'The MFP has bases in and around the Lebanese–Syrian border. Tucked away near Yanta they have an *education camp* for young boys during the school holidays. And we all know what that means.'

'Weapon handling and training.'

'All the basics before they join the big boys who train over the border in Syria. They had a place outside Yarmouk until the rebels lay claim to it. After that calamity the wise elders promptly arrange for their main training camp to operate as a nomadic entity. Here one month, two, perhaps three, then gone.' He emphasised the point with a puff of breath and a magician's fingertip flourish. 'I gather they have also set up a number of shadow camps as decoys. If you *didn't* already know all this, Nicholas, your Arabists are dreadfully dim. Suffering from amnesia are they? My assumption, for all it's worth, is that you're on a black operational footing. Head Office out of bounds is it?' suggested Felix.

Rebounding up into the presbytery a barrage of cheers, whistles and clapping coincidently arrived as Nick very carefully asked his main question he'd kept in reserve. 'The alleged talent spotter you reported. I don't suppose Gabrielle gave a name?'

Waiting for the din from the big top to feather away, Felix gave a lopsided smile. 'It wouldn't be his own would it,' he sneered. 'Gabby was keeping unsavoury company, flirting with men and women that were not always what they seemed,' Felix said, determined any misconception behind his daughter's actions required clearing up.

'Who was he, Felix?'

Holding off answering Nick, the Arabist narrowed his eyes as he had done when faced with contentious issues during his years of making strategic assessments.

'She'd met him on her second trip to the West Bank,' he admitted.

'Introduced himself as a Firas Sahil, a representative of the UN's Refugee Agency based in Beirut's Shatila camp. Gave her the whole sales pitch, how she could make a real difference if she became an agency volunteer. I'd given Gabby enough warnings, so she politely declined. Anyway she'd already made up her mind that she didn't like his manner, that there was something about him not quite right. The next time she saw him he had this other girl in tow, English... Lynda... Lydia... Lynne... something beginning with L. Nice kid Gabby told me, but completely besotted with the cause to the point of obsession. So far as rumour around the campfire went, this kid had apparently become the glowing, trophy wife of a real live Palestinian. Gabby's assessment was that she thought this English kid completely nuts.'

'Something must have given Gabrielle a reason not to like Sahil?' asked Nick.

'He had smarmy written all over him for one,' Felix announced. 'His smile said one thing, his eyes another Gabby told me,' he added, striding over to a walnut bureau, pulling open its lid. He rummaged through papers stuffed in its correspondence racks until he found a photograph that he carried back to Nick, taking a long glance before handing it over.

Staring up at Nick the pensive face of Gabrielle framed by Lydia Hallam on her left and who he presumed to be Firas Sahil on her right; strained smiles all round, their backs to the contested security barrier. Beyond the wire on a rocky, barren plateau the sprawling concrete settlement of Modi'in Illit just visible in the haze. The camera never lies thought Nick, but it often blatantly does, capturing false moments and promises as a constant reminder of times past and times present: Lydia Hallam, a devoted supporter of Palestine, who, to all accounts had transformed herself into a *fedayeen*. 'Mind if I keep this?'

'As long as I get it back.' Accepting Nick's nod as an agreement Felix stretched out his arm, a shepherd guiding one of his wayward flock to the door. 'Now if you've nothing else to ask, I have a stellar guiding session to run. You can find your own way out I take it?'

'I'll use my stellar compass,' said Nick, slipping the photograph into his pocket, heading for the door.

Instead of a holy glow, Nick felt repulsion for Felix's cynical manipulation of converts into believing in a cosmic destiny; fleecing them for all they were worth, hiding his illusion behind the hocus-pocus he fed them. On his way down, Astrid screamed hysterically that Nick had killed Ricco. 'Only his ego,' Nick told her brushing away outstretched hands. A choir of pious youthful voices offering to save his soul followed him to the main door.

Nineteen

It was a morning composed of a light, hazy mist thickened by persistent drizzle. The backstreets of Wandsworth in the ethereal early hours were the domain of dog walkers, half asleep children loitering before school and tight faced delivery drivers on the move before anyone else. Across from a railway viaduct, twin gasometers cast deep patches of shadow over the boarded up Plec-n-Play guitar store. A narrow fronted Victorian relic, it was squeezed between single storey workshops thrown up in the Sixties, all of them vacant. Nick caught the stale taint of charcoal laden smoke from halfway down the parade.

The fire had begun in a third floor room, greedily working out and upwards. Blackened windows in the rooms above were propped open venting each floor. Ducking under a tattered ribbon of incident tape, he passed a Vauxhall Corsa identified as belonging to James Aughton, the one time boyfriend of Lydia Hallam. Slapped at a diagonal across its windscreen a crime scene sticker with its capital directive: 'DO NOT MOVE' soaked by an overnight shower.

'How nice to see you again,' Mike Stanhill observed caustically, a solid plain-speaking Detective Chief Inspector in the Met's SO15 Counter Terrorism Command. He wore a white hard hat emblazoned 'Police' and a high visibility orange vest similarly stencilled that barely spanned his generous back. Bundled inside a short, tweed overcoat he had gained several pounds since Nick last met him. 'I've missed all the chaos you normally trail around after you,' he added, a second hat and vest gripped in one enormous builder's fist, as he shook hands with Nick. 'You must have sacrificed the right offering, your brothers and sisters from Security have agreed *carte blanche* access,' Stanhill confided, adjusting the strap of a torch lantern draped from a shoulder.

He was stocky and could have been in his prime or just past it with too much muscle hanging on a small frame. Creased, wrinkled and careworn, his face burned with an impish charm but was marred from dealing with tragedy inflicted by others. This, together with the way his hands always ran deep in his pockets, gave the unfortunate appearance of a boxer down once too often on his luck.

'That's very decent,' said Nick.

'Don't thank me. I am but a humble servant following the royal commands issued from across the river,' he admitted, nodding vaguely in the general direction of Vauxhall Cross. 'What the wise tsars demand, the wise tsars get. That is *you* to be granted a fully guided tour.'

'Appreciated.'

'I hope it is,' Stanhill said, leading Nick towards a young police constable guarding the door. 'He's invisible to everyone but me,' he explained *sotto voce*, handing the constable the extra vest.

And Roly Blackmore will demand repayment in full for pulling all the right strings, Nick thought, accepting the spare hard hat. Though instead of wearing it he carried it in one hand following Stanhill inside.

'We look but do not touch. Orders from forensics and the fire investigation unit,' Stanhill complained, making room for Nick inside the doorway.

'The initial assessment was accidental deaths, wasn't it?' Nick said aligning the facts supplied by Roly. 'Then it fell into your realm.'

'Roy Orbison could have told you it wasn't an accident,' grumbled Stanhill. He paused to allow Nick to take in the destruction through the lantern's fat beam. 'Fire crews responded to a call of persons reported. They found two, a male and female believed to be your missing targets James Aughton and Shadia Hatab. Both appeared to have been shot, not once, but several times by someone with a bit of a temper. Finished off with a single round to the head. They classed the fire as arson, an attempt at concealment.'

The display of guitars ran from front to back, covering most of the entire ground floor. In a corner bracketed to the tiled wall, an ancient Lamson tube cash carrier that had shot the day's takings to an upper floor.

'I don't suppose we had any decent components left?' Nick wondered, crunching over charred timbers towards the rear.

'You suppose right,' announced Stanhill lighting his way to Nick's side. 'It's going to take a couple of days just to gather, sieve and sort the fragments.'

Harsh faced with shorn hair going maliciously grey at his temples, the DCI tended to inhale heavily through a nose broken more than once playing rugby for the Met's first team.

'Any ballistics?'

On a staircase jammed into a rear passage water lapped down its treads in a waterfall. Hanging the hard hat from a newel post cap carved into an acorn, Nick cautiously ascended one step at a time.

'Going off the number of spent 9mm cases recovered, my guess would be the shooter possibly used a machine pistol. We'll have more idea on the damage inflicted after the post mortems,' the DCI admitted, illuminating their path to the first floor.

'The pair were just the MFP's assemblers,' Nick stated bluntly.

'Read that in your crystal ball?'

'Came to me in a dream.'

'Why the execution?'

'Surplus to requirements... The risk one of the assemblers was compromised... Hard to say exactly.'

'Not a progressive way of treating your comrades is it?'

'The weakest links and all that nonsense,' said Nick, wondering if Jalbun hadn't played him for a fool.

'If our deceased pair *are* Aughton and Hatab, there aren't any indicators of a struggle or show of resistance. That the sort of response you'd expect from an experienced *fedayeen* like Hatab?'

'Devotion to the cause,' said Nick, traipsing down a corridor after Stanhill. 'Perhaps she believed her expertise made her indispensable to the Military Front of Palestine.'

'She got *that* wrong,' Stanhill quipped, swinging the beam of his lantern across the treads of a second staircase.

'Yes, yes she did,' Nick wholeheartedly agreed.

In several places they paused to negotiate badly charred sections, the remnants of carpet wetter than moss.

'The place belongs to Aughton's father,' Stanhill explained, his breathing coming in sucks and nasal bursts when they reached the top landing. 'Far as he understood, his son was in the middle of leasing it to the European Foundation of Palestinian Refugees for conversion into a charity shop. Payment to come from the EFPR's basement office in Bethnal Green. But that's been cleared out, seems they've done a moonlight flit and didn't leave a forwarding address. We've gone through the place, found nothing on the MFP's operational side.'

'Part of the pre-planning for the spectacular,' suggested Nick.

'All the fun took place here.' Stanhill wafted the lantern into an attic room facing away from the street.

On the ascent Nick had passed open rooms facing the viaduct, all of them painted in soot, the window glass crazed. Here in the MFP's bomb making workshop overlooking a narrow yard, the rear wall had deep soot deposits over the Sixties muddy coloured wallpaper. Buckling outwards, the window frame had lost its glass, blown across the corrugated roof sheeting of the empty upholsterers next door.

'The forensic fire officer believes Aughton and Hatab were experimenting or in the final stages of assembling a device in that general area,' disclosed Stanhill, dashing the beam along one side of the room to the charred debris of a large workbench. 'The jury's still out on what they were manufacturing.'

'Fuel-air bomb possibly.'

'That crystal ball of yours again?'

'It's one of Hassan Maghazi's specialities.'

'Seems they hadn't proceeded to that stage,' Stanhill shrugged. 'If they were playing with a couple of cylinders of butane, flammable liquids, aluminium powder and ignition system there's not going to be anything left of this place.'

Nothing would be standing on neighbouring streets either, thought Nick. 'When they sieve the debris, it might be worth looking for fragments from a remote control unit. The type they use on model aircraft and cars,' Nick suggested. The additional components stripped off the device he'd discovered in Jalbun's apartment – ignitors and motors used by rocket enthusiasts, wouldn't have survived the explosion he reasoned.

'Any other needles in the haystack you want locating? Seriously, Nick, look at the state of the place,' urged Stanhill.

Following Stanhill's directive, Nick took in the trail of the fire as it had consumed the technical corner. With barely any effort he could work out the spill pattern of the accelerant's path onto the anti-static matting where it burnt its way through to the boards, then kept going until it hit the joists.

He followed its progress, noting the point of flashover and destruction of everything in the room. Burn and char configurations revealed the intensity of the fire, leaving heat shadows and melted light bulbs. Nick also noted the alligator charring on surviving wooden ceiling joists. At its height, he could imagine the fire sucking all the moisture out of the timber in a rapid feeding frenzy.

'You getting that whiff too? The longer you're in here, the more noticeable it becomes,' Stanhill offered. 'Smell like bleach to you?'

'But it's not,' Nick suggested. The strong, lingering chemical odour trapped in the debris had started to give him a headache.

'We'll bag a sample of the wreckage for a lab analysis, request a search if any traces of TATP were present.'

'Triacetone triperoxide isn't going to be the main ingredient,' said Nick. 'This device Maghazi is putting together is more sophisticated than a batch of Mother of Satan.'

From the pitiful remnants of a small rectangular window in the corner, the clatter of trains wafted in from the viaduct.

'Crystal ball?'

'Crystal ball,' agreed Nick.

'So what *are* we dealing with?'

'The adaptation of techniques used against the Israeli Defence Force in Lebanon by Hezbollah engineers,' admitted Nick. 'And those originated with supervision from the Iranian Revolutionary Guard.'

'Aughton and Hatab were silenced to safeguard this level of spectacular?'

Dashing the lantern beam in a high arc around the attic, Stanhill pinpointed perfectly preserved outlines free of soot, spaced apart on the floorboards where their bodies lay before the fire was set. The graphic white silhouettes looked like the macabre work of a pavement artist, thought Nick.

'We recovered tickets from Aughton's car,' Stanhill disclosed, dipping into his pocket. 'Aughton's companion, Hatab... also booked on the same Beirut flight.'

He handed Nick a boarding pass in a clear evidence wallet claiming Shadia Hatab as its rightful owner.

'They probably also carried out the recce for the attack,' Nick admitted, 'the MFP command would use a cell leader to compile all the target details,' he added, returning the pass. He might also have disclosed that he had good reason to suspect Hatab as being one of Leiston's executioners, how the Palestinian's instant death would never equal Leiston's hours of pain, her torment, her brutal interrogation.

'Something they were handling made a big bang.' Stanhill dabbed his lantern at a gaping, charred hole in the plaster and brick.

Crouched down Nick gradually defined the outline of a lump of twisted metal he presumed had been a gas bottle crushed like a spent artillery shell.

'The device they began putting together is target specific,' Nick disclosed, straightening up.

'Pity the target.'

'Yes,' agreed Nick. 'IDF witnesses to prototype devices in Lebanon talked about the flames being hungry, ravenous, as if they were part of a living thing, a beast.'

'Dust thou art, and unto dust thou shalt return...'

'If the MFP have their way,' said Nick, having seen enough.

'But they won't will *they* Nick?' Stanhill demanded as Nick picked his way back to the stairs.

'I'm working on it,' Nick called back.

Twenty

The delicately restored Georgian house bordered Vincent Square. Its immaculately glossed blue front door glared brightly under street lamps, which on this weekday evening, burnt with an arrogant glow in the sharp, clear air. Propped against the railings protecting Westminster School's fields, a teenage couple entwined in a lusty clinch. Farther along, a sleek black cat brazenly squeezed through the railings, padding out across the cricket pitch on its nightly patrol.

They're lighting my way, Nick thought optimistically, climbing a set of bridged steps taking him from the pavement to the front door. Definitely preparations of some kind were underway he decided, noting every window on all three floors aglow in amber light behind cream jacquard curtains. Maybe it's just a coincidence and they're celebrating a birthday, their wedding anniversary, he reasoned waiting for an answer to his ring; the classical bell chimes slinking off into the depths of the house.

Tall, elegantly built, Natalie Borujeni opened the door with the frantic, desperate energy that accompanies the early stages of a crisis.

'I need to talk to Samih.'

Digging one hand into her hip, the other gripping the door, Natalie waited but Nick didn't offer further explanation.

'It's a not a good time.'

Graced by effortless beauty, Natalie smiled pointedly, clawing back her tattered composure.

'It never is,' Nick agreed.

'He's away on business… visiting a client….'

'He rang the emergency number half an hour ago,' Nick firmly countered.

Refusing to back down, Natalie flailed: 'It was a mistake, he's got a new phone and pressed the wrong number.'

'He called twice, the times and number are recorded.'

'Look, Sam isn't the only bloody Palestinian in London with connections,' she ranted, standing aside for Nick to enter.

But he *is* the only Palestinian in London with the right family connections in the PLO, Fatah and Fatah al-Intifada thought Nick, stepping aside as Natalie slammed the street door with a burst of passion. The lion-head knocker continued rattling in protest for a good couple of seconds.

'A visitor. For *you*,' she bawled up a curved staircase. 'Relax, he's one of *your special* friends. It's *the* Mr. Whitham. You've hit the jackpot, honey.'

Suitcases, holdalls and bags jammed with nappies were dumped either side of the hallway in haphazard piles.

'We're taking a couple of weeks in the sun,' Natalie hurriedly explained when Nick glanced at the luggage. 'Sam's between projects so it seemed an ideal time.'

'*Has* Daoud been in touch?' Nick wondered, deciding Natalie had packed not for a holiday but a rapid evacuation.

'Not with me. He's not exactly a close neighbour, is he?' she icily testified, striding ahead of Nick to the stairs. 'The hero will be keeping his arrogant head down in Damascus or Beirut or wherever he's holed up scheming for the next *bloody intifada*.'

And bloody it would be, decided Nick caught in the powerful wash of Natalie's heady perfume as she opened a stair gate before angrily pounding up to the third floor where her twin boys were bawling in glorious stereo.

'Now you've woken them it will take the night nanny ages to get them off again,' she fumed, scathingly laying into Nick.

'I won't keep him long,' he promised.

'Damn right, you won't,' she vowed, unlocking a top gate sealing off the landing from the stairs like a stockade. 'He doesn't need to get involved any more.'

'Maybe he doesn't have the luxury of making that choice?'

Shaking her head in incredulity Natalie glowered at Nick, her hands spread over her hips. 'Don't you think he's done enough?'

Dark haired, pretty and slender she had the simmering, petulant eyes of a much-harassed mother and wife.

'That's why I need to speak to him,' insisted Nick.

'You know the way,' Natalie sneered, glaring after Nick as he turned for the last run of stairs up to the attic.

At Nick's right shoulder a line of framed coloured presentation sketches celebrating developments conceived by Samih as showcase projects from his architectural practice. A whole gallery of them stacked off-centre to impress clients on their climb to his attic studio. There were brutal concrete office towers, bland brick and glass commercial blocks, dreary superstores and speculative houses wearily imitating Mies van der Rohe's Barcelona Pavilion.

'Mr. Whitham... Marvellous... Great to see you, but what brings you round, my friend?' Samih's opening warm blast was given from a narrow landing where more bags and assortment of plastic tubs were slumped casually together.

'Your distress calls,' explained Nick mounting the final stair.

'*Really*. No... no... not me, my friend,' he protested far too earnestly. Realising that Nick wasn't swallowing his story, he drummed the fingers of one hand on the banister rail. 'Hey... that's it, sure. Listen, Mr. Whitham, I lent Natalie my phone. She's probably gone and hit the wrong button. Butt dialled, know what I mean.' He threw his head back in feigned resignation, turned smartly and withdrew at a fast pace into his office occupying the entire mansard roof.

'Everything's fine then?' Nick wondered casually, following smartly on Samih's heels.

'Sure... sure, Mr. Whitham, you know me.'

Most of what Nick knew about Samih filled a hefty personal file lodged in the electronic registry. After the military wing of Hamas assassinated Samih's father, a respected academic and senior member of the Fatah leadership, Samih – the baby of the family – was shipped off to relatives in the UK when he was a teenager. Under the protective shield of close family he prospered, deciding when he graduated he would skip the stress of returning to Beirut. His eldest brother Daoud remained in Lebanon, taking up his father's place in the armed struggle, as did an uncle who ruthlessly headed Force 17 that began as Arafat's security bureau before it was transformed into a commando unit.

During backchannel meetings between CO8 and Fatah al-Intifada, Samih had become the access agent to his brother – workname Omar – a role he'd revived at Nick's request after the failed extraction of Taurus.

'Daoud's been in contact with you, hasn't he? Is that the reason you rang for assistance?' Nick pushed genially, trailing after Samih.

'I've got Natalie and the kids to think about,' Samih declared.

'What did Daoud tell you?'

'Take care of the family, the same as he always does, I'm his little kid brother,' Samih responded. He spoke with the bullish ease of a metropolitan professional; his accent skewed towards an exotic mock cockney as an affirmation of his credibility.

'Has he warned you, Samih, is that what Daoud has done?'

'That's good,' Samih proposed, his head down rummaging through a desk drawer. 'Warned me, why would he do that?'

'Because of the information he's passed on to you,' suggested Nick.

Listening but in no mood to reply, Samih moved onto another drawer, frantically tossing odd items onto his desk. Swung down beside his face, a screen of shoulder length curly hair revealed strands of grey like filaments.

'How *can* my brother stay in Beirut, my friend, when the MFP discover he's working for you,' he stormed, his hair flailing as he shook his head in frustration. 'I thought you people were meant to protect Daoud.'

'We are,' Nick corrected him quite tersely.

'Of course, my friend, of course,' Samih retorted, slamming the final drawer closed. 'He's told he can't return to his apartment, his usual safe routine is busted,' Samih snapped. 'Restaurants, entertainment, his girlfriend's apartment, they're all out of the window too.'

'It's just a precautionary measure we need him to adopt,' Nick explained.

'Sure.'

Continuing his quest, Samih trooped over to a white, handcrafted bookcase grazing the ceiling. Balanced on a rolling step stool he sifted through a section of technical manuals covering structural materials, then another group containing data on mechanical fixings. Gripping each ring binder in turn by the spine he swung each one from side to side in what was turning into an increasingly frantic search.

'Do you need a hand to make arrangements?'

'No, my friend, I require no help. My family is my responsibility.'

Nick glanced around the long room cluttered with dutiful models of flats, shopping centres and archive racking jammed with rolls and rolls of plans – the work of a man who didn't have a country to call his own.

'The offer's always open.'

Jumping down off the stool Samih gave Nick a contemptuous glare partway through his short march back to his desk.

'Great. I'll make a note of it, Mr. Whitham. That keep you happy?' he declared, his breathing fast and erratic after his exertions.

'Seriously.'

'Okay. I got the deal loud and clear,' Samih muttered, licking a finger and thumb to flick through a bunch of documents he tipped from a folder.

'If you don't pass on Daoud's material, *you're* going to be responsible for his safety,' Nick proposed quite aggressively. He watched Samih compare the number on a safe deposit key with details on one of the documents that served as some sort of *aide-memoire*.

Pocketing the key, Samih finally paid Nick some overdue attention. His vivid dark brown eyes, normally benign and sleepy, were fired-up and distinctly jumpy.

'Okay... okay... I hear you,' Samih fired back. 'I pass this stuff on and you make other arrangements for contacting Daoud,' he insisted. 'I'm taking the family somewhere safe.'

'If Daoud needs to get out of Beirut in a hurry, you tell him the ID and escape papers I promised are still clean and waiting for him.'

'I'll let Daoud know, he'll be impressed.'

'What did he tell you, Samih?'

'Some influential MFP players attended a series of meetings,' Samih reluctantly volunteered. Attempting to stare Nick out and losing, he swung away from the desk, heading for a parallel motion drawing board set in an alcove by the window. 'Khaled al Fawar chief of the Armed Struggle Command and Salem Abu Talib head of security, a brutal Grade-A thug, met up in a Beirut coffee shop,' Samih revealed from a high stool at his board, one arm propped against its raked face. 'Al Fawar was royally pissed off. Daoud said the guy spent the full hour snapping orders into his phone and questioning Talib, who mostly glared at his cup or the table.' Turning away from Nick the architect stared off into the distance.

'And that's it, Samih?'

Removing a half-finished drawing from the paper clamp, Samih diligently rolled it up. 'Another guy turned up. Daoud recognised him, a born *fedayeen*, someone who believes his martyrdom was written in the stars from being a kid. Knowing this guy's reputation, just being in the same café, scared the shit out of Daoud. This guy is known as Hāru. He's hard, cold, a senior battle commander al-Fawar and Talib showed a lot of respect too,' he said, almost recalling his brother's information verbatim.

Not giving any indication he'd hit a vein of pure pay dirt, Nick pointed to a detailed model residing on a large white table in the middle of the room. All curves, cold concrete and glass, there were clusters of masts rising out of its top, and to Nick it had all the charm of the Death Star.

'Did this project ever see the light of day?'

Sliding off the stool, packing the drawing away in a tube, Samih came over to the table. 'Fat Albert commissioned it for a plot he bought in Tripoli,' explained Samih, his reticence making him fidget.

'Fat Albert? What's *he* doing in Libya?'

'He's fronting a consortium getting in ahead of the crowd. He's predicting a property boom is going to happen very soon. He's still optimistic that he's got the deal to pull in backers.'

'Libya? He'll fleece you for everything – things you don't even own. There's not going to be a property boom, Samih, the country is heading for a no-holds-barred civil war.'

'Mr. Whitham, business is business,' Samih contested with a good deal of bravado. But his eyes flashed out dismay from the inner knowledge that the scheme was another dream, another disappointment waiting to happen.

'This Hāru,' Nick suggested, matter-of-factly returning to his rich seam of ore, 'did Daoud know any worknames he used?'

'Daoud said the guy has a pan full,' Samih insisted, his face earnestly reinforcing his pledge. 'Hāru... Firas Sahil... Zaid Khallet... It's the same guy, according to Daoud.'

'Let's stick with Hāru,' Nick suggested. 'Daoud supply any background?'

'You got the lot, Mr. Whitham,' Samih objected, 'honest, that's all Daoud passed on.'

'Nothing else Daoud wanted to share?'

'Sure he did, Mr. Whitham, Daoud's been sitting down with the MFP's Armed Struggle Command. These guys tell Daoud everything. That's maybe why they're so keen to find him so they can have another chat, give him the low-down on their plans. If they don't get hold of him, I'm the next best thing.'

'We're doing everything we can to keep him safe,' Nick explained, wondering if Daoud had already ditched his Operation Nomad workname Omar.

On the floor below, one of the twins did what all babies do in the surrogate arms of a night nanny and cried quite loudly for its mother.

Nick followed Natalie's clipped footsteps out onto the landing, her terse summons for help, then her fast ascent up to the attic.

'If we don't leave in thirty minutes, we'll never make the flight,' she rounded on Samih.

Clinging to the door frame with a raised hand she smiled sardonically at Nick. Leaning her head to one side, Natalie openly taunted Samih to defy her.

'Okay. Sure. Right,' he snapped back.

'This was a public information announcement,' she declared in her best automated voice. Reversing out, she stole off down the landing. Partway along she gave a sardonic rendition to the opening bars of *Magic Moments* that flowed down the stairs in a mocking wake.

'She don't get it,' protested Samih, his head rolling sorrowfully from side to side. 'She don't understand,' he added just to make sure his point was absolutely clear.

'What doesn't Natalie understand, Samih? Is it something else that Daoud has shared and you haven't passed on?'

'That we can never be safe,' he retorted with a touch of regret and a hint of venom.

'She aware of all the family secrets?'

Nodding glumly Samih dragged a part filled holdall onto his desk. 'But she still don't get who we are, why we're here, what Daoud is fighting for.'

'The mystique of the return?'

'Sure...' He began removing photographs, sketches and magazine cuttings featuring design elements from a concept board running from the door to a small kitchenette at the far end of the attic. 'We argue pretty frequently about it,' he admitted, his voice low, rinsed with embarrassment. 'It always ends up the same way, Natalie yelling: "You want to give up all this for a patch of desert?" If I tell her: "Sure, it's in my blood, my genes," she don't talk to me for a week. What's the point of fighting *another* war that I have no chance of winning,' he shrugged folding up a poster of a water tower transformed into a glass and stainless steel cubed dwelling.

'Is there still a war to be fought?'

'Listen, Mr. Whitham, don't even go there. We had this discussion. I am making a point. I had enough of my old man's mantra about the *disaster* of Forty-Eight. All he cared for was "the return" and making the Jews pay for leaving us with nothing. He called it *al-Firdaws al-Mafqūd* – paradise lost.

And that's just what it is. Lost.'

'Daoud doesn't believe that, does he?' suggested Nick.

Glancing nervously towards the door, Samih's ears were cocked for the approach or warning of Natalie's return like a small boy afraid of being caught in the wrong company.

'My brother has been fed Arab ideology since he was a small kid, okay, Mr. Whitham. Israel must be liquidated. The Jews are expansionist – they're attempting to create a State that stretches from the Nile to the Euphrates,' he explained, stuffing some of the concept board's clippings into a black rubbish sack. 'He has devoted his life to the *'ā'idūn*, the returnees.'

'What about the other lead Daoud was pursuing?' pressed Nick. 'Any update?'

'This English woman?'

'That English woman,' Nick admitted irritably.

'All he got is this woman is treasure, she has material the MFP brag is going to be a game changer.'

'He got nothing else?'

'Look my friend, you're chasing the tail,' Samih confided in a conspiratorial whisper. 'My brother heard nothing but rumours since he's been in Beirut. This English woman is normally kept under wraps, personal protection ordered by Hāru. He's a hard guy who makes things happen. People who ask too many questions about him disappear. You figure it out.'

Which would confirm the difficulty of anyone without links to the MFP's circle of influence managing to uncover anything on the mysterious Hāru. A ghost, a legend, a bogeyman who may or may not be a hardened commander also known as Firas Sahil or Zaid Khallet, thought Nick.

'Nothing more? No word on a target here?'

'If there was, you'd already have it, Mr. Whitham. That was Daoud's deal. Look my friend, this all I got. I want no more involvement, okay.'

'If you *do* hear anything, ring the *other* number,' urged Nick, heading for the door.

'Sure.'

Halfway down the bottom staircase Nick stood to one side when he met Natalie on her way up.

'Finished with the family?' she spat, facing Nick squarely from a lower step. 'If anything happens to Samih because he's done your dirty work, I'll go to town with the media, so help me God, I will.'

Her threat over, she wrinkled her nose in disgust at Nick as she swept on up. Behind him he heard the raised voices of Natalie and Samih. Then the spluttering of one of their twins chugged into a full wail: a tiny human engine roaring into life. In a couple of years Natalie will have tamed Samih or broken him, Nick decided closing the front door. Marriage doesn't survive on logic alone, he recalled from his own bitter experience; it demands a comprehensive strategy like a military campaign, but every eventuality cannot be planned for, including rare emotions such as happiness, love and even betrayal.

Lighting a cigarette he glanced back at the house. He thought he could still hear Natalie's voice in a rage, glimpsing a fleeting movement at one of Samih's attic windows. She's laying down the rules of engagement he decided, the yelling dropping out of range as he crossed the road, unable to pick up anything more of hostilities over the continuous hum of traffic. She has demanded all the facts as a condition of a truce he muttered to himself, walking on.

Angie had that power he remembered. His wife recognised when an impasse had been reached.

How she timed it so perfectly Nick didn't know, because he always imagined he held the defensive ground, conceding the Service was driving them apart, admitting his failings as a husband. These attacks happened without any rhyme or reason; sometimes within an hour of his return home, sometimes a day, though rarely did she play extra time, never allowing a week to advance before reacting out of raw anger to something he did or said.

Only after her death did he establish that Angie's hostility was a manifestation of her guilt for entertaining a series of lovers. Perhaps Samih was lucky he decided, entering Rutherford Street at a rapid pace, Natalie might actually care about her husband.

Twenty-One

The explosion was heard a mile away in Mortlake. Much closer, in the immediate area of the Thames in Chiswick, windows shattered and car alarms wailed in deafening arias along the lower reaches of Cavendish Road. Sunday had begun with a bang. Members of a Network Rail maintenance crew completing a track inspection on Barnes Bridge were pelted with shrapnel, some of them tree splinters, one of the team taking a bruising blow to his thigh by a charred fragment later identified as a car's wing mirror.

Several witnesses gave conflicting statements on the exact timing when they heard the blast, covering every second from five to ten minutes past. Though the precise hour given never varied; a unanimous consensus placed the device's activation between 07.00 and 07.15. Of the early rumours circulating within ten minutes of the explosion, a fractured gas main took the credit, then it became a fire at an electricity substation. Then the mobile phone footage appeared online.

A brief, shaky sequence lasting for approximately one minute twenty-eight seconds drew on the exclusive point of view of a runner flattened by the shock wave when she'd surreptitiously cut through the King's House sports grounds onto the Promenade. Overlapping the frantic, breathless woman's: 'Oh my God... oh my God... oh my God...' came vague, distant shouts and yells capped by a dense silence that was actually quite audible before she began gabbling a rudimentary commentary. Over jerky panning shots covering a dense pall of black smoke drifting out of a crater in the car park of the Civil Service Rowing Club, the female witness spurted out her graphic testimony of the devastation on what was about to be anything but an idyllic Sunday morning.

Slotted discreetly amongst an untidy procession of emergency vehicles parked hastily in a secluded corner of the club's car park, a black Volkswagen custom Transporter – its cabin windows a restrained, smoky grey. It was a couple of strikes short of nine o'clock. The van's three occupants stood discreetly by the door quietly observing the latest briefing involving senior officers from the Met's SO15 Counter-Terrorism Command with their harassed friends from Security.

'This Maghazi,' Roly Blackmore began, 'if I've got all my ducks in a row, he's the technical wizard of choice for the MFP Armed Struggle Command. If this is their attempt at a spectacular using a functioning, explosive incendiary...'

'Thermobaric device,' Paul Rossan objected, abruptly correcting Roly's sloppy description.

'More thermobarbaric I'd say,' Roly glibly retorted. 'What I want to know is this, do we conclude this is a sign Maghazi has messed up? Has he done this as a rush job because we're breathing down his neck? That a reasonable deduction?' he continued morosely.

'It was just a trial run,' replied Nick.

'And markedly successful from what I've seen,' added Paul Rossan, staring petulantly ahead as SO15 and Security formed up around the Cabinet Office's National Security Advisor in preparation for his dedicated tour of the site.

'Maghazi was gauging the mix,' said Nick, recalling the stench of fuel soaked into the sump of the crater when they'd had their own exclusive private walk-through.

'Seems perfectly adequate to me,' conceded Roly. 'The damn thing was meant to make a mess and it did.'

And some, thought Nick. They were facing a rear section of the club's main building. One wall had been partly blown in exposing twisted steel beams teetering awkwardly off skewed columns. A decent length of the flat roof had peeled away, its membrane flapping against timber sheathing, some of them bearing wide scorch marks in the style of flames added to the bodywork of custom cars.

'King Charles Street is attempting to minimise how much access Rewall had to classified material,' said Rossan.

'Total crap...' snorted Roly.

'They can only see as far as tomorrow's headlines,' put in Rossan.

'Rewall isn't going to be bothered one way or the other,' said Nick, taking in a host of small red triangular pennants charting the spread of body parts, some of them he noted, had travelled quite extraordinary distances.

'We're already facing a Thermopylaean ordeal,' Rossan conceded, 'without King Charles Street's flawed input.'

'Pure meddling,' flared Roly. 'Penny wise, pound foolish as always.'

Nodding sagely to an explanation from a Met Commander, the national security adviser's little party paused at a corner of the boathouse that had taken the full brunt of the blast.

Nick added a distracted: 'Rewall has certainly got everyone's attention.'

He tried to calculate the quantity of the IED mix capable of such utter destruction, assuming that Maghazi had doubled up on some of the base ingredients as a deliberate scaled piece of research. Insulation flopped down between twisted steel rafters lifted out of their wall plates. A shredded remnant of fabric – a length of curtain, he assumed – shivered in the pale light after being rudely exposed. Hanging off a length of conduit a metal light switch clinked against the breeze block wall, its swaying rhythm set by the stiff chilled breeze.

'So the bare bones as we have them,' declared Roly, 'has our unfortunate victim...'

'Lucas Heligan,' Rossan primly stated. 'Not even the target.'

'... turns up to claim his father's car...' Roly paused for Rossan's next correction. When none came he sallied on: '... after his old man had a bit of a session with his pals following an afternoon on the river. Lucas rolls up, does a brisk once over of the car. Nothing suspicious... nothing out of the ordinary. Wasting time on all those crappy stupid checks before you drive away, that's not for Lucas. Why should it be? He's an eighteen year old with other worldly matters on his mind. Who cares that the old man Donald, a near neighbour of our parish, is the FCO's Head of the Israeli Desk. Who gives a damn that the family are Jewish? Lucas is in a hurry to go a calling on his girlfriend. All that security protocol bullshit is for other people. Blessed with the arrogance of youth, Lucas started up his old man's chariot and spread himself far and wide.'

Roly wasn't exaggerating thought Nick, glancing at ragged chunks of the engine block embedded into a tree. On some of the sycamore's higher branches there were clusters of red pennants snapping to attention in the breeze, standing vividly out against the film of soft black dust and powdered plaster liberally coating the bark.

'If some of the media's paid speculators and *poursuivants* of Rewall's claims are to be believed,' said Rossan, 'they insinuate it is highly likely we have a secret complicit deal with Israel to suppress the rights of the Palestinians.'

'It's the usual misleading dust and fluff they scatter to cast us as the villains,' said Roly. 'They cannot admit an abundance of vehicle IEDs across the continent is the MFP in cahoots with the Blessed Celia Rewall. She can only be revered as their current saint of disclosure. Why would anyone but Rewall have nominated Mr. D. Heligan as a soft target?'

'No one accused the Israelis of being responsible?' said Nick.

'Dear God, do not tempt fate,' Rossan stridently reproached him. 'It would not be too far fetched for some of our Establishment conspiracy theorists to raise that thread as a distinct possibility.'

'They'll be damned pushed to deny our source reports that Rewall's ugly shadow hangs over this,' said Roly, watching the middle-aged cabinet office advisor; stooped, parka clad, he slouched languidly amongst the boathouse debris. 'The venerable Monroe might risk a flutter. He suffers from a fucking severe case of selective inattention when dealing with our representations.'

'He's had numerous entries in C's tardy book,' confirmed Rossan.

'Mostly for not acknowledging our product and source leads,' added Roly.

'Have we had reaction to the MFP's claim that Heligan was a legitimate target?' wondered Nick.

'The edict issued by their Armed Struggle Command hasn't exactly sent shockwaves through Whitehall. The consensus appears to accept the MFP as an opportunist militia amplifying their call to arms on the back of Rewall's disclosures,' said Rossan, handing a folded sheet of paper to Nick. 'How anyone can possibly misconstrue *that* is beyond me,' he snapped.

'The attacks were all designed to fit around Rewall's defection. The one today and the planned spectacular are to coincide with Rewall blowing Operation Nomad wide open,' suggested Nick, reading the MFP communiqué broadcast from Beirut: *There will be no cessation of action until the liquidation of Israel as a State is achieved. Imperialist supporters of the Zionist regime will be treated as legitimate targets. A brave unit from the Military Front of Palestine Commando successfully carried out the necessary elimination of a Zionist enemy in London today. Other strikes will follow.*

'Monroe is one of several major critics whispering that we are deliberately dragging our feet,' disclosed Rossan. 'The mood in Whitehall is not doing us any favours.'

'Since he became the PM's security bloodhound, Monroe has pursued a puerile vendetta against the Service,' snapped Roly.

'We keep him out of the loop as long as possible,' decided Nick, folding the communiqué.

'And what will you be up to, Nicholas?' demanded Roly, 'we fib to give you the time do what exactly?'

'Square the circle,' said Nick. He handed Rossan the communiqué and set off.

•••

Demanding that he must not be disturbed Hāru retreated to the roof of his fortified villa inside its rugged mud brick compound. No one sought him out. His mood became one of violent fury when he received reports of the operation in London. Maghazi had failed him. Hāru expected the death of Heligan the diplomat, not his son. Lost in thought he stared out across the desert plain. The success of the entire campaign rested on his shoulders, a privilege he would not demean by failure. At this moment of uncertainty, Hāru turned, as he always did in a crisis, to his father's words of wisdom.

Turn my son—

Look through my eyes towards the distance where you will see a future running to meet the past. There can be no escape from destiny and violent death. Only fools and cowards attempt to flee, a futile response marked by untended, unknown graves and many wasted sacrifices. We are in a battle we must win with God's assistance and blessing.

Go carefully.

In the future there are traps waiting for us, buried beneath the horizon. Lies, deceit, penances, punishment and destruction must be faced, conquered for our ultimate victory over the Jews. Here is an outline, a plan pricked in blood on the palm of my hand.

Let me explain, expand my visions through my many names and by blessing your senses. See, hear, touch and kill. You are Hāru a faithful son. You are Hāru the cunning hunter. You are Hāru the warrior, and I am your true father.

In the years yet to greet us, we will be united once more. You alone are part living and part dead. You must fight alone to eliminate the Zionists, destroy their souls. We are natural slayers my son. Your time will arrive after mine, when my body has decayed and emptied itself of its passion no enemy can ever destroy. Pay heed to these words my son, I promise a future that you cannot escape. The Jews turned us into worthless shadows, forbade us our natural homeland. But you will repay them, you will drive them into the sea, you will open the gates for the return.

Yet you will never rest on our victory, you must continue the struggle against the allies of Zionism, their bitter reward will be paid in death. Only then can we have a land of a million martyrs.

Victory for Palestine. Victory is yours my son.

'Victory for Palestine,' Hāru repeated softly. A secret war fought against more than one enemy. No surrender, no ghostly echoes, but a promise bound in faith. Hāru smiled, alone on top of his villa, his command centre; a peeling stucco fortress close to a web of mud walled alleys running through smaller compounds. In the years since his father's death, nothing had changed, except Hāru's worknames in place of his father's, added to the list of wanted Palestinian warriors hunted by the Jews. An honour he would die for.

•••

The original fort, a Martello Tower stoutly defended a stretch of English coast where Napoleon could quite easily have mounted an invasion. Expanded and developed at considerable expense, Fort Martin housed an MoD weapons establishment containing ranges and a series of open roofed concrete pens. Having passed scrutiny at the gatehouse, Nick drove between batches of low modern buildings. The concrete road laid in sections, took him out towards the ranges. Red flags whipped briskly, snapping out salutes in the blustery salty wind. Surrounding him, a continuous crack of small arms fire. At a Portakabin used by the safety officers, Nick turned from the ranges setting course for a series of concrete pens. Beside one pen, he recognised a large Service car, the driver diligently monitoring Nick's approach. Strutting along a tight perimeter circuit he saw C's babysitter, Flin. Abruptly halting, she locked her attention onto Nick's car with a gun dog's same motionless devotion.

Parking on a concrete slab spotted with moss Nick found C settled on a rusty tubular chair, its seat and back made of driftwood lashed to its frame. Hidden away behind a grass berm on an access apron, Bailrigg stared out at the marshes. Beyond them, mudflats and sandbars with stretches of quicksand protecting MoD land from assault by the sea.

He just needs a pair of binoculars, a check blanket for his knees, and he could be waiting for the start of one of his beloved point-to-points, Nick decided walking over to the berm.

'Reminds me of the opening to Lean's *Great Expectations*,' Bailrigg announced easing himself up, wafting a hand to the marshes. 'I suppose that sort of film isn't up your street, Nicholas?'

'I've seen it.' But Nick didn't disclose he'd watched it during the four days he'd been holed up in Krakow waiting for the signal to proceed. The dialogue, so heavily dubbed that it resembled a comedy and not the atmospheric original, turned it into compulsive viewing. Nick sat through it from beginning to end in a side street cinema stinking of its patrons' feet.

'Don't care for Pip, not one bit,' ventured Bailrigg setting off a pace ahead of Nick, his route taking him up on top of a berm buttressing a concrete pen. 'Joe and Magwitch... Like Rossan and Blackmore would you say?' he added loftily, gazing at the pale, milky horizon.

Content not to be drawn into one of Bailrigg's vacuous games Nick kept his counsel, watching a line of clouds hooked together in a long train hugging the coast as they thundered inland.

'I was at Downing Street earlier,' Bailrigg said matter-of-factly, 'laying out our hand to the PM. I find him pleasant, but lacking any real intellect, especially when it comes to foreign policy. He can only grasp the shallow, surface forms, not the deep, complex undercurrents. He said, and I quote, Nicholas, that he had been strongly advised to hold us in check because "the Service adopts a stovepipe organisational system flow." Of course we do. But I politely reminded him that we restrict the flow of certain information because that's the nature of our business. Then he raised concerns regarding our ability to "clarify the journey" on our own,' seethed Bailrigg.

'Monroe?'

'Yes, Nicholas, the Downing Street flunkey has written his own invitation to ride along.

'And it's been accepted?'

'Oh, of course it has. Monroe has cast his spell with his usual charm and bullshit. No one in the Cabinet Office suspects Monroe's *Bouffée délirante* symptoms. We are to still allowed the opportunity to "drill down into the issue" but Monroe would prefer that we do not squander *our* take, suggesting expedient disposal be taken off the menu. It is all bollocks as usual. However in this instance, we are prevented from our normal course of ignoring Monroe's meddling. That conniving shit has persuaded his master to accept his recommendations. Rewall, Hallam and Hāru are to return with you to Cyprus.'

'Just like that? One target lift is going to be pushing it for the resources we can muster. Three of them just isn't an option,' Nick furiously resisted.

'The decision is out of our hands,' Bailrigg solemnly declared with a protracted sigh. 'Regardless of whether you or I recognise the PM's hoe as once more stuck fast in the naïve furrow, Downing Street will not alter their line. They see the Middle East fracturing, dizzily buying into Monroe's doctrine that papering over the cracks is the most effective cheap short-term option. Saddled with that baggage, we produce Rewall, Hallam and Hāru tagged and buffed to plump up our bartering rights with friends and allies.'

'Would you like me to have a quiet word with Monroe?'

'No, Nicholas, I do not. If I recall correctly, you do not do quiet. Monroe will be repaid, I assure you of that. I wanted Rewall whipped at the cart's arse,' Bailrigg volunteered with feeling, 'but I doubt you'll have time to administer a good flogging while you're serving her coffee on the return lift to Cyprus.'

Not inclined to argue the duplicity of realpolitik, an uncomfortable silence descended as Nick contemplated the change in strategy.

'We do what exactly?' Nick demanded after the brief interlude.

'The front line MFP *fedayeen* can be dealt with as we see fit,' Bailrigg explained, feigning magnanimity. 'Arrangements are already underway for accommodating and debriefing the higher echelon targets in Cyprus,' he simmered.

'And is Monroe likely to have any operational input?' said Nick, sidestepping an oil drum used a makeshift brazier.

'Oh, do not worry, Nicholas, the double-dealing shit has personally assured me we have total control of *our* operation,' Bailrigg said, laying on the irony.

'He'll have to be kept at arm's-length,' Nick decided.

'I'll delegate Roly, *he'll* ensure Monroe remains in neutral.'

'Good.'

He glanced down into the pen, its sides scorched, heavily chipped after years of test firing explosives. Iron rungs built into a section of one concrete wall were pocked with rust. Hanging at drunken angles in their twisted frames arranged in a square, four door-sized steel plates at the centre of the pen were mangled, peppered by shrapnel and holed by a demonstration of a vacuum IED put on for the Service.

'With their imported technician Maghazi, the MFP have the capability of a device three times stronger,' Nick suggested, recalling the slow motion replay of the IED's power he'd already viewed on his laptop.

After a judicious silence that he spent staring at the damage, Bailrigg decided: 'If I agree to allow you to continue, you do appreciate Nicholas, that this is the point of no return.'

'We've already passed that milestone when Rewall opened the gates for Hāru.'

'Just be aware that if this joint venture with Ni'ram backfires you alone will face the full wrath of Whitehall and its attendant ghouls,' countered Bailrigg. 'It will not be Omri's future cast into the flames of hell. The FS will quite happily allow you to place your neck on the block and turn his back as the Intelligence and Security Committee bring down the axe.'

Nodding a tacit agreement at C's prophecy, Nick stared remotely ahead. High above the pen a deep blue sky slowly filled out with drifting shoals of clouds, a forceful wind bullying them inland as if they had no right to be lingering over the sea. Out on the salt marshes he heard the constant plaintive shrill calls of curlews, redshanks and oystercatchers chiming with the echoing volleys of small arms cracking back over sandbars from a distant range.

'I can't guarantee there won't be any blowback,' Nick proposed, staring directly at Bailrigg who for once didn't seem to care for any form of eye contact. 'You know that.'

'I *am* familiar with the implications of a find-fix-finish operation, thank you, Nicholas. I wasn't born behind a desk,' retorted Bailrigg curtly. 'My intake were the very last to complete the Arabic course at Shemlan before the war crept up to its doors in Seventy-Eight... Lebanon was my playground, it's where I cut my operational teeth, but that was before your time,' he added with a laconic flap of his gloved hand.

A different lifetime completely thought Nick. As far as he could remember, C counted as the highest-ranking member of an exclusive cadre, the Shemlan Descendant's Club, named after the FCO's Arabic language centre perched above Beirut.

On another range a klaxon emitted a short woeful wail before 81mm mortars boomed out in a continuous barrage, setting flocks of geese careering noisily into the air, their coarse honking crushed by further salvoes.

'And still we have no name for Rewall's Svengali other than his nomenclatures Hāru, Sahil and Khalid?'

'It's ultra priority on a number of lists.'

'I take it that you *do* have a strategy for the immediate bagging of high value targets when positive identification is confirmed?' Bailrigg demanded, absently following a cloud of dunlins streaking out towards a sandbar, their forlorn calls swirling behind them in the cold air.

'It's got beyond the planning stage,' Nick admitted.

'And how accurate is the information on the MFP safe houses?'

'We're confident the Plumstead one is still active,' Nick insisted.

'In his most generous display of cooperation, brother Langdon has pledged that we can have open season rounding-up the MFP on home turf. An unusual departure for the Director General of Security, but welcomed nonetheless. You shall have a two hour lead-in time,' Bailrigg decreed. 'Then I shall have to send in my boys and girls to mop your boot prints.'

A full tour of the pen completed, Bailrigg's pace lessened descending the berm's steps, as though putting off returning to his car.

'Appreciated.'

'I can only shield you from repercussions to a limited degree, Nicholas,' Bailrigg confirmed. 'With a general election in the wind, Downing Street is feverishly applying coats of Teflon to anything remotely connected to the PM. That, however, does not include the Foreign Secretary whose failure to make any lasting presence on policy has turned his staff into Dog Soldiers led by his Permanent Under Secretary. I bumped into him the other day as he came out of Number 10's garden entrance, and he had nothing but bile towards the FS. He accuses the FS of using Carlton Gardens and Chevening to keep his head down. To safeguard his own reputation, the FS will have no compunction in naming you as a fallen angel.'

'Every angel has its day.'

Shaking his head at Nick's wilful disregard of his warning, Bailrigg stomped off to his car.

Twenty-Two

They converged on the Plumstead address in two teams of three. Nick in command led the operation from the front on Rutherlean Road. Danny Redman supervised the rear, approaching through a garden backing onto Bostall Woods. Two minutes and twelve seconds past three on a dank February night, a creeping low band of mist claiming everything in sight. From Nick's position in the rear of one of the CO8 tactical team's plain, dark blue Mercedes Sprinters, the playground and crescent of trees at the road's end seemed to be eerily suspended off the ground.

'Tango clear.'

Nick gave a double click on his radio transmit button, acknowledging that their target address was isolated, its alarm box drilled, slowly packed with expanding foam before power and landlines were severed. In a side street in their own converted van parked in the long, clinging shadows beneath a block of maisonettes, a pair of GCHQ technicians initiated electronic jamming on the target property.

The MFP hadn't received much for their investment decided Nick, casting a tactical eye over the shabby semi-detached, its pebbledash the colour of ash, desolately plain. In the downstairs bay window he picked out a Neighbourhood Watch sticker on the glass and cream venetian blinds curled back down their right spine, noting how several grubby veins were twisted after being peeled back to monitor the road. In this pre-strike limbo, Nick counted down the minutes aware they were approaching one of the most risky phases of any operation, what in tradecraft jargon comes under the innocuous heading of *stealing fruit off the tree.*

The lonely strokes of a car's engine swam over the rooftops as it made headway on one of those mysterious night-time journeys. Three doors down a dog in a back garden set of a barked greeting to the unknown driver sharing the long, cold hours of darkness. And everyone, Nick included, froze.

'Romeo: I'm Foxtrot towards hound.'

'Zero,' replied Nick, his callsign used as confirmation.

Now totally awake the dog started to whine then whimper then launch into a series of abrupt early warning barks.

Over the net the operator gave a moment of light relief with her graphic description of the dog: 'Romeo. It's a shagging beast.'

'Zero: Then give it a taster from the pack,' urged Nick. 'Out.'

The 'pack' consisted of two prime cuts of sirloin laced with a sedative secured from a disgraced veterinary. A primary inclusion on many CO8 search and entry operations, the 'pack' through some arcane tradition became the responsibility of the newest member of the teams, which on this occasion happened to be callsign Romeo. In Nick's estimation, which was crude at the best of times, it could only have been just over a minute before Romeo once more came over the net.

'Romeo: It's out... stone cold... or it's dead. I'm going complete.'

'Zero,' answered Nick, wondering what the former vet had laced the steak with? A gnomish man with a palsied complexion he dispensed illegal animal cures and tonics from his flat in Paddington Green. He'd been struck off for creating a formula to enhance the speed of racing greyhounds. Several of the dogs treated with the concoction actually broke track records, but developed the disconcerting habit of dropping dead once they'd cleared the finishing line.

We've always sought out the misfits thought Nick, receiving a confirm call from another raiding party assembled in Fitzrovia. The odd loners with a particular skill or forgotten art, the dissatisfied, the eccentrics, even those harbouring a murderous grudge; we've always been the rightful employers of those adrift in society's dark shadows. And we are the lunatics who run the asylum he decided, giving the command 'Zero: All callsigns. Go...go... go...' into his radio.

As Nick padded up the front garden converted into a paved parking bay, one of his team gently worked open the front door's night latch. Motioning a colleague forward the operator eased back the door wide enough for a stubby pair of bolt cutters to sever the security chain.

In any breach entry there are those initial seconds when the operation gains its 'flow' or, as in a couple of cases Nick never forgot, the operation rapidly descends into an all out messy shambles. That morning Nick had the gods on his side and moving fast, his and Danny's teams silently converged at the foot of the stairs.

The air was cool, musty, releasing the sort of clinging taint occupying an empty, neglected property. A heap of junk mail mixed with flyers lay dumped on a dining chair, its back panel missing. Confirming the assigned roles of each operator using hand gestures, Nick signalled the teams to their positions, signing off with a gloved thumbs up.

A commercial treadmill big enough to form a barricade sat parked in the hallway. The front of its control panel discarded in a pile of components, dumped after the displays and motor had been cannibalised. Stacked on its belt a matching set of hard shell suitcases and a holdall, their baggage tags giving the final destination as Heathrow. As an identifying marker for the reclaim carousel, a cluster of maple leaves were artfully stuck in each corner with 'I love Canada' logos added for good measure.

Leaving two of Danny's team in the hallway Nick started a cautious, gentle climb towards the bedrooms, testing each tread before advancing. Pinned up on the drab stairway wall a large Palestinian flag partially covered oblongs and squares where framed prints and photographs had hung. On the quarter landing a leaded window had begun to bow inwards. Sections of it were taped up with cardboard, the remaining cracked panes let in an opaque grey from the subdued pre-dawn light.

Four paces down the corridor Nick held up a hand, pointing to himself and another member of the team for the main bedroom, consigning operators for the other bedrooms. Counting down from three on his fingers, Nick eased back a silver handle, crashing inside. At that point, quite unexpectedly, the operation collapsed.

Jerking bolt upright in a double bed opposite the bay window, a young woman greeted Nick with a piercing scream. Only when Nick ploughed into her, clamping his hand over her mouth did he manage to stem the hellfire racket. Something close to a scuffle occurred, though it didn't amount to much before Nick's team had the woman subdued, closely restrained.

'I want you to listen carefully,' Nick instructed her softly, bent close to the woman's ear. 'I am going to ask you some questions and all I require from you is the truth. Do you understand?'

The woman frantically nodded, her eyes wide in sheer horror had fixed on Nick's inside his full-face balaclava.

Slowly he lifted his hand away from her mouth, the leather around his fingers and palm covered in saliva trails.

'Where is Hassan Maghazi?'

Sitting upright, shivering in her white cotton vest, the woman shook her head in wild bemusement. 'I've never heard of a *Hassan*,' she vowed. 'It's the truth, I swear to God. Look, can I call the Canadian Embassy? They'll square everything, I swear.'

Firmly rejecting her request with a low stern: 'I'm afraid not,' Nick went after the visiting bomb maker from a different route. 'He might have used David or Dhakwan Mujib?' he snapped.

Grabbing at the lifeline, she nodded vigorously. Clasping her hands around her upper arms she smiled tepidly at Nick in a bid to break the hostility.

'Did you or did you not meet him?' he demanded, his tone unmoved at her attempt to create a personal bond.

'Yes,' she began, goosebumps raised amongst the tiny blonde hairs on her arms. 'But... as... *Dhakwan*.... Not... Hassan Maghazi,' she added and got no further.

In a coordinated move Nick withdrew as Romeo and another female operative supervised the woman as she dressed. Stunned, gripped by total disbelief, she emerged in a loose top, jogging bottoms and flip-flops, her long hair frizzed and tangled.

Her hands were locked behind her back with plastic cuffs. A thick band of tape was slapped across her mouth, and as she stood trembling in the corridor, a dark cotton hood was tugged over her head. Guided and assisted down the stairs, she was bundled over the treadmill. Passed over to Danny's operatives, the woman was run at a rapid trot through the hall and out of the front door, not stopping until she was lifted into the rear compartment of a grey Ford Transit, its engine smoothly ticking over.

After a fingertip search of each and every room scrupulously supervised by Nick and Danny, the bagged items left the property at a couple of minutes past six in the cargo cage of a small cream van. The haul was unusually meagre, consisting of rubbish from three wheelie bins, the contents of fridge and freezer, odds and ends of clothes gathered from dank wardrobes and drawers.

The largest pieces removed for further detailed analysis was the set of hard shell suitcases that had so far yielded nothing but holiday apparel, make-up and dirty laundry. At precisely 06.30 Nick handed the property over to the Service's scavengers who came prepared, their vans stencilled: 'General Building Work. Conversions. Renovations. We Care, We Repair.'

Twenty-Three

It was after seven that evening when Nick retired to a basement flat on Chelsea Bridge Road. In the tight narrow passageway that only Edwardian blocks can produce, Nick lounged beside a gaudy six by three canvas artfully splashed and dabbed into black objects sitting on crackled yellow squares. Rumour had it the piece had been an impulse buy at a student exhibition by a former Chief who fell out of love with it the moment it was hung.

The flat operated as a subsidiary isolation and debriefing centre for officers and assets suspected of being contaminated. For the last forty-eight hours the Service depository for the unwanted and damned served as Nick's base, his solitary home from home.

'Miss Jennifer Anne Ferney is refusing to cooperate any further unless she has consular representation,' Rossan explained, his face flushed in red blotches, the skin under his eyes dark, puffy.

He'd cornered Nick by the canvas between the kitchen and front sitting room when he came in a brisk burst along from a rear bedroom functioning as a technical monitoring suite.

'Well she can't,' Nick rejected the request out of hand. 'We'd lose her Paul, she'd be out of here and screaming blue murder.'

'We can hold her for another six hours, Nick. Perhaps eight with a favourable wind before we decide whether we request an extended stay,' he proposed, his shirtsleeves rolled loosely up to his elbows.

'Her story is still the same?'

'Everything in the same order, nothing omitted, nothing forgotten. Miss Jennifer Anne Ferney travelled to Hebron with no other motives than to display the largesse of a humanitarian. We're awaiting the arrival of a new team of thumbscrews. God knows when that could be.'

'She's been rehearsed,' Nick suggested. 'It's time to up the pressure.'

'We can try,' Rossan sighed in dismay as he set off behind his good friend.

Knocking once on a bare panelled door Nick and Rossan were admitted into the front sitting room by Dearham, callsign Romeo. Nodding for Dearham to return to her gatekeeping duties in the corridor, Nick took a cursory glance towards their guest.

Still dressed as Nick remembered her that morning, Jennifer Anne Ferney, 'Jen' to her family and intimate friends, watched Nick and Rossan enter with the keen eyes of a woman condemned. She remained stiff, awkward, her shoulders tight, her body rigidly locked in the centre of a dowdy floral sofa.

Gazing straight through her Nick strolled past a line of bookcases, their glass doors smudged, dust ground into the corners. He opted for a beaten leather chair wedged between a sideboard and a pair of mature oak cabinets, the wood around the drawers grubby, darkly stained. The continuous flow of traffic grinding away outside gave the room its own mechanical soundtrack. The sweeping rush of headlights dashing against the plain walls deepened the layer of dusk claiming the flat. Completing the sense of confinement, the room was permanently in shadow from mature trees ringing Ranelagh Gardens, the retractable white lattice security grille adding to a dour, sterile atmosphere.

'Your trip to Hebron, let's start with that again,' insisted Nick earnestly. 'Work or pleasure?'

'I already told the other two,' she protested. Taking deep breaths she gave a plausible impression of a much misunderstood, innocent traveller.

'I'm afraid I wasn't present,' Nick said officiously.

Looking round to Rossan on a high back chair just out of the yellow beacon of light from a fringed shaded standard lamp, she pleaded: 'Tell him.'

'He has to hear it for himself,' Rossan said with an apologetic tilting of his shoulders, sitting back like a dance hall chaperone, relegated to the hazy glow ringing the room.

As for Nick's demeanour, Rossan swore that his friend behaved as though his personality had been surgically removed, for there was never a glimpse of warmth, humour or sympathy.

'We do have confirmation that your travel documents are legitimate and that you *are* a resident of Toronto,' announced Nick archly, his authoritarian stare remote, determinedly cold. 'Other than that, I've no idea why you visited the Occupied Territories?'

She laughed, shaking her tapered head at the crazy madness she was trapped in. The movement set free strands of hair wedged behind her ears; the rest remained in place, bound obediently together in a healthy ponytail.

'Look,' she said, sounding desperate, 'I was over there for a month as the guest of the Free Palestine Committee in Hebron.'

'A semi-official umbrella for the international groups pledged to the cause,' Rossan said, acting as scribe, and in way of thanks, received a brief nod of gratitude from Nick.

'The conference...'

'It was on nation and nationhood,' she angrily cut in. 'I'm the coordinator of the Friends of Palestine Society at university.'

'Which would be?'

'Alberta. I'm in my final year of a political science degree.'

'It's all been checked, cross-checked and verified,' Rossan affirmed.

'Other than the conference, what other activities did you undertake during your trip?' Nick's detached gaze never varied nor moved more than an inch from the Canadian's face.

'We went on West Bank excursions,' she retorted sullenly.

'And that's when you met someone?'

For the first time Rossan could remember, Ferney began to treat the interview as a threat, unsure how it should be played.

Starting with her reply, she faltered, and then sighed several times. 'Yeah... I got chatting to another delegate.'

'This delegate... did they happen to be a senior figure with the European Foundation for Palestinian Refugees,' suggested Nick. 'Is that correct.'

'Yeah, I guess...' Ferney grudgingly agreed.

'Yes or no.'

Her manner shifted towards open defiance as Ferney for reasons known only to her, decided to make a stand. Pursing her lips she sat mutely back, her legs crossed, her arms folded defiantly across her chest.

'Does it matter?'

'For me... no. For you? Yes, it matters a great deal,' Nick advised her. 'You knew this delegate was a member of the EFPR?'

'Yeah,' she admitted as part of a long, protracted sigh. 'Look... are you guys Israeli or something?'

'We're something...' Nick rudely retorted. 'The delegates name, was it

Leila Kuatli?' he asserted, retaking the high ground once more.

Suddenly alert, Ferney sat forward as though rudely roused from a light sleep.

'If you're that smart to know all this stuff, then you'd know that I'm just interested in making the world aware of the suffering Palestinians are put through by Israel,' she snapped fully engaged, her eyes brimming with a quite frightening zeal.

Forgoing a hasty reaction to the rant, Nick took a moment's reflection. 'Do we have anything on Kuatli?' He directed his loaded prompt to Rossan who had wisely decided to remain on the outside of the ropes.

As a good cornerman Rossan had come prepared with all the background Nick requested.

'Not only a talent spotter,' Rossan explained patiently. 'Kuatli is a mentor and trainer for girl volunteers joining the MFP's Martyrs Unit. She acquired bomb making skills from her father in the Bekáa Valley.'

'She wires up the vests?'

'Very efficiently,' Rossan agreed. 'The unit is responsible for seventeen attacks targeting supermarkets and cafés in Jerusalem and Tel Aviv. They are believed to be responsible for thirty fatalities and fifty-five wounded.'

'And Kuatli still finds time to recruit volunteers?'

'It's another of her specialities,' said Rossan diligently.

'This is all so much bullshit, it just isn't true,' Ferney protested; her whole body now completely animated. 'You guys are crazy, you're seriously beginning to freak me out,' she yelled, up on her feet.

Entering fast as if to quell a riot, Dearham took up station beside Ferney.

'She lays a hand on me and I'll sue, Jesus Christ, I'll sue,' the Canadian vowed, swiping back a ribbon of hair that had detached from her ponytail.

'We'll be fine, thank you,' Nick assured Dearham who glared a warning at Ferney before returning to her post in the corridor.

'Let's resume with your trip to Hebron, shall we,' suggested Nick with the cool aplomb of soothing a student through a testing seminar.

'Sure... why not,' Ferney irritably agreed, sitting back. Discharging her anger with a brutal slap of the sofa arm, she dutifully relayed the explanation she'd already delivered to Rossan in her very first session. 'Leila... the Leila I *know* and met,' she stated forcefully, 'suggested I round off my trip with a short stay with her in Beirut. I wasn't sure, my funds were pretty low and I had exams in a couple of months. She sold me the trip when she promised to arrange a visit to her mother in the Burj el-Shemali camp outside Tyre. Seemed like a heaven sent opportunity to see the real Palestinian struggle, so I accepted. We...'

'Who drove to Tyre?' Nick interjected.

'Leila.'

'A two hour drive down the expressway isn't it?'

'Yeah, something like that I guess.'

'When you reached the camp, what happened then?'

Kuatli's role as an MFP talent spotter was blatantly obvious he reasoned, if that indeed was her actual name. And the objective behind Ferney's recruitment stood tantalisingly close. After identifying Ferney, the experienced Kuatli charmed her, she wooed her and then she'd hit her with the soft sell. In Nick's experience the recruitment had to contain both logical and emotional triggers, which Ferney confirmed with her very next breath.

'Leila's mom was great,' admitted Ferney buoyed by her remembered enthusiasm. 'She was seventy but looked ninety because of the Zionist cruelty she'd suffered. I just *had* to listen as Leila translated her mom's story of how she'd survived after being kicked out of her homeland. How she came close to being killed in Eighty-Two when the Israeli military thugs poured into Lebanon. It all took its toll mentally and physically. The mom has real bad arthritis, and I guess the start of dementia, but she'd spent a day preparing our meal, stroked my hair and called me her new daughter.'

Cue the tears and convincer Nick thought absently.

'There and then I'd made up my mind I'd be willing to do anything to show my solidarity with this Palestinian family.'

'Did Kuatli ask you for a favour at any point? Ask you to carry out a small deed of kindness perhaps?'

'You're just like the others who don't trust a single Palestinian,' she shouted, fired up once more, 'you're another crappy Zionist appeaser. All the Palestinians want is peace, don't *you people get that? When are you going to stop siding with the aggressors?* Israel is only interested in the illegal expansion of its territory, not for sharing or coexisting.'

She threw out the propaganda with the passion of the initiated, part of the inflammatory rhetoric employed by the radical cheerleaders of both sides; the dedicated supporters who saw only their perspective in stark black and white. Despite the Canadian's accusations, Nick blithely pressed on with his next point: 'When did Kuatli ask for your help?'

Under Ferney's sleek defined jawline she had a beauty spot that she ran a tip of a finger across when under pressure; in the last few minutes Nick noted she did it rather a lot.

'During the drive back to Beirut, okay.'

'I would like the details,' pressed Nick.

Sighing, uncrossing and refolding her legs, Ferney admitted: 'Okay... Leila told me that her mother's health meant she would never see her dreams of a homeland come true. If I'd really like to make a difference to the Palestinian fight for freedom, I could. And that just broke my heart.'

Which probably could not be said of Kuatli thought Nick, wondering how many other gullible useful idiots from the West she had recruited.

'How were you meant to do that? It wasn't by trying to smuggle something in to London was it?'

'Her bags have been cleared,' Rossan disclosed, 'swabbed, sniffed and X-rayed.'

'If it didn't involved you as a mule, then you could be an operational courier,' speculated Nick. 'But there are far more secure forms of transportation, so I don't think they would use you for that. If it isn't smuggling *or* as a courier your Palestinian friends wanted you for, then it must be *you* that is of value,' he proposed earnestly.

From somewhere in the hazy ring of half-light Rossan had decided to stretch his legs and the leather soles of his shoes squawked ferociously on the vinyl flooring.

Possessing, it seemed, all the time in the world, Nick sat back and permitted the silence to gather in strength.

Working up the momentum to speak Ferney stroked the beauty spot. 'It was going to be a public demonstration of solidarity,' she said and quite genuinely seemed out of breath.

'You alright?' Nick asked.

'I think I'm going to throw up.'

Answering Nick's summons, Dearham promptly escorted the Canadian to the bathroom.

Taking advantage of the star witness' absence, Rossan broke cover.

'Honestly Nick, do you believe she is in the operational loop?' he asked pacing remotely in front of the sofa. 'A demonstration... public solidarity... Dear God,' he added, rolling his eyes at Ferney's admission.

'It's the best we have, so let's hear her out,' said Nick non-committally.

Which they did, after an interval of ten minutes.

When the Canadian returned supported by Dearham, she sipped tentatively from a glass of water.

'Better?'

'Sort of,' Ferney said, smiling at Dearham as she withdrew.

The strain, the relentless isolation and tiredness had eaten into her skin. Her paleness made her look dreadfully ill, as did the deep red segments under her eyes.

'Tell me about this demonstration,' Nick gently probed.

'It was going to be my chance to make a difference,' she said, and stopped to clear her throat. 'I would disrupt an event. It would create attention and headlines to keep the Palestinian cause alive.'

'Who is organising the event?'

Flattening her hands palm down on her thighs so her fingertips rested just above her knees, Ferney gazed at them as if really seeing where she was for the first time. 'I wasn't told.'

'Your role, the method of how you were to cause this *disruption*, these details were given to you by Kuatli?'

Nodding morosely, Ferney threw her head back into the sofa's back cushion, closing her eyes as she revealed the part Leila had cast her in.

'Really it was just a matter of making a scene,' Ferney said and even though she chose not see them, she somehow knew she had Nick and Rossan's full attention.

To create maximum effect, Ferney was going to wait until some sort of dinner was underway and make her entrance dressed as a member of the catering team, she explained. 'It was a two act play,' she divulged, her voice relaxed. The first act would involve making a big impression by pitching smoke grenades in and around the tables.

'How many were you going to release?' Nick asked.

'Six, eight, ten maybe,' she said her eyes firmly shut. 'When I'd achieved maximum disruption and everyone was evacuated, I'd hang around for the cops to come and bust my ass.'

'The event is here, in London?'

Delaying her reply, Ferney rolled her head slowly left and right as if determined to unwind. 'I wasn't given the info, it was better for me not to know until the day of the event,' she finally stated.

'Everything we have points to it being here,' Rossan put in.

'And it was just a big scene you were planning? That was it?'

'Yeah,' Ferney agreed, totally at ease.

'How were you going to get access to the event?'

'It was all arranged.'

'Who by?'

'A buddy of Dhakwan's... Jesus... a buddy of this guy Hassan Maghazi,' she said. 'Maghazi's buddy was going to take care of things.'

'No one would be harmed? Is that what Leila told you?'

'In the panic there'd be injuries, maybe some people with heart conditions wouldn't come out smiling, but that crap could happen to them at anytime. We were going to get the attention of the media, maybe a top spot on the TV news, a decent story on page two or three in the papers, a mention on the radio, probably mega clicks on the Internet...'

'A terrorist attack with a decent body count, *that* would guarantee headlines,' suggested Nick, glancing at Rossan. 'I've got a different scenario of how your disruption would unfold. Your big entrance and smoke grenades – all that would take place as promised. Then Maghazi's friend, perhaps with an AK-47, or similar weapon, opens up on the guests. There'd be a stampede for the exits and that's just what Maghazi and his commanders' desire. You were only meant to be the catalyst. On the street parked strategically would be vehicles carrying IEDs. You know what they are?'

Reacting as if slapped hard, Ferney's head snapped forward off the back cushion. Her eyes, wide open, were locked on Nick in a mixture of hate and horror. 'You're lying.' But even she didn't find her accusation quite convincing.

'Each device could easily kill and maim over a hundred. But these aren't normal IEDs, they're different, they contain a mixture of fuel as well. It would be carnage. That would give you your headlines.'

'No...no...no..., you got it all wrong,' Ferney protested, her voice at full pitch brought Dearham into the room.

Holding up his hand Nick kept Dearham at bay, and she stepped nimbly back towards the door. 'Believe me, we *have* evidence that an attack is due to be carried out,' he said patiently. 'Where is Maghazi?'

Struggling up off the sofa Ferney pressed one hand firmly against her forehead, muttering 'Shit...shit...shit,' as she paced frantically back and forth maintaining a straight line.

'Hassan Maghazi,' Nick reminded her.

Glancing sharply at Nick then just as quickly away, Ferney stumbled out a response: 'Er... uh... Mm... He... er... he had to return to... er... Beirut.'

'When did he leave?'

'Mm... *I don't know*...,' she flashed in an angry response, throwing up both arms in exasperation. 'He told me when he met me at... er...at the station when I... er... got in from Heathrow... He told that his mom was real sick... Dhakwan... *shit*... Hassan... er... needed to get home and so he gave me the keys to his place.'

'How were you going to be contacted?'

'Er... Um... Okay... Listen, this is going to help me, right? All the information I've given... that's got to count for something, right? The event... it's got be soon... you got to find out what it is ... so you can stop it going bad...'

For a while Nick didn't answer. His face, his entire taut body seemed absorbed by a different proposition, even though his weary eyes were fixed to the hazy, unwashed window where legs and ankles filed past on the pavement outside, the unknown travellers slipping effortlessly into the thickening shadows of the night.

'Give us Leila and we might have a deal?' proposed Nick having given the arrangements a good amount of thought.

'Dear God,' said Rossan not quite on the same page as Nick.

'Leila is here in London, isn't she?' Nick sounded far from friendly.

'Listen... what if you guys have got it all wrong about Leila... She isn't a terrorist... you got her mixed up with someone else...' Ferney desperately suggested. 'I know her, okay, she wouldn't use me like this.'

She's in denial decided Nick, seeing the tears slither down Ferney's cheeks. 'Where is Leila?'

'Leila's going to keep in touch on her mobile... When everything's prepared, she'll arrange to pick me up,' she volunteered with the assurance of having made the right choice to save herself.

'Has she called?'

'A couple of times.'

'I'll need your phone,' explained Nick.

•••

Alone once more in his temporary refuge following Ferney's departure under the close watch of Dearham supervised by Rossan, the long hours of pre-operational preparation began with Nick selecting two teams of eight. There were a series of encrypted calls to be made which ran on until well after one in the morning. Pouring himself a glass of Laphroaig Nick stretched out on the sofa.

Barely able to keep his eyes open he jumped with a start when a bang and a muffled male voice leaked down from the flat above as if someone bound and gagged was being flogged – which they very might well have been, Nick thought. He had met the tenant in the communal hallway as she brought home two bags of shopping. A ferocious buxom blonde who called herself Lady Sonja, she had a partiality for dressing in leather, for wearing sunglasses whatever the weather; a habit not only lending her a mysterious charm, they were probably also worn to disguise her age, Nick decided. She also ran a thriving business dealing in commercial love of the bondage kind Nick had realised from his first night in the flat, watching the furtive arrival and departure of her many men friends; one of them a respected human rights barrister.

•••

Moving in a fast convoy three pickup trucks bounced along the rock embedded trail, kicking up swirls of dust to mark their progress up from Assal Alward on the Syrian side of the border. Sitting inside the flat bed of a Toyota pickup, Hāru jolted and rolled along with his two bodyguards armed with AK-47s, the Toyota slamming into the deep washboard ruts cut by winter snow and spring floods. Clinging on opposite Hāru, an MFP section leader clutched a rocket launcher, continuously scanning the ridges for hostile activity.

Standing forward on permanent lookout, a fourth member of the pickup's rear party manned a Russian SPG-9, a 72mm recoilless gun, pivoting it menacingly out over the cab. In another ten minutes they swept into Ain el Maara, a village cupped in a high plateau of the eastern mountain range. Abandoned during the Israeli's withdrawal in 2000, the half-dozen houses were more or less cut off from Lebanon, and the area had gained something of a wild reputation.

With the village sitting plumb on an ancient caravan trail popular with Bekáa hashish suppliers, only those with a legitimate reason bothered to make the gruelling trek anymore. Bribery of governorate officials, skirmishes with Syrian rebels, intimidation of charity workers and outright assassination gave the MFP a free hand.

They levied a substantial tax on refugees escaping the civil war on their trek from the southern fringes of Damascus towards the border and the shanty camps around Hammana in Lebanon. Harassment amounted to a daily ritual. Shootings though less frequent still brought a weekly toll of deaths, disfiguring wounds and downright fear that the local MFP commander encouraged his *fedayeen* to inflict on anybody who questioned their control.

Skidding to a stop outside one of the single storey mud block and render houses clinging to the dusty escarpment, the forward MFP base commanded a dominant position above a winding pass carrying the main refugee traffic. On Hāru's orders his two bodyguards dismounted, taking up position by the lowered tailgate. Dressed in Syrian Army combats Hāru jumped down, slapping away outstretched helping hands.

Acknowledging the whispered warning of a solo pickup bumping up the final stretch from Lebanon, Hāru harnessed his thoughts, cut off a question and focused firmly on his duty.

The Nissan truck cut into a sharp right arc to pull alongside the Toyota, four *fedayeen* in its open deck, two to its left, two its right as it halted in a burst of powdery dust. One man leapt over the side wall dropping the tailgate, his three comrades dragged and kicked a hooded prisoner off the truck. Grabbed by his shirt, arms, anywhere that offered a hold, the man was bundled in front of Hāru. Coming quickly to the rear from riding in the passenger seat Lydia Hallam arranged herself by Hāru's side, her combats coated in dust from the drive. On Hāru's nod the hood was ripped off the prisoner. With one backward blow Hallam struck the prisoner across the jaw, a 9mm pistol lodged in her fist.

'You vowed that you would never fail me in your duties, Amud,' Hāru announced, lifting the man's face up from it where it hung semi-consciously on his chest. Turning it this way and that Hāru examined the man's partially closed bruised eyes, the dried blood under his nose, under his bottom lip. 'Why do you wish to betray us, brother?' Hāru asked softly, an uncomfortable question for everyone concerned.

'It is a lie,' Amud grunted, his cheeks and jaw pinched hard in Hāru grip. 'I carried out all my duties. I did everything you demanded.'

'No, brother, it is the truth that I speak. You prefer to work for the Zionists and their imperialist backers, is that not true?'

The MFP man attempted to shake his head in denial, but could only manage a slight painful, jerky movement.

'You were seen talking to an American in Beirut, is that not true? Is it because your life is too precious to be sacrificed? Is it because you have accepted the American's payment? You have stained your family with the stench of a traitor. I can smell it on your skin. Why did you not report the Americans know your identity? Why did you wish to betray our brave fighters?'demanded Hāru, his accusations rising. He released Amud's cheek and jaw his head shaken in pity, in sorrow, at such a betrayal.

'I swear I am not a traitor...'

'Do you think I am so stupid to believe your lies? Did you think that I would not be informed of your acts of treason, of your weakness?'

Saying nothing, Amud's head sank once more heavily against his filthy, bloodied shirt. Nodding Hallam forward, Hāru sighed. 'You have failed our people, your family and your brother *fedayeen*.' On Hāru's next nod Hallam stepped forward, her 9mm Makarov pistol raised. Slowly levelling the barrel she fired one round into Amud's temple.

Wiping off flecks of blood that had dashed his cheek, Hāru stood back as his *fedayeen* dragged the body over to their Nissan. A length of chain tossed down from the truck was attached to the tow bar, its other end wrapped and padlocked around the dead man's wrists.

'Return the traitor to his home.'

'It will be done,' one of the *fedayeen* promised, returning to his pickup. Hāru climbed back onto the Toyota, his eyes locked on the departing truck accelerating away for the Lebanese border, Amud's body tossing, pitching and bounding along behind.

Twenty-Four

Alongside Paul Rossan on the rear seats of an adapted, metallic grey Mercedes Vito crew van, Nick coordinated the concluding measures in the stop and seize operation on Kuatli and Maghazi – codenamed HARP and FLUTE – from a stretch of rough, uneven road on Wharf Street, Plaistow. The time, approaching seven on a clear evening, brought with it a sky peppered by stars. One of them must be lucky, thought Nick.

In their earpieces they had reports from static and mobile tactical surveillance units covering all the approaches to a shuttered workshop on Bidder Street, codenamed: 'Red One'.

Across the street, uneven stacks of wrecked cars and vans peeped above the powdery brick perimeter wall of a desolate, battered scrap metal wharf.

'Hotel: All callsigns. Vehicle making a right at Blue One Four. Two-up. It's a negative for targets, repeat negative. Ignore. Over.'

'Quebec: Hotel. Is it worth doing another walk by?'

'Hotel: Me or you?'

'Quebec: Me.'

'Hotel: Too much of a risk, I have three, repeat three, possible routes from Blue Box. You may lose eyes on Flute if he exits via the rear.'

'Quebec: Remaining static.'

Giving a double click 'yes' as confirmation of having received callsign Quebec's decision, Nick watched one of his pavement teams shuffling on the spot to ward off the bitter evening chill.

'Cheltenham *are* confident they've established Kuatli's location from her phone pinging off that particular tower, aren't they?' Rossan wanted to know, tapping his feet in a quick, steady impatient beat, the old fieldman in him let loose for a rare outing.

'They've given us a generous ninety-two per cent guarantee. Danny's also made a visual confirm on her,' Nick assured him. 'With Ferney on a short lead....' He paused when the door to a pub on the corner banged open releasing a hard faced drinker in his sixties. 'Kuatli shouldn't notice anything out of place. She's paid two visits to the workshop, always in the company of Maghazi,' he added, acutely aware they hadn't identified the target event or its location.

'Do we presume she's controlling the spectacular?'

'Seems to be she's got the baton,' said Nick, his attention on the drinker taking long, satisfied draws on a cigarette.

'We let it unfold along a path of least resistance,' Rossan insisted.

'As long as Kuatli and Maghazi don't decide to make a stand.'

Nodding vaguely, Rossan concentrated on the radio traffic from Danny's team fed through a different network from their positions in Stroud Green. 'Everyone is clear the rules of engagement have been suspended?' he wondered.

About to respond, Nick grimaced as he struggled to hear the latest updates on Kuatli. 'Sierra: Harp showing activity at Green Four.'

'November: Got it. Bathroom light's on at Green Four.'

'Zero: All callsigns. It's just a test of our patience ladies and gentlemen,' Nick advised his teams. 'Sorry,' he said to Rossan, 'you mentioned rules of engagement?'

The moment lost, Rossan smiled, shook his head. 'It was nothing,' he decided. 'You've quite enough to handle.'

We all have too much to handle, thought Nick.

This is where our whole show could become an instant flop. This is where a MFP commander we didn't know about spoils the performance by bursting from their safe house with a squad of highly trained *fedayeen*. Kuatli and Maghazi were sold to us as decoys. The genuine bombers have slipped the net, giving them a clear run to wreak mayhem, carnage and destruction. With a bit of imagination the Foreign Secretary could apportion all the blame for the MFP's reign of terror on me, label me an out of control maverick and seek a solution from another route.

We've one go at stopping Kuatli and Maghazi and we've nothing left. One go and we could mess up, one go and we're left wide open. One go and it all goes down the pan and I'm sacrificed for all my sins.

The limits of his solo and double teams out there worried him. How many times do you pretend that your engine's failed? How long can you hold a kiss for? Tie and untie a bootlace in the doorway of a shuttered sandwich bar? Wait on a corner for a lift that is never going to arrive? Push your luck for that extra minute or an hour? Wait for the targets to make their moves? Nick stared into the night; a void where inhabitants of the day couldn't reach you, infect you, solicit you, worry you, depress you, marry you, divorce you. In the night nothing mattered except your desire to face what you are, what you'd become.

•••

So why had he not called earlier to explain he would not be ready? Glancing at her phone she estimated a window of only ten minutes remaining to guarantee she'd safely hit tonight's deadline for completing the final preparation. With each wasted minute she cursed Maghazi's arrogance, his assumption he had somehow gained total control, how he ruined schedules to suit *his* side of the operation. Because of him she might not even complete her dry run this evening. The longer she left the girl Ferney waiting there was every chance the Canadian could get cold feet, do something stupid to alert the authorities.

Irritated, Kuatli eased into her leather jacket, slipped on her shoes, concentrating on bringing all the different strands together to guarantee her side of the attack was a success. Double locking the front door she kept her head down until she'd cleared the garden path, adhering to her counter-surveillance training of avoiding unnecessary contact with any neighbours. She read the street both ways checking doorways, assessing corners she'd identified as potential ambush spots.

Her steady, dark amber eyes glanced into vans, lingered on front windows searching for that one giveaway shadow of a concealed enemy. Moving fast, her small heeled shoes skimmed the puddles, her long wavy hair flowing over her shoulders. Always at these late stages of operations, her sense of vulnerability became intense, forcing her to listen for that one engine in a thousand, for those footsteps you knew were going to be deadly. A nasty, bitter wind drying the edges of deep puddles raised tears in her eyes. Keeping one hand on the flap of her shoulder bag she brushed them impatiently away with the other.

A hundred yards to cover before the right turn leading her into a ginnel, then she'd have the rough lane between the houses to negotiate. Her behaviour remained natural, maintaining her fast, fluid steps into the ginnel. From experience she avoided anything out of the ordinary, ensured she did nothing memorable to risk the chance of drawing unwanted attention. Confident she had regained control of her routine, she slowed to the same measured pace she always adopted on the gravel lane. Along the short walk to a wide cinder plot she carefully monitored the overgrown crescent of waste ground surrounding garages corralled in 'U' shaped bays.

For the first time on any of her visits Kuatli hesitated. Unzipping her bag she rested a hand on her 9mm pistol. Some of the garages were ancient with apex felt roofs, their creosoted timber walls heavily patched, the double doors triple padlocked. Others were newer, replacements boasting flat roofs sitting over concrete panel shells. She'd hated the place on her first nightly visit, blaming Maghazi for not consulting her before renting what served as one of their temporary stores. The place unsettled her then, and did so every time she made a collection or deposited an item. Patches of dense, heavy shadows seemed to be lying in wait for her between the garages, pummelling her nerves on every trip.

Tonight her apprehension had rocketed, causing her to hold off her approach. Forty paces to their store, the last garage in a row of four lining the right side of a bay. A pair of old lights flung a broad white beam across the wooden doors to their store. On other nights she welcomed the extra safety, blessed its protection. Now those stark lights stung her into extra vigilance when she finally proceeded in a headlong rush to the store.

A trail bike engine throttled up somewhere behind her. Kuatli spun on her heels, the cinders scrunching. Panning her pistol in a wide arc she caught a blur of movement off to her left. Swinging back she aimed at the spot, squinting into the shadows, searching for a target. The bike came at her from her right, its wheels churning the cinders. Smacked hard, squarely in her back by the rider's solid boot, Kuatli went down. Grit under her nails, her palms and knees shrieking, she closed her eyes. Counting to ten she lifted her head. A foot behind her, a rider in helmet and leathers stretched out a hand, a semi-automatic waiting for her next move.

'Stay down,' one of Danny's team screamed at Kuatli. 'Stay down.'

'Place your hands slowly by your head,' another team member yelled.

Almost, just for a second, did she consider resisting, even going as far to raise a shoe up off the cinders.

'*Alllaenat ealayk*,' Kuatli screamed, a knee landing painfully in her back, a firm gloved hand clamped around her neck pinning her down.

'Fuck you too,' someone responded.

'No vest...' She heard one of the voices shout. 'Stay down,' she was fiercely reminded, a military style boot clamped painfully tightly on her right wrist.

'I want a lawyer,' she bawled, shards of cinder grinding into her cheek, her jaw, when she made her choked demand.

Kneeling by her side Danny Redman's dark shape leaned over Kuatli, his finger tapped twice against her exposed temple making sure he had her attention. 'We decide who you see,' he grunted, going roughly through Kuatli's pockets, searching for the garage key, 'that includes lawyers.'

•••

A crackling over the radio net summoned Nick back to the next pressing task of dealing with Maghazi.

'Hotel: I have Flute intending departure.'

'Zero: All callsigns. We want a clean take,' Nick reminded them, having reached his own pavement spot across from the workshop.

'Quebec: Standby... standby. Flute complete.'

'Zero: All callsigns. Flute en route. Let's make sure we don't show our hand until he's in the box. Only engage the van as a last resort, we can't be sure it isn't carrying a viable device,' Nick urged, his orders issued at fourteen minutes past eight.

In a fast relay Nick received the confirmation that his teams were prepared. Then one by one in a smooth transition, each callsign handed over the command of Flute with the clipped efficiency of air traffic controllers. Behind him Nick heard callsign Oscar's Yamaha fire up followed by a BMW M5, one of the team's pursuit vehicles. A couple of yards ahead in a Vauxhall Insignia, their main blocking car, callsigns Uniform and Golf gave thumbs up over their radios. Anticipation rose across Nick's team, he could almost feel it through the airwaves. It's going to happen. It's going to fall apart. Nick peered through the misty evening gloom laying claim to the street. Callsign Oscar on her race-tuned Yamaha remained at the kerb waiting to fall in behind Flute, confirmed as the solo occupant of a Renault panel van.

'Lima: Flute just pulled up on double yellows on Orange Two Four. No contact.'

'Papa: I have Flute foxtrot to newsagents.'

'Zero: Keep close eyes on him.'

'Papa: Roger, out.'

Ignoring other driver's blaring their horns at his van blocking a lane, Flute took what to Nick felt like an hour inside the shop, but the actual duration was actually something less than five minutes.

With callsign Papa given radio priority, mushy static drifted over the net, distinctly racking up the tension. Once Flute resumed his journey Nick's teams broke from their original surveillance posts, taking up fresh positions for the seize. Aware that he had all the balls in the air, Nick's earpiece buzzed with Papa informing everyone that: 'Flute is complete towards Oscar and I am off.'

And you keep driving straight and true Nick silently urged Maghazi, squinting into the oncoming headlights sweeping into the street. The Renault van manoeuvred slowly up to the drop kerb outside Maghazi's rented workshop.

Don't jump the gun, Nick pleaded silently with Uniform and Golf in the briefest of pauses before he gave the 'Go. Go. Go,' command. Working in choreographed precision the Insignia and Audi roared up behind the Renault boxing in the rear of the van in a 'V'. Out of the Audi in record time, Tango sprinted for his allotted covering position facing the driver's door, his C8 carbine levelled. Nick, barely a couple of yards to cover before linking up with Tango, felt the powerful wash of adrenalin heighten his concentration.

Covering the passenger side, Uniform with her HK MP5 and Golf with his Sig P226 made out Maghazi scrabbling under his seat. In close harmony they yelled out a warning.

Inside ten or eleven seconds the world around Nick shattered into a sequence of slow motion overlaps. Viewed in jarring, uncoordinated segments, Maghazi kicked open his door firing a burst from a machine pistol. A collection of screamed alerts ripped from different callsigns. A couple of muzzle flashes burst the van's side windows and windscreen. One moment Tango was standing then he was gone.

With the machine pistol slung around his back, Maghazi vaulted a pavement railing, landing on his toes, slamming both hands hard into Oscar's chest, tumbling her off the Yamaha, her machine clattering heavily onto her right leg. Sprinting on, Maghazi brought his machine pistol around. Half turned, he fired a random burst on automatic behind him. The light weapon rose in a flinch when he fired, each round going high, missing their targets. Bolting off, Maghazi sprinted towards the creek.

Assisted by Golf and Uniform, Oscar righted her bike, accelerating hard, blasting past Nick to draw level with Maghazi. Abruptly halting, he took aim with his machine pistol. Oscar zigzagging wildly kept going. Swinging the bike around in a fast turn the rear tyre smoking, Oscar came at Maghazi again, catching him with a fierce blow to the right of his trim body, tumbling him along the tarmac, spilling her off the bike.

Bleeding from grazes to his face Maghazi scrambled to his feet, squeezing the trigger at Oscar as he ran but the weapon jammed.

He's wound up and hasn't cleared it before, decided Nick, less than five yards behind Maghazi and gaining. Flowing into Nick's earpiece jumbled reports from callsigns handling the chaos at the workshop, streamed in alongside the curt updates from team members attempting to go round the flanks to cut Maghazi off.

His pace decreasing, a distinct hobble noticeable in his right leg, Maghazi frantically glanced behind as he heaved himself over a striped traffic barrier at a side entrance to the scrap metal wharf.

'Zero: All callsigns,' Nick breathlessly transmitted. 'Flute's heading for the creek. Position: Purple Six One.'

A flurry of double clicks rapidly bounced into Nick's earpiece.

'Put down your weapon,' he bawled at Maghazi, drawing his Sig.

Doubled over, sucking hard for breath, Maghazi locked his hands onto his knees like an exhausted athlete, the machine pistol dangling loosely in front of his chest by its webbing strap. Defiantly ignoring Nick, shaking his head in stubborn refusal, Maghazi started to back down a flight of stone stairs cut into the wharf.

Limping, pausing, limping again, Maghazi rapidly cleared his weapon. Tapping the magazine against the head of a metal bollard on a stone landing, he racked back the slide. For Nick remaining on the wharf above Maghazi, the bomber had run out of options, his body out of energy.

Jerking his head round to his left Maghazi momentarily shifted his weight from his lame leg, glancing up at the arrival of Uniform and Golf, their weapons drawn. Not far away and getting louder, a massed band of sirens. Repeatedly screaming *Victory for Palestine*, Maghazi charged the steps, his machine pistol lifted in one hand. Raising his free hand in a clenched fist salute, Maghazi squeezed the trigger. But he was too late. Hit by a rapid volley of rounds from Nick, Uniform and Golf, at least fourteen, Maghazi was dead when he hit the landing.

Twenty-Five

Religiously each morning Nick called Rowena in the Mad House to check on Matt Lorris's – callsign Tango – condition. Without exception his deputy gave the same terse response of 'VSI. No change,' and Nick, his mood rarely rising out of a dark, explosive sense of remorse paced out his anger on the veranda of Lemmings Beach café, resigned that Lorris's very seriously ill status would never improve.

It was a freak wound Rossan repeatedly told Nick during several long, soul searching days immediately after the termination of Maghazi, insisting Nick had no reason to shoulder all the blame or guilt.

But he did. He constantly dwelt on the round's trajectory; the double deflection it took, the first from the van's door, the second from Matt's elbow steering it under his cheekbone, embedding itself behind his left eye, fragments continuing on into his brain. He played over and over the medical team's assessment of Matt as only having a forty per cent chance of survival, and if he did pull through, he would, in all probability, remain in a coma.

After that morose diagnosis, Nick, according to Roly, pulled on his hermit's coarse hood and cloak for an 'off-grid' spot of recovery. The last people to see him on what Roly termed 'the UK's hallowed shores' were Rossan and Danny who partook in a farewell drink of fruit juice with Nick in the bar of RAF Brize Norton's Gateway Hotel before he boarded a flight to Cyprus.

He had been on the island two weeks gearing up for a showdown with Hāru, codenamed Operation Flame. Implemented on the very first day, Nick's routine consisted of an early morning run invariably avoiding the Episkopi Garrison's cluster of cafés and shops playfully nicknamed *Dodge City*. The majority of his course took in the perimeter roads lined with accommodation blocks, the garrison general stores, workshops and transport lines before hitting the uphill dusty tracks towards the range with a turn always taken at the satellite ground section.

On the return leg he would sometimes branch left at the fire station and go part way towards the officers' mess and Kensington Cliffs. On other mornings dictated by his mood, Nick remained steadfastly to the right, passing the medical and dental centre, picking up his pace as he pounded his way down to Lemmings Beach. There he'd make his solitary call to Rowena from outside the café gloomily shuttered until spring.

On today's run the morning was cool, chilly, stacked dense clouds hung over the bay promising a dull February afternoon with perhaps a hint of rain. On his iPod the Black Keys *Howlin' For You* settled Nick into his rhythm for the timed return. A punishing gruelling climb along spidery, ankle grinding tracks up to the escarpment, he felt the climb eat into his legs, his muscles tautened, burnt with each step, his breathing heavy. Checking his time outside the officers' mess, he railed at himself for dropping a couple of minutes on this last leg of the course through Happy Valley.

Bitter at his performance Nick showed the classic signs of suffering from a classic pre-operational obsession, one that demanded perfection in everything he did, spurring him on to greater effort.

During Nick's carefully scheduled preparation, his visitors – which were many – went about their business in a dusty, off-limits compound opposite the garrison's satellite section. Here, in Nick's primitive quarters, military and Service specialists began to respond to his requests. The matter of his identity whilst on the Sovereign Base Area had been resolved with the issue of an identity card – in British Army parlance, an MOD90 – naming Nick as Mike Franklyn. In the garrison ledger he was accredited as a Lieutenant Colonel, and to prove it he wore rank slides.

Eschewing the standard British personal combat system, he went for his normal eclectic mix of pre-loved items of American desert pattern uniform worn informally with civilian attire. To break in his 'combat wardrobe' he remorselessly wore them through every punishing routine, ensuring they had a grubby lived-in look, complete with shabby layers of dirt, dust, sweat and stains. Importantly, Nick ensured they never saw a drop of detergent.

On certain days he sported worn combat tops and blue or beige cargo pants, on others he reversed the combination with plain shirts and desert pattern bottoms. This simple act of making sure he had a complete set of both, merely increased garrison suspicion the scruffy new arrival was one of *Them*, a member of Special Forces who also happened to call the compound home. An operational staging point, during transit stopovers the compound also became a sanctuary for commencing 'decompression' after a particularly arduous operation. Revealing what he called the last of 'his human side', he gradually underwent a robust mental and physical transformation.

He allowed his hair to grow, so that it began to take on an unkempt wild appearance, as did his looks after he avoided shaving, encouraging a partial beard that he kept loosely in check with a secular trim. To top up his weapon proficiency he spent several afternoons on the garrison's range totally focused on getting to know his second-hand SIG 9mm pistol and C8 carbine. Both weapons heavily used, their condition he rated as good. The first time he handled them a protective coating of oil left a slick film on his fingers.

At the range he'd been allocated the unpopular 'end lane' to prevent him contaminating young infantrymen from the garrison's resident battalion with his sloppy dress and unconventional methods. During one of Nick's regular appearances on the range he was sought out by the garrison's Quartermaster; a soulless round man with morose, thin eyes who quietly festered as he watched Nick put his operational weapons to work, diligently zeroing his C8 carbine at one hundred and fifty yards.

'Is this lethality equipment also being forwarded as diplomatic baggage to Beirut, sir?' he asked, pointedly staring at the pistol and rifle.

'No. Aqaba, please,' said Nick, clearing his C8. 'It's to ship as supplies for Exercise Jebel Steel.'

'Jordan, sir?'

'Jordan.'

'And the recipient?'

'Captain Ryal at the Royal Jordanian Air Force's H4 Air Base.'

'Will Captain Ryal be expecting the logistical transfer, sir?'

'Of course.'

And if Danny hadn't already adopted his cover as Captain Ryal to receive the first of several consignments, the move into Syria would be a serious non-starter, thought Nick.

'When you have a moment, sir, the remaining items requested are ready for you to sign off,' the quartermaster announced tersely, severely pained at the prospect.

'Thank you,' said Nick, latching the SIG into his holster.

'Not a problem, sir,' the quartermaster insisted through a rictus smile. 'Always a pleasure to assist,' he added starting up his quad bike. Flicking the machine into gear he lurched off kicking up a curtain of dust.

The rare moments of free time that came Nick's way, usually in the late afternoons, he devoted to acquiring a passable, working tan in a suntrap formed on the lee side of the compound's mini-armoury. And this is where a haggard SBS captain came calling on Nick. He was dozing, a couple of keffiyehs balled in a stuff sack used as a pillow against the armoury's block wall. Splayed open on his lap a copy of Kershaw's *Red Sabbath* its spine upwards. Tangled in his hair a pair of Wiley-X tactical sunglasses.

'Reno became the ideal scapegoat for Custer's tactical errors.'

'Someone always has to pay for their commander's blunders,' said Nick recumbent, his eyes closed.

'Never split your forces...'

'Unless you have eyes on the enemy's positions,' Nick recited the basic infantry mantra at the same time. 'Fight as an integrated group... Fight to win.'

He propelled forward a little too quickly, the green plastic garden chair jolting when its front legs dug into the compact sand. Pulling down his sunglasses Nick smiled as his vision adjusted to reveal Tim Sawtry propped against the armoury.

'No see long time,' said Sawtry, slouching forward.

'Musa Qala,' said Nick accepting Sawtry's firm hand as they met in a soldier's solid embrace, slapping each other on the back in genuine warmth, tiny bursts of dust rising off Nick's top.

'Musa Qala.'

Nick could still visualise the ground they covered around Musa Qala wadi in Helmand. Nick headed a CO8 operation codenamed Roundabout; a two month futile expedition attempting to convert tribal commanders into coming onside before a coalition assault on Taliban forces holed up inside Musa Qala town. The number of conversions Nick and his team achieved was a paltry two. As everyone operating out on the ground appreciated, the local Afghan commanders didn't possess the right type of hearts and minds ever to be won.

At the same time, Sawtry's patrol objective – another joyless task – was to recce the outlying village of Deh Zohr-e Sofla as the site for a feint attack. Skirting around villages and isolated compounds for meetings with assets, Nick's team regularly met Sawtry's patrol to exchange tactical notes from their treks into the bad lands of Afghanistan.

Languid, muscular and slim, Sawtry still had the looks of a professional surfer. His blond hair conditioned by the sun had become thick, rushing in course strands over his collar. On his right wrist he had added another coloured braided cord to his collection of bands. Hanging loosely over his US Marine combat trousers, Sawtry's Israeli Defence Force T-shirt announced: 'My job is so secret I don't even know what I'm doing!'

'I'm going to be your one and only chance to phone a friend,' Sawtry confessed pulling up a plastic crate he used as a stool, his knees forced up close to his chest. 'Air, ground sea... I'm your everything control liaison, your number one watchkeeper.'

'Lucky you.'

'Aren't you going to be a joy to work for,' Sawtry shot back, sliding a tatty ammunition grab bag off his shoulder. 'Your ops callsign for phases one and two is Pirate,' he said dipping into the bag. 'I'm Buccaneer. Thought they had a bit of ring to them,' he continued, pitching Nick an Iridium Extreme satellite phone. 'It's preprogrammed to reach me here entered under mother... and it's for a dire emergency only. So don't try and order a takeaway.'

'Not even an emergency banquet?' Nick turned the phone over in his hands, unplugging and replacing the cap for the SOS button. Bringing it to life, he scrolled the through the menus and numbers he'd requested to be stored.

'You're a funny guy,' Sawtry said, unimpressed.

'Should see me when I'm happy. Our tactical satellite?'

'Monitored by an Israeli special electronics mission Gulfstream providing a live feed to us here.'

For just under an hour Sawtry delivered his significant action briefing. On his knees with Nick beside him, he set out the latest satellite photos overlaid onto tactical maps; part of the items he'd brought along in the grab bag.

'Cheltenham have real time eyes on your secondary players,' he disclosed, dipping into the bag for a printout of the latest string of coordinates. 'Voiceprints and intercepts from identified possible active locations,' he said. 'Here.' He tapped a large area suspected of containing a MFP training camp located close to Qarah with the stubby tip of a finger leaving a light crater in the scaled up map. 'And here.' His fingertip struck a spot between Homs and Aleppo below the Khanaser Plain. 'The good money is on this being your target training camp with Hāru's compound in close proximity,' he added, tapping an expanse of Syrian desert close to the village of Al Hajānīn.

Hāru is a magician thought Nick; his compound appears and disappears at the wave of his hands.

'I've got some other intel from your friend Omri that might interest you,' offered Sawtry. 'Our naughty diplomat has been busy in Beirut again.'

'Shopping trip?'

'You wish,' laughed Sawtry, turning his broad shoulders into the breeze. 'She's escorted by the MFP's security boss man. They don't step anywhere without a pair of bodyguards and a *fedayeen* unit as shadow. Stay for two days, a different apartment each night.'

'After the press release, they're preparing her for a news conference,' Nick proposed. 'Then it's going to be open season on any case officers, assets and irregulars we can't evacuate or protect.'

'Seems like the bad boys are brewing for a strike,' Sawtry proposed. 'Select their targets for retribution, then smack the Nomad material out on the open market.'

'Any location for the apartments where Rewall stays?'

'Ard Jalloul... it's sort of exclusive,' Sawtry explained. 'The bad boys exert a strong influence, tax business owners, recruit teenagers, nurture kids,' he added. 'Our chances of going in – Zero, we'd stand out like rib-eyes at a vegan wedding.'

'That exclusive,' smiled Nick. 'But someone working solo?'

'It's better than going mob-handed, but you'd still be pushing your luck.'

'I'll be carrying my lucky charm.'

'A Mini Gun over your shoulder?'

'It's secret.'

'You're priceless.'

'Thank you.'

'The latest G2 report from Cheltenham's intercepts, hacks and hard drive burrowing,' Sawtry continued, 'gives your bad guys the potential to give anyone they don't like a seriously shit storm of a day. Weapon systems run from the obligatory 9mm pistols, AKs, GMPs to RPGs, mortars, SPG-9s and *Dushkas*. It's a snake pit.'

Nick had witnessed the Russian made DSHK heavy machine gun in action; its 50 calibre rounds made an unholy mess of anyone and anything they hit. 'How many *Dushkas*?'

'From the battle orders Cheltenham have filtered from your bad boys' traffic, they have twelve. Seven mobile on pickups as assault and reactionary units, one in bits waiting for parts, one on the villa roof smack centre in that compound and… three mobile close to the camp.'

'Lucky us.'

'The bad guys' inventory of their muscle power operating in Syria has it around eight hundred give or take casualties and defections. It could be right on the nail or wishful bullshit. You can believe the bad guys' numbers or take them with a pinch of salt, but your real concern are the boots on the ground of the battle tested front line *fedayeen*. From our assessment of the bad guys' order of battle, you're looking at five hundred potential martyrs.'

'They can't all be in our way,' Nick said, running his finger from Damascus up an imaginary route between Homs and Aleppo, the map crinkling every inch of the way.

'It all depends on how loud you turn up the music at Hāru's compound.'

'Pretty loud.'

'Well you'd better not hang around for their roving units to ride to the rescue. It's a twenty minutes max foot on the gas sprint from the training camp.'

'That wasn't on my agenda.'

'As soon as you've given that hornet's nest a decent slap, you'll have a shitful of hate coming after you.'

'I'll be long gone.'

Staring hard at Nick, not for a second believing his assurance, Sawtry broke open a crooked smile, shaking his head. 'You've got balls.'

'Thank you for noticing,' Nick replied with his own graceful smile. Getting to his feet he glanced at his watch. 'Is that it?'

'After you've inserted, it's going to be tough to evaluate the opposition you could run into, the fronts are changing rapidly; one day it's government with their Russian friends, the next the rebels, the next *jihadists*.'

'I'm not going to have time for sightseeing?'

'Not this trip.'

'What about insurance?'

'You got an Israeli aerial overwatch and electronic warfare facility assigned for the compound assault,' Sawtry reassured Nick. 'And our Israelis friends have tasked an aerial Casevac unit to be on call. If I've missed anything I know where to find you,' Sawtry said, folding away one of his maps.

'Thanks,' said Nick turning to leave, clutching the satellite phone and his paperback.

'Do me a favour,' Sawtry called after him 'Don't go eyeball to eyeball with any goats. I seriously don't need the hassle of you falling back on your emergency procedure.'

'I'm a trained goat whisperer,' Nick answered, aware of how other Special Forces' operations had been compromised by unexpectedly running into herders following their goats or sheep scavenging for meagre grazing.

Caught on a warm pulse of wind tugging his shirt, the rich fragrance of wild rosemary seeded along the base of the armoury in dense clumps reminded Nick of different, innocent times amidst his planning for death and destruction.

It's all or nothing he thought, just like Custer. And with that sobering reflection, he returned to his preparations.

Into this remorseless schedule Nick found time to brush up on his Arabic. A retired head of the Middle East Desk spent three hours a day tutoring Nick; revisiting the basics, concentrating on dialects, particularly the colloquial Levantine spoken in Damascus. Tall, his physique on the wrong side of portly, he had wavy light grey hair matched in colour by a full beard. At the beginning of each session he would fix Nick with pale, hazy eyes dulled by overindulgence. When he could fine-tune Nick's language skills no further they shook hands, the Arabist announcing that his pupil had reached 'survival level'.

Surviving what? wondered Nick; for mustering a taxi, ordering from a menu, obtaining directions? Asking if anyone knew Hāru?

The final few days of his stay in Cyprus went at something of a rush. Last minute checks were made as other long and complex briefings by Sawtry demanded his attendance, all in the midst of arranging the covert movement of his teams and equipment to their forward operating base in Jordan.

With under forty-eight hours to go before departure, Nick's packing of his phase one personal gear went at an energetic pace. Sanitising his operational clothing he removed every maker's label leaving nothing remotely identifiable, not even the washing symbols. Nick laid freezer bags full of assorted new batteries inside a pair of cargo trousers before rolling them up to pack tightly into his trekking rucksack propped on the MoD pattern linoleum floor.

Whitehall must only place contracts with suppliers who specialise in utilitarian military design he thought, remembering all too vividly the exact same flooring in shipping containers converted into office bunkers and blast-proof Corimec accommodation in British Embassy compounds in Yemen and Afghanistan.

He slipped compact packs of baby wipes and sanitizer gel sachets alongside syrettes of morphine inside a frayed keffiyeh, stuffing the bundle down one side of his rucksack. Leaning back against a pair of metal personal effects lockers racked by the door, he did a mental inventory of his kit, glancing around the meagre quarters for anything forgotten. There wasn't.

For his last supper on the island, Nick chose to take it at The Royal Apollonia in Limassol. He opted for beef fillet with half a bottle of house red, though neither offered much of a distraction from the forthcoming operation. From his table he had a clear view over an empty terrace to the pool with its tiny atolls of ornate palms and parasols to shade idle summer swimmers. Beyond them nothing but the dark belt of Mediterranean giving the dreamy impression of there being no other landfall. But it was just a geographical deceit, Nick assured himself. Hidden over the horizon in a different war torn cosmos was Beirut, his next stop.

When he eventually made the return journey to Episkopi Garrison that evening, Nick knew there could be no more planning or training. He'd read, he'd run, he'd swam, he'd spent hours in the base's gym; all necessary preparation to fine tune his mind, condition his body.

And in the spiteful light of the following chilly morning when there was nothing else to prepare, he trudged down from his isolated compound to a helicopter landing site clearly labelled by a white circle containing a 'H' that military folklore said stood for 'Here', so as not to confuse the pilots.

His lift for the first phase of the operation was waiting, a Blackhawk UH-60 with its rotors turning. Operated by Israeli Air Force's 124th Squadron it would deposit Nick at its Palmachim base, the staging post for his onward leg to Beirut. On board Nick settled in for the ride, the pilot bidding farewell to the island with a spot of 'Lo-hi-lo' flying over the resident infantry battalion officers' mess on the Kensington estate, Nick fervently hoping they didn't incur what aircrew euphemistically refer to as a CWG: a collision with ground. That would really make his departure one to remember.

•••

Day-to-day living happened in a trance; he ate, he drank, he slept with his wife, his mistress or, less frequently, alone. For those other significant events, a voice instructed the different inner creature inhabiting his skin what mattered and what didn't. Pushing the flaking door he lunged heavily into the dim alley, a side entry into one of the hundreds of foul, dusty warrens criss-crossing Beirut's Ard Jalloul district. Away from the rudimentary air conditioning the night's heat clamped rigidly around Reza Saqiz's damp, plump body despite the removal of his creased linen jacket he'd looped in a thumb to drape over his shoulder.

On his return drive from Damascus, Saqiz replayed the congratulatory praise bestowed on him for his dedicated planning, his essential role in supervising the extermination of the English spy Martens. Saqiz, his family, his wide spread of relations would be favourably rewarded, the emissary of the Armed Struggle Command had sincerely vowed, before trusting Saqiz with new projects. He assured the emissary that he, Reza Saqiz, a loyal obedient servant, would once more show no mercy to the traitors.

Engrossed in this important journey through Ard Jalloul, his bearing, his demeanour shouted of his importance. *If you trouble me there will be severe repercussions* his arrogant swagger warned the fools who may question his business in their filthy, rotten alleys. Not in the least afraid to look them square in the eye, he glared right back at those who even dared to challenge him from their balconies. It took all his inner control from sharing with them his excitement when he would shortly witness the death of more Zionists and their stooges – women, men, children foreigners, Palestinian – it made no difference to Saqiz.

These valued tasks he performed as repayment for his Palestinian birthright; these were chances to seek revenge on the imperialists who had robbed him of his treasured homeland. He would never forget his father's forced exile in Jordan; the fear, desire, longing to be held in those firm hands again, his emotions battered and torn when his father was butchered by the

Jordanians. His mother declared a widow overnight, his dream of claiming the rank of a hero's son in the conquering army of Palestine withered under the shadow of shame cast by the failure of not liberating his homeland. That is when the disillusion grew, when the weed of despair wrapped its tendrils around his heart, crept into his senses locking out the sun of revolution.

He had spent too long living in the shadows, too long having to watch the Jews expand their territory. The tyranny of the Zionists drove him to volunteer, enlist in the MFP who became his family, expanding his training with weapons and explosives. He won honour and respect as a successful intelligence officer. Adapting the skills he used for recruiting assets, Saqiz thrived as the bait to trap MFP traitors.

His method was brilliantly simple; he operated as the friendly, trusted lure to tempt enemy agents and their handlers into the open. He'd perfected his act as the disillusioned MFP insider with secrets to sell. No one escaped Saqiz, the bringer of death, the ghost who prepared traitors and enemy personnel for the execution squad. This is why they had chosen him for this important work in Beirut. He would not fail. Dabbing his forehead, his cheeks, with a crisp white handkerchief, Saqiz hurried on through box after box of stifling air.

Lumbering down another cheerless, stinking alley Saqiz squinted ahead, locking on a thin, perished figure loafing at a small intersection where day labourers gathered before dawn. The fool calling himself Majed had brought a child along for their second meeting, a boy part hidden in the rich gloom. The boy, sporting a Barcelona FC shirt kicked a punctured football in dusty circles as Saqiz waved a spirited welcome to his new friend, his new contact who stupidly believed he was ready to reveal the identity of Hāru.

Concealed in long pockets of shadow with a clear view of his younger brother Majed, a wiry, hardened Palestinian patiently witnessed the negotiations from a rough arched stone gateway, the rear entrance to a villa backing onto the alley. Brought along for a second opinion, Majed's brother was neither stupid nor lacking sharpness from surviving Beirut's backstreets. He read the MFP's man body language, studied how he gestured with his pudgy hands, how he slyly glanced around, the furtive movements of a cheat or liar. From this astute assessment he built an instant impression supporting his brother's sentiments; the man had a pig-headed arrogance about him. The way he stared at Majed cast doubt on his motives, his actual reasons for being there. Impatient, keen for Majed to break off negotiations he would persuade his brother to send word to his English friends tell them of this MFP deception by a man they'd named '*The Hakawaty*' – The Storyteller.

Twenty-Six

A wavering glare leaked from the odd street lamp barely lighting Nick's way. He embarked on his latest odyssey after dusk, his point of departure a traditional *argileh* lounge in Beirut's district of Hamra. Braving the shower that marked his departure, he made it to a branch of Twenty Four Seven in the square, sheltering under its wide canopy as he foraged through packs of sweets enticingly racked near the pavement, his focus strictly on monitoring his status along the route he'd just taken.

Deciding that he had no company he finally made a purchase, selecting a pack of Bond Street cigarettes together with a disposable lighter. His Arabic convincingly fluent if still a little generic, it barely raised a second look from the sleepy clerk at the counter. The rain had moved on and so did Nick. He continued into south Beirut, the heavy clouds running in full retreat out over St. George's Bay, the city spared a regular full on downpour, one of its infamous rainstorms lasting days.

As a means of insurance he kept on an indirect route towards his final destination. He detoured through a sodden Aïcha Bakkar knowing the risks it brought. In his jaded leather jacket worn above a plain grey T-shirt and washed-out blue jeans Nick chose to walk at the road's edge, its gutter a long dark lake.

Implementing the same state of alertness on his trek through the back streets of Mazraa he entered Tarik el-Jdide, his grubby, battered trainers muffling his rapid steps. His nerves were finely tuned to interpret any shift in the 'atmospherics'. It could simply be a change in someone's body language, perhaps the sudden closing of street doors, a look of disgust, the fast dispersal of women and children, the loss of bird song or the instant silence imposed on normal sounds you'd clearly heard a second earlier. Right now Nick was increasingly uneasy.

The alleys were unusually quiet. Since he entered the first quarter he'd had a supplementary soundtrack of top to bottom living: the clash of pots, pans and plates, bubbles of dialogue, the rising swirls of instruments, overheated feuds spilling from balconies draped in worn, fabric sunshade curtains no one bothered repairing, a considerable number holed by bullets. But it seemed far too subdued. This far into unfriendly territory tension had begun to lock itself into his shoulders, setting off a niggling ache in his neck.

All I need now is to encounter a militia patrol and I won't know which side I'm meant to be backing he thought, his focus on reading the nuances of the street scene lined up in front of him. Ticking off the combat indicators he realised something was planned, an event of some kind definitely brewing. The where and when would not be of his choosing.

Ahead of schedule by seven minutes, Nick once more checked his bearings using the compass and map app on his phone. He undid the zipper on his jacket a touch lower, just enough to give his upper body extra room to respond if he encountered serious problems. Leaving a good deal of the sparse light behind, Nick upped his pace venturing into a new quarter.

Here the space between each block had barely enough clearance for motor scooters. Above him a charged buzz from overhead power lines looped like bootlaces into sets of confined, elephant-grey apartments. Lining the alleys a new crop of murals, logos and painted messages of support appeared; all of them clearly in favour of a Christian sect allied to Hezbollah.

In connecting squares the air created its own dense claustrophobic prison. Piles of cast off domestic paraphernalia were dumped in corners – a refrigerator used for target practise, mattresses with soiled coverings, smashed furniture, heaps of rubble from the Israeli blitz in 2006 – all the essentials the local faction would require to construct a hefty barricade in under thirty minutes, Nick decided.

From inside some of the deep shadows loitering around doorways he glimpsed hazy shapes, dim silhouettes. He trespassed into another set of dismal, starved alleys forming dense mazes where only stoic residents loitered after nightfall.

This route should be included on the guided Civil War rambles tourists paid a premium to join, he reasoned crossing another invisible line in district sectors owned by various murderous factions and clans. Around him, alleys slunk into communal yards belonging to hard core MFP loyalists, the fanatics who offered shelter and assistance to the *fedayeen* after their stint on the Syrian front line.

Layers of trapped heat belched out a host of smells. Becoming more potent when apartments packed tight fought for air, there was a clinging aroma of families living on top of each other, the sharp odours of onions, butchered goat, stewed vegetables, stray dogs, soiled, unwashed adults and children.

Sitting under a homemade veranda ahead of him, a pair of backgammon players, veterans of Beirut, its troubles and its good times, their tough creased walnut skin pulled tightly across their cheekbones. Slowly they raised melancholy, all seeing eyes up at Nick. Exchanging critical glances they returned to their game set out beneath a tepid cone of light oozing from a storm lantern powered by paraffin.

And marking the final section of Nick's route, freshly draped flags done in bold paint were crowned by laurel wreaths sprawled across withered plaster; their screaming declaration: 'One Syria One Solution.' He'd reached the heart of Ard Jalloul.

His first indication of a possible setback came with a double circle chalked in blue on the wooden trunk of a utility pole, the agreed code of his asset issuing a warning. Nick proceeded warily through an untidy junction of tangled dark alleys cutting into passageways that never witnessed an hour of sun. The air was fetid. Mounds of waste crept high up the dull, tan walls of four and five floored apartments, ripe middens stinking to high heaven.

He sensed the atmosphere shift as he struck along the same narrow refugee trail Syrians followed to a forgotten semi-derelict district long resigned to demolition; the homes abandoned after the Israelis pulled out.

Most of the blocks were without sewers or a means of drawing running water. Every single one of them had windows glazed with blankets, giving Nick a fresh wave of anxiety, unable to have an early indication of who or what was lying in wait. On each side rows of substantial apartments were near ruins. Some remained intact, bullet pocked, peppered by shells; bare memorials of barbaric fighting.

At a sharp corner where an old colonial villa stuck its backside into the alley, he advanced a pace at a time. Pressed against the villa's solid, high wall he had a diagonal sighting of a set of water barrels ten, maybe fifteen yards ahead. Once owned by the UN they were stacked in a listing heap marking dead centre of the GPS coordinates he'd received mixed in a bunch of texts.

Next to the grubby white barrels Majed waited as promised. A tall thirty year old with coal-black hair curled at the back, his starved body barely filled his tracksuit. He glanced ever so slightly in Nick's direction, a fraught smile of recognition forming. Both arms hung stiffly at his side, the left hand attached to that of his football crazy six year old son, looking skinnier than his father in loose shorts, a short-sleeved Barcelona shirt bearing Messi's name and number. In moments of excitement or fear, the neck seam under the boy's chin had been severely chewed just as it was being done now. Under his left arm he carried a leather match ball, deflated; one side of it hollow like a cwm.

We'll go through the motions of acquaintances meeting thought Nick; then as always I'll have to buy ice cream for the boy, a month's provisions for Majed. On New Year's Eve Majed and his brother celebrated with rounds from AK-47s sprayed into the sky he remembered, his hands out to clasp Majed's shoulder. For providing a little festive colour to the standard *Beirut Salute,* they added tracer.

But it wasn't an AK-47 that made Nick visibly flinch. He only heard the retort of a high velocity round when it struck Majed. Over a wave of piercing screams from Majed's son, Nick latched hold of the boy, dragging him along in a sprint for cover. That was when AK-47s opened up, no more than a second before someone triggered an IED with a command wire.

Clutching the boy under one arm, Nick, in a wild scramble, hit the only secure position available, a recessed arched postern for the villa's garden courtyard. From here they were on the blind side of windows directly facing the killing zone. His back pressed up against the wall's crumbling block work, Nick pressed the sobbing boy into the postern gate. At his feet the baked dusty ground reeked worse than a latrine.

Crouched on one knee he gently eased forward so he could get a line of sight, setting off an avalanche of powdery render tumbling down his shoulder and arm. The blast peppered the outer side of the postern's wall with lightweight shrapnel from the barrels; it also spread Majed up and outwards in a grisly shower. The pressure wave compressed his chest, the blast set his ears ringing, his nose ran as his eyes streamed from the bands of fine dust in the air. His breathing tight, his eyes gummy, the dust lined the inside of his mouth, the back of his throat. Each breath sounded as if it came from a different person.

With a high state of self-preservation kicking in he moved the whimpering boy to one side. Elbowing and slamming his shoulder against the wooden postern gate he rammed it, opening up a small gap.

Using his feet and shoulders in alternate blows, he concentrated on rotten timber boards around its lock and handle area. Pausing for a couple of seconds rest he recharged his lungs after every dozen or so kicks, his bruised shoulder muscles burning. On automatic, he glanced behind not sure if there was likely to be any follow up action. It depended on how determined they are to kill me, and so far they appear pretty fired up about it he thought, battering the gate once more.

Working up an extreme sweat he destroyed the final couple of rotten boards around the lock. With one last heave from his shoulder he tumbled forward into a wild, ramshackle garden. He entered at a headlong rush, the boy clasped to his side, pursued by the zip, zip whine of AK rounds at his heels. He charged through classic ornate beds invaded by thorn bushes, smashed his way over forgotten paths, wild and overgrown.

Joining the AK-47, a higher calibre round zinged close to Nick. The thick bushes and weeds brushing roughly against the boy's bare legs hid piles of battle rubble. Nick knew if he stumbled they were dead.

The villa's rear door consisted of a bead curtain. He crashed through into a ground floor apartment. A startled woman grabbed a young girl, shielding her as Nick burst into their lives. Charging through the apartment's one and only room he deposited the boy, placed a finger to his lips urging silence. But there was no need; the pair stared in dumb terror as he almost rocked the main door of its ancient hinges in his hasty departure.

He slowed to a fast walk wanting to put breathing space between himself and the deadly IED scene. Occasionally he'd glance back towards the alley, barely able to define the thin tongues of smoke as they coiled into a dark night sky. He hadn't seen any emergency vehicles, but he'd heard them converge from different parts of the city. Dashing across the express lane behind the martyrs' cemetery he almost ran into the path of a truck filled with goats; crude blasts from its horn setting off a fresh wave of tingling in his ears.

Knowing he needed to put down more distance, he wouldn't relent on the pace he'd set. He had only a hazy awareness of how far he had to go to reach his primary fallback outside the National Museum. Already passed one waypoint, the crossing of the 'Green Line', the city's old Civil War border, Nick only finally began to slow as he sighted the band of trees around the hippodrome as he neared the Beirut to Damascus road.

Nothing so persuasive as a conversion overcame Nick, just a slight easing of the adrenalin that had driven him on. Close to the cedar tree outside the museum, he called the one number he had for emergency assistance, urgently demanding attention from his one and only guardian angel.

Twenty-Seven

Framed in a mirror slung over an old square basin tinged with a brown, metallic stain, Nick's heavy eyes stared remotely back, weary with fatigue. Only now did he appreciate the horrendous sight he must have presented to the woman and girl when he burst into their world; the sheen of sweat on his face had absorbed a heavy coating of dust along with speckled dashes of blood. His straggly hair and neat beard flecked with fine grey blast particles, gave him the air of a battle hardened desert fighter. Rinsing off the clammy mask he looked in the mirror once more, but he still bore the haunted pallor of a guilty survivor.

You could scrub your exterior clean, he reasoned, reaching the stains on the inside was a totally different matter. Years of witnessing death close up only increased your immunity to savagery; it didn't erase any of the tragedy. It didn't matter that Nick had known Majed's boy for the briefest of moments, the bond was made, his face indelibly recorded; hardwired into an exclusive gallery of characters that ensured his nightmares remained fully stocked for every night's midnight performance.

'Hey... You all right in there?'

'Great, just great,' Nick shouted back, sluicing his face one last time.

He was in the ornate tiled bathroom in a nest of rooms in the city's eastern Christian quarter. One of the dozens of CIA safe houses scattered across the Middle East, this piece of Langley real estate happened to be run by its National Covert Service. Possessing the keys to the part residence, part tactical operations centre run under the cover of a freight forwarding concern, was a doughty, powerfully built Lebanese-American named Seth.

Nick recognised the strategic wisdom behind the location when he'd arrived: a colonial first floor apartment in the heart of Bourj Hammoud. Part of a corner block with a curved balcony, its green window shutters permanently locked. Its scabby plaster had pockmarked scars from a constant scouring by fine grains of desert sand. Rusty stains from rotting rebar oozed through a heavily washed concrete skin. On the ground floor an Ethiopian beauty saloon produced styles popular in the Seventies.

Gripping the basin with both hands Nick leant forward smiling for the mirror: 'Business as normal is now resumed,' he muttered to his ungrateful reflection.

'Feeling better?' Seth idly wondered when Nick returned. Looking his guest over, shaking his head, the NCS man delivered his brutal verdict: 'Man, I've seen healthier corpses.'

'Cheers.'

'So, who knew about the meeting?'

Taking up where he'd left off when he first arrived, Nick concentrated on downing the remains of a neat malt whisky. 'I knew... Majed knew... his brother knew. He had a bad feeling about a new MFP source from their first get together. Majed met him once before, decided he was trouble, broke off all contact. Only Majed didn't know it was already too late,' he answered, the Balvenie streaming through his empty stomach in warm, restorative pulses.

'This *Hakawaty* guy who gave your boy Majed a heavy dose of the heebie jeebies, he'd already pinned the bull's eye on him, right? Marked him as a dead man.' Seth recharged his own dry tumbler, offering up the bottle to Nick.

Declining the offer from his new best friend, Nick dropped heavily onto a leather club chair smelling of mature, aged leather; its haggard condition he guessed would probably have been expensively created in one of the furniture boutiques in the city's fashionable Saifi Village. The CIA's expansive clandestine budgets were a thing of legend.

'That's how it's unfolding. The Storyteller works on targets identified from Rewall's disclosures. After he's made contact, spun his web, he leaves the rest to his MFP executioners,' Nick explained curtly. He was restless; an irritable mood had descended severely denting his patience. 'No one come close to fitting Majed's description of the Storyteller?'

'Sure, there are plenty of big, ugly pig-headed guys who could measure up,' answered Seth, hopping up onto a chrome stool at a stubby breakfast bar.

The tiled counter top was lost under crooked stacks of magazines with phone directories used as book ends. Bottles of water were propped against a fan to prevent it rotating.

'What about the *right* big, ugly pig-headed guy with MFP connections?'

In a corner a selection of spirits, a good few of them various brands of malt whisky including the Balvenie Seth had just returned. Everything was delicately arranged either end of a bubbling tank of tropical fish happily swimming under the glare of their own artificial sun.

'I got to tell you, I ain't heard a single beat from the MFP war drums,' Seth continued, swilling a fresh whisky around his tumbler.

A San Franciscan who toiled under the workname Haaz Choueiri, Seth had rugged good looks, and on his better days could be charming. His hair had begun a slow retreat leaving a light defence of tight frizzy curls a good way back from his forehead. He didn't have a beard as such, just precisely groomed stubble that added to the impression of a natural Beirut resident.

'There has to be a trail, the Storyteller can't just appear and disappear,' Nick persisted.

'In this city some people make a living from being invisible. Listen… let me run with it, do some checking, push some buttons. If I get a needle flicker on the bad guy detector we'll take it from there,' Seth declared.

It's an Agency thing, decided Nick, the glib way those not at the muzzle end of a weapon always appear underwhelmed by operations they don't directly control. Maybe it's a trait they collect during their training, he reasoned, the same way they accrue the professional agility to claim most of the credit.

'I just needed some of the background landscape brushing in before I send Langley the big picture,' Seth explained freely, making it sound a minor issue.

'Now you've got it,' said Nick uncompromising.

'Sure, full colour,' said Seth, moodily contemplating his tumbler.

'*Do we* have crossed wires on any MFP assets?'

Blowing out his shallow cheeks Seth shrugged. 'I got to give it you straight, Nick, okay?'

'That would be appreciated,' said Nick helpfully.

'If it were my call, I'd be happy to declare that we don't have anyone on the leash inside the MFP. No crossed wires, no conflict, no chance of opening the wrong refrigerator in the night.'

'But?'

Sliding off the stool the Lebanese-American refilled his tumbler. In no hurry to enlarge on his oblique point he ambled over to one of the windows, peering thoughtfully through the shutter's louvered slats.

It's Seth's favourite position; his chosen nook where he can check the temperature of the area, decided Nick. He watched Seth arch his wide shoulder into the dark lacquered frame for a reassuring glance along the street towards the whispering traffic at the Dora roundabout.

'You got to appreciate that you're putting me under the microscope for no good reason,' he announced swinging his gaze back around at Nick, his last question deftly cold-shouldered. 'I'm a foot solder just the same as you.'

'Yes, I suppose we are,' Nick countered, drawing back from a full-on pursuit.

'Yeah, but we're as sure as hell not any wiser or we wouldn't still be doing all the crazy dumbass shit,' he declared with a veteran's bitter cynicism.

'Having second thoughts? That's not like you.'

'I got a year of the tour to go, and then I'm frickin out of here man, and out of the frickin Company. I'm starting to triple guess every decision, every single action I take. I've been in the swamp for too long... *you* know that.'

'It's been quite some time.'

Seth came from a family endowed with a strong Baptist persuasion and cussing had been beaten out of him when he was a boy. As long as Nick had known Seth, he employed 'frickin' to vent his various states of displeasure, sometimes to denote the rare highs of serenity.

'Who frickin cares?' Seth lamented.

'We do,' proposed Nick.

He must be nosing up close to forty thought Nick, and the years had treated him with the same lack of respect everyone in our line of work enjoys; an ingrained appearance of being on the verge of exhaustion.

'The whole geopolitical area is paranoid... Come on, man, it's a free-for-all...' Seth declared switching his gaze back to the window. 'Our good folks in Washington... your good folks in London... they've given the Damascus boys and their supporters the freedom to make the play.'

'You still have assets over the border?'

'I lose them by the day,' Seth admitted. 'The Free Syrian Army wanted arming, we're not talking battle tanks and fast air, okay, just a little help in the essential places. And all these guys received amounted to crap excuses. So who steps into the limbo... the *jihadists*, the extremists...Then it's up to guys like you and me to go pick up the body parts.'

'Is the MFP gaining ground?'

'They have their moments,' Seth said with a bitter laugh, his attention out on the street. 'On a good day the FSA guys get into the MFP's forward lines and push them back. There just aren't that many good days.'

'What's the talent spotting been like?'

'Pretty shit actually... pretty frickin embarrassing all told. When you're down to your last magazine, you go find a store stocked with what you need, not a store full of empty promises and hot air. Tight-assed politicians... That's what the FSA guys experience... day after day. It'd be nice to have someone make a decision without thinking how it will affect their poll ratings, how they can justify relegating the war to the back burner until after an election. This carries on and we'll have no one of frickin influence inside the frickin FSA.'

'We've always fought with one hand behind our backs,' acknowledged Nick, troubled by Seth's excitable state. Afraid of the Lebanese-American racing straight over the cliff, Nick needed to ease him back away from the edge. 'It's something we've adapted to.'

'Sure. Pity the White House never got the email about getting their act together and adapting. They get the jitters about supplying weapons that might fall into the hands of *jihadists*, and like that's the end of the road. Man... these guys even talk about *good* terrorists and *bad* terrorists. Can you believe that frickin crap? What do I know, I'm just Johnny on the spot. The FSA don't give a flying pail of shit about long-term trends and eventuality scenarios, they just remember who stepped up to be their friends. This goes on any longer, we're all going to be late for the party and show up wearing the same frickin clothes.'

'I'm really surprised the Storyteller hasn't appeared on your radar?'

'*Man*, this interrogation *wasn't* in the care package,' Seth muttered reaching for a case of Cohiba cigars kept readily to hand next to a twin stack of vinyl albums on an art deco radiogram.

With no idea why Seth would drag his feet, Nick pushed up out of the chair deciding that he would indeed enjoy a second whisky to round over the edges on his gathering frustration.

'Am I alright to...' He held up his glass, nodding towards the bottle of Balvenie.

'Sure... go for broke,' mumbled Seth his attention on cutting and lighting his Cohiba, flapping a hand as additional approval.

Heading for the breakfast bar Nick passed through zones of light blossoming from an assortment of lamps. Seth had arranged them on top of stuffed bookshelves, upright in pairs or alone in messy corners. Cables and wires were clipped across every wall like tiny arteries feeding the lighting arrangements from old shoulder height sockets.

'Thought we were friends?' Nick smiled over at Seth.

'Someone told you we're not?'

Lines of spotlights were targeted at whole walls where they picked out glamorous 1920s Beirut in artistic travel posters. Some of the lamps were antique metal or porcelain and wore no shades. It gave the room a louche period charm Nick thought, adding a meagre dose of Balvenie to his glass.

'Some of my friends insist the Storyteller couldn't have started his career specialising in wetwork.'

'Splash damage?'

'I have no knowledge how they arrived at that result,' admitted Nick as if he truly regretted this oversight.

'Do I know your friends?'

'You may have met them in Tel Aviv or Jerusalem.'

Pushed into a cleft between the magazines and phone directories Nick saw the bottle of Ambien, Seth's magic carpet to help him locate some peace for a few precious hours.

'Listen man, this isn't the deal I was sold,' Seth vehemently objected.

If Seth's sanity was dependent on sleeping pills and tranquillisers as the only helping hand, Nick realised he did have a major problem.

'I thought we had a deal, agreed terms,' Nick stated. 'Wasn't it under the heading of cooperation?'

'Nick... Look man... I understand you're pissed off at the damage Rewall's inflicted. You've had major hits, some nasty losses, but you need to stop trying to hang the blame blanket around my neck... These friends of yours don't consult, they don't listen. You ask them the time and they build you a watch. This the clause where Seth takes responsibility for all the crap? Man it's the first I've heard of it, I haven't had a chance to get to the small print.'

'It's too late to renegotiate,' Nick said, standing his ground.

'You... Me... We do ugly for a living. Some guys don't buy into that philosophy,' Seth pointed out, his cigar tightly fixed between his plump lips. You... Me... Bad things can happen to us. That isn't a risk some of your friends like to accept. They always want to blame guys like us for taking a crap in the pool.'

At a hefty pair of full-length green shutters protecting a set of French doors, Nick glimpsed a meagre balcony through the slats. Beyond the wrought railing Nick knew that from any window in Bourj Hammoud or Naba'a you'd pretty much get the same view of too many people sealed into choked streets waiting for another war to happen. Perhaps one day soon it would.

'All you're providing is arm's-length clarification,' objected Nick.

'Sure, that another clause included in the small print? Man... my understanding was that I was providing succour and emergency facilities. No one notified me that I was expected to be a CO8 part-time contractor.'

'We don't do part-time operations, so you should be fine,' Nick retorted, moving on from the shutters. 'Damascus,' he continued pointing to the Syrian capital on a large map stretched across a decent section of a wall painted a disturbing yellow. 'You happen to have visited recently?'

'Sure,' agreed Seth amicably, returning to his favourite stool at the breakfast bar.

'How's the temperature?'

'Enemy central...' Seated on a high chrome stool, Seth involuntarily jiggled his right leg; levering off the stool's chrome footrest with his toes in a fast, erratic rocking motion.

'Solo venture?'

'Team of six.'

'Any problems?'

'Only before we stepped across the border,' Seth admitted. Forgetting he had company he added a hardened drinker's shot of Balvenie to his drained glass. 'In our last pre-deployment briefing, we had more lawyers than operatives. New rules courtesy of our latest Director... you don't return fire or engage unless they've actually downed one of your buddies... Man, it's like swimming in an Olympic final in your wedding suit...'

'Can the friends you made be contacted?'

Draining half of his Balvenie in one smooth, practised swallow, Seth shook his head.

'They were all picked off, most by the MFP. The last one, a guy with decent MFP credentials, well... they executed this guy Amud before we'd had a chance to fully connect. They blew a hole in his head, and if that wasn't dead enough, they chained his body to the back of one of their pickups. Dragged him back into Lebanon; just raw, pulped flesh and bone when they dumped him.'

'Are they normally so sharp?' Nick had that fieldman's intuition of being led down the garden path.

'I heard their chief of security tightened up their protocols. Look man, I am not here to tell you when you should jump or go take a seat at the back of the aircraft. That level of political crap is outside my lane.'

'But?'

'If it came down to me holding the bare ends of a live cable for a piece of SSI, I wouldn't be the first to head up the line.'

Neither would Nick. Unwilling to reveal that Operation Flame relied on more than a single source of intelligence, he bumped Seth back out onto the runway.

'Surely you must have someone in place inside the MFP ranks?'

Not in the least interested, Seth fully airborne on a heady tide of Balvenie shrugged off Nick's question. 'This little war has given everybody and their jackass the chance of bringing their knife, bowl and spoon to the canteen.' He peered at his guest through his tumbler. 'You need to be careful, Nick, my boy,' he said in an official Washington voice, sitting at something close to attention.

'Of who, Seth? Who do I need to be careful of?'

Waving a finger that he wouldn't be drawn into a corner, Seth continued: 'Different country, but it's same old politicos preparing the same alphabet soup they ladled out in Iraq and Afghanistan to keep the party going. *Progress made...*'

'*...But significant challenges remain,*' Nick completed the mantra he'd heard so many times in Afghanistan. It always came on the heels of another failed British counter-insurgency operation designed to 'clear, hold, build'; only we never did manage to hold onto anything on a large enough scale, recalled Nick.

'Who do I watch out for?' Nick ventured.

'This guy Hāru, that's who. Man, this guy makes the sun seem cold. He's got stairs okay, but they don't reach the attic. He's got ambition and he's got the ear of the Syrians. This guy has managed to coordinate Palestinian factions into a major game changer for the regime. You go over the line and you *are* going to meet him if you don't have someone watching your back twenty-four-seven.'

'This is all reliable intel is it? Who's the provider? *Another* MFP source by any chance? You *know* the Storyteller, don't you Seth?'

'He's a crazy dude, stay away Nick; stay away man.'

Slowly patrolling along one bookcase crammed with hardback editions randomly themed around Lebanese history, a good few volumes on the destruction of the city, Nick suddenly confronted his guardian angel, his long time friend and his host losing his fight with alcohol.

'You've met him, Seth, haven't you? That a fair guess or am I way off track?' Nick insisted.

'Sure,' he admitted defensively, sobering fast. 'I'd spent months trying to cross him over to our side of the street. It was an option, Nick, okay. Man… I badly needed an asset with a full nine yards of influence. Attempts at the centre of the MFP cost me time and an unhealthy slice of my budget.'

Not to mention the other individuals who would have ended up wasted like Amud, thought Nick brushing by pressed shirts returned from the laundry. In clear cellophane shrouds they hung off ornate scrolls on the wooden fretwork panels in the top sections of a room divider reaching up to the high ceiling.

'All I required was a one-off deal, no strings attached. This guy Saqiz, your Storyteller, he showed interest,' pledged Seth emphatically reinforcing his position with robust hand gestures, a stubby tail of cigar wedged firmly between his fingers. 'I listened to his requirements. I passed them on. I waited. Man, did I wait for an answer.'

'What was he asking for?'

'Three quarters of a million, not a cent less. Wanted it as a kiss and tell payment. All notes, used dollars and sterling in mixed denominations. He politely told me that in his humble opinion, my handling of his request might have more bite if I stress his importance. Man… I wanted to bust his head open there and then. I told him: "Opinions! They're like armpits. Everyone's got one and some of them stink." This guy just smirked, trotted out the old Taliban line: *You have the watch we have the time*. Man… he was close to losing his teeth. He was playing me, assessing how much value he'd accumulated.'

'The request was turned down?'

'Approved. Not a single string or condition attached.'

'You processed him, that what you did Seth?'

'Correct. I had my MFP asset and everybody was going to watch the game.'

'And he brought in the product?'

'Correct. The quality wasn't brilliant, but my boss turned it into a main exhibit. A dead in the head profiler claimed that beneath the rabid, murderous exterior, Saqiz is misunderstood. The guy is really a baby.'

'You didn't buy that, did you?'

And in Seth's eyes Nick saw all the pain of a worn-out fighter who'd never make it beyond the first round.

'I got overruled... My big brother at the Embassy was looking to pull up a chair to the main table, so it was Saqiz all the way. Frickin crap and the top floor bought it. So they do what they always do when the cork is stuck in the bottle. They shake it about until junior desk analysts decides what to do with it.'

'Had the Station Chief been provided with a different assessment of Saqiz?'

'We were both reading off the same bookmarked page. Man... it was just like the good old days in Iraq. The analysts' decided they'd put a targeting packet together. Jesus, some of them are so frickin wet, they drip. They don't do basic research, they don't do cross-check, they don't do background. For all I know they spent all of ten minutes on the decision over coffee. Then they actioned it and the packet got mailed out with my name on it.'

'And you had no choice but to proceed,' Nick proposed sympathetically.

'Correct. The latest stuff he brought in took a nosedive in quality. Man... it was just pure chicken shit, a five year old could have told you that. The MFP security chief was playing us with Saqiz. And man, did the Storyteller live up to his name. I knew then we'd bought into a one-sided deal. I let them know my assessment. I let them know Saqiz is an irreconcilable. He can't be converted, he doesn't like us, he hates us. I ignored the directive to comfy up closer with him. Man... I was pissed, I told Saqiz his name would go on the list for expedient disposal. The guy is just unbelievable, he didn't care, told me that he'd be disappointed if he wasn't already on *the* list. Man... I'd had enough. I cut the cord and walked away. They came back with: "You did what?" and point blank insist they're giving me the right glue to stick this thing together.'

'That put you into a difficult position,' Nick suggested.

'Correct. Man... any unfavourable or negative feedback that gains altitude they torpedo. No one at mid-level inside Langley has the balls to take the long walk up to the executive floor and tell them they're not supporting on the ground field decisions just because they run counter to the frickin ops they're attempting to orchestrate. Do I get any career points for my efforts? Man... I got the square route of crap in return. Maybe we don't have our hands tied by Executive Orders, but getting green lit clearance to say "no"... Man, that's a different matter so they cut me out of the loop, handled him from Jordan for a couple of months until he got bored and walked away.'

'My friends and I would like Saqiz to focus on a new target?'

Shaking his head as he smiled at Nick's persistence, Seth did a cowboy style dismount from the stool. 'Man... The guy is sharp, I wouldn't even rate the chances of him buying anything I spooned him above zero.'

'You can find out if you contact him,' proposed Nick.

'If he consents to a meet, it's a one-shot deal. He turns me down and I'm still fully functioning, you don't get another slot, ever. He's exclusive, he picks, he chooses... he disposes. You sure you want this entry into nosebleed territory?'

'See what you can do,' insisted Nick.

'Say I get to Saqiz, who do I sell him as the target?'

'Me.'

'You find yourself in a hole, don't expect International Rescue any time soon, Tracy Island is closed for repairs,' Seth graciously warned Nick, showing him to the door.

Nick be nimble, Nick be quick, Nick jump over the candlestick, he said under his breath working down the crooked, uneven stairs. With much to consider he stole along the narrow streets. Christian crosses in wood, metal or neon were suspended from wires between apartments amongst the jumble of utility cables. In one street not too far away from the disused Family of Brotherhood Mosque, he passed an oversize wooden cross, its head furnished with 'INRI' on a hand carved scroll. Planted in the middle of the road, local drivers never missed a beat when they passed reverently either side of their neighbourhood shrine. Beirut would never change, Nick decided heading back across the old Green Line.

Twenty-Eight

The hotel in Hamra was typical Beirut. Its resolute outer Arab skin boasted a tough masculine style, a down-to-earth resilience, an air of haughty indifference shown to the city's warring tribes. Inside it betrayed its hybrid origins with heady layers of French colonial decadence. The panelled lobby was unchanged since Nick's last visit and probably hadn't altered much since it welcomed its first guests in the Twenties. Low, hand hammered copper tables were still stationed between heavily lacquered ottoman benches with bolsters and fabric in lush reds and golds. The same tall elegant brass lamps still lit the pair of mosaic panels, the same palms still stood either side of the glass arched entrance to the garden courtyard where the same lethargic fountain still dribbled into the same stone well.

Some of the guests were still familiar too. Nick recognised a few seasoned war reporters who followed each and every conflict hanging out in the bar, its décor always on the dowdy side of chic. The corridors, dining room, cellar and pool had their own legends also, the ghosts from when the hotel served as a haven for journalists during the civil war in the Seventies. The pool, Nick recalled from some of the old front line hands in the vicinity at the time, received four direct mortar hits in one day; none of them interrupting the poolside partying. Its reputation as a magnet for foreign correspondents had seen it become the preferred oasis for a spot of R&R away from the grim tragedies they now covered in Syria.

Waiting for the ancient lift Nick spotted the heavily portioned frame of Saqiz the Storyteller parked on a comfortable chair in the lobby. Balding, his flabby chins lapping over his starched white collar open at his stout neck, he'd picked out a spot in the lobby that gave his back a protective screen, allowing him a perfect view of the entrance as he played at being a busy executive, a laptop precariously balanced on his flabby thighs.

His finely tuned instinct alert for any additional threats Nick rang the contact number for Omri, passing on a brevity code signalling they'd had a bite. Now it's out of my hands Nick realised, engaged in a brief tussle with the lift gates on his arrival on the sixth floor.

Up ahead a room door opened, a leather travel bag landed with a dull thud on the carpet's floral pattern, every single rose wilted. Next came a matching rucksack followed by its owner, a male in his early twenties, a bullet resistant vest in an eye-catching blue slung easily over a shoulder; it had 'Press' block stamped boldly on its front panel. Locking his room he started down the fusty corridor.

'Damascus next stop,' he explained brightly in a ripe Midwestern accent as their paths crossed.

Nodding his best wishes Nick strode on.

'If you're coming out on the hunt, look me up. I'll be at the Regal in the Old City. Ask for Jez,' he called to Nick's back.

Nick held up a hand in acknowledgement, pressing on, noting how the wallpaper up here never changed, a perennial combination of brown, cream and orange swirled in a theoretical arrangement. At random intervals to break the hypnotic spell there were framed oils of Paris in the Twenties that hadn't aged so well; the passing of time punctured by thick, glass shaded wall sconces only deepened the flickering gloom. One of the heavy ornate doors with their moulded rosette centres lay fractionally open. Wafting through the gap CNN, Fox or one of the other news channels was blended into a heated conference call that seemed to be about expenses.

It's the American floor Nick remembered, wondering if they'd vetted 'Jez' before allowing him into their fold? Maybe they hadn't even bothered to check if Jez was genuine or one of the smattering of untried freelancers, or a 'parachute reporter' who paid to be guided a couple of miles over the border and no farther, buying their stories from local stringers.

In a discreet cul-de-sac of four rooms he knocked on the last door, an agreed arrangement of three soft and two loud. Opened in a hurry, Alex Moyser glared at Nick. In her left hand she gripped a Taser, her furious eyes suggesting she just might use it.

'Spearhead of another invasion? Or you just came all the way out here to see how I am?'

She did a mocking half curtsey, her left hand swept out in a gracious invitation to enter. When Nick accepted she swore under her breath as he passed, kicking the door closed in a blatant fit of anger.

'Since when have I been your baggage handler?' She pitched the Taser onto her bed, its top sheet hanging off in a clotted ball leaking onto the tiled floor. 'Well?' she demanded, gesturing to his rucksack standing to attention in a corner. 'You could have warned me,' she continued, sweeping back her dark fringe. 'How did I know what was coming for Christ's sakes.'

'Rami delivered it, didn't he? You know Rami?'

'Yes, of course I bloody know Rami. That's why it could have been packed with hash. Now that would have made a good splash as your opening exposé. You joining the real pros, are you?' She glanced at a ballistic nylon camera bag sitting apart from Nick's rucksack. 'Lets see... could you pass as a photo journo from... London? No... New York? No... you'd have a reputation and tear sheets from your features, wouldn't you darling? We'll stick to the plausible... I suspect you're a regional newspaper staffer who is pissed off with the mundane heights of local gossip and suddenly decides to be a war photographer extraordinaire. How's that?'

'Something like that,' agreed Nick examining the camera bag's contents.

Inside he had two DSLR bodies, both Canon, both slightly worse for wear with suitable scratches and parts of their bodies worn bare of paint giving him the veneer of travel his cover as an independent German photojournalist demanded. Snug in their own padded cells he'd been given a selection of lenses, a 24-105mm, 70-200mm and a 20mm wide angle.

'Apparently he's got your *other* item sorted,' she angrily disclosed pointing to the nightstand. 'I bet he blew all your budget too, paying off his smuggling friends,' she added with a sweet insincere smile.

'He'd better have worked out a good deal,' Nick decided, switching his attention to the nightstand.

The unit had started to come adrift from its fixings at the headboard and permanently leant a touch askew. The top drawer stuck and Nick had to give two determined pulls before it reluctantly juddered open. From the bare drawer he got a powerful waft of lavender oil off a dark spill mark in the wood.

'I haven't looked or touched,' she confessed.

'Good.'

He lifted out three individual packages, all bundled in pages from the *As-Safir*. Beneath the newspaper another protective layer, this one of recycled bubble wrap. One by one Nick peeled off the wrapping until he had Rami's special delivery spread out on the bed: the SIG P226 pistol he'd fine tuned in Cyprus, and a vertical pull holster. From the condition of its black ballistic material, a shiny grey, Nick suspected it had a previous owner. Lastly, he recovered two boxes of Russian manufactured Silver Bear 9mm cartridges.

'I haven't seen a thing.'

'I know you haven't,' Nick agreed, removing the lock from his rucksack's main compartment. 'Rami leave anything else?' He eased back the zip, placing his illicit goods inside.

'Under the drawer,' she announced sounding bored.

Removing the drawer he upended it on the bed exposing its base. Positioned more or less centrally, an envelope secured by two bands of surgical tape.

'Thanks,' he offered, meaning it.

Ripping the envelope off its mountings he slit the flap with his finger. Inside fastened to a scrap of card with a paper clip, a printed yellow plastic Dymo label holding a pair of GPS coordinates.

'Rami professing his love for you?'

'Don't tell everyone,' Nick said, stowing the card in a pocket. 'Rami will be so disappointed our secret is out.' He jiggled the drawer back into its opening, sending it home with a couple of bangs with the side of his hand.

'Your wit knows no bounds,' she retorted sullenly.

She slouched over to the minibar fridge grabbing two bottles of water, lobbing one to Nick in a neat curving underhand throw.

'Where's the Bushmills?' Nick remembered how she carried at least one emergency bottle on all her travels.

He'd witnessed her severe appetite when she had objected to a French journalist claiming bragging-rights to front line action he'd never witnessed. Challenged to a duel, Alex chose whisky shots as her preferred weapon, drinking the Frenchman into a stupor, leaving him so embarrassed that he never showed his face in the same watering holes as Alex again.

'Been there, drunk it and had the hangovers to prove it. I'm on the wagon, darling Nick, official.'

'Since when?'

'After my last medical,' she confessed, perching on the corner of a teak sideboard, her legs in yellow skinny jeans propped on an upholstered stool. 'The doc told me the most serious injury I'd picked up was friendly fire to my liver.'

'How's it going?'

'Like a death in the family,' she said, rotating the plastic bottle in her thin hands, running it forwards and backwards between her palms. 'It's akin to turning your back on your one and only best friend.'

For as long as Nick had known Alex she'd spoken with a trill in her voice transforming the 'r' into a rolling 'w'. A gritty, no-nonsense British experienced journalist she'd covered Iraq, Afghanistan, Libya, and was now taking a respite from Syria. Her standing, her reputation, her sheer gutsy determination to reach the front line had brought her awards along with the honour of being the only Brit to share the Americans' floor. As far as he knew, she'd never married and had no children, once explaining: 'I don't have that sort of urge, precious. Sprogs and me don't mix. There isn't the time or the room for them in my life.'

'Thought I was your best friend?'

'You're a different sort of friend, darling Nick,' she fired right back attempting a smile.

Ageing faster than Nick thought good for her, Alex's striking looks had survived week long binges, re-emerging gloriously intact after gruelling parties, but the constant stress of chasing carnage seemed to have finally sprung its trap. Without the foundation she used for her pieces to camera she was pale, hollow-eyed; the creases around her eyes, her slim neck, had grown heavy. From where Nick sat propped on the bed, she had lost an inner spark that not even the slash of a strong red lipstick could conceal. She'd reported conflict as long as he could remember and as she hit her mid forties she'd never lessened the pace. One day he'd read or hear how she'd died in some futile war sending her satellite feed right to the very end.

'Why don't you pack it in?' he suggested, the water in his bottle already warm.

'And what would I do? Write my book? Wait for invites to give talks to budding news hounds at unis up and down the country? That's not me, honey, not yet, not even close. If it bleeds, it leads. And I still want to be top of the bulletin. I might be a little frazzled, but I'm not decrepit, Nick. Anyway I'm harbouring a cold.'

And to prove her point she lunged for a box of tissues. Blowing her nose, she scrunched up the tissue, landing a bullseye in the centre of a mesh waste basket.

Accepting her excuse, though Nick saw no other tissues amongst the rubbish in the basket, he was quite happy to give Alex the impression she was under no pressure and in control.

'But you will be going back into Damascus?'

'Why not? In my trade we're all fleas feeding off misery,' she shrugged, sipping at her water, wincing at the taste. 'We all have different reasons for justifying our interest in godforsaken conflicts. Some of us just want the freedom to report, the need to expose atrocities. Some of us are even honest enough to admit that it's personal; a lust for danger, that ceaseless gnawing personal greed of being there as a witness.'

'Which are you?'

'Which do you think?' It wasn't a question but an abrasive challenge. And not wanting to lose her advantage, Alex turned the tables smartly onto Nick: 'What's your excuse this time?'

'I'm easily bored.'

'No other reason?'

'Don't think so.' And if he'd been pushed by his closest friends and colleagues to explain his motivation, Nick would simply have shrugged; probably muttering it had something to do with the unfashionable concept of duty.

'I'm not buying that. What's the real reason?'

Getting up off the bed Nick left the provocative demand hanging in the air. He strolled to the window attempting to pacify Alex before she worked up a real storm.

'Who's winning?'

'You tell me.'

'The last time you were in Damascus, who would you say had the upper hand?' Peering down into the street he looked for any further indicators of unusual activity drummed up by Saqiz. 'Your opinion, off the record,' he added, letting the voile fall back into place, the make and colour of cars parked opposite mentally noted.

'Current position is the rebels are gaining and the regime forces are gaining,' she answered after a thoughtful pause, her voice drained of its usual enthusiasm. 'The Islamic Alliance has been cleared out of the Mesraba, Maydáa, Yarmouk, Yalda, Tadamon, Babbila, Beit Sahem and Qadam suburbs by the Free Syrian Army. Its only remaining base in south Damascus is Hajar al-Aswad but that's being squeezed by the regime with assistance from MFP units on its southern front. The FSA are coming in strong from the north, east and west, and they now own all the old IA suburbs. Tomorrow it might change, it usually does. Sunni against Shia, Sunni against Sunni, Shia against Shia, Sunni and Shia against Druze and Ismailis, while the Christians in Aleppo are fighting everyone – *and* that includes the Russians. It's not a question of what to believe but who you want to believe. Propaganda is a powerful weapon, it kills just the same as bullets.'

Not wishing to debate the lethal effects of propaganda, Nick paused in the centre of the room, glancing at the television playing an Al Jazeera item on the latest escalation involving MFP units and Israeli Defence Forces.

'Don't suppose you did any pieces from Yalda the last time you went inside Damascus?' he casually asked, his attention on footage of the cross-border attack from southern Lebanon bringing its customary retaliation.

Sliding off the sideboard she grabbed the remote, blanking the screen. 'This is about Wael, isn't it?' she flashed, her torpor swept aside by a show of pure rage. 'Answer me, damn you.'

'We've had a break in communications,' Nick admitted retreating to the bed. Helping himself to a pillow he jammed it behind his head, settling back for the repercussions.

Not long in coming, the storm when it arrived, broke with a foul-mouthed condemnation and Alex's right shoe, an incoming sleek red ballet flat propelled at Nick's head. Ducking sideways and down as part of the same automatic reaction, he heard it smack against the solid teak headboard, bouncing onto his shoulder as it harmlessly fell.

'*Have* you seen him?' He sat back prepared for the long haul, arms folded, legs crossed.

'Fuck you,' she retorted, venting her pent up fury. This her *pis aller* and she made the most of it.

'It's important.'

'He's joined a circus... run away to sea... he's entered a Tibetan monastery... For Christ's sake, can't you bastards just leave him be.'

'We last heard from him a week ago,' Nick explained patiently. 'I need contact re-establishing.'

Returning to the minibar she opted for another bottle of water, this one flavoured with lemon. 'What's the angle?' Composed, her temper and fiery streak under lock and key, she sat crossed legged, her back against the minibar.

'Exclusive.'

She whistled. 'My, you are coming to the table loaded. If that's your opening bid darling, what are you going to follow it with?'

'It's the only bid.'

Taking her time, Alex sipped her water before slowly nodding in agreement. 'What do I get?'

'Inside details of a joint operation,' Nick offered, tugging the pillow higher. 'It's the potential for a feature, a one-off special.'

'Embargoed?'

'For twenty-four hours after completion.'

'Twelve.'

'Twenty-four, and I'm not prepared to give you a second less. It will have to be non-attributable. No names, no official comment, spin or otherwise.'

'I'll need something to hang it off, honey. Helmet cam?'

'Seriously? This time you'll have to be creative Alex, you always are.'

'God, Nick, you're such a... you're so... Let me make a call,' she decided having reached total exasperation.

In a couple of lithe, effortless moves she was on her feet. Taking her mobile phone she used her bathroom as an office to make her call. From the bed Nick heard Alex's raised voice pleading, promising; he heard the lulls between blunt answers, the long gaps when she was forced to listen, grunting at the points made from the other end.

Adjusting the pillow once again he released a fragrant bundle of Alex's scented accoutrements that reminded him of his wife's nightly ritual. When Angie applied *her* lotions he'd had the unsettling experience of not sleeping in a bedroom, but a scented garden. Day cream, night cream, anti-ageing, anti-wrinkle, probably anti-husband in there too he thought, picking up on the piercing silence in the bathroom.

Disguising the deep flush left on her cheeks from an editorial clash of wills, she sank into a leather club chair, her sombre piece to camera face pinned on.

'Embed or nothing.'

Sitting up to swing his legs off the bed, Nick shook his head vehemently. 'Then you've got nothing.'

'It would only be covering the prep. You must have some sort of forward operating base?'

'If we did, you'd still not be going anywhere near it.'

'How about I hitch a ride with your partners?'

'Not a chance.'

'Christ! What do I stand a chance of?'

'The original offer,' Nick declared, his expression suggesting no compromise. 'It's still an exclusive,' he reminded her, retracing his route to the window. 'Take it or leave it, you make the call,' he added, gently easing aside the voile.

Squeezed down both sides of the narrow street, a good few of them bumper to bumper, a different cast of ancient and modern cars, delivery trucks and vans created a counter-surveillance nightmare. But what stood out was not a vehicle. Almost missing him at first, Nick just caught a glimpse of the outline belonging to Saqiz the Storyteller. Slouched against the grille of a goldsmith's, his jacket looped into a fat thumb was draped over his shoulder.

'Reached a decision?' Nick wanted to know, not taking his gaze off Saqiz who now had no laptop with him.

'Do we need a contract or will a handshake do?'

'Handshake every time.' In the brief time Nick had monitored him, Saqiz answered three calls, making two in rapid succession.

'What's so fascinating?' Alex demanded, joining him at the window.

'A problem we're dealing with,' Nick answered. 'Know him at all? The chubby one making all the calls?'

Peeling back her own corner of voile, Alex for a reason she never understood, found her reply delivered in a whisper: 'Started hanging around in the lobby about a week ago. The buzz in the bar is that he's working with the MFP, offering exclusive introductions. No one has committed. If they have, they aren't telling. He's been hogging the same spot in the lobby or a shady corner out by the pool. Everyone's getting twitchy.'

So who *else* have you got in your sights? Anyone in particular or is it just a routine fishing expedition? Nick wondered, scanning along the rooftops opposite, some of them sprouting a bumper harvest of satellite dishes jostling for room with air conditioning units. Across from the hotel on a flat roof capping bruised apartments, a hoarding promoting the local beer *Al Rayiss* in thick smoky blue neon was permanently lit.

On a rooftop half a block farther down two men with stooped, crooked backs hobbled along rows of caged budgerigars, checking their stock for the outdoor bird market. Beneath the knife-edge balcony opposite, Nick tracked Saqiz stepping out from under the canopy. Partway through an animated discussion on his phone he casually walked into the road scanning both ways for something or someone. Braking abruptly alongside Saqiz, an early model Mercedes in bottle green, the paintwork dulled by a top coat of dust.

In a matter of seconds the crowd closest to Saqiz scattered. Leaning towards the passenger's open window, Saqiz realised far too late he'd become a dead man. Nick counted a crack, crack burst of gunfire. There were screams: some of fear, some of panic and a couple of loud, yelled warnings. Only managing a quarter turn away from the Mercedes, Saqiz staggered; his legs giving way, he sagged into a half crouch.

Drivers behind the Mercedes were starting to blast their impatience when another volley cracked out, this one automatic, delivering fatal shots into Saqiz's upper chest. In what Nick literally classed as overkill, a determined burst from the same AK-47 smacked into Saqiz's heavy body when the shooter and his driver abandoned their Mercedes, bolting flat out in opposite directions. No more tales from the Storyteller Nick thought; the street a scene of utter pandemonium.

'You okay?'

Hunched on the tiled floor Alex had jammed her lightweight body tight against the wall. Staring up at the ceiling she eventually nodded. Arching her legs she folded her arms across them, her shoulders slowly relaxing.

'Christ! Was that *you* taking care of a problem?' she flashed, glaring fiercely up at Nick, some of the colour feeding back into her ashen cheeks. 'I wasn't prepared... You bastard!'

'It's natural, you're off duty,' Nick assured her. But he recognised how her nerve had deserted her, maybe marking the beginning of the end for Alex's front line career.

It didn't matter how much of a robust personality you possessed he thought, in the end something inevitably gives when you're immersed in lies, betrayal, misery and death on a pretty regular basis.

'I'll be fine,' she smiled, knowing it was an act.

'If you need to talk...'

Shaking her head she accepted his hand, allowing Nick to haul her up.

'I just need a moment,' she decided.

'Take as a long as you want,' said Nick as she brushed past him into the bathroom.

It's already crept up on her Nick decided, recalling how he had operated with officers from the Service who never gave a hint of how they were inching closer to a meltdown, slowly coming apart inside after witnessing one too many damming incidents. Refusing assistance, rejecting any suggestion they were suffering post-traumatic stress, one of Nick's oldest friends, a member of the same new entry cadre, didn't wait to resign, choosing a bridge over the northbound lanes of the M1 to end her misery. He recognised the identical tragic symptoms beginning to claim Alex; soon she'd be exhibiting 'social welfare issues' – Service shorthand for being psychologically compromised.

'When are you due back?' He adjusted his position at the window, minimising his profile.

The chaos after an assassination followed its usual depressing course; inflamed groups of men and adolescents baying for revenge, the hardliners capturing the scene on their phones, contacting family, friends, auctioning their story.

'Four days.' She glanced in disgust at her armoured vest and helmet in dull grey dumped by the wardrobe.

The entire street was in uproar, the typical Beirut three-ring circus. Seasoned taxi drivers had turned off their engines, congregating in huddles around their vehicles, cigarettes passed round as a gesture of solidarity while they discussed the incident, each point underlined with animated arms, poetic hands.

'Extend it.'

Shoving his way towards the body, a lone *Forces de Sécurité Intérieure* in grey urban combats urgently chattered into his radio. In the distance the shrill bleating of emergency sirens fighting their way through clogged city arteries completed the dénouement.

'Come on darling, if I'm not there, they'll only bring in a younger, hungrier correspondent. Not many of us have the nerve or decency to bite the hand that feeds us. Christ, listen to me... spouting moral fortitude... it might as well be a concept from a lost age.'

Nick had seen quite enough from the window.

'Who's babysitting?'

'Dirk, ex-Seal, he's okay, he's been on the circuit for a couple of seasons.'

'I'd like you to get a message to Wael,' Nick said. 'You can do that?'

'He's busy trying his damnedest to get himself killed.'

'It's important that he knows I'm on my way to meet him,' Nick explained collecting his bags. 'He'll need to send someone to collect me,' he added, hoisting his rucksack onto his shoulder. 'I'll let him know where, I'll let him know when,' he insisted, shrugging the bag into place, spreading its weight across the straps. 'Where are you roughing it in Damascus?'

'The Four Seasons and they're charging a premium. It's become the foreign correspondents club. Used to be reception would ask which view from your room you preferred – the Old City or mountains. Now it's whether you want to face the rebels or the government. We've also got Russians in abundance, claiming to be journalists, but they're obviously mil advisors. Moscow isn't interested in peace. It's just the same play they made in Africa; divide and misrule.'

'Are you still using the same fixer?' Nick had reached the door fully laden with his bags.

'He's reliable but can bounce either side of the net. You get what you pay for, Nick darling, and we don't pay the local support all that well. Not so ethical trading, but don't tell the viewers.' She offered a broad smile, the warmest Nick had witnessed since his arrival.

'Don't waste Wael on a lost cause,' she warned.

'He's already made his choice,' he said, the door open.

'Thought we were both on the same train heading for the same station?'

'I changed trains,' replied Nick, softly closing the door behind him.

Twenty-Nine

There was no one to see Nick off when he struck out after sunset. Behind him the lights of Beirut flared against a lavish night sky in their own glorious constellation. During the twenty-four hours before his departure he intensified his tried and tested pre-insertion routine. He kept showers to a bare minimum; those he took he did so using plain soap with lashings of barely lukewarm water, avoiding any product containing fragrance. He carried only what he classed as essentials in his rucksack. Around his neck he wore one of the Canon's equipped with a 24-105mm lens as a means of verifying his cover; providing what veteran operators term 'giving legs to your legend'.

Acutely aware of how far Seth had descended into his own dark labyrinth, Nick, concerned that tradecraft might be the last thing on the Lebanese-American's mind, elected to make his own arrangements for the outward journey. Rejecting outright the option of travelling by taxi, he boarded a minibus at Beirut's Cola intersection. With the dishevelled appearance of a nomadic long distance voyager he attracted only the odd, initial disinterested glance from his fellow passengers, the majority stoical locals enduring the return passage home. Setting off as he meant to go, the driver lurched away in a cloud of diesel exhaust.

Squeezed beside Nick a round, ancient woman combining a heady perfume of goat and wood smoke, clucked uproariously when the driver blessed his passengers to his favourite Arab musical medley played at volume, drowning the protests of motorists he'd offended. Which happened to be a considerable number on the one and half hour drive into the foothills of the Bekáa Valley. Occasionally the woman nodded to Nick as they sped precariously through villages she knew as another stage closer to home. Nick grinned back with the enthusiasm of an idiot from behind his pack wedged between his knees. Each and every time the minibus slowed or made a stop he discreetly assembled a collection of his fellow passengers' expressions, most taken in side profile. He counterpointed these with the raw landscape outside his window so that if stopped and questioned, his camera would have its own background story too.

The driver unconcerned by an endless succession of hairpin bends negotiated them at suicidal speed, showing the same reckless skill when he screeched into a rocky passing strip marking Nick's requested stop; a crossroads on the ragged fringe of a steep escarpment. After wishing Nick well with a friendly slap on his arm when he alighted, his recent travelling companion watched him from her window as he hauled on his pack; her eyes and wrinkled smile this time bore the sadness of someone who knew the true reason for his journey.

For a couple of hours he climbed relentlessly up along crumbling trails on a south-east bearing, halting at timed intervals to take a GPS reading. In these short interludes he also listened and observed, tensed for that one piece of tumbling rock, the chatter of a radio or misplaced foot hitting hard against the slabs of brittle limestone outcrops. Content everything was clear he'd holster his SIG before pushing relentlessly back into his rhythm.

At one a.m. precisely, three minutes ahead of schedule, Nick, his breath coming in hard surges, reached a ridge above a ragged walled gorge. Braced against an angled rock face he fixed his position as a scattering of light snow fell from heavy swabs of cloud. There was no moon and no stars; the only visible light came from the valley floor. Below him to the west in the Bekáa, tiny dabs and pricks of lights were sprinkled across the valley like ships on a dark sea. Farther to the south-west, the traffic darted quicker than fireflies through a twisting pass.

With no real cover and the night air plunging, his lips were dry; in several spots they were already cracking. Tucked into a narrow cleft the bitter, chilled wind streamed around his body, cooling the band of sweat he'd worked up ascending to just under six thousand feet on the Anti-Lebanon range. The base of the snowline was a couple of hundred feet below him in the poplar trees. And so were the patrols; regular Lebanese Army forays aiming to intercept *jihadist* fighters using the lower worn trails to ship out casualties and ferry in supplies. Flexing his shoulders he shifted his pack to reposition the straps that felt is if they had worn ruts into his muscles, cutting grooves in his collarbones. In his mind he blamed it all on the camera bag that he'd looped through the sack's top fasteners. Temporarily relieved, Nick cracked on.

He knew the latest contact had occurred between a Lebanese *Maghaweer* Regiment's mountain combat unit and an MFP-Syrian Army outfit on the slopes of Chaabet es Sourr less than a mile and half away. The increased activity had forced him higher, 'off-piste' as Roly would have put it, onto frighteningly stupid narrow goat tracks. In some places it was touch and go, the tracks barely wide enough for his boots in single file.

At steady intervals he had to navigate ragged fissures. Lacking time to find alternative routes he made do with short run ups paced as burst sprints; each time his luck held. Clambering away without incident he muttered prayers of thanks to the mountain gods. He broke the journey down into two or three mile spurts, but they still seemed to be an endless march, the straps on his pack sinking further in, his boots opening raw patches on his heels when he scrambled over wicked crags.

He marked the halfway point in a steep cleft he deemed suitable for a temporary shelter. Curled up tight against the cutting wind he ate a honey and fruit energy bar. Rolling back the cuff on his down jacket, the luminescent hands and numerals on his watch confirmed his positional check was overdue. Under the red light of his head torch he hit the pre-dial on his satellite handset, bouncing him through a designated IDF satellite to CO8's forward operating base in Jordan then bumped on to the Episkopi Garrison in Cyprus.

Aware that if he stayed on the link for more than ten minutes he risked being compromised, he signed on with his callsign before providing his GPS position. On the move again he started a horseshoe descent towards Syria, once more staying clear of herding trails snaking down to Nahle and Younine. His ears buzzed from concentrating on identifying any excess sounds; the careless noise from unfriendly forces prowling through the darkness of their hunting grounds lower on the mountain.

On this side of the range the punchy gusts of wind arrived laced with particles of desert. Scouring Nick's face the dust pricked his eyes, leaving them smarting with watery deposits. At this height he got advanced warning of another day commencing; already the first raking strands of dawn began to slowly corrode the dark grip of night suspended over the plain.

Losing altitude along with his cover masking his intentions, he worked prudently through steep gullies hewn out of high walls of loose boulders.

Every time he halted to plot his next section he heard the whisper from granules of shale tumbling under fragments of rock; stone cascades escaping pell-mell down the mountain. In the air he picked up the merest hint of a scent from wild herbs rooted in pockets of rocks; miniature alpine gardens trailing over outcrops in coarse, tufted mats.

If he continued directly east he'd have begun a hell of a walk into Iraq, so he swung north towards the Syrian village of Falita, consulting his combat maps at frequent intervals. He needed to be aware of the positioning of mines, or any recent IED strikes in the heavily contested area where control see-sawed between Syrians and the rebels. By sunrise he'd been on the go for close to twelve hours. Aching from his neck down, his shoulders were raw patches of fire from his loaded sack weighed down on its straps.

From other difficult operations and forgotten dusty military exercises, Nick had become adept at reading his own body signs; alert to when he'd passed the ultimate point of exhaustion, when he could no longer safely operate, or sensing if his blood sugar levels were dropping. He had the opening symptoms now; the slight nauseous tide in his stomach brought with it a weak niggling headache, both warning of a general energy sapping lethargy turning his muscles to string. He rooted in a side pocket for his dextrose tablets, not caring about the recommended dose he popped six as a fast countermeasure.

In all it took a further twenty minutes for Nick to recover completely, his guarded descent onto the mountain's barren apron threatening to render his schedule useless. Spread out ahead of him in glorious widescreen, a rugged valley that only the Middle East possesses. Smack down the centre of its spine the one passable dirt road tailing away towards Ras Maara before finally hitting Damascus. Increasing his pace he started across a flat terrace of olive trees that hadn't been cultivated for years. His movements fast, a shadow ducking between the wild branches in an uneven one horse race of beating the arrival of daylight.

Down a steep escarpment to his left a rutted track had taken direct hits from high calibre canon rounds peppered from Syrian jets and helicopters. One air attack had wrought havoc on a pair of pickup trucks; their burnt, twisted frames rested on the track where it entered a forsaken terraced village, a signpost of how far the war had meandered up the valley.

Moving fast he darted off, a cautious run down a rocky slope, his legs buckling as the mountain dropped away with each step. Light snow spun in his face, cooling his hot skin. Now he was operating on pure adrenalin. He had new points on his compass, the bearings distinct and unambiguous – a pumping station in a glade of poplar trees where he would lay-up, wait for his contact. Bent double he set off in a weaving and winding run for a waist high stonewall hedged by a grove of walnut trees. In the poor light he mistook the distance between the banks of a dry stream, jarring muscles and bones in one leg as he hit the opposite bank at a bad pitch, throwing his whole body and pack off balance, a sharp pain flickering over his ribs.

He took cover in the half ruined pumping station that had provided water from its isolated site above the village. Only a portion of one wall survived the attention of the Syrian Air Force, defiantly rising up out of scorched, blackened rubble. The generator and pumping gear had taken a deliberate hammering, much of it scattered in tatty shards crunching under his boots. Larger chunks had been driven outwards in a sweep of lethal shrapnel.

Below a sooty, smashed control panel, a technical service logbook swung gently in the dry wind. Held with a string through a punched hole in its spine to a wall hook, Nick steadied it to read the date of the station engineer's last visit, recorded some two years ago. He'd have a fit if he could see the place now, he decided.

Such a concerted Syrian operation to deny the enemy resources in this top half of the valley was meant to deter rebels from setting up camps Nick reasoned, making himself at home. Swinging off his pack he cleared a square on the concrete pad, shaping a rough space in the rubble big enough to lay comfortably with a clear view of the dirt road tailing lazily into the village. Wriggling down onto the cracked slab he got a potent draft of diesel fuel that irritated his nose, lodging down at the back of his throat.

At his side he'd arranged his compact binoculars, his SIG by his right hand. As he lay there, Nick's reactions were primed, his state of readiness high. So was the tension; a niggling appreciation that every move, each individual action he made could end his life or leave him irreparably damaged. Right now his world consisted of locations identified only as strange map coordinates. Simple grid references representing obstacles to be taken, objectives gained. Cold, detached targets in another dirty war to be reached; you carried them as desensitised facts; never people, never faces.

At the far end of the village precision ranks of overgrown orange and apricot orchards converged on a tight turn on the dirt road, a feature that began to concern him. If a vehicle happened to stop or slow in the lee of the turn one or more occupants could debus giving them the benefit of concealment from Nick's position. With only his SIG, he knew the odds of surviving an unfriendly encounter were less than slim if the wrong people came calling. After several failed attempts he managed to establish a satellite connection to the base in Jordan, relaying confirmation of his arrival at the set of coordinates codenamed 'Hammer Fast'.

Constantly scanning the head of the valley through his binoculars for any spouts of vehicle dust, he ate a frugal breakfast of a fruit bar complemented by sips of bottled water tasting stale. At some time around mid-morning during his tedious bouts of watching, of energy sapping waiting, he heard the low murmur of an engine way off in the distance.

Listening intently he picked up the strident growl of an attack helicopter circling farther down the valley. Occasionally it sounded to be drawing rapidly in over the village before fading away to virtually nothing. Searching the sky through his binoculars in clockwise segments, Nick couldn't locate anything resembling an airframe despite still hearing the echoing slap of rotors paddling against the clear air. He put it down to weird mountain acoustics, the effects of a shrill wind screaming in over the summits, amplifying the high engine noise from above a distant valley. He finally relaxed by several degrees.

In the hour before dusk his vigil was rewarded when he tracked spurts of dust pop, pop, popping like puffs of smoke above the road. Kicking up enough gritty sand for what he assumed must be a tank, Nick gradually made out a flatbed truck driven manically fast into the village. Slowing and stopping at the same insane moment, it came to an instant slurring halt. With its engine gruffly turning over, the truck rested on the right hand side of the roadway as it was meant to do; a couple of yards beyond a junction where two main alleys converged, which Nick gratefully accepted as a good omen.

The Isuzu truck's flatbed was partly loaded with knotted piles of scrap metal pitched inside an improvised wooden pen. Hanging from its top rails, homemade banners in Arabic offered the best prices for salvage from the 'Scrap Iron Company' in Al Nabk. One more recognition symbol Nick dutifully ticked off. Totally relaxed in his crew cab the driver had his window down, tapping his hand on the outer skin of the door panel to a powerful rhythm belting from his radio.

Hauling on his rucksack Nick ruled out a direct, once and for all approach. Padding softly out of the scorched ruins he set his first objective as a gully providing maximum concealment. Scaling mounds of stone rubble, once the pumping station's boundary wall, he bent low as he entered the gully, hugged close to its twisting sides. He stopped to listen for any sound of the helicopter but nothing claimed the sharp air except the driver's music. Sliding lightly down into a dry riverbed wadi twisting behind the village, Nick threaded his way along its rock and boulder lined course, estimating the distance travelled before he hit a parallel line with the truck.

Reaching what he gauged was more or less his ideal position, Nick scrambled up the wadi's flaking bank. Peering over the hard baked rim, sharp grains of dust whipped straight into his face, tossed down the valley by impatient, hostile gusts. Some twenty yards ahead of him at the end of a narrow alley steeped in shadow, he got a partial view of the truck's rear end.

Moving up the alley, his pack scraped hard against ancient plaster walls deeply stained from punishing, harsh seasons. Reaching the junction where the alley met the road, Nick took the safety off his SIG then returned it to its holster. Down on one knee, he ran through the permutations of what could go wrong between now and his rendezvous with the driver who was supposed to be his FSA contact.

Convinced he had enough options for escape and evasion, he slipped towards the truck using shadowy recessed doorways to traverse down the dirt road. Swinging off his rucksack he flipped open the lid to retrieve his Canon. For the last couple of yards he walked casually towards the cab, the camera his only cover.

Drawing level with the cab Nick took the initiative, making sure the driver could observe his friendly wave that he presented alongside a broad smile.

'*As salam aleykum.*'

'*Wa aleykum as salam,*' the driver replied not smiling. 'You seen enough of the sites up here?' he pointedly asked, a northern European undercurrent standing out when he presented the agreed coded wordplay greeting in English. Abiding by the rules he gripped the top of the steering wheel with both hands.

'What do you suggest?' Nick left an arm's-length gap between himself and the driver's door.

'There's plenty of action in Damascus.'

'You know someone who can get me close to the fighting?'

'Depends which side you want to cover.'

'FSA,' said Nick, 'can that be arranged?'

'It can be arranged,' the driver offered and revved his engine.

Before stowing his backpack on a crew seat in the rear of the cab, Nick circled the truck collecting a dozen or more images on his Canon; a visual backstory should he need to prove to any Syrian officials his photojournalist credentials. Welcomed on board into the passenger seat by an indifferent grunt from the driver, Nick sat as upright as possible in the hope that his uncomfortable position would prevent him sleeping.

When he awoke to the trill of the driver's phone ringing he was in one piece and still inside the cab, the truck stationary on a rough compact strip of sand at a Castrol station on the fringes of Yabroud. For the duration of the call the driver never uttered a word, his wide head bobbing patiently in agreement. Rubbing away the remaining grogginess from his eyes, it took Nick a couple of seconds to focus. When he did, he was staring at a convoy of assorted headlights bearing straight at them as they barrelled down the road.

'Fighting's got serious in Al Sehel,' the driver commented matter-of-factly to Nick after his call ended.

Nick counted seventeen logistic vehicles in total, all Syrian Army, all Russian built, all in an unmistakeable rush. As the heavy transport trucks darted past in a filthy, bedraggled column, Nick felt each and every pressure wave as they buffeted the Isuzu's cab.

'Syrians and MFP are reinforcing,' the driver explained, cupping his square chin in his hands, his elbows resting on the steering wheel. '*Jihadists* want to retake Al Sehel. That's not your problem,' he added, snapping up straight after catching a glimpse of more headlights in his mirror.

They belonged to a beaten ZX Admiral pickup that made for the truck in a reckless, aggressive manoeuvre from behind. In the driving seat a man with the stare of a hardened veteran, though to Nick's fleeting glance he looked barely older than twenty.

The pickup came to a brisk halt slewed in front of the truck. Throwing open his door in a single fast movement, rocking it back on its hinges, the driver leant out of his seat directing Nick over with furious hand signals. In silence, the scrap truck driver waited for Nick to unload his rucksack before ploughing back down the strip in reverse. Dumping his sack into the back of the Admiral, Nick had barely climbed into the front before the pickup accelerated away in a swirling ball of dust.

'Wael agreed to see you,' explained the driver.

'I thought he would,' answered Nick. Welcome to the FSA he thought, seeing the first sign for Damascus reflected back by the pickup's headlights.

Thirty

At the Damascus Excelsior Hotel Nick requested a first floor room and didn't care about the view. What mattered was having the means of escape – which he did; six paces along the corridor to the emergency stairs. If he didn't have the luxury of that much evacuation time, he'd risk a direct exit from his room. After he'd wriggled through the end window there was a good eight feet to drop and with a bit of effort he could, if he swung out hard enough, land in the hotel's pool, or so he'd earnestly convinced himself.

For over a week Nick sat on his hands. The urgent rendezvous arranged with Wael never materialised. Somehow holding in his increasing despair, Nick's mood at these daily no-shows veered between dour acceptance and volatile impatience.

As all sound fieldmen do when waiting for the operational cogs to turn, Nick lived his cover. He roamed through the Old City storing background colour on a compact point and shoot camera. A natural, accomplished photographer, Nick's quirky framing, perspective and angles are all there in the sets he took of Al-Hamidiya Souq, the Souq Medhat Pasha, and the Street Called Straight. On high alert, practising evasive counter-surveillance measures, he never once relaxed his guard; taking marathon routes, stopping rapidly to perform a U-turn or selecting a strategic corner where he would smoke a cigarette as if passing time until the arrival of a friend.

His respect for the *Shu'bat al-Mukhabarat al-'Askariyya* was absolute. He knew the Military Intelligence Service's methods of detention were far from pretty; how their first choice in any interrogation would certainly be of the extreme and inhumane kind, a considerable number of them involving the imaginative use of electricity. To preserve every last inch of his cover Nick confined his photographic excursions to a basic core triangle in the Old City, maintaining a varied routine on every single outing.

Over a Turkish coffee at an outdoor café, the sharp crack, crack, crack of gunfire wafted in solo and multiple bursts from the suburbs. The middle-class patrons around him continued with their mid-morning refreshments immune from the bitter struggle for control of their city. When 81mm mortars unleashed a rapid-fire barrage away to the south no one at the other tables showed anything but passé indifference, as if the retorts from weapons were birdsong. It's collective amnesia or bloody-minded denial he thought.

Leaving a small tip, he edged his way through a huddle of conversation onto the roadway, wondering how long the residents' self-deception would continue? He recalled being in other cities under siege when people blithely insisted life had to go on; until eventually the civil war, uprising, rebellion or revolution arrived unannounced.

On the following Tuesday a pro-FSA supporter delivered greetings from Wael, topping off the courtesy visit with a dedicated time and grid reference. Needing transport and needing it in a hurry, Nick paid three times the going rate to charter a vehicle and fixer-driver for Thursday, even insisting on a receipt as any intrepid photojournalist would; another small piece of verisimilitude added to enhance his fabricated legend.

The small fortune Nick paid brought him a pickup truck patchily resprayed in various hues of brown. Dressed in its budget desert camouflage it arrived complete with tears of dried blood across the back seats, worked into the mats, streaked in rashes across the inner door panels. As a makeshift battlefield ambulance its open, bed floor was lined with a sheet of plywood doused in the blood of living and dying casualties. In Nick's verdict the pickup was a complete and utter pig. When it started or when the gears were changed, its exhaust belched out more smoke than a tank.

The truck's owner, the fixer-driver for the duration of the charter had come highly recommended by Alex. A jovial grandfather sliding happily towards his sixties, his choice of cologne or hair oil reminded Nick of mouthwash stocked by dentists. Raed disliked the government, he disliked the rebels, he disliked the *jihadists* or so he owned up five minutes into their trip. After his avowed confessions Raed gave a catfish grin, his dark, lively olive eyes reading Nick's face for any hint of a response.

'I don't understand why they fight for religion,' he ventured. 'Their God is my God, the difference is only in people's hearts.'

'That's a wise idea,' Nick agreed.

He had one camera slung across his shoulder, riding down his right side ready for immediate action. He'd discarded the lens cap, fitting a UV filter and hood to cope with glare. In the sling bag riding next to his hip, along with his spare camera for back up, he'd cached his 9mm with a round chambered, his only access to deadly force for when that one incident he wouldn't be able to walk away from came along.

'You think?' Was Raed's stock response to any question, to any comment Nick offered; his top lip heavy with a grey bristle moustache, rolled back to reveal two missing gold teeth, one either side. When the revolution threatened to sweep through each district, he'd had them removed to stash away as insurance.

'Yes, I think,' heralded Nick's closing part in their familiar little ceremony with its own short litany.

The heat in the cab gripped Nick's body. His casual shirt, his loose cargo pants, stuck to him within moments of Raed grinding through the gears on their departure. He felt the sweat trapped between the creased material creating a barrier next to his skin; a sticky layer that had also found its way into his lightweight boots. Everything he wore came from the same colour swatch, a nondescript tan. That even went as far as his discreet body armour, a tactical vest with ceramic ballistic plates.

For long periods along their meandering approach route, Nick just nodded agreement as Raed gave a warts and all commentary. Lost in deep concentration, Nick analysed the destruction as an experienced military commander might; assessing the problems involved in street-by-street urban warfare, this strain brutal.

Away from the Old City on the drive through suburbs won back by the regime, Nick noticed how those that had no choice but to survive weeks of all-out fighting didn't have the same energy to go through the motions of carrying on as normal with a mid-morning pavement coffee. The block-by-block battles had eaten their way into new districts, flattening neighbourhoods in its rampaging footprint, leaving behind hollow-eyed scavengers. Normality would have meant food vendors on the streets, packed local souqs in manic squares, but he saw only desperate women and children clambering over heaps of spoil.

Laid out in temporary pitches under dark concrete spans of highway bridges he passed raw improvised stalls manned by farmers, their meagre selections of fruit and vegetables barely worth harvesting. Whole districts were caught up in a nightmare; and none of them know if it is ever going to end, he decided.

As Raed threaded his pickup towards the northern boundary of the Yarmouk neighbourhood, he stopped without warning.

'No good here,' he stated. He didn't bother with his smile or grin.

Locals have an inherent sixth sense for instantly recognising the danger signs, Nick recalled. He'd witnessed it in Iraq, Afghanistan, and Northern Ireland in its various forms, a dialled-in inner radar alerting them when something wasn't right.

'This is fine, I'll walk from here,' he suggested.

'I drive for you, I come back for you,' Raed insisted.

Shaking his head, Nick adamantly refused: 'You forget that we met, you forget where you dropped me. You make sure that Miss Moyser takes care of my things back at the hotel. Do all that and I'll throw in a bonus.'

Nick gave his ultimatum half out of the Toyota's cab.

'Trust me; you and me are friends,' insisted Raed piously.

He had his first gear already selected. The moment Nick clicked the passenger door closed Raed pulled slowly away, not hitting close to five miles an hour as the tyres gently crunched towards safety.

From under his boots Nick heard the same grinding with each step. It was everywhere. There was no avoiding it, a thick veneer of splintered window glass, tile shards and blown out masonry fragments were mixed with white, dust coated debris from collapsed apartments. To Nick it sounded very much as if he was cutting a trail through a landscape of crisp, virgin snow. Farther east in Yalda, a neighbourhood he calculated to be no more than a mile and a half's hike away, the intermittent solo cracks from semi-automatic weapons gradually intensified into the rising overture of a determined firefight.

Kicking up a storm of powdered debris, five armoured personnel carriers rattled by at full speed leaving a slipstream of acrid diesel exhaust flavouring each mouthful of dust. Behind them and in the same no-nonsense mood, a dozen pickups flying MFP flags carried a quick reaction force into battle; four *fedayeen* in army surplus combats jammed around a heavy machine gun in the bed of each truck.

Quite sure he'd pushed his luck beyond its narrow confines, Nick picked his way through shell and bullet pounded remains of a wasteland. He had only travelled a short distance down what had been a main thoroughfare and the dust had settled on him, claiming him as one of its own. Most of the apartments were concertinaed into the road burying shops, stores and workshops. And from the putrid eddies sticking to the humid air, bodies remained trapped so deep under mountains of rubble they just weren't recoverable. There was no electricity, no phone signal, no food, and barely any water. In poster-sized letters, 'GOD IS GREAT' was daubed on standing walls.

At one corner a mature yew tree slowly perished from its wounds. Its main trunk split; the upper portion leant dejectedly towards a mosque that had lost its minaret. The yew's branches hung hopelessly in bare, barbed wire coils, the leaves stripped by different calibre rounds of heavy crossfire. The front of one residential block was completely missing, peeled away by high explosive ordinance. The apartments were rudely ripped open like the rooms in a doll's house, and there for all to see, the private lives of its residents.

Above shattered concrete panels clinging to twisted skeletal sections of dull steel, a splendid orb chandelier hung in what had been a graciously decorated living room. At a far window, a firing position constructed out of bags of white cement included a sofa furnished in pallets as its raised firing step. They hadn't bothered to take down the swagged curtains in their haste to hold the neighbourhood, Nick noted; streaked in powdered, white dust they flapped like bizarre battle pennants. In a separate room he noted a cot, a mobile attached rotated gently in the grit soaked breeze.

For some strange reason the nursery irritated Nick no end. He captured both scenes from a number of angles on his main camera, absorbed in recording the eerie quirks that go hand in hand with war. It was this seamless transition from peace to barbaric hostility that some people found unsettling. Families had moved out, the fighters moved in; that was all there was to it he reasoned, pushing nimbly onwards towards a little pocket book war running at full pelt no more than five blocks away.

When he came to what he identified as vulnerable points Nick adopted a quite different routine. At junctions he made quick, non-stop dashes from one pavement to another, his camera gripped tightly into his body. At crossing points in the rubble he avoided straight, predictable lines, bolting from one side to other determined not to stop a round. When he encountered blind corners he'd take slower detours through peaks and valleys of debris. On one occasion he covered several hundred yards in a continuous, unbroken run scrabbling along inside the shells of adjoining buildings, not willing to risk drawing fire from regime or rebel snipers. A reckless frontal approach out in the open would only be attempted by the plain stupid, or martyrs he decided, counting the bodies felled in the open; more or less a draw for each side.

As Nick advanced, the exchange of fire rose street-by-street. Then he hit the battle proper. Pinned down inside a set of rubble foundations, sweeping arcs of half accurate fire had him laying nose to the ground. The fiercest came from a general purpose machine gun, the ricochets hurling stone chips directly over his head in dusty, zinging bursts. Small, very personal contacts would erupt around him, then intensify into a broad front fought across the strip of no man's land hiving off a quarter of the neighbourhood.

Welcome to the delights of urban civil war he thought, bracing for the impact when a couple of MFP 107mm incoming rockets streaked erratically overhead. The impact from high explosives removed a corner of an apartment block, the rumbling shock wave rushing through Nick's prone body. Then came the dust. It moved in a bitter tasting swirling wall, slowly shrouding everything it touched; the sun, commercial buildings, burnt out vehicles, apartments and stores remorselessly blown apart, all of them were silently wrapped inside the thick grey haze. Only by breathing slowly through his nose cupped into the crook his arm, did he overcome the natural urge to withdraw. He waited half crouched like an athlete on the startling line until the GPMG rate of fire slackened, allowing the dust to roll over the forward line positions like an early morning mist. Then he broke cover.

At that precise moment he actually felt naked without any serious personal weapons, preferably a C8 carbine with an underslung grenade launcher. He had by his reckoning slipped around the regime and MFP's flank, putting him squarely amidst FSA units. Lining up what scraps of basic cover he could find Nick doggedly stuck to his GPS coordinates, a lone buccaneer on the trail of treasure. Wild automatic rounds tossed up spurts of dust just about everywhere he ran. If he'd been in Iraq or Afghanistan leading a CO8 patrol his radio headset would be buzzing with the familiar motet relayed over the net: 'Zero... This is Lima Charlie Zero. Contact. Wait Out.' If his lucky star was shining he might even have Cheltenham feeding him the real time communications of the opposition commanders.

Here he possessed no support and still had more deadly ground to cover.

The central FSA firebase was compressed inside a collection of narrow alleys barricaded by blitzed cars, reinforced by buses hoisted end on end, tatty sandbags and walls of tyres. To reach it Nick had a main thoroughfare to cross but it wasn't traffic that kept him hanging back on the pavement. Catching his breath he tucked his back against a high, ornate wall disfigured by the pocked scars of shells, bullets, rockets and God knew what else that had been ferociously exchanged in the battle for a block of ground no wider than a football pitch.

A major supply route for the FSA, the thoroughfare had an MFP unit blasting at anything that moved with their pickup mounted *Dushka*. Edging forward Nick saw a pair of FSA trucks taking turns to dart out in a cat and mouse game of returning fire. Poking out of the pickups' rear beds monopod heavy machine guns resembling seaside promenade telescopes spewed out high calibre rounds instead of picturesque sea views. The racket during these volleys bouncing back off the high alley walls began to affect Nick's ears; not so much a persistent hissing or ringing, more of a flat buzzing almost costing him the acknowledgment call from his good friend Wael. Across the street exactly where he was meant to be, an FSA fighter held up his hand to Nick in the stop gesture. As a pickup prepared to reverse at speed back down an alley opposite in another heavy calibre duel, Nick's guide rattled off an order into his radio. Holding its position, the pickup's gunner hammered out covering fire as his guide beckoned Nick forward, a frazzled attendant crossing a child at a crazy junction.

Each alley was more or less a ruin choked with an uneven bed of smashed block walls. Here and there, the remnants of water pipes surfaced like ragged fingers grasping for air. In other ruins there were strands of scorched cables and splintered chunks of timber churned in with household items. Every dusty step he took disturbed a piece of somebody's life.

Every so often above the sapping staccato din of AK-47s, he picked out the whoosh of random RPGs aimed hopefully towards the front line of regime troops. Accompanying the dull explosions of an accurately aimed warhead, the yelled salutation '*Allahu Akbar*' from FSA fighters lifted in an uneven chant. A return volley of machine gun and automatic rounds slammed into the pulverised walls kicking out little dust spouts.

Where some of the alleys ran in parallel, the regime troops were less than twenty yards away in their own rubble fortresses. In some places the actual midpoint of no man's land was bizarrely marked by makeshift screens of rugs, bed sheets or ancient tarpaulins slung over nylon lines strung between decimated buildings or severed tree trunks. The whole lot was peppered by different calibre rounds, and for the life of him, Nick couldn't see the point. The incoming rounds zipped and whined across the alley, a permanent background note in the opera of war.

At strategic peaks of rubble FSA fighters, some in assorted, ill-fitting combats, some in jeans and T-shirts, made a dash to the top of rubble mounds, firing bursts from their AK-47s before charging back down the steep banks, their legs barely able to keep up. In other sections of the alleys, crude sangars fashioned out of shell debris had a beachcomber air about them, including the scrappy pieces of cherished rugs used as firing mats for general-purpose machine guns. Every fast stride Nick made he scattered brass ammunition cases and empty links smeared in battle dust. A gritty white substance, it clung to everything, a ghostly camouflage coating the living and the dead.

Only once did Nick and his guide deem it expedient to take cover. It came when the regime opened up with a fusillade of mortars topped by RPGs and 107mm rockets. After the last high explosive slammed into an abandoned clinic blowing a wall outwards in concrete shards fierce enough to remove Nick's head, a strange, brief moment of tranquillity smothered the thrashing noise of battle. From where Nick knelt in a serious crouch the muted stillness sounded painfully loud. Reduced to dim, fast moving shadows in the cloying horns of dust, Nick vaguely made out Wael's men as they legged it in and out of apartments reduced to their bare, concrete and steel bones, evacuating casualties in exchange for reinforcements.

A swathe had been cut right through a side alley by tanks or artillery, levelling everything to stumps of rubble. No more than a couple of paces along a trail twisting through wasted concrete shells, the ripe, coppery stench of blood dammed up at the back of Nick's throat, sticking fast to the dust lining the inside of his nose. From the splatter pattern across several reinforced beams, Nick estimated there'd been a number of clean kills by a regime sniper. Intent on improving his odds of not catching a piece of 7.62 he accelerated; his head, his shoulders hunched low. How many pieces of gold was the going rate for a foreign journalist? he wondered, outsprinting his guide.

Thirty-One

It took an intense twenty minutes for Nick and his taciturn guide to thread their way along wasted, rubble packed alleys to the FSA's forward line in an MFP tactical HQ they'd just overrun. The headquarters, a technical college on the northern boundary of Damascus' Tadamon suburb once offered hope on all of its six floors. Now there were no students and only two floors. Both of them pounded into a ragged, lopsided shell. The windows were gone, blown in during an earlier battle. Sooty tongues from severe fires had lapped eagerly up the block walls giving the place an air of defiance.

With a clear view to withstanding an immediate counter-attack, the holding pattern of security around the HQ actually impressed Nick. There were fighters covering the approaches with AK-47s supported by RPGs. Filling the gaps he recognised a couple of Kalashnikov PKM machine guns ready to pump out lethal area fire. The entry point had a chicane built of twisted steel beams set in a bank of rubble to prevent VBIED attacks. The HQ, generously decorated by incoming machine gun, rocket and assault rifles, was the biggest ruin left in the square. Nick counted at least six bodies lying in and around mashed buildings, slowly festering like overripe fruit carelessly discarded in the sun.

Two of the dead wore shredded militia uniforms, a decapitated older fighter lying alongside a younger volunteer cleaved in two from the chest down. In this half world of brutal affiliations, it mattered a great deal how far you were prepared to demonstrate your allegiance; make too much of your loyalty and sooner or later you'd have no choice but to stand up and prove it. And that was often fatal thought Nick, ducking under a concrete beam, stepping exactly in his guide's dusty boot prints.

Inside the HQ emergency lights fed from humming generators were taped together in bundles. Glowing at less than full power they leaked a feeble, lacklustre white, rinsing classrooms, labs and corridors in an eerie monochrome. Ragged man-sized mouse holes were hacked through interior partition walls allowing rapid movement. Sprayed in colour beside them, arrows marked the routes to what had been MFP firing sectors.

The whole building had a noticeable list. At a junction of two corridors standing rigidly like a drunk attempting to hold himself straight, the FSA Area Commander watched Nick approach.

They greeted each other in a warm embrace as if they had been friends for much of their lives. Which in different circumstances they very well could have been. Wael, lean and slim with the Middle Eastern charm concealing an ark of conflicting emotions, had known Nick for exactly six months after their first meeting in Jordan at Operation Nomad's temporary training base. Staffed exclusively by CO8 and Special Forces instructors, the courses furtively taught FSA officer recruits advanced battle planning and urban combat tactics.

'When are you going to join us in the fight? We need you, we need a hundred like you,' Wael declared, his big smile dissolving, the anxiety of a commander once more established.

Put on the spot Nick could only shake his head. 'London recognises your position...'

'We do not wish for an invitation to a pity party, we wish for direct action before our ranks run dry,' he insisted, escorting Nick deeper into the tactical HQ, his prize after two days of heavy fighting.

Raising his AK-47 as a salute to his men gathering for a patrol, Wael snapped out a list of orders on his radio. Blessed with dashing, subtle good looks enhanced by a worn set of US desert combats, Wael could have been a poster boy for any revolution.

'How bad is it?'

'We have few reserves. We manage. We have success for now, God willing... but the future cannot be predicted. But if we had you, and people like you... If London didn't have tin ears...'

'You don't need me,' Nick insisted, 'you've achieved all that you have done because you believe in what you're fighting for,' he declared passing through a hastily established comms room. Most of the equipment appeared captured or primitive and if this electronic bric-a-brac pays off it will be a miracle thought Nick. 'The items you urgently requested are in transit,' he added, receiving cool, diffident glances from the comms specialists who in a different life were probably students.

He reeled off a précis of the resupplies he had managed to put together; some bits and pieces were skimmed from Special Forces' stores, a good deal of the medical kit came from the Americans. He'd had no option but to beg, barter and scrounge when no assistance or interest was ever likely to emerge from the MoD or Whitehall.

'It will help,' Wael admitted with a trace of calm grace, unable to totally regulate his disappointment.

'What about the MFP's main camp between Homs and Aleppo?' Nick shouted when an FSA mortar furiously thumped out rounds in retaliation for an attempted regime advance.

'We have made progress,' he explained, his smile fixed, 'My FSA brother... the one we call the Ferryman... the commander for that sector... He has agreed to be your support when you have paid an advance toll in Krugerrands.'

'*Toll... Krugerrands*?' Nick struggled to contain his anger. 'You were meant to negotiate with him, not for him to put the squeeze on us. Barter, Wael, you remember how it works? We pay in supplies; we provide funds for *you* to make a deal with the Ferryman. Then we all get what we want.'

'It is his sector,' Wael admitted languidly. 'No one moves in or out of his sector without paying the toll. He's a shit... total shit.'

'Well this shit is now *your* problem. Sweet talk him Wael, promise him medical supplies, an ammunition resupply drop... anything. I need him there watching our backs.'

'He's a total shit... we suspect he maybe has links to other militia around his sector, *jihadists* and *fedayeen*.'

'MFP *fedayeen*?'

'We have a saying for this war, Nick. I told you, remember? You are my sworn enemy until a better enemy comes along, then we fight as one,' Wael admitted, giving Nick his *no comment* look before concentrating on answering his radio.

'Have we any confirmation that our target *is* in residence at that compound?'

'The shit tells me he does one surveillance as a favour, his show of good faith to a FSA brother. Any other tasks we need can be arranged as extras to the toll. No toll, no eyes on the compound, no support.'

'What happens if the Ferryman decides to share our interest with

Hāru's people?'

'Okay, Nick, I hear you, I understand your concern,' Wael avowed, one hand raised in a placatory gesture. 'Maybe the shit already shown his hand too early.'

'How could he do that, Wael?'

'His surveillance of the compound,' Wael confessed, a hand held in front of him. 'Maybe it not too subtle, not too discreet,' he added. 'Nothing's changed.'

'Nothing?' Nick snapped in a hostile challenge.

'Not much... Hāru's *fedayeen* maybe reinforced the defences, maybe added more to their security detail around the compound,' Wael reluctantly volunteered.

'*Maybe*... Well that's a relief, Wael. For a moment I thought we had serious issues.'

'We got it covered,' insisted Wael, shaking his head at Nick's lack of faith before launching into a long, heated dialogue into his radio.

And Wael's relaxed approach only intensified Nick's rising concern.

'This is the big deal,' Nick curtly reminded him. 'Forget the Ferryman, you'll have to supply the extra support.'

'I got that covered, I already started selecting my best people,' Wael said, his resolute gaze challenging Nick to question his claim.

'Can they handle it?'

'They'll need convincing, they'll want something in return,' Wael replied with a snort of disdain, upping the pace.

Above the next floor on what counted as the fortified roof, a hail of concentrated fire opened up in the same instant Nick recognised the high rotor slap of a helicopter. Halting on a set of concrete stairs blown off their mountings so they rested wedged at an angle, Wael roared a command into his radio. A fine dust drifted across Nick's hair, shoulders and arms after RPGs and rockets on the roof joined the attack.

Two detonations, seconds apart rocked the ground. Nick couldn't say which came first, the noise or the violent tremors that danced through the HQ. He knew it wasn't a direct hit but he estimated it to be close. The roof and walls were pelted with debris; a heavy shower of shrapnel mixed with chunks of brick, block, tiles and concrete. Then a fine pattering of smaller particles fell from a pall of dust tumbling over the building.

'Barrel bombs,' Wael explained, dusting himself down, quite stoical.

'Can you convince your men to support us?' Nick asked, joining Wael on the second floor landing.

'If I deploy my men, I got some suggestions for the strategy of our support operation,' Wael said breezily. 'It's important my men know I have hundred per cent input.'

Which Nick knew would be bad news. Good commanders rarely made changes for changes sake. Others, justifying their rank, endlessly tinkered and meddled so that when simple effective plans ascended to the top, they came back down as complex, illogical and total bollocks; a menace to everyone on the ground. And that, Nick decided, might summarise Wael's likely involvement.

'That's not going to happen.'

'My men will question why I permit external forces to use them as mercenaries in a battle that has no part in *our* war,' he retaliated.

'Aren't we fighting for the same result?'

'For FSA fighters it is their belief that they did more than their duty for their brothers. They understand when they awake for the next day some will live, many will die. It is what it is, God has chosen a path for them. Come... Come Nick... Let me show you,' Wael insisted setting off at double-quick pace, beckoning Nick to keep up.

Refusing to answer Nick's questions, Wael steamed fast down a series of shattered corridors, disappearing into the remnants of a door less room labelled 'Laboratory 7'.

A small cohort of senior FSA officers were gathered into one corner where a jagged line of concrete wall blocks finished roughly at head height.

'One of yours?' Nick asked quietly. He knew it would be bad from the stench of blood, sweat, piss and shit.

Wael nodded. 'My second in command, he was separated from his men during our initial assault,' he divulged, his voice direct without a trace of emotion.

It's not the just the physical battles, the close quarter firefights that makes anyone immune to savagery thought Nick, not seeing one sign of emotion registering in Wael's expression.

He was well educated, someone who provided good company, Nick remembered. Always softly spoken; a twenty-six year old former news cameraman who had broken into Alex's steel lined heart and probably still did every time he met her. Now Wael accepted death as nothing out of the ordinary. It's when the war seeps inside us the problems start Nick reasoned; it is the conflicts that become personal that slowly eat away at our humanity, become open lesions on the thin skin of decency.

Shuffling apart for their commander and Nick, the officers revealed a naked male lashed upright to a heavy grille propped against a wall at a tilt. Nick could tell from the injuries that the man's release through death couldn't have come quick enough.

Dismissing questions from an aide with an irritable glance of having more pressing matters to consider, Wael launched a series of his own questions at a thin, bald officer studiously commencing an examination of the deputy commander's corpse.

He'd given them everything decided Nick; this is pure revenge, payback big time. There wasn't an inch of him they hadn't touched, he realised. The man's features were unrecognisable; a bloody, inflamed mess that Nick knew would conceal broken bones. His ribs had been given special attention, so too his arms and wrists which were clearly fractured.

The way his feet had discoloured Nick guessed that his soles had been savagely beaten, his ankles crudely broken. It was hard to distinguish where the islands of bruises on his torso ended and tattoos of cigarette burns began. At some point they'd attached clips to his testicles for doses of electric shock. But the power from the generator must have fluctuated he thought, noting the severity of the burns.

The slow fuse of anger at what he was witnessing as a dubious voyeur spilled over. Roughly elbowing his way out of the circle Nick retraced his steps back down to the floor below knowing the longer he stayed, the greater the chance a personal quest for justice would erode his objectivity. And that would not be good news for the operation he warned himself, lighting a cigarette.

•••

How, or where it happened, Nick never disclosed. The first inkling London had of Nick having cut all ties with Wael and the FSA came the following morning, relayed through Sawtry, his SBS liaison in Cyprus. By then Nick had put the last of Damascus' checkpoints behind him. Armed with fragments of signal intelligence supplied by Cheltenham confirming the main compound east of the Khanaser Plain as the location where they believed Hāru had gone to ground, he drove north in his pig of a truck he'd had fully overhauled, insisting on watching the mechanics fit run-flat tyres.

He'd stacked the truck's rear bed with empty poultry crates as a slim form of cover. Under a blanket on the stained passenger seat he'd stored a folding stock AK-47 with extra magazines as insurance. For the entire drive he wore a keffiyeh tucked around his neck, and a short sleeve blue check travel shirt hanging loosely over his cargo trousers. Staying clear of expressways, he opted for the hard-surfaced roads, dirt trails and remote tracks for his first stage on a north-west heading towards Qarah.

Breaking the drive into bridging zones he negotiated each of them with restraint, seeking out lying-up places before continuing. As much as Nick felt the need for a full-on charge up towards Aleppo, he deliberately made it slow going to give him a healthy distance from regime forces and rebels; nominating them all as more than likely to be extremely deadly or unfriendly.

On a rough east-west tack across country he gradually crept north. In villages so small they didn't feature on standard maps he read the trauma in the children's eyes, the vacant stares asking 'why'? They'd lost their mothers, fathers, brothers, sisters, sometimes their grandparents without ever having an answer to the madness they couldn't begin to understand. One boy's small eyes were dark, baggy like an old man's. When they hit Nick's fleeting glance, he felt as if he'd been cursed.

He remembered the child casualties in Afghanistan; the blackened chunks of corpses their families couldn't recognise, those left limbless from stumbling on IEDs or mines. He'd learnt to ignore their faces, concentrate on their wounds, a process of desensitisation so that lifeless eyes couldn't return to haunt you because they have history attached; the short lives lived, the future years lost.

When he ventured into areas he knew were under the jurisdiction of radical *jihadists* around Homs he drove at night, adopting a no lights routine. At hourly intervals Nick would halt, take a GPS reading he cross-referenced on his map under the red glow from his head torch. During one of these stops where he selected his next objective, he had pulled a good way off a dirt trail, reversing into a wadi. Out of the pickup in the cool night air he stretched his legs, jogging on his heels and toes to ease the numbing ache in his lower spine.

Working out a route to skirt around any villages, farms and compounds lying in the darkness up ahead, he'd knelt within reach of his door studying the possibilities on his map. He felt the first vibrations of the convoy before he saw its chain of headlights in the distance. Slowly levering himself up Nick reached across to the passenger seat withdrawing his AK-47 and spare magazines from under the blanket.

If they have night vision I'm going to have a contact to remember, he thought, taking up a prone defensive position a yard or two from his truck. Of all the places to be 'bumped' this wasn't one of them he reasoned.

Folding out the stock he nestled it firmly against his shoulder, racked back the cocking handle then flipped the safety lever down one notch for automatic. The tremble passing through the compact top layer of sand worked its way through Nick's body when the long column of land cruisers and armed pickups began rumbling by. The cruisers and pickups, either cream or white, were hauling *jihadi* fighters to another fluid front. It struck him how the fighters swaddled in black with their black flags hoisted above the white cabs had an unnerving resemblance to a medieval army on the move, invaders en route to a siege.

Pressed as low as he could go he took each breath slowly in a familiar, controlled rhythm. He'd estimated it to be a thirty strong convoy, and after the last vehicle slipped into the darkness his final tally came to thirty-eight. A few of the cruisers he'd seen had heavily tinted windows and no number plates; the standard commanders' transport.

From the silhouettes he knew the majority of the pickups – in military jargon 'technicals' – were equipped with PKMs, at least a dozen were fitted with *Dushkas*. For a healthy ten minutes he stayed in the same firing position, aware there was always the chance that there may be stragglers attempting to play catch-up with the column.

None did.

Out of the wadi Nick resumed his trek, following a different heading for the last hour, entering Al-Rahjan on the heels of a misty dawn. Moving through ruined streets he saw only children and women roaming in dazed, famished packs; the men press-ganged into a war no one seemed like winning. Along his route he noticed competing helplines urging wealthy relatives of kidnap victims to call. Applied in high letters on walls and burnt-out vehicles like political slogans, he knew how abduction had become a profitable sideline for local tribal gangs or militias when they needed to raise quick funds.

Slowing to a crawl, then accelerating, he sped through a junction partially blocked by a Russian T55 tank with its turret blown off. Farther along he came across regime personnel carriers scorched, blasted apart. On the road into Al-Hammam he drove by a rebel units' pickup ripped open by heavy calibre weapons. The bodies hadn't been removed. From a distance they looked to be draped in black mantillas. Only when he was closer did he realise they were packs of flies come to feast. In this remote front line, the only medical assistance rebel units could call on was usually a sympathetic local dental surgeon.

Artillery and air strikes rumbled off in the distant like constant summer thunder. When the wind picked up it brought snatched exchanges of small arms coupled with heavy weapons. To use the remaining daylight hours for rest Nick struck out across the semi-arid, rugged terrain until he found a suitable lying-up position inside a dry ravine on the mountain fringes running to the southern tip of the Khanaser Plain.

• • •

They had assembled to listen to Hāru. Freshly trained *fedayeen* sitting cross-legged in the centre of the camp as a cool evening gradually eased over them. Each and every one a noble volunteer pledged to continue the armed struggle, all willing martyrs in the war to liquidate Israel. A cadre of young men brought together from every corner of the Palestinian territories reared on hatred for the Jews, a loathing for their Western allies. All of them believing their homelands composed the MFP's front line.

Beckoned into the camp's main compound by the training cadre – men hardened by years of armed struggle – there was a palpable sense of expectation. It was almost as if a mild electric current flowed through the volunteers' bodies, connecting them together as a new generation of warriors.

In the weeks they had lived on the edge of civilisation in Syria, their camp became the centre of their universe. Unquestioning obedience to orders had been brutally enforced from the second they arrived. The days were measured, precise, leaving nothing to chance in their military training. Some buckled at the gruelling routine, others embraced it; but they all suffered the same routine in the name of victory.

After morning prayers they would divide into groups for physical exercise, toughening their bodies on the assault course before political classes reinforced their grievances as Palestinians. The afternoon always consisted of training on weapons where they learnt first how to break apart their 9mm pistols, moving on to assault rifles then light and heavy machine guns. Marksmanship was expected, so too was close quarter combat skills emphasising fire and manoeuvre tactics.

Later in their training they would be divided again into specialised teams for the heavy calibre weapons, with the truly gifted receiving personal tuition in engineering improvised explosive devices. Those revealing leadership potential would be given extra political instruction in preparation for running their own European cells or commanding a fighting unit.

Their training was in the past, now they waited to hear about the future.

Hāru's arrival heightened the atmosphere of celebration. It also marked an unexpected break with routine because a female warrior walked proudly at his side; a Westerner Hāru had taken as his bride. They knew her as Amatulla Salhab, a dedicated, accomplished bomb maker – her background unknown, as was her capitalist name of Lydia Hallam. Strolling out to address them Hāru cut a dashing figure in impeccably pressed combats he'd topped with a beret. Embellishing his image as a freedom fighter he wore his keffiyeh hanging loosely around his neck. At his side, similarly dressed, Hallam gazed proudly out at the graduates. They both had AK-47s gripped casually in one hand, Makarov 9mm pistols holstered around their waists.

Holding up both arms Hāru called for attention.

'Brothers of Palestine this moment will live with you forever. You are ready to become men of vengeance. It is the day you truly join our ranks as MFP warriors,' he began earnestly, his voice sharp, its clarity heightened by the pure desert air. 'The Jews have occupied our homeland for too many generations. They are thieves, murderers. They have dispossessed our people; they butcher men, women and children to give *our* land to Zionist settlers,' he declared as though reciting a prepared statement. Which he was, jointly scripted by fellow members of the Armed Struggle Command.

'All of you, my brothers, have seen the true faith. You have pledged your loyalty... your lives to making judgement on the Jews. We know in our hearts that they are guilty. Together we will pronounce our own death sentence on the malignant, criminal Israel. As dawn breaks tomorrow you will leave here, your work in this camp is complete. By sunset you are to begin a new phase in our war. You, my brothers, are the chosen executioners; you will be the strike force to overthrow the Zionist colonisers. Never forget my brothers, that the whole of our homeland *is* a Holy State, intended for Muslims.'

Taking a moment for his wisdom to circulate through the ranks of the faithful, Hāru continued: 'You, my brothers, will cleanse our homeland of Jews. *You* are the warriors who will plunder the will and spirit of their imperialist puppets in Washington and London. It is they who are now your enemies and they will be eradicated for stealing the soul of our people. It is you who will punish the imams of infidelity in Britain and America. All of you should rejoice in making our enemies cower.' Bringing up his AK-47, Hāru fired off a long burst into the evening sky.

Other AK-47s from the instructors swelled into a barrage, an established revolutionary anthem before the new fedayeen joined in; a refrain from expendable MFP martyrs.

Thirty-Two

A mile or so before the GPS position he'd been working so faithfully to reach, Nick spotted the first set of tyre tracks. He viewed them from different angles, confirming that they were from an adapted quad bike operating as a forward scout. He traced the bike's direction of travel across the rough, weathered semi-plains cupped in the northern arm of Mount Shubayt. He also clearly saw where it had been joined by another machine, its tracks leading away to a different compass point. Then overlapping in opposite outer sweeps, they'd used their tracks to improvise an advanced greeting in strict adherence of the operational procedure demanding radio silence.

Fighting to get his truck into gear, he cursed it to hell and back before he rolled off along a pair of tracks left by the quads ridden side by side. He drove in low revs to negotiate the unforgiving terrain, but even with the moonlight he couldn't avoid every serious rut, hump or shallow depression. Tensing each time the jolt reverberated up off the front axle, he urged, he cajoled, he openly threatened the pig of a truck that while he was at the wheel it would not shake itself apart. In just under three and a quarter back wrenching miles he nursed the grinding, squeaking truck to a halt at his final rendezvous near Al-Hammili, an eerie, desert ghost town.

Sitting cross-legged on the warm pickup's bonnet to fend off the night's departing chill, his AK-47 resting across his lap, he used his compact binoculars to scan the horizon for any telltale spume of dust. Dutifully checking each quarter of an hour he saw nothing. No dust, no sign of the planned reception party. In the distance at high altitude, a plane flew along the rim of dawn unzipping the fragile morning. The arrival of a lighter sky fluted in thin red slivers revealed a vehicle travelling fast. He'd locked his binoculars on it after it first appeared as a black dot. As it neared he started to pick out the details; an Iranian built Pazhan 3000 – a cloned Land Rover Defender – that had somehow found its way from the Syrian Army into the hands of the Jordanian Special Forces. One of two 'wagons' Danny Redmond had supervised during their adaptation into open-topped desert fighting vehicles, it seemed to skim across the crusty desert like a dust devil.

He's gone and modelled it on the SAS's old style 'Pinkies' realised Nick, tracking the Pazhan. Danny's reliving his days as a NCO in the Mobility Troop he thought smiling to himself, ticking off the upgraded features. Not blessed with the same power or suspension as a Land Rover 110, Danny had still managed to pack the wagon with an impressive punch, noted Nick. The main armament mounted in the rear was a .50cal machine gun. For the sort of extra firepower Danny once relied on, he'd had a GPMG fitted up front.

'Forget I was coming?' Nick yelled sliding off the bonnet when the Pazhan came within range. 'You're an hour behind schedule,' he stiffly reminded Danny and his driver, Mark Lindeth, when he reached the heavily laden wagon. 'Tactically misplaced?' he added.

'A dozen surface to air missile launchers were kicking up dust. Looked like 2K12 KUDs,' Danny avowed to nodded agreement from Lindeth.

'Any threat?' called Nick starting to unpack his truck.

'Spotted them over six klicks out from our PB, but we weren't bumped,' Danny explained.

'Were the KUDs setting up?' Nick wondered, transferring everything from the pickup to the Pazhan, which now became his wagon.

'Heading north... they'd pulled out of Rasm al-Ahmar after an overnight stop. Disorganized, a shambles, total bollocks,' Danny added, stowing Nick's gear into the wagon. 'Got a bit chocka, so we laid-up, took stock and detoured around Wādī Ja'ār al Gharbī,' he added.

'Any other hostile movement?' Nick enquired, considering the possibility that Hāru's compound might be out of their reach given the heavy volume of enemy traffic moving up to Aleppo.

'Syrian mil mostly, infantry, looked like conscripts. Had *jihadi* technicals roaming up front as scouts,' conceded Danny.

The last thing Nick needed would be to clean slate the operation if FSA fronts around Aleppo collapsed. 'Okay, let's crack on,' he decided.

To 'deny' Nick's truck to regime or rebel scavengers who might start wondering why its owner had abandoned a working pickup, he coaxed it down into a twisting high-sided gully.

The last rites were deftly administered by Lindeth packing explosive charges inside the truck, the fuses relatively short, a manual system rated at ninety seconds. On top of one demolition pack Nick placed his AK-47 and spare magazines.

Off and rolling with something close to eight and a half seconds to detonation, Nick glanced back from his commander's front seat in the wagon when the charges blew. For a split second the pig of a truck peeked cheekily above the gully walls. Then it was gone, ripped into shrapnel cascading down across the desert floor in a metallic hail shower.

'How far to the PB,' Nick yelled to Danny manning the .50cal in the back.

It could have been five miles or a thousand that Danny shouted in reply. Whatever the distance it was to the patrol base, it was lost under the snarl of the engine then snatched away by the wind screaming past. Nick just nodded, tightening his grip as Lindeth fought the Pazhan over a nasty band of rock hard washboard ruts.

As patrol bases go, this one, aptly named *Furnace* by Danny, really had nothing much in its favour Nick decided within five minutes of his arrival. From the surrounding bleak, empty terrain he knew Danny had no other real options. He'd selected a sweeping bend in a narrow stretch of a deep wadi where an outcrop brought partial shade. Nick spent a couple of minutes with Danny sheltering from an unforgiving sun, then he was off, touring the remainder of his CO8 combat team.

Chris Loftus, running a critical eye over the .50cal on the wagon Danny would command nodded a cheery greeting, Pete Anston breaking off from cleaning his C8 carbine gave a brisk thumbs up.

They wouldn't admit to anything but being ready thought Nick, checking with Tony Hagley nursing the satellite comms in the unarmed Liberty, before finishing his grand tour with the four other team members. A couple of feet away he found Lindeth deep in thought fussing over his carry system, but assuring Nick he was fine. Absorbed with essential maintenance on their quads, Neil Stipden and Alan Welney nodded a greeting. Finally he received Steve Tew's upbeat report as he prepared Nick's wagon.

He knew none of them would let him down, but was he about to demand the impossible from them? He didn't know, which concerned him a great deal, occupying his thoughts until Danny returned from his shift on stag, his vigil as lookout taken by Anston.

'Cheltenham have harvested the latest phone and Internet traffic from the compound,' disclosed Danny, dusting himself down. 'They've had voiceprint hits,' he continued, 'which we've confirmed from our ISTAR. We have Hāru, Hallam and Rewall in residence.'

'What else?'

With barely a pause, Danny unrolled the intelligence, surveillance, target acquisition and reconnaissance gathered by the team in the days before Nick's arrival. 'There's been a big buzz at the training camp,' he admitted, pointing his C8 carbine in a north-west heading. 'We can't decide if someone's rattled the cage or if it's planned, but newly minted *fedayeen* are being shuttled out.'

Nick thought of Saqiz the Storyteller's elimination, he thought of the FSA sector commander's over zealous surveillance; how long could they ride their luck before Hāru responded?

'So who's left?'

'Eight instructors pulling the camp apart,' said Danny, preparing two coffees.

'The distance between the camp and compound?'

'Three klicks.'

'Numbers in the compound?'

'Sixteen ...,' announced Danny.

He pulled out two A5 booklets their covers laminated, as were the pages; they were CO8's operational Tactical Aide Memoires. Normally issued twenty-four hours ahead of an operation they contained grid reference guides, tactical codes, radio frequencies and a personal profile section holding photographs of targets, their height and weight, with one line notes on any visible identifying features.

'Hāru has a bunch of guests staying,' Danny continued as if bearing bad news, handing Nick his own Tac Aide. 'We have eyes-on Hadi Semnān, boss of their intelligence outfit,' he added, tapping a page. 'Salem Abu Talib their security champion is here, and Walid al-Nubani a confirmed *Akab 1* representative is the number one guest from the special treatment they ladle on him. And they're not here to play happy families.'

'No they're not,' Nick agreed, thoughtfully flicking through the profile pages in his Tac Aide. In the jargon beloved of certain Whitehall officials, Hāru had convened a gathering of stakeholders, the only item open for discussion being Rewall's Operation Nomad treasure, suspected Nick.

'That gives us ten *fedayeen* operating as defence and security,' Danny disclosed. 'Two on the roof at all times for a three hour stag, then a new pair take over on the KPV-14.5 and LMG. The other six are all mobile in the compound. Weapons are AKS, 9mms and RPGs. This bunch seem like new recruits, no finesse,' he admitted. 'Hāru's close protection are different. Two mean *fedayeen* or instructors. Hāru doesn't step outside without them. A second pair work split shifts, one always solo patrolling around the guest annexe which also seems to be Rewall's accommodation.'

The likelihood that Hāru could also now have clearance to call in heavy, loyal support from the regime crossed Nick's mind. How far away any assistance may be, and what it amounted to in numbers and firepower had Nick worried that they might just have lost all their advantages.

Leaning back against a wheel on the Liberty he quietly absorbed the remainder of Danny's full briefing.

'What about the farm half a klick north-east?' Nick wondered kneeling at the edge of a map they spread out between them, their C8 carbines holding the sides flat.

He'd asked for profiles on anyone in a settlement close to Hāru's compound; a tactical insight into their normal daily routines – Did they have frequent visitors? The number of vehicles they owned? Did they openly display their sympathies? Could they be armed? Would they lend a defensive hand?

To these last minute concerns Danny provided answers compiled from a number of close target recces. Supplemented by satellite images, the recces supplied detailed visual clues for what they could expect in Hāru's compound. From an approximate height of the compound walls, to the possible size of windows, internal and external doors, Danny gave a mental tour of the villa and its guest annexe.

If Nick was satisfied he didn't show it. He had the normal commander's curse of playing through each proposed operational action and scenario, double-checking, triple-checking that he'd overlooked nothing of importance.

After the midday heat mellowed, the late afternoon dragged its lazy shadows towards evening, where at a preselected hour Nick delivered his pre-op briefing. Opening proceedings he reminded everyone it was their responsibility to adhere to CO8's operating procedures; insisting that no item of personal combat kit was to be traceable except as readily available surplus commercial equipment. There wasn't anything close to a full military uniform between them anyway.

Their tactical body armour vests with ballistic plates were an eclectic mix of American styles based on personal preferences for different carrying systems. On such an isolated operation the need to preserve and share ammunition was also critical, so the standard pistols were SIG P226s in thigh holsters. For close quarters stopping power they opted for PDX1 hollow-point rounds. As his last point, the one that always drew sighs, Nick reminded them that if they hadn't made their wills, now was a good time as any.

Given the podium, the bonnet of his wagon, Danny outlined the current intelligence on Hāru's personal quarters located on the villa's third floor, emphasising the MFP commander's daily routine, dissecting the Palestinian's normal activity twice in forensic detail. Their approach would be dictated by the lay of the land, which happened to be flat, mostly featureless and a factor very much in Hāru's favour. What they could, and should expect, would be heavily armed resistance – a 'target rich environment' – according to the Americans, or in British parlance, a contact that would be a 'bit sporty'.

Now Nick owned the 'ground truth', his reading of the 'live' situation rather than relying on assumptions made elsewhere, his anxieties heightened.

Comparing maps and plans of the compound with feed captured by their drone's night recces replayed on Nick's Toughbook laptop, he made sure that everyone knew their limit of exploitation, what could and couldn't be sacrificed in the prime objective of taking priority targets alive. If they could bag all the principals and the main players they'd hit the jackpot.

After sorting out his main technical support, Nick loped off to a quiet space for his own prime time. He found it in a cleft of rock that swept majestically down into the wadi bottom. Here, undisturbed, he ate a beef jerky teriyaki, washing the industrial sauce away with a hot chocolate, flavoured – only the Army knew why – orange, followed by a hardy raisin bar. As much as he attempted to rest, Nick's mind would have none of it, stubbornly running through a number of possible outcomes for that night's operation. What they had wasn't ideal, but it's all they had.

He knew realistically it was only the first minutes of any operation you can plan and train for. Even with everything rehearsed using unit standard operating procedure – identifying individual and team tasks, flagging up the expected responses to situations that could arise on the ground, there were never ever any guarantees of success. After the first contact if things go awry, and they usually did, the only option would be thinking on your feet, which meant improvised solutions and carrying them out fast. Wondering how much that capability would be tested in a matter of hours, he belatedly began to wind down.

•••

She crossed the compound still unsure of why she had been summoned. Celia Rewall quite happily sympathised with her MFP comrades' decision to place her under house arrest; she was, after all, a proven traitor. She had done it once, would she do it again? Was she, they might wonder, a double agent? With that heavy-duty baggage came a bundle of restrictions until she proved her loyalty. Though this, like the reason she came, remained ambiguous; an unspoken clause she accepted as a challenge. They could have asked my husband if they hadn't blown him to smithereens she reasoned; poor lonely Graham was too weak. He was too absorbed in Western materialistic pleasures, its soul numbing dogma to understand her commitment to the Palestinian struggle for freedom, her passion to destroy, humiliate the enemy.

A missed opportunity of proving her unconditional loyalty, but there would be other situations where she could demonstrate how she would never turn back the clock. Held at the villa's main door until the bull of a sentry received clearance over his radio for her to enter, Rewall inwardly groaned at the petty rules. Did all guerrilla armies go through this stage of doltish bureaucratic control?

'You're expected,' the sentry snapped, his expression mordant. 'The meeting room.'

Forgive me if I am not worthy, she felt like saying, but held off as a gesture of peace to all *fedayeen*. Nodding once that she understood her directions, Rewall slipped inside the villa's entrance into a cool, shady hall.

After her climb up the marble tiled stairs to the second floor, she made for the meeting room door set alone at the end of a dark corridor. From inside she heard a laugh and the rumble of low voices. She hesitated, uncertain suddenly of why they had sent for her and what would be expected of her. She pushed back the door.

'Hey... glad you could make it,' Hāru cordially announced.

'Glad to be here,' Rewall smiled back at the MFP's golden boy. He sat beside Hallam on a low sofa, both of them grinning like two besotted teenage lovers.

The meeting room had windows leading to a balcony, their glazed bars slightly open letting in a smell of hot, sandy earth and goat flesh from the compound along with curious, drowsy flies. The furniture had a second hand low quality style, leather sofas and chairs polished and cracked so dark the hide seemed too shrink from touch. Spread around the available seats Rewall slowly recognised other members of the inner court she'd only fleetingly met: Talib the bruising head of security sat apart, a fresh date skewered on a cocktail stick he appeared in no hurry to eat. Propped to attention in a club chair, Semnān the dictator of everything intelligence related, glanced at her with disinterest, his attention flicking straight back to something on his phone's screen.

Gallantly aiming her towards the only vacant seat – a stubby legged side chair – the man she knew as al-Nubani, an *Akab 1* officer, smiled, an avuncular uncle welcoming his niece.

'We're going to rearrange our disclosure schedule,' Hāru sadly admitted, convivially opening the forum. His expression, his whole tone gave the impression of an impromptu meeting.

'Do I get to ask *why?*'

'No...' Talib snapped, launching straight into a planned offensive of shutting her down.

'Yes...'

'Of course...'

Semnān and al-Nubani answered as one.

'It is time to recover the Nomad material you cached,' Hāru suggested as if it only involved a trip to a local market.

'I thought we'd agreed that I'd release more disclosures first?' Rewall objected mildly.

'This is not possible,' declared al-Nubani.

'You made sure the material would not be found?' Talib barked.

'Our sister has volunteered to travel with you,' Semnān added, picking out Hallam with a curt glance.

And it was at this particular instance she realised a number of hours later, in the solitude of her room as she unwound and recovered the thread of her thoughts, that her role, her contribution was rapidly losing some of its sparkle. The confirmation of a reverse in what she'd assumed would be a smooth acceptance by her MFP comrades arrived later that night in the bitter mood displayed by Lydia Hallam.

'We leave the day after tomorrow,' Hallam curtly opened when she was inside Rewall's room, her back against the door, her arms knotted across her chest.

'Have you got a grievance against me Lydia?'

In the couple of seconds after Rewall attempted to clear the air Hallam was on her. She slapped, she punched, she lashed out with her feet; snarling, hissing as she set about Rewall with unbridled venom.

'I've seen how you look at him,' Hallam panted, standing off, her attack wound down, her aggressive outburst subsided. 'He never loved you,' she spat, her sides and chest heaving with the effort of catching her breath.

Taking refuge on a simple metal bed, Rewall shook her head, running her fingers over the bruised, puffy skin around her eyes. 'It wasn't Hāru I loved,' she explained, wiping the blood of her lip with the back of her hand. She drew up her legs, folding her arms around them, her back tucked safely in the corner. 'Not in the sense you understand. I love him as a symbol of his people, of his country,' she confessed. 'I am willing to die in the fight for a Palestinian homeland. Are you?'

Biting her lip Hallam started to form a response, her face dipped in a scowl, her eyes flooded with a lonely sadness. Shaking her head in pitiful contempt, she turned, walking briskly from Rewall's room.

Thirty-Three

Retreating from the brittle tension in his villa, Hāru slipped away to a small primitive mud brick dwelling in a meagre alley close to his compound. He'd reached his earth walled sanctuary through a tunnel dug for escape or to spring ambushes. Climbing a handmade ladder, its rungs fastened with sturdy twine, Hāru strode to the edge of the flat, sun baked roof, surveying the surrounding district.

Below him a handful of similar ragged dwellings inside their own tiny mud walled compounds; the partial ruins of a tribal village emptied by his *fedayeen* when Hāru claimed the villa as his own. Farther out towards the horizon he gazed at the flat, pitch dark Khanaser Plain. Ebbing away, the plain lapped against the spread of Mount Shubayt silhouetted against a cerulean desert sky bursting with stars.

He stared intently at the darkened peaks, the crests, the ridges, his heart heavy with sorrow as he remembered a family legend.

The moon is a mover of mountains... his aunt told him when he was a child, wrapped and tucked neatly under sheets and blankets in her home. Hāru's favourite aunt, his beautiful mother's sister, butchered in cold-blooded retaliation by Zionist settlers who set fire to her house with his aunt inside.

The moon is a mover of mountains only when you're ready to face great danger, when you grow into a warrior, when you're ready to give your life for your people. Only then will the moon move mountains, his aunt promised, stroking his forehead, her voice a soft, poetic melody gently leading him towards sleep.

'They *will* move...' Hāru quietly vowed, his eyes pricking with the strain of staring long and hard into the distance.

Hearing footsteps pad along the alley, Hāru brought his AK-47 around off his shoulder. Stepping deftly backwards until he judged he had enough distance, he took up a firing position on one knee, his barrel aimed where the roof and ladder met.

'Al-Nubani requests you should return,' Lydia Hallam informed him clambering onto the roof.

'He can wait,' snapped Hāru rising. Lowering his AK he let it swing freely at his hip.

'A captain from the artillery base is here...'

'Let Semnān take care of him,' Hāru ordered, abruptly silencing her, 'he does nothing to justify his status.'

'What's wrong? What's eating you? Tell me, I can help.'

'Really... is that what you think, my pretty little Lydia,' Hāru angrily flared, briskly striding across to her. '*You* are my salvation, is that what *you* think? Only *you* understand me?' he spat, toe to toe with Hallam.

'I am your wife,' she hissed, her face twisted in outright fury.

'Go,' he instructed her, his voice strangely calm, a distant tenor to it. 'Go deal with the officer of artillery. Better warn him that I have patrols out. Tell him if he doesn't want his beautiful bus shot up, he should confirm his route with Talib. Go,' he snapped. Crudely snatching Hallam by the shoulder, Hāru spun his wife towards the ladder.

•••

Prior to their departure at 2345 hours on what had turned into a bitter Syrian night, the team scrupulously bagged up any trace of their stay. As Nick made a final inspection using his red head torch to walk the patrol base, satisfying himself that nothing remained, he heard the metallic notes from a final weapon and magazine checks on GPMGs and .50cals clacking in the darkness around him like nasty, lethal insects. Nick's very last piece of personal admin saw him turning his spare magazines upside down in his pouches preventing dust jamming them.

After testing the frequency on their personal role radios for one last time, Nick gave the command to move off. Instigating a no light routine they started to plough their way on a selected route towards Hāru's compound, the terrain a strange, glowing luminescent green through the teams' panoramic night vision goggles. Nick's wagon, placed second in the convoy, clung to a steady dust stream thrown up from the roving quad bikes riding ahead to sniff out potential trouble. And less than a kilometre out from their forming-up place, they found it.

The first Nick knew about running into a forward line of enemy troops came with a salvo of heavy calibre fire, then over the radio in a rapid transmission from one of the quads: 'Charlie Oscar One... Charlie Oscar Four. Contact. Wait. Out.'

He'd got as far as responding to Stipden's callsign: 'Charlie Oscar Four...' when a stream of green tracer looped towards the quads' last position. 'All Callsigns... Charlie Oscar One. Go mobile... we need fire support for Charlie Oscar Three and Four. Repeat, mobile and fire support,' Nick instructed his team. He yelled for Lindeth, his driver, to head east towards a cluster of low, block built workshops marked on the map as a gas pipeline field station.

Nick cocked his GPMG as they belted over the rutted desert floor, opening up in a chorus to Tew banging away with his .50cal. Their tracer rounds spurted in rapid dash dot dash jets at three pickups that had swung out on a short service road between the field station's north and south sections. Through his goggles Nick's view consisted of a rapid exchange of white-hot tracer with brilliant popping flashes of intense light from a *Dushka* and a hulking, lethal ZPU-2 anti-aircraft gun mounted on a pickup.

We've only gone and woken every militia, rebel, regime and *jihadist* units in the area Nick dismally thought, swinging his GPMG around on its pintle mount, engaging one of the pickups breaking away from the field station.

For a matter of minutes it was, in Danny's valid opinion, 'fucking mayhem'. And if Nick had been able to hear him through his PRR headset he would have wholeheartedly agreed. But he couldn't hear a thing. Callsign reports were scattered into garbled fragments under the insane spatter of his GPMG and the blistering boom... boom... boom of Tew's .50cal. In any case Nick had no need of yelling directions through his PRR's mic, the whole team were wise old hands at fire and manoeuvre, mounted or dismounted.

Working off each other's positions, the wagons and quads deployed as individual units. The pickup Nick and Tew had in their sights hadn't moved since it had been caught out in the open. In Nick's view of the action – a weird saturated green – the pickup had half tipped; its driver's side lifted a couple of feet in the air. The smoke streaming from its engine confirming the vehicle and its crew, twisted and torn on the sand, were unlikely to bother them again.

Sat up on his quad Stipden would pop away at the two pickups behind the field station with a 40mm grenade launcher slung underneath his C8. After loosing off a random number of area rounds he'd drop back into the saddle and throttle away, covered by Welney's LMG on the second quad. Far from slackening, the rate of fire rose in intense salvoes as the remaining pickups took turns to lurch out from behind the field station attempting to pick off one of the wagons or quads.

Breaking off to change a belt Nick bent low shouting his instructions close to Lindeth's ear, receiving a smart thumbs up response. Accelerating as Nick closed the GPMG's latch on his fresh link, the burst of speed sloshed spent cases backwards and forwards in the footwell, a jingling brass swell washing against Nick's boots.

Somehow managing to obtain Danny's attention over his PRR, Nick clung on for dear life when Lindeth pitched the wagon in a tight, controlled right turn. When Danny's wagon came alongside, Nick shouted across his plan. Danny reviewed it for a couple of seconds before bawling back: 'Why not.'

Nudging Lindeth in his side three times with his boot, Nick braced hard for a fast disengagement Lindeth achieved in a flowing series of gear ratios matched by the wagon's raw power.

He knew he had no more than a window of seconds with nothing to spare, and they started ticking when the pickup slogging it out with Danny and the quads drew back behind the field station for the handover. Giving Nick everything the wagon had, Lindeth set a direct course for a point midway along the outer, southern station building.

Berthing the wagon alongside the eight foot cracked render wall, Lindeth gave a fast 'Go...go...go' gesture with one hand. Nick, perched on the spare tyre clamped to the outer panel behind his door, made one leap, missed and tried again. On the third attempt he latched hold of a concrete lip on the flat roof's low parapet. Digging in with his knees, his boots and elbows, his stomach muscles tightening in a vicious clamp, he shimmied his way up to the top.

Hauling his legs over the parapet he flopped into a prone position not moving, listening for any yelled shouts of alarm rising above the duty pickup taking its turn to smash out *Dushka* rounds. Leaning his head and arms over the parapet he held open his hands catching two fragmentation grenades Lindeth pitched up to him one at a time, followed by his C8 carbine.

Down on his belt buckle Nick crabbed across the roof, tucking himself into the far parapet. This close to the *Dushka* hammering away, the whole roof vibrated, small tremors riding up from the service road immediately below. Running through the pickups' changeover routine in his head, Nick strained to hear the first signal that it was about to happen. In the noise of what had indeed become a very sporty contact, he just caught the silent *Dushka* below him being cocked.

Nick didn't lob or throw the grenades. He dropped them. One after the other in a precise routine – pin out, go. He'd eased slowly up, glanced rapidly down onto the idling pickup, calculating a rough crossover point where it would meet the withdrawing firing unit. The grenades detonated consecutively, two blasts Nick roughly timed at five and seven seconds. Because of the cosiness of the buildings either side of the narrow service road, the confined blast was intense, devastating.

For Nick, face down on the roof's concrete skin, the violent shock waves actually felt as if the building swayed; that same strange moment of disorientation a Royal Marine experiences when he goes to sea for the first time. Covering his head as best he could with his hands and lower arms, he still managed to get a gash below his left ear when parts of the pickups fell back into the service road. Along with grit in his eyes, he had dust in his mouth, nose and ears. From somewhere below him there were two single shots. They sounded a couple of miles off at least thanks to the faint humming in his ears. Joining a very short, intense firefight, Nick put round after round down, laying into the remaining *fedayeen*.

The aftermath of any contact is never pretty. It's more often than not a right royal bloody mess. There are no winners, only those fortunate to survive, and they don't have the luxury of being able to switch off, write it up as job done. The final procedure was one every combat soldier loathed with a passion; the site sensitive examination demanding a thorough search and recovery task. This involved the messy collection of personal items and recording images of the dead for identification, for intelligence analysis. Nick knew the carnage he was stepping through would be another carving on the totem pole of horrors he carried deep inside; one more macabre scene automatically edited, added onto the nightmare spool suitable only for adult viewing.

There was little point bothering to photograph the *fedayeen's* faces to check if one of them was Hāru. They had no faces. One of them didn't have anything recognisable, except, bizarrely, a right leg and foot still laced into a bargain buy training shoe. The two fighters Danny had humanely put out of their agony had dragged their badly pulped remains a little way from the mangled pickups. Every step Nick made he knew it was going to be on body parts: lumps of flesh, muscle, limb, brain, pools of blood, streams of body fluids and leaking fuel.

Against the blackened wall that absorbed a good deal of chunky shrapnel, Nick found the last *fedayeen*. There was nothing left below his waist. His naked torso just sat there on the hard packed service road, a brilliant white trail of intestines leaking into the sand, like roots urgently trying to probe their way underground. The fighter's nose, eyes and jaw were missing, so too were fist sized pieces of flesh from his neck and chest. Identification was impossible.

The first pickup they neutralised out in the open had a rudimentary radio badly damaged by .50cal rounds. On the driver's door the MFP pennant had taken a severe mauling.

'If they notified the compound, we've got an issue,' Danny said, pointing out the smashed radio unit when Nick joined him at the wreckage.

'We'll have to deal with it,' Nick said, flapping open a clear sack Danny filled with the *fedayeens'* personal effects: prayer beads, mobile telephones, wallets, coin purses, a notebook, a picture of a child, a broken pencil, a comb with teeth missing. 'Portraits done?'

'Stipden's got what he can,' said Danny.

'Time to go and pay our respects to Hāru,' decided Nick, the adrenalin swilling through his system.

Thirty-Four

A hastily arranged bonnet brief was held shortly after they drew up into a rough circle at 0145. Gathered around Nick's wagon they listened intently to the quick battle orders. He spent no more than ten minutes designating new tactical objectives assigned into territorial boxes; each box the responsibility of individual team members for the duration of their compound assault. The main 'ops box' would be the villa itself with Nick heading the high value target team.

'Because of our little entertaining interlude back there,' said Nick, nodding his head towards the field station, 'Hāru will be either in the wind or preparing to make us pay for ruining his sleep. No matter what we run into, our prime task is to bag him and any other MFP friends. We need them alive, kicking and breathing.'

After Nick's pragmatic speech they mounted up, every member of the team trying to disguise the soldier's expression of grim realisation this may just be their final battle. Then without any ceremony Hagley in the unarmed Liberty with Stipden on his quad as escort formed the advance, slipping away before the others to recce Nick's chosen forming-up point.

Moving off when Hagley reported no opposition, no problems, the run-in brought no further contacts though Nick didn't regard that as a bonus, it raised a whole new set of issues to add to his heavy list of concerns. Was that a regular MFP patrol or a fluke they had run into? Were they the last instructors to leave the camp? Has Hāru prevented others from pulling out, ordering them into the compound as reinforcements? Unable to provide adequate answers, Nick concentrated on being Lindeth's second pair of eyes as they bumped along, his vision suffering from 'green fever', a niggling, fuzzy strain from peering intently at the terrain's features through his night vision goggles.

A couple of miles out from their target compound Nick signalled for an immediate halt.

Something on the crisp desert floor where it sneaked into a valley a good way ahead of them troubled Nick. So much so, that he sprinted over to Danny's wagon, returning with his second in command at a brisk trot.

'Shit...' Danny stated, catching his breath, staring at the footage on Nick's Toughbook balanced on its Pelican case.

'Exactly,' said Nick, following tracking shots coming back from their drone way ahead of them in the distance.

'Regime,' speculated Danny.

'Seem to be,' Nick stared at the screen.

Standing on its own, to all the world completely stranded, a pig-ugly, vintage jingly bus personalised with tasselled curtain window blinds. Around it twenty feckless regime conscripts loafing about. Nervously smoking, chatting or wishing they were somewhere else, they stood in groups with a couple of NCOs hawkishly watching over them. At the rear peering into the engine compartment, its driver shone a flashlight hopelessly around its guts.

'Let's hope their bosses included recovery in their breakdown membership,' suggested Danny.

'Yes,' Nick agreed.

Confronted with another risk of having his operation compromised, Nick ran their options past Danny, neither of them wanting to risk another contact, not even with conscripts, not this far down the line. The solution, not optimal, but nevertheless practical given the circumstances, involved a fast, Hail Mary, looping manoeuvre.

Assured everyone understood the plan, Nick gave Lindeth the nod to bring their wagon up to a smart walking pace. Around him, the quad and Danny's wagon eased on their throttles in the same routine. Once they began to skirt the jingly bus on a diagonal bearing, Lindeth floored the accelerator. In a matter of seconds and with plumes of gritty sand spuming up around their wagons and quad, they shot away from the bus, Nick not caring to glance back.

In all, it cost an expensive forty minutes for their small convoy to regain their momentum, switch back to their primary heading. Once they were roughly positioned in line with their territorial boxes in a shallow, rocky re-entrant, Nick jumped down.

• • •

Hāru bristled in, no greeting, no smile. The room wore a scent of lemon blossom from petals arranged in neat copper bowls. Hurling down a spare AK magazine, he dropped onto a low sofa, nudging plum cushions aside. He propped his chin on the palm of his hand, balancing an elbow on his knee, staring quizzically at Celia Rewall.

'It seems we may have an unexpected change of plan,' Hāru began, his voice low. 'My patrols have failed to report in… I hear weapons exchanging fire… Who is responsible I ask myself? Has someone betrayed us? Has someone given our location away? Who is it out there? Which of our enemies is preparing to visit?'

'She is a traitor,' Lydia Hallam announced at Rewall's side.

'No….' Hāru angrily cut her off. 'No… No… No…,' he continued, his raised forefinger sweeping backwards and forwards in an admonishment reserved for a small child. 'No, my dear wife, you do not speak. This is not the time for petty jealousy.'

'Am I a liability?' Rewall answered.

She was perfectly composed. With some primal instinct she'd harboured from the very first moment she'd willingly given Hāru her body and soul, she'd anticipated how one day he would eventually have no use for her. This was the day; of that, she was sure.

'Celia… Celia… Celia…,' Hāru smiled, 'my dear Celia, you have proved loyal, you have my respect for what you have achieved. I will never be able to repay you for your dedication, the great service you have given to our cause. This…' Hāru broke off giving a light-hearted shake of his head.

He sat back, folded one leg over another, lit a cigarette; all the while lost in a deep bout of contemplation. Gazing at her intently Hāru quietly smoked, his cigarette held the traditional Arab way, high up between the fingers towards the knuckle.

She suddenly felt intimidated by Hāru's coolness. She loathed the charade he was performing; she loathed having bloody Lydia as her shadow, her jailer.

The road she had set out to travel as an enthusiastic, dedicated MFP supporter seemed so uncomplicated at the outset, more of a super highway taking her straight and true in her chosen direction. Now the road had suddenly narrowed, the way ahead unclear. More than once recently she'd panicked she had no energy to continue, a deepening desire to curl up and howl as events budded open around her. She'd planted the seeds, nourished them, diligently tended them, hoping, praying for them to bloom into a natural Palestinian spring. But she had lost control, couldn't bear to watch her flowers wither.

'We need action from the heart, Celia,' Hāru declared, grinding out his cigarette with a heel of his combat boot. 'Are you prepared? The decisions we take now will be seen in years to come as brave and heroic.'

'I have made sacrifices. I have made my life the gift of the Armed Struggle Command to do with it as they wish,' Rewall stated, rather too formally, smiling at her silly desire to impress.

Nodding gravely Hāru reverted to a man of action, the illustrious senior battle commander, the director of commando operations.

'Is everything prepared?' he demanded, snapping his attention on his wife.

'We are ready,' Hallam pledged, her body, her eyes, radiating devotion from Hāru's attention.

'Okay, good. We are leaving soon, Celia,' he disclosed, striding swiftly towards her. 'Lydia will take good care of you,' he promised his face close to hers. Gripping her by the shoulders he kissed one cheek then the other.

Very nice, Rewall thought, watching her one time lover sweep out. A kiss on the cheek from a Palestinian hero like I was his flaming sister; well that's some reward. You go Celia, the next time he might even shake you by the hand.

•••

When Nick joined Hagley at the Liberty's tailgate, the drone was climbing away towards the valley once more. With less than a thousand yards to the compound, Hagley put the drone into a climb. Squatting at the head of a low, wide valley, Hāru's compound came into focus on Hagley's Toughbook. Large, prestigious, constructed of concrete block, it must have belonged to an elder or tribal leader and his family reasoned Nick, seeing the villa flow onto the screen.

The compound dominated an abandoned settlement packed tightly around it in a natural hollow of a steep escarpment. In a series of bluffs, the escarpment rose in outcrops stretching away to Mount Shubayt. Compact, high earth walled compounds sheltering modest mud brick villas were linked by ribbons of alleys backing out into the valley.

The last thing Nick expected was for the villa and annexe to be lit from top to bottom. Each time the drone made a high, circular pass, Nick waited for each light on every floor to go dark, to go combat ready. But they remained defiantly on.

'Maybe they're going to throw the towel in,' Danny proposed, 'MFP don't fancy a good kicking.' But even he didn't sound close to being convinced.

'The pattern of activity is all wrong.' Nick checked the roof, he checked the courtyard, he checked the perimeter of the villa including its guest annexe. A pair of *fedayeen* continued to cover the compound and surrounding alleys with a LMG and a Russian KPV-14.5, an impressive anti-aircraft, anti-vehicle, anti-anything heavy machine gun.

Down below them the regular *fedayeen* security detail strolled through the compound, apparently oblivious to what should have been a no noise and no light routine, merrily chatting and sharing a cigarette. They stopped to check two additional pickups worryingly armed with *Dushkas*, substantial escorts that arrived with Hāru's guests. Thirty paces on, they looked over four prestige SUV's parked in their own exclusive corner, sharing admiring nods at the VIP transport.

'What do you want us to do?'

Staring hard at the screen Nick didn't answer. 'What's that?' he demanded. 'There... the alley... behind the main compound. There's movement...' he explained, pointing at an area heavy with shadow on the extreme left of the screen.

'Got them...' Hagley repositioned the drone. 'There... two of them... Both have AKs... one an RPG... There... There... They've slipped into an empty compound butting right up to our target destination,' Hagley added, whispering his commentary.

'Show me.' Nick squinted hard at the screen. 'There... another twenty yards, ten o'clock, third compound... two more.'

With delicate, precision hand movements on the remote control paddles, Hagley gracefully positioned his drone over an alley between compounds.

'Reinforcements?' Danny craned forward picking out two armed *fedayeen* in urban combat uniform leisurely propped against the wall of a single storey villa.

'Can we go back around?'

Sending the drone in for a second look, Hagley nursed it through a slow flypast starting at the gully. 'I make that four additions to the opposition,'

Nick volunteered.

'Not sure,' Hagley said adjusting the drone's height.

'Driver escorts for the VIPs,' Danny proposed. 'Sent out to play on foot patrol.'

Nick stared hard at Danny, his decision already made. 'Let's move.'

Formed up behind Welney's quad, the wagons, Liberty and Stipden's quad covering the rear, were nudged close to the re-entrant's craggy spurs. Hugging the contours they traversed on a bumpy course parallel to the compound, low gears, revs kept down. Drawn into a protective laager inside a gully marking their line of departure Hagley once more launched his drone. From over Hagley's shoulder Nick watched the drone take up position high above the villa and compound. A warm film of sweat coated Nick's fingers, settling into an itchy band around his neck.

To Nick's disquiet each window in the villa remained gloriously ablaze. He knew they would be up against the clock, he knew he alone possessed the authority to call-off the operation. After a group debate on the consequences of accounting for the extra *fedayeen*, Nick his decision reached, gave the 'Go' code over his PRR.

Calculated to the second, phase one began at 0245 when Lindeth and Loftus slipped away from their wagons, entering the alleys from the gully chute on foot, suppressed sniper rifles slung over their backs. Their overwatch positions preselected, they had a tense five minutes to set up after reaching their allotted rooftops employing the assistance of a telescopic ladder.

Guided through the maze of alleys by Hagley's drone eye view directions, Nick led the high value target team of Danny, Stipden and Welney in a heated sprint to the rear of the main compound. It took Welney two attempts scuffing up and down the base of the perimeter wall to locate a half buried utility box housing the villa's main electrical feed. With the supply interrupted, Welney took out the landline to the phones at the same time. In the seconds after the villa went off grid Nick heard Lindeth and Loftus transmit their 'ready to engage' signal. After he'd guided the drone on a different course, Hagley talking directly to an Israeli Gulfstream orchestrated electronic jamming.

Occupied by holding his ground after scaling the compound wall on a rickety telescopic ladder, Nick barely registered Lindeth and Loftus engaging two *fedayeen* inside a village compound, or their neutralising the gun crew on the villa's roof with one shot apiece, fired simultaneously. Up to that point Nick had thanked God, the angels and all the saints for their good progress when a *fedayeen* sent to investigate the loss of power trotted around the corner on his way to the backup generator. Fumbling his AK-47 to aim at Danny he lost valuable seconds. Hit by three rounds from Nick's suppressed C8 he bunched up, bouncing onto his side in an unflattering heap. 'Welcome to the party, boys,' Nick muttered into his PRR when the rest of the team scaled the compound wall.

According to Nick's reckoning, they were fifteen minutes adrift. In pairs, working in tandem – Nick with Welney, Danny with Stipden – they swept round the east and west side of the villa. From the front of the compound they heard yells, a string of bawled orders. They also heard Lindeth and Loftus select new targets, engage them. When Nick broke cover from his side of the block and stucco villa, a *fedayeen* lay in his own sticky blood alongside the backup generator he'd attempted to start. The other confirmed kill was a *fedayeen* on the roof, a hasty replacement trying to bring the KPV-14.5 into action.

Gathered around reinforced metal double entry doors Nick, Stipden and Danny went firm as Welney, down on one knee, finished attaching his strip of shaped breaching charge rigged with two detonators in case one failed. During the count down for the breach, a rapid exchange of semi-automatic fire in the distance carried into the compound, coming somewhere close to the guest annexe. The team turned to Nick who shook his head equally uncertain of what was happening.

Braced for the charge, his spine pressed to the wall, a hot lick of foul air from the back blast hit Nick when the explosion came. With an indecently heavy boom, the shock wave hurled both doors a good way into the villa. Now they know they've got visitors he thought, slipping in behind Danny.

In the smoke tinted dust it took a few seconds for Nick's focus to adjust. When it did, he saw one door had slammed into the staircase, jammed at a twisted slant across the first dozen treads. The other door, with nothing to halt its progress, was embedded into the block work across the hallway.

In the centre of this destruction Nick counted one *fedayeen* severely mutilated by one of the doors, his screams were up there alongside the worse Nick had heard.

Using standard CO8 entry tactics Nick and his team pushed on into the hallway. Clambering across the door blocking their advance, Nick's boots squawked with every step along its smooth metal skin. A full burst from an AK on automatic chipped the marble stairs a tread in front of him. Returning a volley up the stairwell Nick pelted up to a half landing, covering fire pouring up above him from Stipden and Welney.

Legging it into a first floor corridor Nick took a fast in and out peek up the stairs, noting the body of one *fedayeen*, his combats doused in blood, tattered from the weight of rounds slammed into him. Given the all clear to proceed, Danny rapidly sprinted up to a hold and fire position. Stacked up behind Nick, they both instinctively ducked when the tail end whoosh of an RPG fired from the third floor streaked past them down into the entrance. A single pulse like lightning lit the short upper corridor. In the darkened villa the blast reverberated with the deep tone of thunder over mountain valleys.

'Charlie Oscar Two: We require fire support. Concentrate on third floor, repeat third floor,' declared Danny over the net.

Opening up on the .50cals from the gully Tew and Anston blasted away at Hāru's living quarters. Nick listened, awed at the devastating pounding shattering everything on the third floor. Heavy folds of dust packed with fine debris tumbled down the stairs in a thick bundle, seriously hampering Nick's view. The irony of his dilemma was not lost on Nick. His options as he hurriedly reviewed them were positively limited; the more extreme bordered on the downright suicidal.

Thirty-Five

Signalling for Danny to cover his back, Nick manoeuvred down the corridor swinging doors back on their hinges, the laser pointer on his C8 carbine probing ahead of him in sweeps and quadrants through each room. Below, the noise from the ground floor sounded like Stipden and Welney were in a full-on contact, the rate of fire heavy, unrelenting. On his right Nick glimpsed movement in a doorway. A figure peered out with a 9mm pistol raised in a two handed grip. Reacting and firing at the same moment, Danny brought the target down with clean double head shots.

Watched over by Danny wedging the door open with his boot, Nick performed an instant profile check on the body. He confirmed the termination of Walid al-Nubani, the *Akab 1* representative, his blood lazily pooling between Nick's boots. The nerves in one of Nubani's leg were twitching, small convulsions jerking his lower body. Nick put two more rounds into Nubani's head; then slowly inched across the threshold, finding the room deserted. Relaying they had cleared the first floor over the net, Nick called a halt to the .50cals punishment before he and Danny spun back to continue their upward advance to the third floor. At the meeting point between corridor and stairs Nick diligently made a ten second assessment, giving Danny the hand signal they were ascending. Crunching through heaps of plaster, shattered tiles, splintered wood, Nick treated each marble step with healthy caution picking his way up to the third floor.

Grabbing everyone's attention another accelerating whoosh rushed out from somewhere at the rear of the villa. To Nick's urgent demand for clarification of: 'What *was* that?' Lindeth from his rooftop position gave the hearty response of: '...too fucking close... RPG... bastards... Rear of the compound... we've got a blind spot.'

Discussing the situation in their own technical way, the snipers could be heard demanding Hagley re-task the drone for an aerial view of the compound directly behind the villa. Reacting to suspected hostile movement one of them dutifully aimed and fired. In an instant they had at least one AK-47 snarling out returning fire.

An age after Loftus had reported he was fine, he'd suffered no damage, he was still holding his position, Lindeth came over the net informing Hagley he'd received a minor wound, stoutly confirming that 'No fucking way' did he need to disengage or evacuate his position.

Reaching the third floor landing Nick and Danny fanned out down the corridor. Tucked close to the wall they eased forwards working in tandem on opposite sides, clearing rooms in their tried and trusted standard procedure. Gripping the first handle to a door directly opening onto the landing Nick turned it slowly. Nothing happened. He tried again, gently applying pressure with his shoulder. Stepping back Nick fired a quick sequence of rounds into the door's top and bottom panels.

No one screamed, no one moaned, no one moved.

Using his boot as a mark-one breaching tool, Nick kicked the door open. Flung inwards it rocked against an object. Taking cover on both sides of the doorway Nick and Danny rolled in stun grenades. As the last of double charges blew like a howitzer, Nick and Danny roared inside. Behind the door they located nothing but piles of holdalls riddled with .50cal rounds. Aware there might be booby traps Nick gestured for Danny to hold his position as he edged deeper into a cripplingly strafed bedroom.

Striking through Nick's concentration, Hagley's report came loud and clear into his earpiece: 'All callsigns... Charlie Oscar Three... Drone is down... Repeat. Drone Down...' Now they had no eyes on anyone operating at the rear of the villa. He could still hear Tew and Anston pumping out .50cals from the wagons on new coordinates; just what they had in their sights Nick didn't have the vaguest notion.

Once more with his PRR playing up, Nick worked the room. A double bed rested at its centre, unmade. The ripe odour of bodies, of sweat and deodorant were pungent. In one corner a desk. Beneath it, a laptop, a bundle of papers and phone. Fitted along the length of a wall, a full-sized wardrobe robbed of its doors, its interior jammed with box files. Facing him another door he guessed opened into a side room, most probably a bathroom.

Heading for the bathroom Nick caught a movement out of the corner of his right eye. Swinging round he saw a length of bullet shredded lace curtain shuffling in the breeze from shattered windows. The tiniest dry squeal from a hinge on the bathroom door brought Nick pivoting around, his C8 instantly engaging a fighter in a combat pattern T-shirt and jeans. A couple of seconds too late on the trigger of his AK-47, Nick's rounds virtually cut him in two. Glancing briskly at the dead fighter Nick provisionally pencilled him in as one of Hāru's close protection team.

A figure kicked open a second, smaller door, the muzzle tip of an AK appeared, a burst of rounds fired in a catch-all sweep.

'LEFT,' Danny warned, opening up with his C8.

Manoeuvring fast, Nick went low firing on the target sector identified by Danny.

The intense exchange lasted for a matter of seconds, the rapid crack, crack crack of rounds replaced by silence. Holding their positions Nick and Danny waited.

'I'm hit... I'm hit... coming out...' Yelled a male voice, educated, the English tinged with the touch of a European and American cadence.

The door opened slowly. Taking one small limping step at a time a tall figure, his hands raised above his head, shuffled towards Nick. Through his night vision goggles Nick made a visual hit on their priority target Hāru.

'I'm hit... I'm not armed,' the MFP commander declared, kneeling as gestured by the muzzle of Nick's C8.

'Face down. Arms and legs spread apart,' Nick barked, and then issued the target acquired code into his PRR. Keeping his carbine aimed at Hāru. 'Hallam and Rewall?'

'Indisposed,' Hāru grunted, his face forced against the tiles by Nick's boot.

'Where you hit?' Danny snapped out the question as a command.

'Leg...' grimaced Hāru.

'It's a graze,' Danny reported over his shoulder to Nick. 'Combat veteran my arse.'

After that sharp exchange, everything seemed to jog along at a rapid pace. Nick and Danny had the plasticuffs on Hāru, roughly hauling him to his feet, leading him out onto the landing. Twice Nick tried to raise Welney on his PRR, each time he got only a weird squelch.

Fired from the rear of the compound, the RPG slammed into the second floor bedroom at 0330.

Nick had travelled no more than four stairs pushing, jostling Hāru towards Danny who'd moved down on the next landing to receive their first bagged target. The rush of hot air from the blast threw Nick off his feet, slamming him heavily into the stairwell where he hammered into Hāru. Knocked flat, Danny watched helplessly when Nick clinging to Hāru, tumbled past, the filigree balustrade prevented them free falling into the hallway below. His body bouncing against the balustrade once too often, Nick ended sprawled in an ungainly heap next to Hāru when they came to rest at a turn on the first landing.

Bruised, cut, his hearing muffled, Nick was coated in a coarse concrete and fine plaster dust irritating his eyes. Somewhere during his journey down the stairs he'd lost contact with his carbine, his NVGs were knocked askew. Propping himself against the stairwell Nick's cotton wool hearing relayed dull rifle cracks from below, a bawled call of 'clear'.

'Hold that,' Danny yelled, applying his own field dressing to a deep gash on Hāru's neck. 'Snapped wrist and a couple of busted ribs,' was Danny's crude diagnosis. 'He'll live.'

Nick sincerely hoped so, hobbling off down the stairs to recover his carbine. At a set of five steps down into to the guest annexe Nick found Welney. Sitting up dazed beside an opened door, Welney, buzzing with adrenalin, bled from his mouth after losing several teeth in a nasty encounter with the stock of an AK-47. He greeted Nick with a rapid shake of his head.

'Got one... two legged it... Smaller of the bastards might have been Talib...the other... bog standard foot soldier like his mate in there... She'd already been taken care of...'

Through Nick's NVGs the pitch dark room had a green, sickly wash but he could make out the sparse furniture in sharp detail: the daybed, a couple of odd chairs and two occupants. Lying three quarters into the room where Welney had dropped him with an accurate burst of rounds, the blood spattered body of a heavy, bulky fighter. Stranded in a corner, slumped at an angle, Celia Rewall bled from her chest. Sliding towards unconsciousness she looked up at Nick, her dry, cracked lips urged into a wry smile.

'I got my wish... to die as a martyr,' she announced, her voice drained from the effort of getting her breath.

'You'll be fine... Stay awake,' Nick shouted, reaching into his map pocket for his first field dressing. Pushing it tight over the entry wound he heard a slight sucking noise. Running his hand behind her body he found the exit wound and, worryingly, he felt a good deal more blood.

Responding to Nick's urgent call over the net, Stipden, the team's nominated medic, clattered into the annexe. Shooing Nick away Stipden set down his combat trauma bag, chatting quietly and calmly to Rewall during his assessment of her wound, rating her condition.

'See what you can do,' Nick advised him during a rapid briefing in the doorway, 'we need her.'

'I'm not qualified to administer miracles.'

Limping back into the villa proper Nick's day at the office seemed to be heading for a bag count of exactly one; if it continued he'd be invited for an interview without coffee if they made it back.

When he returned to where he'd last seen their rogue diplomat, things were much as he'd left them. Looking up from his casualty, Stipden shook his head when Nick, using the door frame for support, enquired about Rewall's condition.

'The round must have deflected upwards and travelled across. I think it's nicked an artery, maybe the left subclavian,' explained Stipden, 'I've done all I can,' he nodded to the Asherman chest seal. 'Even if we arranged a Medevac here and now, she's lost too much blood.'

'There must be something you can do?'

'No, nothing.'

'She's still coming with us,' Nick insisted, limping off to supervise their tactical withdrawal.

His mood during the final sweep of the villa was downright ugly. It wasn't even the pain swimming through Nick's ankle that could be held responsible. Nick's persistence in demanding to know how Lydia Hallam could simply vanish brought about a rummage that verged on outright destruction. Tearing a cold store pantry apart Welney uncovered a trapdoor feeding into a deep concrete chamber connected to a large, dry culvert pipe. A brief probe by Danny into the dark void took him out under the villa, about three quarters into the compound where the pipe ended, branching off into two smaller tunnels.

'They could be in any of the compounds,' Danny told Nick, hauling himself back into the pantry his face, hands and arms baked in fine granules of sand.

'We haven't the time or resources to look for them,' Nick snapped, furious.

Harassing the team to complete their search and recovery phase if they were not going to blow the extraction schedule completely, Nick prowled where he could, his swollen ankle notwithstanding, consumed by a growing sense of frustration. He repeatedly checked on Rewall who was beyond saving. On each hobbled journey he made through the central ground floor hallway where Hāru waited for departure Nick positively glared at the MFP commander, finding excuses why he shouldn't just break his neck.

Totally unmoved, Hāru's stare, tipped with assured confidence tracked Nick as he hobbled away.

Having to factor in how Hallam, Talib and at least one fighter were on the loose, quite possibly preparing another IED or an all-out attack with RPGs and AK-47s, Nick scrapped their planned withdrawal. Exiting by the front gate was a no-go he told Danny, proposing a new strategy instead. Using spare breaching charges Welney blew a rough and ready doorway in a section of the rear compound wall.

Going firm, Nick's PRR behaved long enough for him to get through to Loftus and Lindeth already working their way around the compounds; Lindeth's right leg peppered with RPG shrapnel hampering their progress. Taking a different return route towards the gully in judicious stages, Danny, Nick, Welney and Stipden took turns hauling Rewall's body.

Regrouped into their vehicle formations they were ready to pull out in Nick's revised order; instead of three phases, there would be two. In the end because of the struggle involved in getting Hāru into the back of the Liberty alongside Rewall's body – Danny only physically restraining Nick after he'd landed two mean blows on Hāru – they moved off from the gully in one column. Swapping places with Lindeth, accepting the role of driver for their wagon, Nick stuck doggedly behind the Liberty on their final journey from the mountain fringes onto the dry, scrub plain.

The opening movement of another day brought a sluggish, febrile dawn. With it came a fierce wind scooping up a loose top coat of fine, flinty sand, whipping it into low, misty waves reducing Nick's visibility, forcing him to constantly rack back and forwards with his gears, decrease or increase his speed according to the terrain he could barely decipher. Each gear change fired pure pain through Nick's ankle.

On three occasions one of the team called the column to a halt, claiming they could swear a helo was heading in on a south-west heading. When everyone listened all they heard was the wind strumming against the aerials on their wagons and quads. No pilot answering their call on the tactical satellite link, no engine, no whisking rotors, no helicopter, no lift home.

About half a klick out from their extraction point Nick examined their position against the grid reference guide, knowing they might be slightly off course, which they were, but nothing they couldn't compensate for with a minor correction or two.

What if Omri forgot to book the IAF Sea Stallion for their return? Nick wondered, unloading his wagon at their rendezvous point. Around him all the vehicles were being stripped; weapons, ammunition and equipment too sensitive to leave behind lay in neat piles beside personal Bergens.

Keeping his concern low-key, Nick was actually considering reloading the wagons to make a crazy run back to the Jordanian border if there was still no contact with the helo. In the middle of plotting a southerly course, including essential stops to take on fuel and water anywhere but close to Homs and Damascus, Nick glanced up, listening. The other team members stopped to listen also.

When Hagley gave a thumbs up and began liaising with the pilot over the TACSAT, the pace of the final preparation became hectic. One by one the wagons, quads and the Liberty went through a process of being checked, parked in a tight, square formation, then rigged with charges timed to blow and deny the vehicles once the team were safely in the air.

Special provision was made for Hāru, supervised by Nick. For the final time the plasticuffs were changed by Stipden who examined the MFP commander, checking his wrists, his ribs; spending more time on the wound to his neck. The only incident in the whole extraction came as a hood was tugged over Hāru's head. Spitting viciously in Nick's direction he had to be forcefully dumped into a sitting position when the Sea Stallion landed in a brown out as its rotors slung grit and sand in a stinging circle.

The last to board, Nick loitered on the ramp counting everyone on, having to explain to a young loadmaster that the body bag didn't contain a member of the team. After a seconds pause Nick shouted 'She was a victim...' And he supposed she was. Not in the way she had died, he reasoned; he saw the end of Rewall's journey from a different, profound viewpoint. She was a victim of her ideology he thought, choosing beliefs that would inevitably consume her, he decided, glancing back towards the villa before the tail closed, the lassitude that came with command finally hitting him.

Thirty-Six

Of the haul that eventually made it to Cyprus via Israel, there were a few decent items in the villa they'd actually bagged for analysis. Danny had recovered a laptop from the shell of the third floor bedroom, a couple of memory sticks, along with bundles of documents packed in clear sacks.

The initial consensus along Whitehall delivered after a nose in the air assessment, suggested that anything ultra sensitive had been probably removed from the villa before CO8's arrival.

Anticipating how such a discriminating view would rouse a furious reaction in Nick during his decompression at the Episkopi Garrison, Paul Rossan forbade any communication from the Mad House or Head Office to his old friend. So Nick once more idled away the days slowly coming down.

He kept in shape, but abandoned the strict training regime he'd practised in the run-up to the operation. He read more, returning to Orwell's essays, dipped into the novels, swam an odd time or two when the sea felt reasonably warm enough, walked isolated trails by the coast or striking inland to villages ringed by wild orchids, anemones and cyclamen.

As a mark of respect, he attended the scattering of Rewall's ashes in a remote area within earshot of the garrison's ranges. Standing alone after the chaplain had retired to his quarters Nick stared off into the distance, where, within the British Sovereign Territory, a secluded safe house with a private drive, even a pool, had been prepared in advance for the senior MFP detainees. Where at that moment, Nick knew Hāru would be being treated like royalty.

But Nick had ruined the party, he'd arrived home virtually empty handed; the whereabouts of the other coveted trophies – Hallam and Talib – were unknown, sheltered somewhere in Beirut's backstreets, or planning future operations from another secure desert location. Also out there and unaccounted for, Rewall's treasure, her prized Nomad stash the Service was already offering a handsome reward to secure its return.

And Nick was in no better frame of mind when he ventured out of the garrison early one afternoon behind the wheel of a rented Toyota Rav, heading southeast along the Paphos Road. His journey in total covered two and a half miles, including a smooth access road to the Sanctuary of Apollo Hylates. There, three cars stood in a visitors' area, and only one – a BMW – contained an occupant; a starched faced babysitter in wraparound sunglasses even though the blue sky was a prisoner behind leaden, miserable cloud.

The man's rugged features, his intensity, didn't come close to Nick's impression of a classical scholar. A talented, natural watcher, he attentively tracked Nick as he brought his Toyota to a halt in a quiet corner, scrutinising him still when he paid his modest entrance fee at the kiosk.

Omri's arrived early Nick decided inside the ruins, it's the old soldier in him unable to resist seizing the ground. Spaced evenly apart as Nick would have placed them himself, he counted Omri's close protection teams. A couple hand in hand, traipsed amongst the rubble littered foundations, lingered by lonely standing columns as they patrolled in an arc, guarding the rear. To their left and right protecting the flanks, two further attentive couples studied the information boards or took it in turns to set up elaborate souvenir photographs ensuring they kept Omri squarely in their viewfinder.

And like an ancient priest or senator embroiled in a devious conspiracy, Omri welcomed Nick with a threadbare, weary smile standing in the remains of a colonnaded portico.

'So Hallam and Talib wriggled out of our net,' Omri began, 'You did all you could Nick, of that I am certain,' he said in a rare burst of philanthropic indulgence, glancing around at the rubble footprints of the shrine's auxiliary buildings.

'We didn't even save Rewall,' Nick forcefully admitted, striding up onto a stone ledge to join Omri.

'In war, my friend, there are always other occasions to make amends.'

'Are there?'

'Of course, we are warriors, my friend, we accept defeats on the road to victory.'

Accepting Omri's point, Nick shifted his attention to Hāru.

'Is our star terrorist cooperating?'

'We're still pulling all the associative strands together,' Omri warned. 'From the picture we so far compiled, one of our psychiatrist's suggests Hāru's personality code may indicate *paranoia*,' Omri added.

'Is he talking?'

'He is reticent, reluctant to engage, perhaps believing he will soon be freed or exchanged. But we have confirmed his identity,' Omri disclosed. 'Ilyas Maroujd, and he has been a very active player, my friend,' he added. Holding Nick in his steady gaze, Omri quite mundanely provided his good friend with Mossad's rapid summary of Ilyas Maroujd, the fighter known as Hāru: 'He's twenty-nine, born in the West Bank territories. His father, Babak, celebrated Hāru's birth by organising the murder of three Israelis in a Larnaca marina bar by a unit from the PLO's Force 17. The whole operation was conceived and controlled by Babak in retaliation for the capture of a Force 17 commander.'

'Impressive role model,' said Nick.

'Babak was not the only influence,' Omri answered softly: 'Hāru also has his grandfather to thank for his fighter's blood. The grandfather was a key figure in the Palestinian resistance after the *Nakba*, the catastrophe in Forty-Eight. One of the early PLO commanders after the Six Day War, the grandfather played his part in creating the movement's military structure, overseeing training and selecting targets. We suspect he led the attack on an El Al flight in Athens in Sixty-Eight, but never had total evidence to proceed against him.'

'Hāru certainly inherited a solid base of Palestinian fervour,' Nick proposed.

'Of course,' Omri agreed, 'Babak and his brotherhood of terrorists raised their sons as fighters, adhering to the main principle of Article 7 of the Palestinian Covenant. "It is a national duty to bring up individual Palestinians in an Arab revolutionary manner." All the basics a boy needs to know for martyrdom,' added Omri.

'And Hāru has certainly put them to good use.'

'As a tribute to his father,' Omri suggested, 'he owes his father everything. Babak tutored his son to think and behave like a terrorist. Babak's trusted *fedayeen* trained the young Hāru, passed on to him their skills in killing, in surviving. After his thirteenth birthday, Hāru went underground with a dozen other young fighters. He became a ghost.'

'But an active ghost all the same.'

'He resurfaced as Hāru, Firas Sahil or Zaid Khallet to lead a new cadre sworn to the MFP cause,' Omri confirmed.

'So who steps into his shoes?'

'There will be strategies in place,' Omri conceded. 'If he did not discuss the question of a successor with his comrades on the Armed Struggle Command, he will have trusted his adored wife Leila Kuatli to make his recommendations.'

'Kuatli?' Nick repeated, caught cold. 'What about Hallam?'

Omri shrugged. 'What about her, my friend? She is an incidental feature Nick, another means to another end. Hallam is English, Kuatli is Palestinian, it is not difficult to understand why he prefers Kuatli.'

'And we bagged his one true love.'

'Of course, but Hāru has not reacted to her capture. He will wait until he's ready to bring Kuatli home. He will wait, months, years if he has to do so, he will wait for the right moment. He's shrewd, he realises that everyone has a price, a weakness that can be exploited.'

'Maybe someone's already decided to cash in,' Nick suggested, raising another troubling issue. 'Omar still hasn't surfaced,' said Nick, part of him concerned that his prime Palestinian asset, Samih's brother, would never be seen again.

'We have tried to locate him as requested,' Omri admitted. 'Anyone connected to him is also at risk,' he stated bluntly.

'Payback?'

'Of course, why would he otherwise disappear? My team in Beirut confirmed Omar met with representatives of his movement two days ago. He has not been seen after this rendezvous,' Omri disclosed. Gesturing down the colonnade like a charitable host, Omri motioned they walk.

'Do not blame yourself,' he advised Nick, moving towards the preserved remnants of the baths. 'You did all you could for him... more than others would do in your position.'

'Who got to him?' Nick really wanted to know, an important precursor to looking Samih in the eyes when he explained the fate of his brother.

'His own people have sold him out, that is the story circulating in Beirut.'

'Who put up the bounty?'

'Fatah al-Intifada... the Popular Front for the Liberation of Palestine... the Palestine Liberation Army... the MFP... one or all of them,' Omri disclosed, glancing at his close protection couple playing romantic fools at a corner of the path. 'Revenge is always taken as a symbol of the faction's strength,' he continued.

'As a deterrent, a means to maintain prestige,' Nick offered. 'There's no need to spare my blushes, Omri,' he continued. 'The bounty...'

'Hallam and Talib,' Omri admitted.

'From Hebron?'

Omri shook his head, smiling. 'Beirut. The most recent sighting of them was forty-eight hours ago, my friend.'

'Sightseeing?'

'They have *their sights* on targets, we're pretty certain of it, Nick.'

'Anyone in particular?'

'They're still scouting, my friend, deciding who and when. We got a few sightings of them across the city. All we're receiving is hearsay, rumour at the moment. Fragments in the wind that always contradict each other. They are playing an elusive game, Nick, totally elusive,' admitted Omri evasively.

'Until now?'

'Until now,' Omri agreed. 'Until they make a mistake,' Omri explained. 'Talib is clever, he observes a strict security protocol. But Hallam... she is careless, sloppy, thinking too much of Hāru. We've already got our *Duvdevan* guys in Beirut prepared. With a little persuasion, some IOUs called in and arms twisted, I've got a volunteer *Sayeret Mat'kal* team ready to go in. You've worked with these *lochem* before, you share the same warrior spirit,' Omri suggested.

'I'd get in the way,' reasoned Nick.

'It's your call, my friend,' Omri proposed. 'But we still have one or two loose ends to be tidied away before our business on this occasion is completed,' Omri reminded him.

'I'll leave the arrangements to you, Omri.' Nick decided as they crossed the site, its uneven ground pitted; shattered fragments of stone scattered in a wafer thin carpet. 'It's time I took a step back.'

'I'll let my people know they may have a special visitor, *just* in case you have a change of heart, my friend,' Omri unilaterally decided.

In the role of inspired visitors they trailed through partly restored baths under a protective canopy preserving chunky blocks of mosaic. Diligently stopping to read information boards, their roles demanded a revered silence until they emerged once more into the light.

'Can the MFP survive losing Hāru?' Nick wondered absently?

Pursing his lips, Omri offered a grave nod of his head. 'For the short-term, yes, my friend. Others will take up the sword of course, but we will now be ready for them,' he confessed darkly. 'Jerusalem is re-evaluating its plans on how best to confront MFP *fedayeen* and commanders from their havens on Lebanese and Syrian soil.'

'All thanks to Hāru?'

'No, my friend, all thanks to you,' Omri declared.

Having reached the surviving grandeur of Apollo's temple; two upright early Corinthian columns supporting part of a pediment, Omri stared back over the headland. 'Look, my friend, I am worried for you. When everything is completed, come visit me, we'll blow the walls out for a couple of days, unwind properly.'

'I might just take you up on that,' vowed Nick.

'Well all we require for now, my friend, is to relax.'

And some thought Nick.

'In the old days I would take a month off,' declared Omri, offering his hand as a broad, generous smile lit his face. 'But now my superiors would not permit me.'

'Some of mine would pay handsomely to guarantee I never returned,' Nick admitted, gripping Omri's powerful hand in farewell.

• • •

None of the witnesses questioned by *Forces de Sécurité Intérieure* patrol officers claimed to have noticed Jerry Lewiston enter the toyshop situated behind the Jounieh-Beirut coastal highway. After all, it happened to be an oppressive, humid Friday afternoon in the Jal El Dib neighbourhood. People had the weekend on their minds, family business to arrange, friends to see.

'Who stands about watching toyshops,' a reluctant witness protested, even one so popular where foreigners counted as regulars.

The patrol officers could locate only one credible eyewitness, a wily taxi driver, a resident of Beirut of some sixty years. Taking a break from the down town mayhem of crazy traffic jams, enjoying a respite from the mayhem, the driver found space in a parking bay marked by low planters teeming with laurel. Facing him across the street, a café beneath a squat banking tower with a lower floor mall dedicated to upmarket jewellery, clothes and restaurants favoured by clients of European and American origin.

Leisurely smoking as he recounted his testimony, the driver first spotted the foreigner when the man left the café. He only took notice because the foreigner took a call on his phone, not a normal call, the taxi river speculated, something serious making the foreigner almost walk smack into a street sign.

Which was more or less true, Lewiston's Lebanese business partner had rung to report they had a catastrophic problem with one of their major contracts.

The driver also noted how this foreigner seemed to take the call badly, staring at his phone, absently picking up yesterday's copy of the *International Herald Tribune* from the stand before sleepwalking into the toyshop.

'Was he sure about the newspaper? Was he certain?' the patrol officers demanded.

As sure as he was that the city would never go ahead with its plan to introduce real pavements, the driver retorted. Anyway, he'd read that paper, remembered the front page headline, recalled the photograph of a visiting Chinese delegation.

'What happened next?' the officers prompted the driver.

For once the driver wasn't sure. The foreigner set off from the toyshop, walking briskly to his car. Halfway into the road the foreigner hesitated when he saw a neighbourhood street supervisor working his way down the line of cars.

Again correct. The last thing Lewiston wanted was a ticket and he almost halted in mid stride, sorely tempted to abandon his blue Ford Fusion before he got a hefty fine or sank into haggling rights to settle on an amount for a bribe. But Lewiston determinedly kept going, believed he could reach his car, climb in, start it and be away before the supervisor reached him.

That's when the other car almost ran the foreigner down, the driver explained, lighting another cigarette.

'Which car?' the patrol officers asked, somewhat perplexed.

The white Fiat came at Lewiston faster than he anticipated. He had to surge forward out of its path, head and shoulders jutting forward building up momentum, a runner pushing for the line. He cursed, a short vindictive 'sod' as the Fiat driver continued hitting the horn long after it had sped by.

Once again, an accurate observation, though rather than posing a danger, the Fiat may actually have attempted to slow Lewiston down.

'The Fiat never stopped?' one of the patrol officers demanded.

'What about the people in the Fiat? How many did you see?' his colleague wondered.

Unable to say why or who happened to be inside the Fiat – and 'yes, it didn't stop, it didn't slow down' – the taxi driver returned to what the foreigner did next.

Turning his attention back to reaching his Fusion, Lewiston noticed the supervisor approach a big dark coloured Jeep with tinted windows parked directly behind him. The supervisor looked up once, only for a couple of seconds, so Lewiston shrugged his shoulders and gave a 'that was lucky' smile. The supervisor returned to scribbling in his notebook, his face set hard, not registering Lewiston's attempt to draw him into his world.

Reaching his car, Lewiston fumbled in his pockets for his key fob, deactivated the alarm. Instinctively he glanced left then right before opening the boot to put his toyshop purchase away – a handmade pull-along mother duck on wheels with its cute ducklings linked in a train. He pitched the *Herald Tribune* in after the parcel when his phone rang again.

Sliding into the driver's seat Lewiston took the call, repeated 'hello... hello' as the supervisor tapped on the driver's window of the Jeep behind.

Lowering his window, the Jeep driver smiled, a charmers' smile, nothing too cheesy, but balanced as he had always done. 'Rather you than me', Lewiston thought firing his ignition.

'And?' encouraged one of the patrol officers, prompting the driver who stared ahead, his head shaken in wonder at the memory.

'It happened. That is when the people in the Jeep were shot...' the driver disclosed, shrugging his shoulders that he had nothing else to offer.

Hours later after a member of the British Embassy's Consular Section paid a visit to the scene, an initial sitrep cable reached London. Filtered through the FCO, it reached the Service around two in the morning. Containing only the bare bones of factual information, the cable detailed how the Embassy's representative found Lydia Alicia Hallam in the passenger seat, a neat bullet wound to her forehead. Slumped beside her over his steering wheel, Salem Abu Talib, his brains liberally coating the windscreen.

What the representative added next earned a red flag complete with immediate priority circulation. During the *Forces de Sécurité Intérieure* immediate street-by-street search of the area, they discovered a Westerner had booked a room in a one-star boarding house. The room in question stood on the very top floor, and with it, came a prime view that happened to overlook the toyshop. The clerk retrieved the registration details along with a photocopy of the male guest's passport, handing them over for official scrutiny. The room it transpired had been vacated that very morning, not more than ten minutes after the shooting. The guest, by all accounts, appeared to be a German citizen, a photojournalist, who the clerk swore, preferred his own company, a hard man who looked as if he'd been through many, many wars.